LUX ET VERITAS

ARCHANGEL

THE BOOK OF MAMMON

LOX ET VERITAS

BLACK MIKE

AUDERE BOOKS

The Book of Mammon is the first book in the Archangel series.

ISBN 978-9925-7869-3-0 (Paperback)
ISBN 978-9925-7869-4-7 (Hardcover)
ISBN 978-9925-7869-5-4 (e-Book)

black-mike.com

Contents

*For those who will not forsake virtue
despite the vice that surrounds them.*

The Fall of Grace

Grace strained against the chains binding her wrists. The cold metal bit deep and even though it was only gold it was still too strong for her to break. The gag in her mouth was silk, but that didn't make it any more comfortable either.

She was in a small room, dark and cold. It was probably some kind of closet. She'd been blindfolded when they brought her here. *That* she'd managed to free herself from, a small stab of hope that was quickly withering in the face of the gold chains around her wrists and ankles.

Grace's eyes stung but did not tear. She wasn't going to cry! She hadn't done anything wrong! She shouldn't be here. She wouldn't be here. If she could just break these fucking chains.

If only the agent who had burst into her apartment had believed her! Had been able to see the monsters in the air all around them! But he hadn't. He hadn't believed her.

No one had believed her.

She'd just been doing her job! Her boss had asked her to show his boss's boss around the office, and she had. Creepy old fuck. But Grace had played nice. The man owned the whole fucking company; of course she'd done as she was asked. He gave her a thumb drive with some files on it he said needed to be incorporated into their database. She finished the tour, plugged it in, and transferred the things.

Had she opened one, out of curiosity? Sure. But there was nothing inside but a bunch of strange diagrams that made not a lick of sense to her.

She closed it out and didn't think anything more of it until she began seeing...things. First it was just flickers at the edges of her vision, like the dancing spots you sometimes get from rubbing your eyes too hard or looking at the sun and then away. But then she started to catch sight of hazy forms drifting around certain people. Not just at the office but on the streets and in her building.

Eventually, they came into focus and that's when Grace's real problems began. They were horrific, the things she saw, and no one else seemed to see them! Her work became erratic, she stopped sleeping, and the whispers began.

She didn't know if people were actually whispering about her at the office or if it was the things she was seeing. It got so bad that she requested a leave of absence, using up all her banked holidays and sick leave.

Grace had been three days into her break, not that it had been doing much good. The strange forms she saw were all around. Even in her apartment! Golden eyes seemed to stare at her from everywhere. Mirrors were the worst, though at least the monsters she saw reflected in the glass were silver, not gold.

She wasn't sure why that was better, but for some reason it was. They were less menacing, less immediately dangerous.

Three days in and a one-man SWAT team of some kind had exploded into her apartment, shoving her to the floor and shouting about her being some kind of terrorist! She wasn't a terrorist! She'd tried to explain, to tell him what she had seen, that she was innocent, but he hadn't listened. She'd thought she saw a flicker of kindness in his eyes, but he hadn't listened.

And he still turned her over to his superior. A fat man smoking a disgusting cigar. Who gave the agent that had taken her down a bag that clinked heavily. She'd still hoped, then, that she was being arrested, had breathed and told herself that a lawyer would sort it all out, but when she was shoved into the back of an unmarked sedan, she wasn't taken to jail.

She was driven to a deserted stretch of road and the fat man with the cigar had hauled her out and passed her to these lunatics. The men who had wrapped her in golden chains and gagged her with silk.

The ones who were holding her prisoner.

The sound of a key in the lock broke through Grace's reverie. Though it was hopeless, she nevertheless persisted in trying to break her bonds. Golden light, bright and warm, spilled into the darkness blinding her. Strong hands grabbed her and hauled her out, carrying her kicking and screaming through her gag, only to dump her bodily onto a cold, slick expanse of raised marble.

An altar.

Robed figures stood all around her and Grace bucked and struggled as she was bound in place with yet more chains. These also gleamed like gold but there were scratches on the surface, strange imperfections that Grace's panicking mind seized upon. The chains weren't pure gold, merely gilded iron.

Not that that would do anything to help her.

Tears streamed from her eyes, turning the candle flames all around her into dancing globes of fuzzy golden light. Words were echoing off the vaulted stone above her, voices chanting, and the sound of…coins? Coins falling all around her.

One word stood out from all the others. A name.

Mammon.

Then a figure was standing over her. Grace tried to scream but again the gag kept her silent. The cowl of the robe was pushed back revealing a cold and smiling face.

A face she recognized!

She screamed through the gag, but it was no use. A knife glittered in the candlelight, rising and then falling with a swift finality. Grace choked on her own blood, her last thought just the words *But I'm innocent!* screaming through her fading mind.

There was no one left to protest when Grace's body was removed from the altar, no one left to see when two strong men hauled her body away, her lifeless eyes glimmering golden in the night.

No one saw them drive away. No one saw them digging a shallow grave several yards deep into a copse of woods off the interstate. No one saw Grace's body turned out of its shroud of a tarp and unceremoniously dumped into the hole.

A few shovelfuls of dirt and even if Grace had still been alive she would no longer have been able to see the starry sky through the skeletal branches of the trees all around her.

Then even the men were gone, leaving behind only a small mound of dirt strewn haphazardly with handfuls of leaves to mark their presence.

Golden fireflies rose from the freshly turned earth, blinking aureate in the blackness, though there were none there to see them dancing in the dark.

CHAPTER 1

Wakeup Michael

"None are more hopelessly enslaved than
those who falsely believe they are free."
— *Johann Wolfgang Von Goethe*

Michael ignored the trickle of sweat creeping down his back. The surveillance van was hot from the screens and various equipment running inside, hot from the sun beating down overhead, and hot from overcrowding, with five people cramped inside the small space. His eyes never left the screens, however. This was his op, and he was in charge of making sure the terrorist they were tracking didn't kill anyone else.

"What's that on five?" Michael directed the question to Tanner, one of the younger men on his team, a genius at the tech angle of things.

"Looks like maintenance personnel," Tanner answered. There was a bit of a quaver in his voice. Tanner was better with tech than he was with people. Or high-stakes situations.

"Can we get another angle? The cap is blocking his face. Could be our guy."

"On it," Priestly said, her hands dashing across the keyboard. "Nothing, nothing, there! On three."

Michael glanced at screen three. The angle wasn't great, but a partial face was visible. Though there was a goatee, it wasn't enough facial hair to stop the recognition tech they were running.

"Not even a partial, sir. I don't think this is our target."

"Where are you?" Michael scanned the screens, looking for anything out of place.

The van was parked in a nearly empty lot surrounding a decrepit warehouse. Two streets away there was a thriving street market, full of knockoff handbags, tech that had "fallen off the back of a truck," and, for the discerning terrorist, a brisk trade in illegal weaponry. Not what you'd expect in Queens, really, but hey, New York was New York, and the unexpected was pretty much what you signed on for when you arrived.

Laughter erupted in the van, though it was quickly cut off by professionalism. Michael glanced over at the screen everyone seemed focused on, but he'd missed whatever it was. What he didn't miss was that one of their people on the ground was in clear shot, and there was a bit of a disturbance around him.

"Focus, people!" Michael snapped. "We're professionals here. You all right there, Miner?" he asked, touching a hand to the toggle on the communications panel.

A man on screen four, one of their plain clothes operatives, seemed to scratch his cheek as he answered.

"Fine. Just startled me is all. Why the fuck would you have severed goat heads for sale? It's fucking Satanic is what it is."

"You're drawing attention. Move on. Find a new vantage point. We don't want anything spooking our target."

"Yes, sir."

Michael watched screen four as Miner moved away from the butcher stall. Priestly and Weston were still shaking with laughter. Michael frowned. They needed to focus.

"Stay sharp, people. Our target is looking to take part in an arms deal if our information is correct. Whatever they're after, we don't want them getting it, got me?"

"Yes sir!" His team spoke in unison, straightening in place.

Well, as straight as they could get in the cramped van, anyway.

"Now where are you?" Michael leaned forward to look at the screens again, the blue light flickering and playing across his face.

The screens showed a dizzying mix of angles, mostly from covert cameras that had been placed around the market by operatives like Miner. Though the screens washed everything out to shades of black and blue and grey, the motions of the people and the stalls gave the impression of color. A huge crowd of people shifted and juddered all around, buying, selling, laughing, gossiping, everything that humanity does when it comes together in a place like this.

Suddenly Michael froze. A man was standing alone in the crowd, people moving around him like he was a stone in a river. He was looking directly at the camera. It felt like he was staring directly into Michael's eyes.

Wake up, Michael.

Michael jerked back. When he glanced at the screen again the man was gone. Vanished as if he'd never been. Only the roil of people remained.

"You see something?" Tanner was looking at him, panic clearly rising in his eyes. "Are we go?"

"No, no—I thought—no." Michael shook his head. "False alarm."

What was that? Too much heat? It was damned hot in here. No one else had reacted to the voice. Everyone had been intent on their screens.

Now they were all looking at him. Michael reached over and snagged a bottle of water. It would be lukewarm and taste of plastic, but at least it would keep him hydrated.

"Stay sharp," he repeated, jerking his chin at the screens before taking a swig from the bottle.

His people turned and focused back in on their jobs.

Not a bad idea for him, either. Michael needed to get his head in the game. Lives were at stake here.

He picked up the dossier on the side and flicked through it again, looking for anything he might have missed that would help them spot their target. There was the usual background stuff about the organization—they thought the target here was part of a larger group that called itself The Resistance—and a summary of the reports cobbled together from a couple of C.I.s.

Michael's department had been cracking down hard on illegal arms dealers recently. A lot of the regular sources had dried up or pulled up stakes temporarily until the heat died down. It was forcing a lot of troublemakers, like the one they were tracking, to expose themselves in searching for new suppliers.

It was a nice side-benefit of the work.

Michael flicked over to the next page and frowned. The background on The Resistance made it seem like a big operation.

There were a lot of hints, pieces of evidence his gut told him pointed to something larger, but if so why hadn't he heard of it? A domestic terrorism operation of this size?

Something didn't add up.

And their target. They weren't acting like part of a well-funded, well-organized terrorist organization. If so, why would they need to come here to get arms? That should be handled on a larger scale, possibly smuggled through the docks by a dedicated branch of The Resistance. Looked like some kind of home-grown religious fanatics from what was in the dossier. White Christian nationalists.

Domestic terrorists were the worst. And it seemed like more and more of them cropped up every year. Idiots with a gun and a grudge, most of them.

Michael flicked back to the pages with the interview transcripts from the criminal informants. He began to scan through the interviews themselves, having only read the summaries before. Sometimes the analysts left something useful out in their need to be concise. Not their fault; it was part of the job. Saving time meant leaving some details out, and you could never know what was or wasn't useful until you laid eyes on it.

And then, Michael did. One of the informants specifically mentioned that their target had been asking about distance scopes and high-efficiency ammo. Sniper gear.

He cross-checked the other interviews. No. None of the others mentioned anything this specific. They all just left it as "wanted to buy a gun."

It was worth checking.

"Priestly," he said, "any of our known arms dealers have any sort of specialty or sideline in sniper gear? Or military gear, failing that?"

"Two of them that I can think of offhand. Let me run a quick search." Priestly began clacking at her keyboard.

"Give Tanner the two names you can think of first," Michael said. "I want eyes on them now. We can cover that with the cameras we already have in place."

"Should I ask Miner or Stowe to move to cover?" Tanner's left hand hovered over the communications toggle even as his right brought up the requisite views on screens four and five.

"No. Not yet. This is just a hunch. Let's not pull too far out of position yet."

Michael studied the screens. The two arms dealers in question had very different stalls and were on different ends of the market. Either one could be the destination of their target, based on the winding layout of the place. Both stalls looked perfectly innocuous, one selling mostly cheap-looking phone cases under a sign talking about getting your tech fixed, and the other an array of cheap cleaning supplies.

A fixer and a cleaner. Cute. Not really subtle, but not so blatant anyone would pick up on it. If you knew, you knew.

Michael scraped the nail of his thumb against the nail of his forefinger, lost in thought. There were other arms dealers hidden throughout this market. It might not even be either of these two. He needed to cover all the bases.

"Priestly, where are we with that list of suspects?"

"I've got three more so far. I'm chasing down records on two others, but the wireless connection here isn't as strong as I'd like—"

"You're doing great. Pass what you do have to Tanner, and—"

Tanner broke in before he could finish, his voice tight with adrenaline.

"Sir, I think we've got something."

"Show me." Michael leaned forward.

"Screen two." Tanner pointed. "Right there. Baseball cap and backpack. It looks pretty empty, but that brown paper bag they're holding? That's got something in it. And they're on a direct path to Argon's position."

Argon was a Russian arms dealer with ties to the mafia and the Wagner Group, a cadre of mercenaries that were rumored to be a private arm of the Russian military dictatorship, often employed on missions for the deniability it granted the government. He'd certainly have access to the sniper materials their target was likely after.

"Send Miner and Stowe to intercept," Michael ordered. "Now!"

Michael's eyes flicked to the screens. He saw the two operatives pause, then shift direction, moving purposefully toward Argon's stall. They were moving a bit faster than they should, pushing aggressively through the crowd, but it couldn't be helped. They were too far out to get there in time if they moseyed on over.

"Come on, come on," Michael muttered, his eyes moving from screen to screen, tracking the progress of his operatives against that of their target.

The target paused, looking to either side of themselves. Then they stepped back and ducked into an alleyway, out of sight. They must have seen Miner or Stowe moving to intercept.

"Shit! They've made us! Go, go, go!"

Michael burst out of the surveillance van, blinking in the sudden, bright light. Two other agents followed him. Tanner and Priestly would remain in the van, directing them using the cameras scattered throughout the market.

"Fan out," Michael ordered. "We can't let them slip through our net. Go!"

Not waiting to see if his orders were followed—he knew they would be; he worked with good people—Michael took off at a sprint down the main thoroughfare of the market, a direct line toward the target's last known position. He rushed through the crowd as fast as he could. Michael was not a small man, and even though he was flexible and agile, he was still faced with trying to get through hundreds of people who were all themselves only barely moving. It was like trying to run through honey. You could do it, but it wasn't easy and it wasn't fast.

Certainly not as fast as he needed it to be.

"Bear right! Target is fleeing down Goethal, heading toward an alley," Tanner's voice echoed in Michael's ear.

He adjusted course, still struggling through the crowd. At least the target was heading towards him. He should be able to catch sight of them any minute now.

Michael pressed forward, eliciting shouts of anger and alarm as he pushed through the crowd. Come on. Come on!

There!

Michael spotted the target and recognized the hat and backpack.

He pushed through the crowd faster. He didn't bother shouting for the suspect to freeze. They never did. All that would accomplish is giving away his position. Right now he had the advantage of surprise and he had no intention of giving it up.

The crowd thinned. They were both nearing the edge of the market where they could move more freely. Michael spotted Stowe struggling through the crowd to the left.

The other agent was closer, but neither of them was making as much headway as the suspect. The target was surprisingly agile. And damned quick.

Michael broke free of the last of the crowd and managed to shift up a gear into a full-on sprint. His long strides ate away at the distance between himself and the target. There was a flash of reflected sunlight from the suspect's glasses as they glanced back to see who was pursuing them.

It was an oddly familiar gesture.

Before Michael could wonder why it seemed so familiar, the target stumbled as they tried to hook sharply around and down an alleyway. Michael surged forward, following. This was it! Just the two of them in the narrow corridor. He was going to nail this creep!

Then suddenly there was someone in front of him. The man from the surveillance cameras, the one that seemed to be looking right at him. He locked eyes with Michael and spoke.

"There are none so blind as those who will not see. But you *will* see, Michael. *Lux et veritas*."

There was a flash of light and the man was gone. Michael blinked wildly, trying to clear his vision. His eyes felt gritty, sandblasted.

When he could see again he cursed. No sign of the target.

Shit.

"There was someone else in the alley, waiting. I lost the target! Talk to me, Tanner, Priestly!"

"Sorry boss, we've got nothing." Priestly chimed in his ear. "No camera coverage there."

"And nothing from satellite surveillance. Nothing useful anyway," Tanner added.

The target had escaped.

"Sir?' Stowe's voice came from behind him, at the mouth of the alley.

Michael turned around and had his gun in his hand before he could think. That was Stowe all right, but there was a monstrous black worm, segmented and leaking red fluid coming out of his back! As Michael watched it spasmed and heaved, red gunk dripping to the pavement with a hiss.

At the sight of Michael with a gun, the man took a step back, raising his hands.

"Sir? What is it? It's just me."

Stowe. It's just Stowe. There's no way what he was seeing could be real. Giant black worms like that don't exist. And if they did, and Stowe had one on his back like that, other people would notice. Other people would be freaking out. But the few people he could make out beyond Stowe were just walking past. No one was reacting.

He wasn't seeing anything that was really there.

Shit.

"Stowe," Michael said slowly, lowering his weapon, "we've got a situation. Our target had an accomplice. I think he hit me with something."

CHAPTER 2

An Unexpected Partner

"What the hell happened out there?"

Michael's boss, Joseph Garibaldi, was a stout man whose drastically receding hairline was kept in the sharpest of buzzcuts. Hell, the only thing shorter than Garibaldi's hairline was his patience. He had the look of a career soldier and the gut of a heavily-muscled man whose body was slowly turning to fat from being stuck behind a desk after a lifetime of active service.

It also looked like he also had something or some*things* living in his mouth. Michael could only see flashes. A dark, segmented body, needle-sharp teeth, sinuous movement—any time Garibaldi went to take a sip of his coffee or a bite of his danish, those things were there, gnashing and tearing, swallowing down the food before Garibaldi could.

It was far from the worst thing Michael had seen since that asshole dosed him a few hours ago. It had to have been some kind of hallucinogenic drug. Maybe something custom? New? The whole trip back had been like this. Flashes of horror. The only mercy was that it faded in and out. The things, the visions, weren't there all the time.

But they kept coming back. It was worse the longer he stayed in one place, for some reason. That certainly wasn't making this interview any easier.

"We were made," Michael answered, keeping his answers short and to the point, fixing his gaze on the wall just beyond Garibaldi's stocky form. That way he didn't have to look at whatever the drugs were making him see. "We pursued, but the subject outpaced us and made use of a fire escape to, well, escape. Sir."

"I hope you don't find this situation amusing, Lieberman."

"Not at all, sir."

"You know why you're in that chair. Why I put you in command." Garibaldi squinted at him with his piggy eyes.

One of the *things* living in Garibaldi's mouth coiled out as the man talked. It was segmented and chitinous, like a centipede from hell, and there was a fatty, golden sheen to its exoskeleton. It tasted the air and Michael got the sense it was trying to taste *him.*

"Yes sir," he said, clenching his teeth. This wasn't real. It was a hallucination. And fuck Garibaldi for always digging up old shit. He'd done what he'd had to do; he'd gotten the promotion he deserved. Now he just had to live with it—and with Garibaldi yanking him up short every time the sleazy fucker was annoyed at something.

Garibaldi gave him the hairy eyeball for a long moment, then grunted.

"This," his boss said, tapping the file on the desk between them with one meaty finger, "was a disaster. It cost the taxpayers a lot of money and we don't have anything to show for it."

Michael refrained from pointing out just how much of the taxpayers' money Garibaldi had spent on refurbishing his office. The room looked more like a wealthy man's study than a civil servant's office. Even a corner office.

"I understand, sir. We'll do better next time." Michael remained standing at attention.

"See that you do. Dismissed."

Michael didn't allow his spine to relax even a bit until he was outside the office and back into the general maze of cubicles in the center of the office floor. It was a relief to get away from Garibaldi. It was a relief to get away from whatever he was seeing in the man's mouth.

He made a beeline for the kitchen area. He needed something hot to drink to help him relax, never mind that it was scorching outside. And maybe, if he was lucky, staying on the move would help keep the hallucinations to a minimum until whatever this was, wore off. He grabbed a folder from his desk as he breezed past. Might as well do some work while he waited for his brew. It would give him something to focus on other than the flashes of hallucination that were still haunting his eyes. Plus there was going to be a line, or a malfunction, or something. There always was.

And if he was reading, then maybe no one would bother him.

His eye wandered down to the page, reading as he walked. It worked fine up until the moment it didn't. Michael had stepped around several people on his way to the coffee machine, eyes glued to the page, but it was always the one you missed.

And the one he missed was a doozy.

Michael slammed into someone, sending papers flying everywhere. He managed to retain his grip on his cup of coffee, thankfully, so no one was doused, but the person he'd walked into was less than pleased about the fact.

"Watch where you're going!"

Michael looked up into two hazel eyes, all but spitting sparks at him. Their owner was a slimly muscled woman, nearly as tall as he was, wearing the woman's version of a detective's best suit and dirty blond hair pulled back in a ponytail so tight it could have wound clock springs.

She wasn't trailing a hallucination, but there was a sharpness and a clarity to her that was unnatural all the same. Like a polished knife waiting in the kitchen block. Sharp. Businesslike. Dangerous in the right circumstances. But something that was always to hand, always reliable, and always trustworthy.

Why did he think that?

"Sorry—" Michael began.

Began was all he had a chance to do.

"Damn straight you're sorry! What the hell were you thinking swanning around with your nose in a stack of reports like that? Idiot." The woman snorted.

"I was thinking I'd do my job," Michael replied with a bit of heat.

Who the hell did this woman think she was? Not someone he recognized from this office, that was damn sure. And if he didn't recognize her, she was either new—which wasn't likely, not with the state of their budget—or a visitor. And if she was a visitor, she had no place lecturing him how to do his job on his turf.

"Nice." The woman sniffed. "Real effective there, Sparky. Watch where you're going next time. Some of us have real work to do."

Before Michael could formulate a response she swept off. He shook his head and continued on to the kitchen area. He really needed that coffee.

Tanner and Stowe appeared out of nowhere just as he was settling in with his cup. The younger man, so tense in the field, was downright relaxed here. Stowe, on the other hand, looked impatient with the surroundings. Michael was pleased to see the man was no longer visibly hosting a gigantic worm-like parasite on his back.

Maybe the stuff was wearing off.

"Still walking, I see," Tanner said. "I thought for sure we'd all be toast after that mess."

"We're not far from it," Michael responded. "It was a mess and we're going to need results on the next op."

Stowe grunted. He didn't often say a lot, but once you spent some time with him you could usually pick up on his moods just from the sounds he made. This one indicated he was frustrated, maybe blamed himself a bit.

"Not much you can do if you can't see where they went," Michael offered.

Stowe nodded slowly, but Michael could tell he was still irritated.

"It took us long enough to secure that lead," Tanner complained. "The Resistance is pretty discreet, pretty professional for a terrorist outfit. They have no right to be this clean in the way they do business."

"Garibaldi—" Michael began.

"Garibaldi only cares about looking good and securing more funding for the department so he can snazz up his office a bit more," Tanner interrupted.

He really was bold as brass when not in the field. Michael had seen him stand unflinching in front of the commanding officer's wrath on more than one occasion. If it didn't involve a chance of bullets or bombs, Tanner was unflappable.

Too bad he couldn't keep that cool while in the field. He'd make a fantastic field op if he could. Until he did, though, he'd be stuck riding in the surveillance van.

Michael and the others continued the conversation long after the coffee was finished, speculating on where they might catch their next break, the motives of The Resistance, and where their target might have escaped to. More to the point, where the target might go to next in the attempt to acquire sniping gear.

"It's a good lead," Tanner said as he rose. "I'll take it downstairs and see what the analysts can put together for us in terms of options. It'll be a stupidly long list, but it's at least a direction."

"Tell them to have copies of whatever they find on my desk in the morning. I'll—"

"Lieberman! Get back in here!" Garibaldi's voice echoed across the office.

What now?

"I'll go see what the boss wants," Michael finished wryly. "See you two later."

He'd hoped to head home and get some rest, but it looked like that was too much to ask for. Garibaldi said he didn't seem drugged, whatever he may or may not have been dosed with, and the man was too cheap to give him any kind of day off for his health, even half of one, so why wouldn't he have more work for Michael?

"What took you so long?" Garibaldi barked when Michael made his way into the office again. "We're wasting time, officer! And time is money, which around here comes from the taxpayer! Let's not waste any more than we have to. Lieberman, this is Officer Sara Wilson. She's the break in your case. Your lucky star."

Garibaldi gestured to a woman standing next to his desk—the one Michael had just run into, in fact, then spun on his heel and stalked off toward one of the conference rooms, leaving Michael to stare blankly after his boss, cold cup of coffee still in hand. Sara followed, glancing over her shoulder to flip Michael an impatient look. Michael stared after them for a moment, trying to mentally catch up to what just happened.

"She's my what?"

Garibaldi led them to the big conference room. Naturally. He loved to show off, and the big conference room was the one he'd ordered refurbished as soon as he took over.

On the taxpayers' dime, of course.

It was impressive, sure. It looked nice. New. There were several of those fancy clear plexiglass whiteboards and markers for case diagrams. A large central table, all of one piece, dominated the space. The other conference rooms had collections of smaller tables simply shoved together to make one larger table, more useful but less aesthetically pleasing. This fancy room wasn't nearly as useful or as comfortable as the smaller conference rooms, but it looked good, and that was why Garibaldi chose it.

"This is my partner, Detective Bryan Overstreet,' Sara gestured to a powerfully built Black man with close-cropped black hair holding a cardboard evidence box. "We're the ones who caught the case originally."

Michael ignored the warning in her voice. Standard jurisdictional pissing contest. The police force was never happy when Federal stepped in. Like anyone here was really after glory.

He glanced at Garibaldi, lording over the room from the chair at the head of the table.

Well, almost anyone.

"I'm not sure what you mean," Michael said, bringing out the diplomat. "This is the first I've heard of any criminal case related to the—," he flicked a glance at Garibaldi and got a small nod before continuing, "—terrorist activity we've been tracking."

"We're not so sure it is related," Overstreet said, setting the box on the table with a thump. "Someone is, though, so here we are. Playing nice." He removed the top of the box and began pulling out files and folders.

"A murder," Michael said, catching sight of a couple of the photographs as they spilled out onto the table.

"More like a contract killing, or an outright assassination," Overstreet said. "You would not believe—"

"That's speculation," Sara cut him off. "Though some of the elements of the case are…unusual, for a regular murder, yes."

"Who's the victim?" Michael began picking through the files, absorbing details here and there. If there was something here that could lead them back to The Resistance, he'd happily put up with Officer Wasp and her lunkhead partner.

"Robert Hug," Sara said, "he's—"

Michael let out a low whistle. Robert Hug was very well known. He was one of the richest men on the planet. Possibly one of the top ten or even top five! This was a high-profile target indeed!

He was about to ask a question when his eye fell on one of the other pictures. There was a small boy in the background, crying and in the care of a pair of police officers. No. Surely not—then he noticed the background to the crime scene photos.

It was a playground.

"That's his grandson," Sara said softly. "The assassin got to him because he insisted on having less security around when he took his grandson to the park. Apparently, he felt it scared the other children."

"I see." Michael stared at the photo a moment longer, then shook off the emotions threatening to rise up. "No wonder you were calling this a contract hit."

"Right?" Overstreet asked.

"But what's the connection to our case?" Michael had been looking, but he didn't see it. Sure, there had to be a sniper involved, but—

Sara pulled out another set of photographs and spread them across the table. Michael swore and snatched one of them up. Same frame, same hat, even the same backpack. It was the suspect that had gotten away from them all right!

"I expect you two to play nice and sort this out," Garibaldi said. "Fast. Time is money you know." The fat man shot one greasy glance at Michael. "I expect you to handle this, Michael, with your own particular brand of effectiveness. Whatever it takes."

Another dig at the past. Michael's hands tightened into fists but he kept his face neutral. How long was he going to be paying for that choice, with interest?

Well, at least he had another lead, even though working with the two detectives was likely to be a headache and a half. And Michael already had one of those. At least the day was nearly over.

***

Michael took the scenic route home. He wanted some time to think, to go over the events of the day. He drove along the river, not minding the snarl of traffic and the aggressive jockeying of the taxis. Michael liked to drive, and he was good enough at it that he could think and navigate all at the same time.

The setting sun glittered off the water. Michael replayed the day's events over in his head. Could he have done something differently? How had the target escaped them? Why did something about the subject seem off or different to him?

Michael didn't end the drive with any more answers than he began it with.

He parked his car in the underground garage beneath his building, locked it, and headed towards the stairwell. The sodium lights bathed the concrete around him in an actinic yellow and his footsteps echoed slightly in the cavernous space.

Something moved in the corner of his vision and Michael paused, throwing a quick glance its way.

Nothing.

Michael resumed walking toward the stairwell, not hurrying, keeping a sharp eye out. Was that a flicker of movement in the car mirror? For a moment he thought he saw a familiar face, but glancing around he still didn't see anyone.

He paused at the top of the stairs for a good two minutes, waiting to see if anyone followed him up. When no one appeared, he relaxed, slightly, and continued up to his apartment. It had been a long, disappointing day. He must be imagining things.

Michael took the lift up the several floors to his level. The doors dinged open and Michael cautiously stepped out, glancing up and down the hall. Still nothing. He felt himself relax as he walked down the hallway to his apartment. He'd only been in this building a few months. His last promotion had come with a nice raise and he'd moved into a nicer, larger place then.

Michael pulled the keys out of his pocket. They jangled slightly, almost too loud in the silent hallway. He reached out to let himself in but when his fingers brushed the knob the door shifted slightly.

Someone had been here. The door was unlocked.

— CHAPTER 3 —

Eyes In the Shadows

Michael eased the door open with the point of his pistol. It swung inward on silent hinges, still too new to have developed any telltale squeaks. Light spilled across the threshold, illuminating the entry hall. It glinted off the mirror by the door and danced across the toes of Michael's too-polished shoes. Priestly always teased that they'd give him away, because no one other than a cop or a soldier keeps their shoes in that good of condition.

Side table was still in place. Drawers closed. Bowl for keys and spare change hadn't moved. Nothing looked out of place so far.

But the unlocked door, the day he'd had…no. Something felt off to Michael and he wouldn't feel settled until he'd checked every inch of the place.

He eased inside, slowly swinging the door closed behind him. No point making himself a target as the only shadow backlit by the lights from the hallway. The door closed behind him with a soft click and he froze.

He stood stock still for one minute. Two.

Nothing.

Michael eased further into the apartment, moving more quickly now, a changing pace to throw off anyone who had been watching, waiting. He surged to the corner and whipped around, gun first, checking all the points of concealment from memory.

This room was a combination open-plan kitchen and dining room. Nothing behind the fridge, and no one crouched behind the island. All the knives in their block. No scent of gas.

Between the time he'd taken driving home, and the scenery he'd admired while wrestling with his thoughts, the sun had begun to set. It dropped fully away between his pulling into the underground garage and making the ascent to his floor. But plenty of light spilled through the vertical blinds from the city outside. Enough to see by.

The bathroom was clear. The guest room was clear. There was no sign that the picture of dogs playing poker with its heavy and ironic gilded frame had been moved. Michael ran a hand along it to be certain, just in case. Nope. Not disturbed. The secrets in it were still safe.

But the door to the balcony was unlocked.

That gave Michael pause. He always kept it locked, no matter how many floors up he was. Call it force of habit, call it irrational, he knew he'd left it locked.

Just like he always double-checked he'd locked the front door when he left, morning or night.

Something beyond the glass caught his eye: a large, white feather caught at the base of the railing, shifting slightly in the constant breeze rising from the hot street below. Michael stared at it, then deliberately locked the balcony door. Strangest bait for a trap he'd ever seen, if it was. Probably just blown off a seagull or something.

Damn big seagull, a rebellious part of his mind whispered.

The only room left to check was the bedroom. The door was already open, so Michael swept in, gun at the ready, checking all points. The bed was clear, as were the closet and the attached bathroom.

Nothing.

Michael did one more sweep before holstering his gun. He was the only one here. That didn't mean his place *hadn't* been broken into, however. Someone might have been planting bugs. It wasn't like everyone working in counterterrorism didn't have to be on the lookout for that, as well.

He swept for bugs, checking the light fixtures first, then the photographs. There were several hanging on the walls. Most were art prints, pieces he liked by the likes of Raphael, Caravaggio, and Buonarroti, but there were also several framed pieces representing his family. A few were photos, several were drawings.

There was a single photo of his parents together, young and laughing. They'd died so long ago he barely remembered them.

The photo, framed, had been a gift from some old family friend that Michael had barely known. He'd appreciated it, though. It was nice to have something to look at when his own memories had grown so fuzzy.

He paused when he stopped to search the art drawing he'd had done of his sister Hannah. That loss was much more recent, much more painful. Hannah had disappeared over a decade ago now. Michael had looked, asked, even called in favors at the office and with some of his old service connections, but she'd vanished. Gone without a trace.

Leaving him alone.

Michael carefully ran his fingers around the frame before gently taking it down. This would be hard to replace. Hannah wasn't around to sit for art pieces anymore. Not that it was ever easy to get her to sit still. She was always in motion, moving like a Santa Ana wind.

Strong and fast, that was his sister. His big sister. She'd taken care of him after their parents died. Managed to stick it out between the orphanages and foster homes. Helped keep his spirits up, told him dirty jokes to make him smile after the endless sermons and beatings from the friars at the orphanage, or the belt-buckle beatings their second foster father would mete out when Michael didn't say or do what was asked of him fast enough.

It was clean. Michael gently replaced the frame and continued on his search.

He turned up nothing. No bugs, nothing overtly out of place. Nothing seemed to have been stolen or altered. Maybe it was just his imagination. Maybe he'd left the balcony unlocked. Maybe he'd forgotten to check the door was locked behind him this morning. It had been a stressful day. High stakes.

Having turned up nothing, Michael triple-checked the locks, put his stuff away, and started cooking himself some dinner. Nothing fancy. Chicken, some blanched spinach, pasta, a little pesto. He flicked on the news for a little company while he worked.

"…cryptocurrency is rising in popularity, led by the increasingly in-demand PitCoin, named for its creator, Mallory Pitman, one of the richest men in the world even before his custom currency began to take off."

The next segment was lost in the sizzle of the chicken hitting the hot, greased pan. Michael flipped the food and began chopping spinach. The simple action was relaxing, just what he needed after a day like this one.

"...in other financial news, the United States legislature remains trapped in conflict over whether or not to raise the debt ceiling, for—"

The news certainly wasn't helping. Michael wiped his hand on a dishtowel and flicked through the channels until he hit some music videos. Better. Much better.

The phone rang just as he was removing the chicken from the pan. He narrowly avoided burning himself on the pan as he jumped. Damn. Still on edge after the day he'd had.

Michael glanced at the caller ID on the screen. Tanner. The kid really needed to learn to leave the job at the door when he left.

Yeah, as if Michael was one to talk. He hadn't set the job down in at least three years.

With his off-hand (grease-free!), Michael swiped to accept the call and tapped it into speaker mode.

"What is it, Tanner? I'm in the middle of cooking dinner."

"Sorry, boss! I've got that list and I wondered if you wanted to..."

Tanner chattered on. Michael only half listened as he sliced the chicken and tossed the pasta with some pesto and the blanched spinach.

"No," he said when Tanner finally paused to take a breath, "I don't need to see it tonight. We've all done enough work today. Leave a copy on my desk. Do *not* email it to me. Then print one out for yourself, take the digital files off your stuff, and then go home and relax. That's an order. I need everyone fresh tomorrow, and none of us are going to get there gnawing at this thing like a dog at a bone. Clear?"

"Clear, sir," Tanner said. "I'll see you tomorrow."

"Have a good night." Michael flicked the cell closed and sank onto the couch with his bowl piled high with food.

He turned the music up a bit higher. The apartment was too quiet on nights like these. Hannah used to scold him for not trying to find someone, for not dating more, but who had the time? He worked in counterterrorism. Hardly a nice, safe job. Anyone he dated would need to sign up for a solid chunk of danger and a whole lot of stress.

It never really seemed fair to do to anyone. Not that he would have minded the company. Company would be nice.

Well, he'd have to make do with a nice meal and a hot shower. Michael finished his food and rounded off the meal with a cold beer from the fridge. He was big enough that just one didn't even get him a bit of a buzz, but the cold and bitter bite was refreshing, and it took the sharpest edge off of the day.

Right. Cold beer, then hot shower.

Michael rinsed the dishes before loading them into his aging dishwasher. On the way to the bathroom, he double-checked the locks on the balcony and front doors one last time before turning off all the lights except for the ones in his bedroom and bathroom. The shower spat and hissed as water began to flow. Michael slowly shrugged himself free of his clothes. The damn thing always took so long to warm up. In a new building like this the water pressure really should be better and the heat more responsive. Contractors probably cheaped out. Anything to line the shareholders' pockets!

When he finally stepped into the shower half the tension of the day dissolved under the all-but-scalding water. The chase scene began to play through his mind again. The way the target had moved, how quick they had been. Slimmer, slighter than he would have thought. Strong for their size. Not that terrorists came in a standard model. He'd arrested men and women, large and small, broad and thin. Hate didn't discriminate which hearts it germinated in, ironically.

Michael shook his head to clear it, sending water droplets flying everywhere. Enough! He was supposed to be unwinding!

He toweled off and headed to bed.

The sheets felt cool on his skin. Another small luxury after his last promotion. Tanner wouldn't shut up about how nice the things were after a long day, so Michael had let the guy talk him into a set.

He wasn't wrong. It was like sleeping on a cloud. And Michael could use any advantage he could, coming home wound up as often as he had to, in his line of work.

Tonight though, it wasn't quite enough. Even as he drifted off to sleep he still felt like he was being watched.

Like there were eyes in the shadows.

— CHAPTER 4 —

Gabriel

Michael awoke to the sound of something tap-tap-tapping at the glass. He came awake immediately, a smooth snap into consciousness, and his gun was in his hand before he could think about it. His feet made not a sound as he padded to the door, pausing to listen at the crack of it.

Tap tap tap.

Something was out there. Michael eased the door open and stepped into the hallway, a maze of blue-black shadows. He padded toward the balcony, the carpet soft beneath his feet.

The first thing he noticed was how cold it was, a fresh, clean cold, like mountain air. The balcony door was open and the cold air came coiling in. It set the vertical blinds to waving and the cord that controlled them, that was what kept tapping against the glass.

But who opened the door? Michael moved closer, gun at the ready. His eyes darted from side to side, checking for anyone who might be in hiding as he went.

Don't be ridiculous, Michael.

Michael whipped his head around, searching for the source of those words. The apartment was empty. He saw nothing.

You're the one who is hiding.

"Who's there?" Michael said, finally. There didn't seem to be any point in acting like he hadn't heard whoever it was. "Show yourself!"

There was a flicker of movement, a reflection in the glass. Michael whirled around, gun pointed.

He saw no one.

"This isn't funny, asshole!" Michael began tracking back and forth with his pistol, eyes looking for something, anything out of place.

Do you hear me laughing? On the contrary, I am in deadly earnest.

Someone moved in the shadows to Michael's left. He squeezed the trigger and a shot rang out.

Nothing.

Movement again, this time to the right. Michael squeezed off another shot, taking three quick and careful steps back, to give himself more lead room. That one seemed closer.

The air on the back of his neck was sharp and cold, yet light as a feather.

That is entirely counterproductive.

The voice was right behind him!

Michael whirled around, gun leveled, but there was no one there. No one and nothing stood on the balcony. Beyond the railing shone only stars.

Only stars?

Michael! Wake up, Michael!

The voice was behind him again! What was happening? This time when Michael turned he found himself nose to nose with a face he recognized.

"You! You were staring at me through the monitors at the stakeout today!"

Was I? The stranger's lips didn't move. *How curious of me. Wake up, Michael! We're running out of time.*

Michael tried to bring the gun up but when he raised his hand it was empty.

"What?"

Fine. We'll do this the old-fashioned way.

"Wha—"

Before the word made it all the way past his lips, the strange man in front of him exploded into action, whirling into a spinning kick that landed dead center of Michael's chest and sent him flying backward, through the open door and over the balcony railing.

Michael screamed as he fell.

He screamed and then he wasn't falling.

He was flying.

Michael opened his eyes and all around him was nothing but an expanse of starry blackness as far as he could see, in every direction. Muscles strained in his back and he heard the beating of powerful wings.

His wings.

He was flying.

Dreaming. He had to be dreaming. There was no way his mind would have whipped up this hallucination.

But do you know when you're dreaming?

Sometimes. Lucid dreaming is practiced even amongst the mortals, Michael.

The man from the apartment. The one who had kicked him over the balcony. He swept down and hovered in front of Michael, who felt a twinge in his back as his own wings flared to catch the air and hold him in position.

"Who are you?"

Come now, Michael! Is that any way to talk to an old friend? You know who I am.

"I've never met you before in my life! Today was the first time I've ever seen you!"

First time that you remember seeing me, perhaps. In this life, anyway.

"This life? What do you mean this life?"

Clouds began to whirl around them, vast conglomerations of cosmic dust condensing into nebulae. Inside were flickers of light and life, visions teasing at the edges of Michael's awareness. It was like memory, yes, but memory on the other side of glass. Not something he could reach out and touch, even if he could catch a momentary glimpse.

I'd tell you to wake up again, but I believe at this point you might take it entirely the wrong way. But you need to remember yourself, Michael. Time is running short. Mammon is moving and you're the only one who can uncover his intent. We will help you stop him but you have to be the one to lead us in this.

As you have in the past.

"I told you! I don't know who you are!" Michael gestured wildly around him. "I don't know what this is! This isn't even real!"

Oh, it's very real, Michael.

Gabriel–that was his name! Gabriel!–shook his head as he hovered in front of Michael.

"Gabriel?" Michael tried the name on for size. It certainly fit the person he saw before him, but that would make sense in a dream, wouldn't it? An angel, appearing out of nowhere? What other name could there possibly be except Gabriel?

Michael, a treacherous part of his mind whispered to him. *Michael is the other obvious name for an angel. Michael or Raphael or Uriel.*

He shook his head to clear it then, with a shrug, pinched himself hard on the forearm.

Michael swore. That stung! No. That didn't make sense. How could he test if he was dreaming in a dream? Something about reading?

It's a dream, yes, but that doesn't mean it's not also very real. Else what force does love have? Or language? None of these things have the material reality you're seeking to cling to, yet they are very real nonetheless. Have a little faith, Michael.

"Not really my thing," Michael replied, not seeing any alternative to continuing this conversation. What would it take to wake him up?

Gabriel threw back his head and laughed at that.

Your surroundings might indicate otherwise.

"I don't follow?"

What is faith if not finding beauty in the face of the void? That, or the fact that you're flying amongst the stars on angels' wings?

"I probably undercooked the chicken."

Gabriel threw back his head and laughed again.

And what? Are those chicken feathers growing out of your back? I'm not sure I'm convinced.

Michael twisted his neck around to catch a glimpse of the massive wings working behind him. They were broad and powerful, and an unexpected tawny gold with black stripes, like the feathers on a golden falcon. The wind from their movement played about his fingers and fanned the nebulae nearby into a swirl of beautiful chaos.

Wait, how large was he that his wings could do that to a nebula? This had to be a dream. Not that he ever thought of himself as this creative, but maybe his subconscious had hidden depths.

Stop hiding from yourself, Michael. Wake up.

Michael started as Gabriel's words unknowingly echoed his thoughts.

"No. This isn't real. This is just a dream. Stop talking to me!" The last was a shout he hurled at Gabriel like a thunderbolt.

Michael's wings flared, then swung downward with titanic force, propelling him away from the angel before him and toward the unknown deeps of space around him.

Michael, wait–!

But he was already light years away. Star systems and nebulae flashed by, then whole galaxies; he flew by black holes and dying stars, through the endless void of space, trying to put anything, everything, between him and Gabriel.

Memory clutched at him as he flew. A voice–his father's?–calling to him from impossibly far away. So far away that all he could hear was the love in the tone of it. The words themselves were a mystery. Unknowable.

Words of arcane power hummed in the radio static emanating from pulsars, and constellations spun around into sigils and runes. Lines of power billions of years old twisted before his eyes, promising meaning that danced just out of reach of his mind. Some were familiar, others seared into his eyes like living mockeries.

There the seal of Solomon. There the ward of John Dee. A hundred sigils, each distinct and precise in its power, flashed through his mind and Michael recognized many of them. Somehow he remembered them. There! That one was the so-called Sword of Simon Magus, a sigil that could cut through wards and protecting enchantments of white and black magic alike.

Michael flew faster, trying to escape this wellspring of knowledge within him. This was not something he knew! This was not something he wanted to know! It was not a part of the life he had lived.

Flashes of his mother's eyes winked at him from blue dwarf stars, older than he remembered them. Her voice came to him on the stellar winds, calmly telling him to turn back, that she would see him soon if he just turned back.

"No!" he shouted. His wings carried him faster and further away. The stars around him were fading now, vanishing into impossibly small motes of light as he left the observable universe.

Come back…

The voice that whispered to him was dreadfully, terribly faint, a thread trying to pull a drowning man from the storm-wracked waves.

Michael himself was the one that stopped. The endless black void, rising all around him, was colder and sharper than the interstellar winds that had supported his wings thus far. There was something hungry out here, a yawning need that clamored to consume all light, and Michael somehow knew that it would never be satiated, never full.

Michael…why do you pause? Come to me, Michael. I can show you more than your father ever would.

This voice was different. This voice was new. And yet it was also somehow familiar. Like encountering your childhood bully when you are both adults, when you have both changed, but somehow your ear still recognizes the timber of cruelty in the voice, as identifying as a fingerprint.

No. No, no, no. This was not escape! The silence began to pulse around him, ringing like some kind of great and terrible bell as the weight of that unfathomable and hungry gaze bore down fully on Michael.

Come to me, Michael. Give in! You will have rewards such as you never dared dream of! Your father has left you behind, Michael. You have been left all alone. Here, where other angels fear to tread you have dared to fly. It is but a little further, Michael. Fly just a little further into the dark.

"No!" Michael woke with a shout of defiance, sitting bolt upright in bed, his body drenched with sweat and the sheets a tangle of silk around him.

Sunlight, pale and clear, streamed in through the window, and the city was sharp and glittering beyond the glass. His city. Reality.

A dream. It was all a dream.

He let out a sigh of relief and shook away the last of the cobwebs clogging his brain.

Michael winced as he hauled himself out of bed. The muscles between his shoulder blades were absolutely killing him. He turned to make the bed and froze.

There, lying upon his sheets, was a single, massive feather, golden in color with black stripes.

CHAPTER 5

The Sword of Simon Magus

Michael gulped recklessly at his coffee, the hot liquid burning his mouth but he didn't care. After the night he just had, any reminder that he was awake and in the real world was welcome. Thankfully there had been a street-seller right outside Sara's precinct. He didn't have to feel bad about flinging yet more money at a faceless corporation for an inferior cup of joe.

It was getting harder and harder to do. Seemed like every street had at least two corporate coffee shops. Of the same chain even! How did that make any sense?

Making his day even worse were the files that Tanner had couriered over to him first thing. He'd leafed through it and there, on the fifth page, staring at him like a beast rising out of the murky depths of the sea, was the symbol from his dream last night.

The Sword of Simon Magus.

It had been custom etched into the bullets their target had ordered. One of the leads Tanner had been running down. Not that many people supplying snipers, after all.

But the image haunted him, misty and half-remembered, though this dream was more stubborn than most.

What did that mean?

Michael shrugged off the thought and made his way into the precinct. The desk sergeant checked his ID and gave him some direction. Up to the second floor. Third door on the right. Halfway back.

It was easy enough to find his way.

Sara's desk was a morass of half-completed reports, empty coffee cups, case files in various stages of completion, food wrappers, and all the other detritus of a career law enforcement officer who was a bit too dedicated to the job. Michael had seen it before. He'd *lived* it before.

The desk's occupant was, by contrast, crisp and orderly, but wasn't present. He had to show his badge to get her cubicle neighbor to show him where she was. Michael was led to an interrogation room and left there. Professional courtesy, at least, seemed alive and well in this precinct.

Michael looked through the mirrored glass into the room where Sara and Overstreet were interrogating a prisoner. He was pleased to note there wasn't any residual effect from the hallucinations. She no longer looked hyper-real and sharp. Their voices came clearly over the tannoy.

They were well into the interrogation, by the sound of it. Sara, Michael was surprised to note, was playing bad cop. She reached across the desk and slammed the suspect's head into the table.

Very bad cop.

"So do you work for?" Sara demanded.

The suspect spat on her face, blood and spittle.

Sara reached over and slammed his face into the desk again and again, repeating her question with each impact.

"Who. Do. You. Work. For?"

"Max! Max Ashton!" The guy finally screamed.

Sara stood, breathing hard. Michael could see tension thrumming through her figure. She'd gotten what she wanted but it didn't seem to make her happy.

Overstreet tossed her a handkerchief and she cleaned off. Michael glanced around the room he was in. There was no one else. The recording equipment was off.

This was off the books. It smacked of something personal. Sara's reaction told him it was personal.

Not his business. Michael slipped out of the room and chose to wait outside the door to the interrogation room. Sara would be out soon enough.

And she was. She was remarkably composed, looking as if nothing had happened, though Michael spotted a small speck of blood on her shirt cuff before she tugged her jacket down to hide it.

"Good. You're here." Sara reached down and retrieved a ring of keys that had been juggling at her belt. "Follow me and let's get to it."

Michael followed, saying nothing more than the usual empty greetings and chat you used in unfamiliar environments.

Sara led him to one of the precinct conference rooms. Unlike the showpiece Garibaldi maintained, this was far more in line with the ones Michael was used to. It was small, utilitarian, and sat in a row of similar spaces, all with their own gruesome store of information splattered across the walls like viscera across the crime scenes so many of them recreated.

The room had actually been locked, a precaution Michael was surprised Sara had taken. Most detectives wouldn't bother, the evidence in question being smack dab in the middle of a police station, one of the safest places it might conceivably be. But Sara pulled out her keys and unlocked the door, turning on the lights to display everything pinned up to the boards around the room.

"Here we are," she said, "though there's not much you can see here that you wouldn't have gotten by just looking at the file we gave you."

"It's helpful to see it all laid out," Michael said, not mentioning how helpful it was to see her thought process all laid out as well. Well, hers and her partner's.

Thankfully, Overstreet had not come with them. Probably gone for coffee and doughnuts, meaning Michael was temporarily spared his looming presence. It made it a lot easier to focus. He wasn't sure why the man seemed to have taken an instant dislike to him, but it certainly wasn't going to make things easier.

"Hugs was in a small private park, the kind that requires a high-tech key to access. You know the ones." Sara began, starting to take him through everything they had.

"Yeah," Michael said, "only the people that own in the high rises around the park have access, never the renters, and they're always impeccably maintained and beautiful to look at through the tall black iron bars. I know the type." He'd walked past them often enough, tailing suspects. Terrorists often had backers with very deep pockets—and very exclusive lifestyles.

"Hugs was here, taking his grandson out to play on the little swing set and slide combo the park has. Apparently it was designed by a famous modern artist or sculptor or something. It's technically a sculpture entitled *Fleeting Innocence* and it's worth several million dollars on its own." Sara shook her head. "That kind of money just for a children's toy."

"And the shooter?" Michael paced around from photo to photo, trying to get a sense of the angles. The shot had to come from somewhere higher up, but it was hard to predict angles from all the two-dimensional photographs on the board.

"Here," Sara tapped one of the images with her pen. "See the scaffolding? We think that's how the assassin was able to gain entry so easily, and how they were able to make such a fast getaway. By the time anyone figured out where to look, it was too late. The culprit had dashed. Down the scaffolding, into the alleyway, out the other end, and blended into the crowd."

"You have an image?" Michael glanced up from studying the picture of the scaffolding.

"Maybe," Sara said, her eyes suddenly veiled. "What about you? What have you seen so far that would fit with—as your chief thinks—this shooter and the one you were tracking being the same?"

There was a note of challenge in her voice. Michael bristled at it. Why should he have to prove himself here?

"How many snipers have you had come through the city in the past year? Past five years? How many murders were you able to trace back to an M.O. like this?" See if she could answer that off the top of her head.

"None this past year," Sara replied immediately. "Three over the last five." She smirked at him. "Why don't you try asking something a bit harder than the obvious, Columbo?"

"So we've got four deaths now that fit the profile. It's obviously not common, for all the gear isn't *that* hard to get a hold of if you know where to look. We know our target was in the market for some replacement gear, and obviously, you found some bits on the scene, or we wouldn't be here having this conversation. No prints though, I'm guessing."

"No, that would be too easy." Sara snorted. "What else? This is all pretty circumstantial."

Pushy. Michael crossed his arms and looked at her. Sara mirrored his position, leaning against the edge of the small table.

"Convince me you belong here," she goaded.

"Convince me it's worth letting you continue to work this case rather than calling jurisdiction and having this all boxed up and shipped to my office where my team can deal with it."

It was an empty threat. It didn't work like that. Michael knew it. Sara knew it. But Michael wanted to see how she'd react.

"You could try," came the response. Sara's eyes were glinting, but her tone was controlled.

Her posture was too rigid, though. Michael could see the idea bothered her, but she was cool-headed enough to keep it from showing too much. Grudgingly, he had to respect that.

"That's still not an answer, though," she went on. "I'm not seeing anything here that would convince a schoolteacher of your logic, let alone a judge."

She kept pressing him, though. That could get really old, really fast. Michael pivoted back to the board.

"Depends how much of the story isn't here," he said. "Depends if, say, your boss got some requests for added security from other wealthy people afraid they'll be next." He shot a glance over his shoulder.

The way Sara grimaced told him his guess had been correct. Something bigger was going on here than a single murder. His gut had told him that would be the case. Why else would his target have been in the market to replace sniper gear?

"Speculation," is all she said. "You got anything else, or is this what amounts to 'police work' in your department?"

Michael hesitated. He did, in fact, have more information. He even had it with him. Tanner and the rest of the team had done fantastic work in digging up some intel from a criminal informant that linked some more pieces together, but he wasn't sure he wanted to share it. Sara was being aggressive, and territorial. If he handed it over that easily, she might seize the reins and run roughshod over his whole operation.

And he couldn't risk that. Not with this many lives on the line.
He *could* tease it a bit, however.

"Maybe," he said, throwing her own teasing word back in her
face. "Could be that we've got a source that may have insight into
the order that a certain arms dealer had in stock. Strange custom
job."

Michael didn't say anything about the strange request for
lead bullets or the etchings they were supposed to come with. The
etchings he'd first seen in the dream he had last night and then
again in the file Tanner couriered over. The etching that formed a
shape he felt he strangely knew. The Sword of Simon Magus.

A chill traced its way down his spine. As if an assassin and a
terrorist weren't enough to deal with. Then there was the memory
of that voice out of his dream.

Michael refused to think of the name. He was an atheist, first,
foremost, and forever. His subconscious was just playing tricks on
him.

Sara had come alive at his hint, however. Her arms were
uncrossed and she was poised, tense as a coiled spring, hovering
next to the table she had been leaning on only moments ago.

Michael could see her eyes flicking across the detailed
photographs of the etchings on the bullet—no, *bullets*—they'd
found at the sniper blind overlooking the little private park where
Robert Hugs had died. Wheels were turning behind her eyes.
Michael said nothing. Let her make her own conclusions and share
a bit more of her intel first.

It was going to be exhausting if they had to play these games
the whole way through the investigation.

"You've seen the suspect," she said slowly, as if realizing it for
the first time. "You engaged in foot pursuit."

"I did," Michael acknowledged.

Sara turned and began flicking through a folder buried at the
bottom of a pile. Interesting. So she didn't keep everything up at
all times. Or, she'd taken it all down before she first left the office,
knowing it was likely she'd have to show her case files to the feds.

Michael opened his mouth to say something as she handed
him a photograph, but his voice vanished as his eyes latched on to

the grainy picture. That slim figure, that hat and backpack. They were the same as his suspect had worn! It was impossible to say for certain that the faces were the same, but the similarities were undeniable.

"Ha!" Sara said. "Now *that* is some circumstantial evidence I can get behind. You clearly recognize that person. Maybe from your own recent sting operation—sorry it went South, by the way."

Michael didn't ask how she knew that. It would have been easy enough to pick up from office gossip when she had been visiting earlier. Instead, he asked a different question, since she was suddenly so forthcoming about her evidence.

"What else did you recover from the scene? Anything interesting."

"A few things," Sara said, turning again to rummage through the closed boxes. "Including Hugs' phone. The guys in IT got it unlocked. Took them a while. They had to request permission for Federal-level decryption. This thing was locked up tight."

"Call log?"

"Yeah, that's what we thought. Nothing obvious. Did get some of his frequent, recent calls, though. A guy named Marvin Drummer was up there, as was a guy named Darren Kerbs."

Kerbs. Drummer. Why did those names sound so familiar? Then it hit him. The victim in Sara's case was a billionaire. So it stood to reason the other two might be wealthy as well.

"The industrialist and the hedge fund manager?" Michael asked. Each of them was routinely on the *Forbes* list; each of them commanded vast financial empires and was routinely seen in the papers in the city.

"Bingo," Sara tapped the phone in her hand as she frowned. "Drummer seemed nervous for some reason. Kerbs though, Kerbs was just an asshole. Snapped at me for calling the number, threatened to have my job over it. Really raised the chief's hackles."

Sara didn't seem too bothered by it, however. Michael found himself smiling at that.

"No one is above the law," she said, eyes hardening for a moment. "Seems like someone needs to remind Mr. Kerbs of the fact. I doubt it will be me, not with the way he seems to have shaken up the department, but someone will do it. No one is above the law," she repeated.

"No," Michael agreed. "One law, fairly applied. Screw how much money you've got. Right is right."

Sara cocked her head and looked at him. Michael had the impression of passing some kind of test. The detective tossed her keys in the air and caught them with a flourish.

"I have an appointment to speak with Marvin Drummer tomorrow. Want to come along?"

"Yeah, actually." Michael blinked, surprised. "Yes, yes, I would. Thank you."

The rest of the morning was spent with Sara walking Michael over the case from her end, with him offering extra context from their investigation. Michael could tell Sara was irritated that he hadn't brought copies of the bureau's files with him, so he made a point of calling Tanner to ask that copies be prepared and sent over. The kid would know what to keep back and what to share, what to make look like an oversight so their asses were covered. Michael liked Sara and thought he could trust her, but there was no reason not to play it safe to begin with.

He could tell she had a tendency to seize the reins and go her own way. He didn't really want her to do that with what he still thought of as his case. Departmental cooperation be damned.

"Right," he said finally when they'd made their way through as much as he could absorb, "I think it's time for lunch."

"I've got some paperwork to get through," Sara said before he could suggest that they grab a bite together and get to know one another a bit better since they would be working together. "I'll see you tomorrow for the meeting with Drummer."

Michael took that for the dismissal it was and headed out. He was a few blocks past the precinct when a voice caught his attention.

"Michael?"

He turned around. Something about the voice was familiar. Then he saw who it belonged to, and the bottom dropped out of his stomach.

"Hannah!?"

CHAPTER 6

The Sister and the Otherworld

"Hannah?" Michael stared at the woman in front of him. It looked like his sister, but it had been so many years since he'd last seen her—at the orphanage—and she wasn't nearly as tall as he remembered.

Or as happy looking.

"It's me," she replied, "I need to talk to you. Come on. Let's go someplace else."

Hannah glanced over her shoulder, clearly nervous about something. Her hands tugged at the cuffs of her blouse.

It looked new, some part of Michael's brain noted. As did the slacks she wore. The sneakers, though, those were well-worn and very much in the style of the sister he remembered. Those sneakers, as much as anything else, convinced him to follow her.

Hannah reached out and linked arms with him as they walked. Michael was surprised to discover he was actually taller than she was! It was surreal. Though to be fair it was far from the most surreal thing he had seen recently.

"There's a coffee shop I like a couple blocks from here," he suggested. "They do a really nice—"

"Actually, we're here," Hannah said, pulling him around the corner into an alley.

Michael had just enough time to register the design drawn across the brick in thick lines of chalk, all lines and angles and improbably sigils. The hair on the back of his neck began to rise, but before he could react Hannah shoved him. He stumbled, reached out a hand to stop himself from slamming against the brick—

—and fell right through the wall.

He was caught in a firm grip—Hannah's—before his lack of balance sent him crashing to the pavement. Michael righted himself and quickly pulled away from the woman who claimed to be his sister.

"What? What—"

"It's all right! Really! I'm sorry I had to spring it on you, but it was way easier than explaining and hoping you'd believe me." Hannah stood before him, two hands held up in a placating gesture.

Michael was not in any mood to be placated, but the pause gave him time to register his surroundings. He was in what looked like the same alleyway. Almost. There were some…differences.

It was a subtle thing, at first. Everything just seemed…more. Or maybe clearer? It was hard to put into words. Clearer, but at the same time hazy with an inner glow? Everything had this hyper-reality to it.

He reached out a finger to trail it down the brick wall he had just stumbled through. It felt like brick. It felt hot and cold all at once, wet and cracked, like every brick he'd ever touched, in summer or winter or in between.

Michael snatched his hand back.

"There's more to the world than you know, little brother," Hannah said, voice heavy with irony. "And I'm sorry to show you this, but I'm hoping once I do you'll listen to me and go back to living your life, just as you did before, before that asshole Gabriel fucked with it."

She bit the name off savagely. Michael looked at her. His head was swimming. Gabriel? How did she—?

"Come on," Hannah gestured to him, clearly not comfortable trying to link arms again so soon after she tricked him, "I'll explain as we walk. Follow my lead. We should be safe enough here, but you never know when something dangerous might surface from the Deeper Realms."

"The wha—"

Hannah didn't answer, striding off swiftly around the corner. Michael, left with little other choice, followed. He didn't know what was going on, but his sister seemed to be his best chance at finding out.

He made it as far as stepping onto the street before he stopped and stared. Awe and horror battled in his mind as it struggled to come to grips with what he was seeing.

On one level, it was just the street. People walked up and down it; cars drove to and fro. They were all just slightly out of focus to his eyes, except Hannah, though that was not what gave him pause. That honor fell to everything *else* he was seeing.

There were all sorts of *things* mixed in with the people walking up and down the street. Some walked or floated by on their own power, like the men and women he saw just going about their day. There were men with goat's legs and giant pulsating slugs twice his size in more colors than he'd seen before, women with the wings of a bat, and eerie masses that seemed to be nothing but wings and eyes. Though these seemed almost normal compared to some of the others.

Almost every normal person he saw trailed something behind them. One man had long, streaming things that looked like giant tapeworms nibbling at his eyes. Another woman had a massive black worm attached to her back, like the one he'd seen on Stowe. As he watched, one of the balls of wings and eyes swooped down to harry the tapeworm-things away from the man's eyes. They hissed and struck back, a mid-air battle ensuing.

Michael shuddered and looked away, not caring to see who won.

"What is all this?" he asked.

"People call it different things," Hannah replied. "The Near Astral. The Dreaming. The World-Soul. The Otherworld. It doesn't really matter what you call it. It's basically a spirit realm that sits alongside and overlaps our own. Don't ask me to explain the geographies or geometries of that. It's enough that I know how to get here, and what that means."

"How *did* we get here?" Michael spared a glance at his sister before being drawn, inevitably, back to the panoply of horrific wonders in front of his eyes.

"Magic," she said shortly. "I'm not very good, but I'm solid on the basics. Especially the ones I need for the work."

"Work? What is it you're doing these days?" Michael let out a weak laugh. "Please don't tell me you fly around the city with the aid of a sentient cape casting out demons."

"I don't have a cape," was the only answer he got.

Michael almost asked her again if she could fly, but then the memory of his recent dreams resurfaced and he shut his mouth with a snap. The idea hit a little too close to home.

"Look," Hannah said before he could think what to ask instead, pointing to a man walking along relatively unmolested by the swarming spirit-creatures all around. "I think he's about to get some bad news."

The man's face was screwed into a frown, and as Michael watched first one, then another, of the strange creatures flitted near, then backed away, seemingly frustrated. A small creature with purple fur darted forward and at first, Michael wasn't sure that it had done anything, but then a flick of motion caught his eye.

The little bastard had untied the man's shoelaces!

"They can reach through to the real world?"

"This world is just as real as the one we came from. It's practically the same one. And yes. Some of them can."

The man, shouting into his phone, stepped on the lace and stumbled, nearly tumbling into oncoming traffic. Michael started, trying to lunge for the man, but Hannah held him back.

"You can't affect things from here, not without magic or some other power."

Michael heaved a sigh of relief as the taxi zooming past narrowly missed the man.

His phone wasn't so lucky, however. The man, pale as a sheet, began to swear. This time when one of the strange creatures drifted close it managed to attach itself to him, swirling around his head like a pink cloud that grew steadily more crimson as the man sputtered and swore, his anger surging to cover his obvious fear.

"You're standing in a dangerous world, little brother. You need to listen to me. Go back to your life. There are dangers enough there without stumbling into this one. It's too easy to lose people, and I don't intend to lose you too. Avoid that asshole Gabriel, and keep your head down. It's safer that way."

"Taking my name in vain again, Hannah? That's hardly polite."

Suddenly the man that had blocked Michael from catching the terrorist earlier—the one that had drugged him!—was standing next to them. He wore a tan trench coat and mirrored sunglasses and his short-cropped hair danced lightly in a breeze Michael could not feel.

"You—"

Michael took a swing at the man, but Hannah got there first. Her hand simply passed through the man as if he weren't even there, however. Michael blinked and stepped back.

"You never did fight fair," Hannah said sourly. "Go on. Leave. You have no right to be here. This is a *family* matter."

"I'm here to advocate for Michael's best interests," the man—Gabriel—replied calmly. "If you had your way, he wouldn't get a choice in the matter at all, and you know how I feel about that."

"Like enchanting him and turning him loose with the Sight was any better!?"

"It was temporary," Gabriel said. "Just a little dose, to get the ball rolling."

"You had no right—"

"Excuse me," Michael said, breaking in, "I think I'm the one that gets to decide that." The shock was beginning to wear off, driven away in no part by a growing ember of fury kindling in his chest. He'd been dosed—or enchanted, whatever—haunted, shoved through a wall into a strange spirit world, and now his big sister was arguing with a mysterious man about *his* future? After she'd disappeared for years?

No. No way. Some pain had carved deep creases in his sister's face, and he'd missed it. He wanted to know what, and there was no way he was going to lose track of her again.

"I don't know how I know this is all real, but I know it's real," Michael said, gesturing to the insanity around him. "As fucked as that is—"

"The Light of Truth shows the truth," Gabriel said. "You know it's true because the Sight reveals only that."

"Fine. Whatever. But *I* am the one that gets to decide how to react. *I* am the one that gets to decide what to do with my life now that I know. Not you," he pointed to Gabriel, "and not you," he pointed out Hannah. "Me."

The smile that had flashed across Hannah's face when he castigated Gabriel vanished as he leveled his finger at her.

"I don't know what you're thinking, Hannah," Michael said, running his hands through his hair, "but you've been gone for years. Years! I don't know who you are anymore. I'm not the little boy you left behind. What? You think I'll just do whatever you say because you say it?"

"It's for your own good—"

"I don't want to hear it!" Michael snapped. "I need time to process this. Time to think about…everything."

"If you have any questions, I'm happy to answer them," Gabriel offered.

"You?" Hannah snorted. "Under your watch, he'd be selling himself off piecemeal at the goblin market by the dark of the moon."

"And if you have your way he'll be completely helpless for any of the things that will inevitably come for him," Gabriel shot back. "At least my way he can learn to defend himself. Ignorance may be bliss but is no excuse and certainly no defense. Not for him."

"Enough!" Michael waved his hands at them, drawing the attention of some of the nearby spirits. "Hannah, take me home. Now. I want to think things over. And when I call you, you damn well better answer. I want to know where you've been all these years. You don't get to just show up, drop a bomb like this, and disappear again."

Though he had no way of knowing she'd listen to him, Michael felt confident she would. If she didn't still care about him she wouldn't have shown up to try and warn him off of…whatever this was.

Michael's phone buzzed. How did he have signal here, wherever here was? He pulled it out and looked at it. It was a text.

It was Gabriel's number.

"If she won't answer," the strange man said, "I will."

And with that, he vanished.

"Come on," Hannah said wearily, "I'll take you home."

Michael thought he heard her mutter to herself that this whole afternoon had been a mistake, but he chose not to call her on it.

His sister was back and what's more, she knew magic.

CHAPTER 7

The Philanthropist

"We'll have to park on Ninth and walk over," Sara said.

Michael was in the passenger seat of Sara's Crown Victoria. He couldn't believe she still had one. The Crown Vic had been a staple of the force for years. Solid, dependable, and discreet, but the company had stopped making them years ago. The sedans the force used nowadays worked fine, sure, but Michael did appreciate classics like this one.

"Seems like parking gets harder to find and more expensive every year," he remarked, watching the buildings flash by as the taxis whizzed around them like suicidal hornets.

"It does. Last year, some real estate company persuaded the city to let them redevelop a few of the midtown lots that had been used for parking. You know the ones. Got what looks like a massive elevator stack system for cars? They're putting up high rises, luxury housing in their place. Less space, more demand."

"And higher prices." Michael shook his head.

He and Sara walked and made small talk for a few minutes then began discussing the particulars of the case. That, in turn, gave way to a discussion of the man they were about to interview. They had plenty of time. Traffic in the city was always a nightmare. Particularly as they got closer to Drummer's building. It was in that part of midtown where the high rises with penthouses full of the rich and powerful butted up against the theater district and all the homelessness and poverty that clogged those well-trod streets.

"What do you have on Drummer?" Michael asked as a taxi swerved around them, nearly clipping off one of their rear-view mirrors.

"Just the standard stuff. No criminal convictions or even arrests, but a slew of legal challenges and scandals deep enough to drown a horse. He's got more money than God and that always means a lot of trouble. Not that they ever seem to mind much. The perks must make up for it."

"I can imagine," Michael said. "I'm actually surprised he was willing to speak with us without a warrant."

Sara grunted agreement before continuing.

"Drummer had a wife—his third—and two children from his previous marriages. Both of them are grown. Neither currently live in the city. For that matter, neither does Drummer, officially, though the address we're headed to is in his name."

Michael nodded along as Sara rattled off what facts they did know about the man. A lot of it was supposition culled from files and reports. He donated to charity, of course, in the flashy way that most rich people in the city did. It got them invites to all the most exclusive cultural events. He seemed to care particularly about museums of history.

Most of his holdings were industrial in nature. He made a killing off of each of the last few fuel crises. Drummer seemed to be a canny operator, always knowing when the next shock was just about to hit.

Must be nice to have friends in high places to discreetly tip you off whenever something was about to go down. And Drummer was big enough that there was no way the SEC was going to nail him on a bit of insider trading, even at this scale.

If they even went after guys whose net worth was in the twelve-figure range anymore.

"I had my team look into business connections between Drummer and our victim," Michael offered. "They haven't turned anything up yet. I'm sure they will eventually. They're sharp, and both men were far too rich and involved with far too many businesses and ventures not to have crossed paths at some point. It's just going to take time."

Michael checked his phone again just to make sure. Nope. Nothing new yet.

"It's always a needle in a haystack with rich people and corporations," Sara complained. "It was bad enough with multi-millionaires and multi-nationals a decade ago, but now? Billionaires running around the city? The assets are all so complex and tangled, even when they aren't held in a never-ending Matryoshka doll of nested shell companies, it's a nightmare sorting anything out."

Michael made a noncommittal sound of agreement. Sara was not wrong. That's why he was so glad Tanner liked that aspect of the job. More than made up for any weaknesses the guy had in the field.

"Here we are," Sara said as they neared their target. "Now all I need to do is find parking."

***

There was a *ding* as the elevator door slid open, revealing the interior of the penthouse level of Drummer's building. Michael and Sara stepped through, past the massive wrought iron gate that could be locked across the elevator doors, and onto a plush, Persian carpet that ran the length of the entry hall. It was clearly custom work, flowing and branching like a river along the hallway and its offshoots. Art practically dripped from the walls, hanging in massive gilded frames, and tasteful statues, busts, vases, and other precious artifacts stood at attention along the walls at even intervals.

The place screamed old money and new, and made no bones about showcasing the wealth.

There was even a butler waiting for them.

"Mister Drummer is in the study," he said. "If you will follow me, please."

They were led directly to Drummer's sanctuary, a large room lined with mahogany shelves, niches for works of art, several leather-bound books with indecipherable titles, and a window that showcased a spectacular view looking out over the city. Michael and Sara stood just inside the entrance. Their host was across from them.

Drummer stood behind a massive desk, the kind that could have served as a wrecking ball in its spare time, it was so solid, and clearly had to be air-lifted in through the window. He was pouring himself a drink from the selection of crystal decanters at the sideboard. Michael suspected that that one glass of booze was worth more than he'd make in six months of work. It was just that kind of room.

The man was a match for it. His manners were as polished as his desk and he moved with a limber ease that belied the snowy-white mane of hair on his head. Drummer's face was lined, but in that way that the wealthy alone have, indeterminate of true age. The man might be fifty or eighty. You couldn't tell simply from his slim frame or the healthful vigor that suffused his movements. Money could buy a great deal of rejuvenation care. And his bespoke suit, expertly tailored, was cut precisely to show him to greatest advantage.

This was a man that understood the power of presentation.

"Detectives," Drummer began, "what's this about poor Robert being murdered?"

Michael didn't bother to correct the man's assumption. Not only would it be useful, but the fact that the man started by demanding something from them, rather than opening the floor to their questions, rankled. He was treating the whole thing like an update on one of his minor business concerns, as if Michael and Sara were his employees.

Yeah, that was it. He was treating them like employees. The feeling made Michael's teeth itch for some reason.

"We were hoping you could shed some light on that very subject," Sara said, smoothly reclaiming control of the conversation. "The deceased's phone lists you as the last person he spoke with. What were the two of you talking about that day?"

"We were discussing dinner plans for later in the week. I'm only in town about two weeks a year, and I do like to entertain while I've got the house," Drummer gestured to the room around them. "Robert spent much more of his time here, but he did appreciate my art collection, so we make—*made*—a point of having a little get-together whenever I'm actually using the place."

Two weeks a year. This penthouse apartment was used just two weeks a year, and the rest of the time it just sat up here, locked and empty. Michael pivoted to move slowly around the room, taking in the details, while keeping an ear on the conversation Sara was having with Drummer.

There were several gold statues in a pseudo-Greek style. Satyrs seemed prominent, and kings. Oil paintings, too, were evenly spaced about the room. The one closest to Michael was a portly man sitting on a throne with two named figures at his feet. The man was wrapped in cloth of gold and had a pile of moneybags on his lap. The lower right corner of the painting had a signature, something that looked like "Watz," but Michael couldn't quite make it out.

Most of the books were on the shelf, neatly and expertly in rows. One stuck out a little further than the others, however, so Michael glanced at the title. It was Book Two of Spencer's *The Faerie Queene*. Huh. Not the kind of literature he'd expect an industrialist to favor, but it was probably a valuable first edition or something, bought for its value rather than any inherent interest Drummer might have in the subject.

Or maybe the man liked to read four-hundred-year-old literature in his spare time. For fun. There was no accounting for taste.

There were all kinds of objects d'art as well, including an ornate dagger with a golden hilt. Michael cataloged that right away as part of his initial scan of the room. It was always worth knowing where your exits were, and what weapons—improvised or otherwise—were close to hand. Even in seemingly normal situations like this, you never knew when someone might get desperate or do something stupid.

"No, I can't say I can," Drummer was saying. "You can't *not* have a very long list of enemies when you have as much money as I do—or Robert did. People who feel they've been wronged by you in some way, though you'd not know them from Adam if you were in the same room as them. People who want what you have, or just think you shouldn't have it." Drummer waved his hands airily about over the desk. "The list is quite literally endless."

"There have to be people that are more likely as suspects, though," Sara pressed. "Surely you can think of some. If your business and personal relationships were as close as your description has led me to believe."

Sara was watching Drummer carefully as she said that, but she was focused on his face. Michael was looking at the man's hands and he thought he saw them tighten around the glass he was holding. It was only a flash, so he couldn't be certain, however.

"Probably. If you'd like, I can draw up a list and have Smithers send it to you."

"That's your butler?"

"Yes. I always hire him temporarily when I'm in town. He does such a good job airing the place out and getting everything stocked and in order before I arrive. Honestly, most services are useless at things like that. The little details escape them. They think unlocking the door and sending a cleaning crew through is enough!" Drummer snorted. "Hardly."

"If you had to guess, though, right now, who would you think the prime suspect would be?" Sara tried to press Drummer on the issue.

"A disgruntled employee," he said immediately.

Michael had to repress a laugh at that. How many former employees, even in terms of the kinds and number of people working for a billionaire, had a sniper's skill set? Interesting that that was the first place he'd go to, as well. Were all bosses *that* conditioned to view their employees as the enemy?

"You seem very sure of that," Sara said, perhaps mimicking Michael's thought path.

"It's simple logic, my dear girl!" Drummer either did not see or chose not to see just how much those words made Sara bristle. "Envy arises from what one can see, resentment from those ill-equipped to recognize proper authority. Employees are in a position for both things to be true." The billionaire sighed and downed the last of his drink. "And these days? No one wants to work! No one appreciates what we do for this country."

"We?" Sara glanced around the office.

"People like me," Drummer clarified. "Job creators. Businessmen. Engines of industry. 'That of my plenty pour out unto all,'" Drummer gestured broadly with his arms. "'Ten times so much be numbered frank and free.'" The billionaire nodded at the book Michael had eyed in his circuit around the room. "Edmund Spenser."

"Pretty," Sara said, though Michael could tell she thought absolutely nothing of the words.

"You think of yourself as a philanthropist, then?" Michael asked.

"What rich man isn't?" Drummer smiled. "Even were I to give nothing to charity, the number of people I employ? The jobs I've created? That is a great deal of good done, my boy. A great deal, indeed."

"We'll look forward to receiving that list," Sara said firmly.

It was clear she thought this guy was as ridiculous as Michael did. The detective and the anti-terrorism agent exchanged a glance. It was clear this guy was full of himself, but he definitely didn't seem like a suspect. There was a genuine fondness for his friend Robert Hugs in his voice, though the man could just be an excellent actor.

He certainly had the means to hire a sniper and remove a business rival. Though the motive for that would have to wait on Tanner and Priestly and their friends in forensic accounting. Something told Michael that Drummer wasn't their guy, though. None of the instincts he was used to relying on were telling him that Drummer was anything other than what he appeared to be: a self-involved, old, white, rich man.

Sara looked like she wanted to continue interrogating the man, but she didn't say anything. There weren't any more obvious avenues for questioning. So she fidgeted with her suit before reluctantly bringing the meeting towards its close.

"Thank you for your time, Mister Drummer. I think that is all the questions we have for you right now. Though we may of course need to reach out to you as the case develops." Sara tugged at her sleeves.

"Thank you, Mister Drummer," Michael echoed. Might as well keep things on a polite footing. There was every likelihood they'd need to talk to the billionaire again, if only to try and get his help in accessing other hard-to-reach parts of Robert Hugs's life.

"Here, take my card," Drummer reached into the breast pocket of his suit and pulled out an antique silver card case. He flipped it open and pulled out two business cards, passing one each to Sara and Michael. "I've had my number changed again. Can't have it out there where anyone can phone in. I'm sure you understand." He smiled with too many teeth in Sara's direction. "That's a direct line to my personal assistant."

So much for direct access.

"Of course," Michael said before Sara could snap back. The card stock under his fingers was heavy and smooth, the highest quality, and the gilding of Drummer's name and contact details was a rich old gold.

"We'll be in touch," Sara said, grim promise in her tone.

"I would expect nothing less, dear girl. Nothing less." Drummer smiled.

Smithers appeared, opening the doors and standing just to one side, a clear invitation for the two of them to depart. If he instinctually knew to open the doors then, Drummer wasn't paying him nearly enough, but Michael suspected the billionaire had tripped some kind of silent servant-summoning alarm from behind his desk. Sara looked as if she wanted to say something, but instead she gave the butler a long and thoughtful look and moved to make her way out of the study.

Michael followed.

"Enjoy the remainder of your afternoon, Agent Lieberman," Drummer's voice floated after him, a note of amusement in it.

Michael started. He'd not told the man his last name, let alone his title. Before he could turn to face him, however, the doors closed behind him with a resonant *click*, a heavy sound like the final stone sliding into place on a tomb.

***

Drummer watched the detective and the agent leave. No sooner had his butler escorted them out than he had retrieved a sleek, black phone from an inner pocket and hit speed dial. There was a *click* as the line connected.

"You'll never guess who was just here. Yes, the detective, but she brought someone else along. He's calling himself Michael Lieberman, but he's the spitting image of—" Drummer paused as the voice on the other line spoke. "Yes. Exactly."

A heavy silence fell in the study as Drummer listened to the voice on the other end of the line.

"Yes," he said finally, "we should definitely take care of it."

CHAPTER 8

The Falling Spire

Stepping out onto the sidewalk, into the cooling evening, was a breath of fresh air, in spite of the tang of rot and garbage rising from the gutters. No street in this city escaped it, no matter how exclusive the postcode. Michael smiled at that as he stepped onto the sidewalk.

"Stuck up, but at least he wasn't as big an asshole as Kerbs," Sara muttered, walking next to him.

"I'll have to take your word on that," Michael said.

"Here, let's walk through the park to get back," Sara said. "I want to stretch my legs a bit after that, look at something other than dead wood and gold for a bit."

"Sounds good to me," Michael agreed easily.

"I don't think he had anything to do with Hugs' death," Sara said as they walked. "I don't think he's telling us everything, but I don't think he had anything to do with it."

"Agreed." Michael squinted in the afternoon sun. The sidewalks were beginning to fill with people. It was that time of day. Schools were out, businesses would be releasing a wave of employees soon, despite the longer working hours of a city like this.

Sara and Michael hurried across the street. As they reached the other side, the greenery of the park just on the other side of a low stone wall, a pigeon fell out of the sky and landed on the sidewalk next to them with a wet *splat*. It didn't move.

"If that isn't a sign of the day, I don't know what is," Sara said, stepping around the gruesome bit of flesh and feathers without batting an eye.

Live in the city long enough and most people start doing the same. Dead rats, dead pigeons, all manner of critters poisoned in the eternal war between humanity and those lifeforms it classed as vermin raged on. You'd think that it wouldn't be so obvious, but ever since the last administration gutted the Environmental Protection Agency to open up strip mining of national parks, companies had felt justified in hauling out all manner of banned pesticides. Michael had seen a lot more rats—some over two feet in length!—dead in the street where they'd crawled out of the sewers to die, poisoned and in pain.

It wasn't the greatest of municipal gains, really.

Michael followed Sara into the park. Well, not so much a park, really, as a very large churchyard that had been turned into a public green space. The church had been de-consecrated long ago and the churchyard long since turned into a de facto park. The place was currently the focus of a battle between the local branch of the historical society and some city real estate developers. If the signs posted all over the place were to be believed, anyway.

The press of people eased here. There were a few mothers together with their children, most of whom were running and shrieking with laughter across the grass. It was nice. Peaceful. The press and stress of the city, though it was just over that small stone wall, seemed suddenly far away. It would be a shame to lose this place to yet another high-rise development.

Michael followed Sara around the church along the little cobbled path. An afternoon breeze swirled around them, setting the leaves overhead to rustling. It was almost as if they were speaking. Michael had the unnerving feeling that he could understand what they were saying, if he just concentrated a bit, if he turned his ear in just the right way.

"So what's your next move?" Michael glanced over.

Sara was smiling up at the trees as she walked, a surprising look of peace on her face. She was enjoying this! Michael found himself smiling in response.

At least until she turned to look at him and frowned. His smile died as quickly as the pigeon had earlier. Sara was suddenly all business again.

"Kerbs, if I can get in to see him. I suspect I won't manage it. He was a real piece of work on the phone. I expect if I show up anywhere within a hundred feet of him without a warrant, he'd have my job like *that*." Sara snapped her fingers. "My boss would give it to him too. Spineless conformist fuck."

"I've known plenty of bosses like that." They'd reached the end of the loop around the church already, but Michael kept walking because Sara did. They headed around again. "I still haven't heard back from my people on the financial trail. Says a lot about how tangled it is. Tanner lives for this kind of thing and he's damned good at it."

"I could tell." Sara smiled. "He reminds me of my brother, a bit." The smile flickered and died. "Not that that has any bearing on the case." She cleared her throat. "I'll head back to the office and go through the evidence again. Maybe there's something there that I missed, some new lead we can follow."

That spark of vulnerability had been nice, Michael realized. He found himself wanting to know more about Sara's brother. But there was no way he was going to ask right now. That seemed like a terrible idea.

A man breezed past them, talking on his phone. Michael frowned at the rude behavior. A faint unease kindled in his gut. The behavior seemed particularly out of line, in this place.

Sara and Michael moved in silence for a few moments, navigating between several mothers pushing strollers and a few businessmen clearly taking off work early. Then a familiar face caught Michael's eye. Was that Gabriel? Michael blinked, but where he'd thought he'd seen Gabriel was just another businessman, charging ahead while staring absently at his phone.

"Do you know him?" Sara asked after the man passed.

"No," Michael said. "Thought it was someone I recognized but it wasn't."

"That happens to me all the time," Sara said, shaking her head. "I swear it's all the mugshots. We spend so much time staring at pictures of people, surveillance photos and footage, suspect pictures, perps and decoys in a line-up, you get a lot of faces stuck in here, you know? And your brain thinks they're all important, because at the time they *are*, but then you just have this library of people you don't really know in your brain and you start to see familiar faces everywhere, even when it's just another stranger on the street."

"I'd never thought of it like that." Michael blinked. "Makes sense, though."

"Too much sense," Sara agreed. "Bryan thinks it's bullshit, but anyone could see I'm the brains *and* the brawn in that partnership."

Sara flashed him a smile. Michael answered with one of his own and found himself laughing.

"I'm surprised he let himself get left out of this visit."

"He hates interviewing old white dudes. Especially the rich ones. We did him a favor." Sara shook her head. "Last time? The guy actually mistook him for the chauffeur and started yelling at him for not waiting in the car."

"Ouch. I can see why he might prefer desk duty. Never thought I'd see the day where anyone would say that, but in this case, yeah. That tracks." Michael decided to see if he could get Sara to open up a bit more since she was feeling chatty. "You two been partners long?"

"Four years now. We—"

Whatever Sara had been going to say next was interrupted by a small form, darting between the two of them.

"Matteo! What did I tell you about running? Slow down. You almost hit those nice people."

Michael smiled and waved to the mother, trying to fit the whole idea of "It's fine, we really don't mind" into that single motion the way people do. The kid stopped, turning to grin at him. Michael smiled back.

Then he froze. Something was wrong. Every instinct he had screamed that something terrible was about to happen, but he had no idea what.

"Matteo!"

There was a sharp *crack* from overhead.

Michael looked up. Time seemed to slow. He saw the spire of the church shudder and shift to the side, beginning to slide slowly—oh so slowly—off the top of the building. It was headed right for him and Sara!

He turned in place, the air feeling like molasses all around him. He shoved Sara away from him, away from the path of the falling spire, onto the nearby grass where the soft earth would catch her and keep her from injuring herself.

She flew away from him, still so slowly.

The spire was plummeting towards him. Slow, it moved so slow, but the very air was fighting him, grabbing at his arms, sticking to him and clutching at him with desperate fingers. Michael saw the boy, not three feet from him, staring up at the death falling toward him in shock.

He wasn't going to make it. The boy was going to die, crushed beneath two tons of stone.

No! He couldn't allow that to happen—wouldn't allow that to happen! Michael felt his jaw crack under the strain of trying to scream his frustration to the heavens. There was a sharp, blazing pain in the middle of his back and it was like the air snapped around him.

Suddenly he could move! Not freely, but faster. Fast enough to reach the boy. Fast enough to outpace the falling spire.

Michael caught the boy up in his arms, curling himself around him protectively as he made it just a few feet beyond where they had been standing when the spire—surreally slow or not—finally caught up with the ground. There was a series of sharp *cracks* as the paving stones snapped beneath the weight of the spire, part of a massive *thud* that shook the ground. Shrapnel went flying like bullets. Michael felt the impact of several pieces on his back. It was a strange counterpoint to the soft form huddled in his arms, stranger still that he was still moving slowly enough through time to notice such a thing.

He felt curiously light. Like air or like lightning. Like a feather on the wind.

Michael felt it when his feet touched down again, thrown as he was by the impact. He felt solid, painfully, sorrowfully solid. The suddenness of it hit him like a great wave but he didn't have time to consider what it might mean. There was someone else he was far more worried about.

"You're all right," he said to the boy. "You're all right. You…
are all right, aren't you?" Michael blinked dust out of his eyes and
tried to focus on the boy.

The kid nodded, brown eyes wide. He was still in shock.
Michael couldn't see any blood, didn't see any bruises or what
might be broken bones. He was fine.

They were fine.

He stood. His back screamed in agony and several spots of
pain blazed to fiery life. Michael almost collapsed to the ground
right then, but the boy had grasped his hand with all his strength,
and Michael couldn't—wouldn't—fall now.

The spire was embedded in the ground, shattered stone all
around it. The stone cross that had adorned the very top lay
broken in pieces right in front of Michael's feet. Across the way,
the rubble between them, Michael could see Sara staring at him.
The detective was still lying on the ground where she had fallen
after Michael had shoved her. Her gaze caught his, eyes wide.

He almost didn't notice when the boy's hand pulled free from
his. Almost didn't notice the hysterical crying of the boy's mother
next to him. He just stood there, staring at the ruin in front of him,
but the broken stones could offer no explanation to him as to why
they had chosen that exact moment to fall.

What the hell had just happened?

Michael. Well done.

CHAPTER 9

Unnerving Revelations

Michael sat on the couch, a cup of coffee slowly wafting steam in front of him. It was untouched. He didn't even register it, his eyes lost in the middle distance.

What was happening? Murder and a terrorist plot? His sister appearing out of nowhere? And she had magic? Interviewing billionaires and then the thing with the church and the falling masonry?

His back still throbbed. It'd been nearly a whole day since the mishap, and his back still throbbed. Michael lifted a hand to twist around and grope between his shoulder blades but let it fall before he could actually follow through. Did he want to know? What if he found something there? Like the monster he'd seen on Stowe's back? Or in the Spirit World when Hannah had shoved him sideways through that brick wall and into another world?

Did he really want to know?

Michael's phone sat on the coffee table in front of him, next to the steaming mug. Hannah's contact information glowed on the screen. Or would, if the phone hadn't gone back to sleep. Michael had opened and almost dialed his sister more times than he could count this morning.

He was pretty sure he already knew what she'd say. Forget about it. Go back to his old life. Don't ask questions, don't look for answers.

Be safe.

But safe from what?

Michael huffed out what might have been an ironic laugh if he'd had more energy. Safe. As if his life had ever been safe. He, like many other orphans, might have had the dream, but he certainly hadn't had that reality. Not then, and not now.

Not with the things he'd done to survive, to build a nice life for himself.

Though there was another option for answers. Someone else he'd met in the Spirit World that made him an offer. The mysterious man in the trench coat and glass. The walking stereotype. Man of mystery.

Gabriel.

Michael flicked on his phone and pulled up the number. It glowed on his screen, promising a lot. Answers. Danger.

One really pissed-off sister.

He set the phone down and took up the coffee. It was practically tepid. Michael grimaced but didn't rise to freshen the cup.

Answers. He couldn't make an informed choice without them. His sister wouldn't give them, and even if she did, would he be able to trust them?

Could he trust Gabriel?

Michael tapped his chin. He could probably trust them to cancel one another out. If he talked to both he could compare information and possibly thresh out something like the truth from the wheat and chaff the two would throw to him.

Yeah. He'd do that.

Plan sorted, Michael reached for the phone. Gabriel first, he decided. He'd already had some bits from Hannah, and he knew her well enough—he *used* to know her well enough—to read her reactions, get some context that way.

The phone rang twice, but the third ring was echoed, almost overlapped, by the doorbell. Michael glanced from phone to door. Something told him to hang up and open it, so he did.

Gabriel was right outside.

"How—no," Michael held the door open. "Come on in."

"Thank you." Gabriel breezed past. "Though you should be more careful who you invite into your home." Before Michael could say anything, he continued. "Vampires."

"Really?" Michael closed the door. "Vampires?"

"I'm joking!" Gabriel smiled.

Michael relaxed. Spirits were one thing, but if he had to deal with vampires as well—

"Little jest to break the ice. No, vampires needing an invitation is a myth." Gabriel paused. "Well, for most of them."

Of course.

"Would you like something to drink?" Michael reached for politeness, not quite sure what else to say, not quite ready to ask his questions and get answers he may not like.

"No thank you," Gabriel's said, moving to seat himself in a convenient chair across from where Michael had been enchanted on the sofa. "We should probably get started. I expect this will be a lengthy conversation and I could be called away at any minute."

"Right." Michael crossed the room and reclaimed his position. "I guess—"

"Why don't I just rip the bandage off? The world, Michael, is like a human being. It has a body, the physical world you can see around you, and a soul, the spirit world you stepped into the other day. There are various beings that inhabit each, and deeper depths to the Spirit Worlds than any sane being really plumbs, but the analogy works well enough." Gabriel pushed his sunglasses up the bridge of his nose. "And you, Michael, are a product of both."

"What?"

"You're half-and-half. One mortal parent. One spirit parent. That's why you can do what you can do. Move too fast. Shoulder off several hundred kilos of falling granite. That sort of thing. You, Michael, are—what's the closest mortal term you might recognize?—an archangel."

That…was a lot. If it was true.

"It's true," Gabriel said as if reading his thoughts. "Here, we don't have time for this. Do you have a sword or some kind of holy book? Some symbol of truth or justice?"

Who keeps a sword in their apartment? Though, given some of the things he'd seen, maybe he should start. No holy books, unless Marlowe counted. Maybe something like, ah. Michael pulled out his badge.

"Will this do?"

"It'll do if you believe in it," Gabriel answered, somewhat cryptically. "Might as well try."

He reached out and tapped a fingernail against the metal of the badge. It rang out with the sound of a vast bell.

Michael almost dropped the thing.

Gabriel nodded.

"Looks like you believe in it, enough anyway. Go ahead, put your hand on it and try to lie."

Michael did as he asked. He opened his mouth, but nothing came out. He tried again.

Still nothing.

"Major invocation," Gabriel said. "Now, try saying something you know to be true. Pay attention to how it sounds."

"The sun seems to rise in the east because of the direction of the Earth's rotation," Michael said.

He blinked. Every single word rang in his ears. Like each had been somehow spoken by a carillon of bells.

Then Gabriel reached out and took up the badge.

"I am not here to lie to you. I am here to help you. You can trust the words I speak are the truth."

Every syllable rang like a bell, and Michael found he couldn't help but believe them.

"Good?" Gabriel looked at him expectantly.

"Good," Michael managed.

"Here, maybe this will help as well." Gabriel took off his glasses, revealing his eyes. "There's a bit of truth to the saying that eyes are the mirrors to the soul."

They were unnerving, Gabriel's eyes. Oh, they looked human enough but the *color*. Michael hadn't known that strength and duty had colors, but there they were, mixed in the eyes of the man sitting across from him.

Then a pair of vast wings, the feathers matching Gabriel's eyes, flared into existence behind him.

Michael's back spasmed in response. He flicked a glance to the television screen, a black mirror, but it was just him sitting on the couch, normal as before.

Still, his back throbbed and whispers of that dream flight susurrated through his mind.

"There are many things I could tell you," Gabriel said, "but as time is limited I will try to focus on the important ones. You've seen some of the Spirit World, though you should be thinking of it less as a separate place and more of something that occupies much the same space as the world as you know it. The closer regions of it, anyway."

"It's inhabited by beings of all kinds, many of which have been seen by mortals throughout history and given rise to all manner of myth, folklore, and legend. Some you might think of as good—"

"Like angels?" Michael asked, eyeing Gabriel's wings.

"It's a word that works, though my kind—our kind—can be good, evil or anything in-between. Angels, demons, kinnaris, swanmays, tengu, we've had many names. Wings are common, as is a connection to ideas or ideals. That's why you get the idea of angels who guard or demons of wrath or lust."

"Demons," Michael said. "Demons are real too?"

He could believe it, actually, considering some of the things he'd seen in the Spirit World.

"Oh yes," Gabriel said softly. "Very real. And something you desperately need to know about. In fact, it's one of the reasons I think your sister is incorrect to try and keep this world from you. Whether either of you likes it or not, the world will come looking for you."

"The world? Or a particular demon?" Michael thought it certainly sounded like Gabriel's had someone specific in mind.

"I mentioned some of us have connections to specific ideas, can draw a great deal of power from them, in fact?" Gabriel waited for Michael to nod. "There is a being of great and terrible power, a being who draws his strength from avarice. Sometimes mortals call him Mammon."

Michael might not be religious, but he'd been raised in a Catholic orphanage. He knew his Christian lore. Mammon was the archdemon of greed. One of the greatest of the angels that fell from heaven.

Though it didn't sound like Gabriel was saying there was a heaven. Or a hell.

This was…a lot.

"And you think Mammon has some sort of interest in me?" Michael found that hard to believe.

"He is largely the reason you ended up in that orphanage,' Gabriel said quietly. "He is incredibly powerful and has all manner of agents that do his work for him here in the physical realm."

"He can't just reach out and do whatever he wants?" That was part of the problem Michael was having with all of this. If there were all these powerful beings, why wasn't the whole planet just their playground?

"No. Stronger spiritual beings tend to come from deeper within the Spiritual World. Places like the Deep Astral, or Faerie, or Pandemonium. The stronger they are, the harder it is for them to get a proper foothold in the physical world. It's a small blessing, but even small blessings are to be counted."

The conversation carried on, Gabriel taking Michael through a crash course on multi-world metaphysics, the various kinds of spiritual inhabitants he was likely to encounter, some of the rules, etc. Angels and demons weren't the only beings wandering the world. Vampires, werewolves, fairies, yokai, and more were to be found all over the world. You could even find them in the city! New York was a melting pot for supernaturals as much as it was for humans from around the world. There was even, apparently, a goblin market that appeared from time to time, though Gabriel warned him repeatedly not to try and buy anything there unless he was very skilled or truly desperate.

Of all the things Gabriel explained to him, how to do magic was not one of them. Not yet. If Michael wanted to learn, yes, Gabriel was willing to teach him, but not before Michael had made his decision—exercised his free will—and made some commitments.

"There is a group that opposes the—as you call them—evil forces assailing the physical world. Call it "The Resistance." It's had many names down through the ages, but most of them are ridiculous, if not entirely out of date. More than that I will not say, not without certain oaths being in place."

"Is Hannah a part of it? This Resistance?" Michael had a sudden instinct. It would explain a lot. Her facility with magic. Her disappearance. How close-mouthed she was about some of the subjects he'd tried to question her about.

"I think that is something for your sister to confirm or deny herself," Gabriel said, sidestepping the question.

Michael filed it away with the list of questions he was mentally assembling to ask his sister as soon as Gabriel left. He had quite a few stored up at this point. Though Gabriel's next words distracted him entirely from reviewing them.

"There's one more truth I have to tell," Gabriel's said solemnly. "It's about your parents."

CHAPTER 10

Family And Friends

His parents? Michael blinked at Gabriel. His first thought was what could his parents have to do with any of this, but if it was true—that he was some kind of angel, like Gabriel—then it had to come from somewhere.

Like his parents. Well, one of them, anyway. Gabriel had said he was half-and-half.

Still, no reason to jump to conclusions.

"What about my parents?"

"Mammon took a particular interest in them. I don't know why. He had some plan, however, and it either involved using them somehow, or they got in the way of it." Gabriel's voice was softer, now. "I suspect the demon had a particular use for them. And, possibly now, for you. You are, after all, your parents' child."

Michael shoved the unpleasant part of that thought away, for now. This was all getting to be too much, too fast. Though part of him—the professional part that had seen action and knew the value of intelligence—rebelled. Still, there was another question burning in his mind more brightly.

"Did you know them?" Michael asked. "My parents. Before…"

"Oh, this information came to me much later,' Gabriel said, dismissing the question with a flick of his fingers. "Though yes, if I could have intervened, I would have. I—" the angel paused and his wings quivered. "Ah. I see. No. Your parents did want you. Very much. And before you ask why, I cannot say for certain. I do know that your mother believed that Mammon was still searching for her. Searching for you. She was convinced that hiding you and running away was the only way to protect you."

"How can you be sure?"

"Letters that I have seen. Things that Hannah has said." Gabriel sighed "We had such a good working relationship, for a while."

"What did Mammon want with my family? What do I need to do to defend myself?" Michael's hand itched for a gun, for a knife, for a rock—anything he could use to defend himself, but which of those would be any good against a demon?

The apartment was quiet, save for the sound of the wind across the glass of the windows. Gabriel shifted, his wings rustling around him. He cocked his head to one side.

"I don't know, is the answer to the first. I'm trying to find out, but I have yet to discover any useful leads. As for the second," Gabriel shrugged, "there are a few things. Though perhaps your mother was right. Perhaps your sister is right. Perhaps hiding as deeply as you can in a mortal life is the safest thing you can do. Though you'd need to find a new one. I'm afraid you've become quite compromised here."

Michael rolled that around in his mind, leaning back into the thick padding of his sofa to think about it. He could do that. He had the skills to disappear. Find work as a mercenary. Get a new name. He even had a stash of emergency cash and supplies he could use. It would be easy enough to go tonight. To just disappear.

But he wasn't sure if that's what he wanted to do. Michael wasn't really one to back down. And he'd only just managed to reconnect—if you could call it that—with his sister.

"And if I want to fight?"

"Then that is something you can learn to do." Gabriel's eyes seemed to stare right through him. "Though there is, of course, no guarantee that your personal power will be enough to challenge a being of Mammon's might and influence. Still, here on in the physical world, you would have an advantage. And yes, before you ask, I am willing to teach you, as I said. If certain conditions are met."

"I'll have to think about that," Michael said carefully.

"Do. Consult with your sister. Verify as much of what I have told you as you can." Gabriel stood, his wings flaring. "But for now, I must go. There are other people and other places that require my attention. Have a good night Michael. I hope you have found our discussion useful."

"It's certainly given me a lot to think about," Michael responded.

Gabriel inclined his head. His wings flared and a flash of brilliant white light answered. When Michael's vision cleared, the self-professed angel was gone.

"Well, that was something," Michael said to the air.

He didn't move for a moment, just listening to the racing beat of his heart in his chest. It was overwhelming, everything he'd been told. But Michael was trained for stressful situations, trained to take the information he had at hand and quickly evaluate it to decide on a course of action.

Of course, this situation was a bit outside of all the ones he'd drilled for or lived through. He didn't know nearly enough about the capabilities of his enemies, or what force he might be able to bring to bear in the future.

"Fuck." Michael sank back into the sofa.

It was too much. Too many things. Though he could break it apart. No task was impossible if you broke it down into smaller pieces.

He needed to talk to Hannah. See what she could tell him. He even picked up the phone to dial, but then he stopped himself.

No. Not right now. There was too much in his head. Talking to Hannah would only add to that. He needed to deal with what he could, first. Sort out what Gabriel had told him. Make up a list of priorities and questions, and then talk to Hannah.

It was too much. He needed a drink. Maybe someone to talk to, at least about the revelation about his parents. Well, as much as he could say about it anyway.

He could call someone. Meet up at a bar. It was still early.

Michael came to a decision, picked up his phone, and dialed.

"Hi," he said when it connected, "are you free?"

***

New York City had more than its fair share of bars, pubs, clubs, and gin joints in general. Michael made his way to Midtown, where he'd be spoilt for choice. There was a place called 47s that might be thought of as an Irish Pub if the place bothered to give a shit, but it didn't, so it was just another storefront bar like all the rest.

It just had decent Guinness on tap and more than one cider bottled in the fridge.

Michael slid into a seat at the bar and ordered himself a pint. The wood beneath his hands was sticky with the residue of decades of spilled drinks and food grease. The place was busy enough that you felt comfortably a part of life in the city, but not so crowded you couldn't have a conversation or hear yourself think.

"Hey," Sara said, appearing to perch on the stool next to his. "Thanks for the invite."

"Thanks for coming out." Michael signaled the barman. "What'll it be?"

"I'll have what he's having," Sara said as the barman appeared.

They didn't say anything as they waited for Sara's drink. Michael could feel the tension between them. A bit wary, but tempered with a bit of respect.

Fuck. The churchyard. That had happened. It seemed like forever ago, but it had to be up there in Sara's mind. He could see it in her eyes, her posture.

Too bad he didn't have any answers he wanted to give her.

Too bad he didn't have any answers he wanted to give himself.

Gabriel's words flitted through his brain.

"Cheers," he said, raising his glass when Sara had hers.

"Cheers."

The clink of the glasses was lost in the general din of the bar.

They started with general chat. Talking about the weather, local politics, office politics, the general sort of nonsense people say when they don't have anything to say, or worse, when they do but they don't want to get into it.

Then they got into their pasts. It took a few drinks, but they made it. Michael talked about growing up an orphan and elicited an unexpected reaction from Sara.

"I lost my parents young too," she said. "Mom died before I was old enough to remember her, and then I lost my dad as well when I was nine."

The way she said it made Michael think there was more to it than the odd heart attack or stroke, but Sara didn't elaborate.

They bonded a bit about how shitty the system treated foster kids, then moved on to safer topics.

Every so often Michael caught Sara looking at him. Weighing him with her eyes. Eventually, she worked the conversation around to the other day.

"You've got good reflexes,' she said, absently spinning her glass on the counter. "You're fast. So fast. I've never seen anyone move like that."

"I didn't know I could move like that," Michael said. It was the truth, anyway. He took a sip of his drink, the last, then signaled the bartender for another. "Glad I did though."

"Yeah," Sara said. "That's the thing, isn't it? The best part of the job."

"Helping someone? Yeah." Michael wasn't sure why he said that. He hadn't had nearly enough booze for a conversation this honest or this maudlin. "It's too bad it doesn't happen more often, though."

"Try working in a police precinct." Sara let out a bitter bark of a laugh. "Not a lot of helping gets done, all things considered. Too many assholes in it for the chance to abuse what little power the system gives 'em. Too many trigger-happy wannabe heroes hoping for fifteen minutes of fame."

"Overstreet seems like a good guy though. Good partner." Michael didn't really have a follow-up to Sara's observation save that his department wasn't much different. That was just depressing though and he wasn't here for depressing conversation.

"He is. Overprotective idiot, but a good guy." Sara smiled and took another swig of her beer. "Sounds like you've got a good team working with you too, though."

"I do, yeah. I really do." Michael let a smile slowly slide across his face. "Took a while. Teams aren't easy to build. And most days I'm not sure the extra headache of being in charge is worth the perks of being in charge, but when it comes to my team, yeah. Worth it."

"That's nice," Sara said.

Michael could tell she was looking at him again, but this time it felt different. Like he'd passed some sort of test or she'd come to some sort of decision.

"It was good, that day. Something to remind me that things can go right, after that dead-end of an interview with that smarmy fuck Drummer. It's nice to see someone make a difference, use their talents for good." Sara let out a long sigh and took another drink. "It doesn't happen often enough."

She wasn't wrong. Even Michael, working with his unit, put in a lot of hours for debatable gain. It wasn't something you could measure, really. It was nice to have a reminder that there were things you could do with obvious, concrete benefit, sometimes.

"It was," Michael agreed. "And it doesn't. At least we both have good people to work with, though. That helps."

"It does. And it's great to have someone at your back that you can trust."

Michael felt her attention again and felt an irrational flash of guilt. He wasn't exactly being totally forthcoming. Not that he could without getting himself committed.

"I mean, how else are we going to take care of one another, take care of everyone out there, if we can't trust the people we're working with?" Sara paused. "Though it helps if you work with friends, or friends who are like family."

That was it. That was what it was all about. Protecting what he loved.

If he was going to do that, he was going to need all the help he could get. All the power he could learn. Even if it did mean walking into a whole new world.

"To family and friends, old and new," he said, raising his glass.

"To family and friends," Sara echoed.

CHAPTER 11

Lux Et Veritas

Michael squinted in the afternoon sunlight. It was a clear, crisp day and the small park around him was lushly green and manicured to within an inch of its life. Residential high-rises loomed all around them, a forest of Art Deco stone and steel, with this little park a small glade or oasis in the center. Inordinately playground equipment, looking more like modern art than anything that would be enjoyed by a child, clumped together to his left, empty and quiet.

Police tape and scattered location cards marked out the area of Hugs' murder, completing the scene. Though the body was long gone, and any blood lost amongst the grass, this was where the billionaire died.

"The grandson was over there," Sara was walking him through the scene. "He's been interviewed by a child psychologist attached to the force. You've read the report already."

Michael had.

"Bodyguards were around the perimeter of the park," Sara continued. "Took them thirty seconds, maybe a minute to respond. Ballistics estimates that the shot came from," she crouched down near the body mark and pointed to one of the buildings clad in pale grey stone, "there. About two-thirds of the way up the building. We're still canvassing residents and building staff, looking for anyone who might have seen anything. So far we're coming up empty. There's no evidence that any of the rooms have been broken into, not so far anyway and it's taking forever to try and contact all the residents who aren't in the country right now."

Sara's face looked slightly disgusted.

"That many people own property in the building but don't even bother to live there?" Michael guessed.

"Yup." Sara shook her head. "It's a nightmare. Any one of them could be the staging ground and the paperwork alone—"

she groaned. "Not that we have many other leads. That's why we approached you, hoping you might have something more than we did, once we were alerted to the links between our cases. All we've got left right now really is more interviews. Like Hugs's personal assistant. She should be expecting to meet with us after we finish here. Unless you turn up anything else we can use."

"We can hope."

Michael paced the perimeter, taking it all in. He wasn't super hopeful that a regular review of the area would result in any new information, but it helped to see the place in person and get a feel for the scene.

"Does something about this feel personal to you?" He asked.

He wasn't even sure why he said that. Some new instinct? But there was something about the place that screamed to him that this was more than an impersonal hit. Fuck knows why.

Of course, if the last few days had taught him anything it was that there was always more to a place than meets the eye. At least than meets the physical eye.

Michael struggled to remember. What were the words Gabriel had used? They had allowed him to see through to the spirit world, or something similar. Was there anything here he might see with them?

If he was truly half-spirit, half-angel, shouldn't he be able to see things naturally?

A stab of pain knifed through his eyes as he squinted, trying to see through to that other world. What were the words? Lux et veritas?

There was a flicker. The world briefly changed and he saw a swarm of strange beings hovering over the place where Hugs had died. It only lasted a moment, but Michael was sure of what he saw.

"You alright?" Sara was looking at him funny. "I think you've got a nosebleed starting. Here."

She passed him a napkin, stamped with the logo of a nearby coffee cart.

"Thanks." Michael dabbed at his nose. Yup. Little bit of blood there.

But it had worked. He'd definitely seen something. What it was and what it meant, he had no idea, but he'd seen it.

What else might he see if he tried again?

Even if he did see something, could he use it? Though Michael and Sara seemed to have established a solid bond of trust, especially after their drinks the other night, it was still new, and Michael doubted it was up to withstanding a revelation like the one he would unleash if he told her what he was really seeing.

He wasn't even certain he trusted his own sanity. Trusted this new reality. How could he expect her to?

Of course that depended on him actually finding something with these new eyes of his. Michael put the moral dilemma to one side and focused on the magic. There are none so blind as those who will not see, but that wasn't him. Focus!

Lux et veritas.

Pain spiked in his eyeballs once more. A tiny swarm of *things* appeared where Hugs's body had fallen, as they had before, but this time the vision held and Michael could see they weren't the only ones. There was a trail of smaller ones following a line in the air between where Hugs had been shot and about two-thirds of the way up the building opposite, as Sara had indicated.

He squinted.

And that wasn't all. There was a small cloud of them near the top of the building as well, it looked like.

"Do you have any binoculars?" he asked Sara.

"Got a pair in the Crown Vic. One sec."

The detective disappeared to fetch them. Michael dug his fingernails into his palm to distract himself from the pain in his eyes and try to keep his vision focused on the other realm.

Sara reappeared and passed him the binoculars.

"Thanks." Michael glanced through them, hoping his enhanced vision would work through the device.

It did. There was a small swarm of the things hovering over what looked like a window-washing rig. It was currently resting on the roof, but Michael could see the moveable crane arms that could swing out to raise and lower it.

"What if our suspect didn't use any of the apartments inside to stage the hit?" He asked, offering the binoculars to Sara. "Rooftop. Have a look."

"I'll be damned," Sara said after a minute. "You think our perp used the window-washing rig to stage the hit? That's a tough shot for anyone, let alone at this distance. Doesn't seem humanly possible. The wind shear, movement in the cables—"

Sara kept rattling off the difficulties a sniper would face in these circumstances, but Michael had caught on to the phrase humanly possible. There was a lot he now knew that was beyond the human. Were they chasing something from the other side? And if they were, did he have to tell Sara?

"Maybe not, but it's probably easier to try and get permission to check the roof on the off chance than to wait on all the paperwork for those apartments with A.W.O.L. owners, right?"

"If you think it's worth the time." Sara didn't seem convinced.

Michael wasn't sure either, and even if he was right about the window-washing rig being used as the mobile platform for their sniper, that didn't mean there would be any evidence left behind. So far their target had been careful, canny, and more than capable of slipping pursuit.

That didn't mean it wasn't worth the time to follow up on it. Especially if there wasn't a better lead at the moment.

Did Sara have a better lead?

"Any luck with Drummer?" He asked. Sara had been trying to find an angle that would let them pressure the man a bit more.

The billionaire had to know something useful. Michael's gut told him that much. Sara's gut agreed, but when he'd asked about follow-ups she hadn't had anything. Maybe she'd found another angle though.

"No," Sara shook her head sourly.

Or maybe not.

"He's got too much money and too much clout. I was told in no uncertain terms to leave him alone."

"I'm honestly surprised he didn't lawyer up before we got a chance to meet with him the first time," Michael said.

"Drummer's canny. Someone like that has faced so much litigation he has to have a pretty good idea of what lines he can and cannot cross."

"You can work around it, sometimes. Request records, do some light surveillance—" Michael massaged the bridge of his nose. His eyes were throbbing after forcing himself to see into the spirit world. Hopefully he hadn't done any permanent damage.

"Interview the staff?" Sara waved him off. "Tried all of that. He's wrapped up tighter than Fort Knox."

"Normally I'd say that just makes him guilty, but you don't get to be a billionaire without being guilty of a whole helluva lot, so that doesn't really help in this specific case." Michael let a wry grin creep across his face.

"Exactly." Sara sighed, her shoulders dropping suddenly. "Exhausting. Seen enough? If so we should move on. I'll put in the request for roof access. Not sure how long it'll take though."

"I don't think we're going to get anything more out of this visit," Michael said. "Might as well try the next lead, even if it's a tenuous one."

Sara sighed.

"Let's go interview the P.A."

CHAPTER 12

More Questions

Sara drove them in her Crown Vic. Michael was quickly coming to appreciate the smoothness of the ride. The car was heavy and that made all the difference.

It was a long drive. The woman they were headed to interview lived all the way out in Queens. Michael didn't want to think how early she had had to wake up to make sure she had been at Hugs's side in the morning to handle his schedule. Still, if you wanted affordable, you wouldn't find it in Manhattan. Not these days.

It was a nice drive, actually. The rapport he and Sara had built after that night in the bar was holding strong. They discussed the case, daily life, and even got into an argument over the relative merits of Styx versus Queen.

Before he quite realized how fast the time had flown, they were pulling up to the curb in front of a small house, tidy, but with robin's egg blue paint beginning to ship off the siding and rust beginning to eat into the white metal of the window awnings.

Michael let Sara lead the way. It was technically her lead, so let her talk to the woman first.

"You sure Brian doesn't mind having to sit this one out?" Michael asked. He couldn't imagine Sara's partner was too happy about that fact.

"He's chasing down another lead. One he claims is better." Sara shot Michael a smile. "I can't wait to rub it in his face when we prove him wrong."

Michael grinned back before settling a look of cool professionalism in place. Sara already had her game face on as she strode up the few steps to the front door and rang the bell. There was no sound, but with these old houses it was always impossible to tell if the bell was broken or just quiet.

Sara knocked after waiting a few moments.

Nothing.

Sara frowned and knocked again.

No answer.

She jerked her head at Michael. Getting the message, he immediately moved to try and find a way around to the back of the house.

He checked the windows as he went. Blinds down. Can't see inside. Standard for New York City, even out here in Queens. No one wanted passers-by just looking into the lower levels of the house. Which helped Michael's recon not at all.

A battered wooden gate allowed access to a thin strip of cracked concrete running along the side of the house to the parched back lawn. Michael peered around the corner of the house. No one in sight. Back door appeared to be closed. No idea if it was locked or not.

Michael did a quick survey of the backyard. It was brown and withered, and not terribly large. There was a rotting garden shed at the far end. A cracked cement patio extended from the back of the house, under what was probably an illegal raised back patio and set of wooden stairs.

To get to the back door he'd have to walk under the platform decking. There were supports, but they were thin. Nothing that would provide much cover if things went South.

"NYPD," Michael heard Sara's raised voice from the front of the house. "Everything all right in there? Ms. DeSousza?"

They'd had an appointment. No reason for the woman not to answer. Michael edged the safety off his weapon and watched the back door for any signs of movement.

When nothing happened after a long moment he closed in. He could see through the window that led to the kitchen, the thin white-and-yellow curtain not doing much to obstruct his vision. It was empty. No sign of anyone.

Michael tried the door. Unlocked. He eased it open and slipped inside. From somewhere ahead and to his left he could hear Sara entering through the front.

"Shit." Sara's voice was low but clear as day. "Woman down! Lieberman! Come cover me."

Michael sped through to the front of the house, where he found Sara, gun in hand, standing over a woman splayed out in a pool of her own blood.

Ms. DeSousza, presumably.

As soon as Michael appeared, Sara holstered her weapon and crouched down to check for a pulse. Michael caught the detective's eye but she shook her head. The woman was already dead.

For an instant, Michael saw another face in place of DeSouza's. Innocent, she had claimed, but she'd also been face-down in her apartment, though it was Michael's boot on her neck, not her death, that kept her there.

He shook off the memory.

"I need to call this in—" Sara said before there was a faint *creak* from above their heads.

Someone else was in the house with them.

In an instant, Sara's gun was back in her hand. She jerked her head at Michael and he moved to the archway separating the living room they were in from the entryway where he could see a set of stairs leading upwards.

Sara flashed past him, moving quickly and surprisingly quietly to the foot of the stairs, her gun aimed upward. The two of them froze, listening. For a long moment, nothing happened. Michael slowed his breathing to keep it and his gun arm steady.

Then it happened again. A faint creak from the floorboards above. Sara set one foot on the stairway leading up when they heard it—a clattering sound from the back of the house.

The external stairs!

Michael bolted for the back door. He could hear Sara right behind him. Cutting down the hall he dashed through the kitchen and paused at the back door, trying to get eyes on the suspect. There was a flash of motion at the foot of the stairs and a figure running toward the back of the yard. Michael could only make out a tall, athletic frame, jeans and a fitted shirt.

There was no way to get a good shot from this angle, and yelling "Stop! Police!" had never worked once in the history of law enforcement. The suspect definitely had a gun, as that was what killed Ms. DeSousza.

All of this flashed through Michael's mind as he made a split-second decision to pursue.

Michael dashed out the door. He could feel Sara not far behind him. The suspect was sprinting for the back fence. It was high but easy enough to hurdle. There was an alleyway behind, or the suspect could hop another fence and hide in one of the nearby houses if the pursuing duo weren't quick enough.

The suspect took the fence, flashing a quick look behind him—Michael could now see it was a man, tall, Caucasian, well-muscled—before vaulting easily over.

"Son of a bitch!" Sara's voice rang out from behind him. Then she rattled off a request for backup into her radio.

Michael didn't stop. Sara had backup handled, and he knew she'd be right behind him. He upped his speed so he could vault over the fence as well.

He cleared it, easily. Too easily, really, but he ignored the thought for now.

Michael landed lightly on the cracked asphalt of the alleyway. There were bags of garbage piled here and there, with scattered trash choking the various nooks and crannies. There were oil puddles from passing cars, flickers of movement from an alley cat or a stray dog hiding amongst the rubbish, but no sign of the suspect.

The man was gone.

***

Michael and Sara returned to the house, securing the scene as they waited for forensics to show up. Something was clearly eating at Sara but Michael didn't ask. They weren't on solid enough ground for that.

Sara took the opportunity to carefully examine the house without disturbing the scene.

The place was a disaster zone. From the state of the place, it was clear that the murderer had been looking for something, or several somethings. Drawers were opened, cabinets rifled through; general chaos reigned throughout.

"No sign of a laptop or phone anywhere," Michael confirmed.

"He didn't have a bag on him though," Sara complained, "and there's no way she didn't have one for work. So where is it? Did he take it or did she leave it somewhere else?"

"Maybe she kept it at Hugs's," Michael called from the office. There was an old desktop computer there, but the housing had been opened and the motherboard removed. "He was certainly taking—or disposing of—everything that looked like it could hold information."

The bookshelves had been torn apart—some of the books literally.

"There's no way he left here with more than a phone and a few sheets of paper in his pockets," Sara protested.

Unless he had some kind of magic. The thought was not one that sat easily with Michael. But this was new territory, with new players. What did he truly know about Hugs, for example? The man could have been any manner of spiritual in hiding, using who knows what talents to accrue his obscene fortune.

Maybe he should request to see the body before the coroner had to surrender it up for the family's funeral.

That would have to wait, however. Here and now he had a fresh murder to deal with. And he had a way to see if there was more here than met the eye, even if it was unreliable. Still, it had provided him with a clue last time. Might as well try his luck again.

Michael muttered the incantation under his breath this time, in case that made it easier.

It didn't. It still took him several attempts and cost him a spike of pain through each eyeball. And even then he was nearly blinded by the result. Not because the magic hadn't worked, but because it worked too well.

That is, it revealed too much.

If the little spiritual parasites that had hovered over Richard Hugs's murder site were bad, this was a hundred times worse. The place was so swarming with monstrosities Michael couldn't see the floor around the body.

The air all through the house also seemed to swirl with something. Michael would have called it snow but it was larger and grittier and grey. Some of it landed on his lips and the chalk and smoke of it told him exactly what it was.

Ash.

What had gone through here?

Michael moved through the whole house carefully, but nothing leapt out at him as an obvious clue, other than the odd manifestation of ashes, which were fading even as he moved from room to room. He had the creeping feeling that their murder suspect might indeed be more than he appeared to be.

Fuck. Just what he needed.

"There's no real way to tell what's missing," he said at last, "but it definitely looks like he was here to steal or destroy some kind of records or information. Those are the only commonalities I can see."

"She'd certainly have access to all kinds of stuff that people would want to exploit or keep safe. Even Hugs's personal schedule would be worth something." Sara had crouched down to shine the light from her phone under the couch, in case something had slipped under there.

"Well, whatever it was, it's gone now." Michael paused, hearing movement outside. He glanced out the window and saw the forensics van pulling into the driveway. "We're not going to figure it out ourselves, not right this second, anyway."

Sara stood and sighed. She moved over to join him by the door.

"They'll let us know if they find anything. I'll put out a request for canvassing. Maybe one of the neighbors saw something, saw where our suspect went. He can't have just vanished into thin air."

Unfortunately, Michael knew Sara was wrong on that one. Again, he felt like he should tell her, but that can't be a good idea. Could it?

"I suppose we'll have to wait and see," he said instead. "Who knows? Maybe we will get lucky. Until then, I guess we move on."

Sara shook her head, a disgruntled twist to her lips.

"Just what we need. More questions."

CHAPTER 13

The Hidden World

After Michael had exhausted his usefulness at the crime scene, he excused himself and caught a taxi back to the city. He wanted to file some paperwork and check-in. Maybe Tanner had turned up some new leads.

Today certainly hadn't resulted in anything concrete.

His driver was old-fashioned, the kind that kept the radio on and simultaneously kept up a non-stop stream of chatter as they drove. Michael only had one ear to spare. His eyes were killing him, but the whole seeing through to the spirit world thing wasn't fading. Not yet anyway.

"Can you believe this shit?" His driver complained, thumping a hand against the dash just above the radio. "These politicians! Unbelievable! Fighting over this stupid debt ceiling thing. Every six months it seems like we gotta listen to this crap. Playing with people's lives is what it is. My cousin, who works down in Washington, explained the whole thing to me. They don't pass this debt ceiling bill thing, and the government goes into shutdown, worse, other countries get antsy, think our money ain't so good no more. I don't understand all of it, but I know it's not the politicians who suffer. You know it's going to be the working stiffs like you and me!"

Michael made a noncommittal sound that might have been agreement. In any case, it was good enough for his driver, who continued ranting about politics. The things he could see outside the car were more than distracting.

After nearly twenty minutes trying to squint to bring things into better focus, Michael suddenly felt something shift. It was like the way your vision changed when you closed one eye, and then another, and things seemed to move without moving. Somehow, it was like he had another eye he couldn't see but could almost sense.

By the time the cab deposited him outside the agency offices, Michael had started to get a feel for turning his spiritual perceptions on and off. It wasn't quite something he could control, yet, but at least his control seemed to have progressed to a degree that the spike of pain from his mangled spellcasting was fading. And he didn't seem to need to re-invoke it to see again.

Hopefully he hadn't somehow damaged himself.

"Heya," Stowe called a greeting as Michael passed the designated smoking area outside the back entrance. "Anything good?" The man took a long drag of his cigarette.

Michael couldn't help but stare. The worm he had seen before was still embedded in Stowe's back, but this time it pulsated wetly with every drag the man took of the cigarette. Was it some kind of nicotine or addiction demon?

He blinked away the sight. He couldn't hold up a conversation with that in his eyes. Michael shook his head.

"Nothing solid. Tanner or Priestly turn up anything?"

"Dunno. Garibaldi has had me running up intel on a woman that might be connected to the case though. Not sure where the tip came in from. Tanner should be going over it now."

Michael got the message.

"Enjoy the rest of your break." The words felt like ash in his mouth.

Stowe just nodded and took another puff.

Michael made a beeline for his floor. Tanner wasn't at his desk. He was about to check the lad's other haunts when a familiar voice leapt across the office and yanked him up short by the collar.

"Lieberman! Get in here."

Michael sighed and headed toward Garibaldi's office. There was a twinge in the middle of his forehead right as he walked through the door and Michael braced himself. His vision seemed to have a mind of its own.

Garibaldi sat behind his desk like a toad behind a brick. The man's complexion—sallow at the best of times from too much drink and too many cigars—was positively waxen. Golden fat dribbled from the corners of his mouth and all of his fingers were liberally slathered in the stuff. When he spoke, Michael could just make out the whirling, undulating *thing* he had seen in his superior officer's mouth the last time he had been in this office.

It was not improved by repeat viewing.

"NYPD have any good leads?" Garibaldi demanded. "We need to nail this terrorist scum and nail them yesterday."

"Two leads, both run dry, sir," Michael reported, again focusing his gaze just beyond Garibaldi's ear, on the wall. "NYPD is running paperwork to get us canvassing and access to another potential crime scene. We've got a second murder linked to Hugs. The P.A. NYPD is running forensics there now."

"It's not nothing, but it's not something. I want something, Lieberman. Don't waste the taxpayers' money!" Garibaldi eyed him. "And don't think I don't see you going soft on that detective. You remember who put you where you are…and who can bust you right out of the agency. Don't test me, boy."

"Sir. Yes, sir."

Garibaldi waved his hand, dismissing Michael and sending small globs of golden fat flying across the office.

Michael all but fled the scene, fury flaring in his guts.

***

His stomach twisting from what he'd just witnessed, Michael decided to check the kitchenette for Tanner. He moved through the office, not able to help looking at each of his co-workers, men and women he'd known for months and years, and seeing, literally, some of the demons that plagued them. It wasn't anything anyone should know.

Ignorance really was bliss, more often than not.

Then he made it to the safety of the kitchenette. Sure enough, Tanner and Priestly were there, files on the tiny table between them, drinking coffee and cleaning up the last of the morning's doughnuts.

Neither of them had anything hideous crawling in, out of, or around them, and fuck but wasn't that a relief.

"Stowe says you have a new lead?" he said, forcing a nonchalant smile across his face.

"We do indeed, bossman," Tanner smiled. "Priestly and I—"

"—with some legwork from Stowe," Priestly added, shooting the young man across from her a look.

"Yeah, with some help from Stowe, we managed to canvass the area and cross-reference with the streets and shops and managed to get a visual on our suspect. The one that got away."

Priestly flicked through the pile of folders in front of her and spun one around for Michael's perusal. She tapped the grainy image with one finger as she explained.

"Tanner and I calculated all the routes someone could take from that part of the market to get away—"

"Even the ones that cut through the sewers," Tanner interjected. "Did you realize there was a storm drain only a few feet from you?"

"Even the stupidly unlikely ones, yeah," Priestly said, glaring. "Anyway, we then figured what the five most likely options were, checked them, found two that looked like they might have had someone matching our suspect's description pass by on the cameras we could access—"

"Then we sent Stowe out on foot to check the local businesses and see if there were any angles their security cams might have caught that we don't have access to," Tanner added excitedly.

"It was a long shot, but it paid off. We got this. The outfit matches, the bag matches, time stamp lines up—I think this is a pic of the terrorist that slipped through our fingers." Priestly looked more than a little bit smug. "We got her. No idea who she is, but we're running facial recognition now. Hopefully it turns something up in the next few hours."

Michael just stared. That face. He knew that face.

It was Hannah.

A thousand thoughts went screaming through his head. This whole thing just got so much more complicated—if this was even true. Michael didn't know what to believe anymore. Angels, demons, spirits, magic—Hannah a terrorist?

"Good work," he managed to say. "Keep me posted on this. I want to know the minute you have something." Michael shook his head. "Much better luck than I had today. Got a new murder, and a whole lot of new questions. Caught a suspect at the scene—"

"Could it be her?" Priestly leaned forward, eye slight.

"No. Caucasian male. I clocked him close up but he still got away."

"Not having such great luck with the foot pursuit," Tanner observed. "Maybe you need to hit the track."

Michael managed a weak laugh at the joke. Then, with a Herculean effort, he managed a few more minutes of small talk before finally excusing himself. The thoughts in his head were beginning to scream so loudly he couldn't hear himself think.

"I need to go." Michael stood abruptly. "I need some fresh air after the day I had."

His sister?

***

Michael stalked along the street. He could have grabbed the subway or hailed a cab, but he wanted the fresh air, the grounding of the city, to help him make sense of all this. A twinge in his forehead made his eyes water and suddenly all around him, he could see *things*.

He saw the spirits harrying and helping humanity all around, but that wasn't all. He could have sworn he caught a glimpse of red flashing in the eyes of a woman leaning in the door of a club. A thin man in a business suit—a defense attorney Michael had seen around the agency, in fact—had a long pair of sharp tapered ears rising to either side of his head and impossibly violet eyes.

There was a whole Hidden World threaded over and through the New York he thought he knew, and if he didn't know his city, how well did he know himself?

The space between his shoulder blades twinged like they had the day after he had that dream of flying, but this time it was more than that. He *felt* the weight of something settle on his shoulders and suddenly he was conscious of all the tiny whirls and whorls of air around him. The breeze tugged at him and his bones felt simultaneously too heavy and too light all at once.

Michael paused, the slowly fading light of afternoon giving way to evening, and turned to look at himself in the reflection of the storefront to his right. Like so much of New York's midtown, it was all but solid glass, treated to stay clean and therefore as good as a mirror, most days.

His reflection stared back at him.

And it had wings.

CHAPTER 14

Looking For Hannah

"Hannah, you need to call. Me. Back." Michael left yet another message on the number his sister had left him. He supposed he should at least be glad it was still connected. He could have Tanner run it through the system if she didn't call back soon.

One way or another, Michael was going to have words with his sister.

He'd prefer it without the rest of the department getting involved, if possible. At least to begin with. Especially with that toad Garibaldi sitting there with his fingers in everything.

The alleyway around him was strewn with the standard heaps of stinking, New York City garbage. There were several split, black plastic bags in a large pile from the restaurant to the left, and overflowing dumpsters that nominally held all the refuse from the small apartment block to the right. There were also several piles of cardboard—ersatz mattresses for the homeless population.

That was why he was here, actually. Not having any better leads in front of him, Michael had taken a copy of the photo of Hannah and returned to the place he had last seen her. Canvassing was always hit-or-miss, but it was worth a shot.

He'd started with the bodegas. There was almost always one on a nearby corner. That or a pharmacy. Bodega owners were usually a gregarious lot, very keyed into the local community. Elías was no different.

"Yeah-yeah, I saw a woman that looks like that. Few days ago. I remember because she asked for chalk. Not many people ask for chalk. Sometimes the neighborhood kids buy it, or their mamis or papis, but they don't need to ask, you know? Everyone knows where everything is. But this lady, she asked, so I remember."

Michael had thanked him by buying an overpriced bottle of freshly squeezed juice, an apple, and a packet of chips. He had to keep his energy up after all. Pounding the pavement was hard work. He polished off the chips and the juice as he stood outside under the awning, pocketing the apple for later. Then, and only then, did he follow the lead he'd gotten from the bodega owner.

He'd walked down the street until an alleyway appeared on his left. He turned down it and skirted the trash cans and other rubbish choking the mouth of the alley. His eyes flicked to the rusty, black metal of the fire escape. Plenty of ways for a suspect to flee.

Michael moved carefully down the alleyway. There were plenty of places for an assailant to hide, as well. No one jumped out at him, however, and in the middle of the alleyway, in a space left behind by a scene of dumpsters, he found several stacks of cardboard—improvised mattresses.

One was even occupied.

Michael's pace quickened for a moment, even though he could tell with a glance that it wasn't Hannah, hiding out. But he knew she'd been here. He knew Elias had seen her duck down this alleyway. So maybe this man had seen something as well.

"Excuse me," he said, loud enough to wake the man.

"What you want?" A pair of rheumy eyes peered up at him from over a greasy beard. "I ain't hurting nothing or bothering no one."

"I just want to ask you a few questions." Michael pulled out his wallet and retrieved a couple of bills. "If that's all right with you, that is."

"Sure, sure. What do you want?"

Michael passed over the money. It wasn't that much, and he was more likely to get honest answers if the guy didn't think the payout was contingent on saying the right thing. Then he took out the picture of Hannah.

"Have you seen this woman? Anytime in the last few days, maybe?"

The homeless man squinted at the photo. Michael waited calmly as he thought.

"I think so, yeah. Not sure what day it was, sorry. They all seem to run together now." He shook his head. "But she walked past. I remember because she kept stopping to tap at the bricks for some reason. Only on that side, though," he jerked his chin toward the apartment building side of the alleyway. "She didn't find what she was looking for, I guess, because she didn't stay. Just kept moving along."

Hannah must have been looking for a particular spot to draw the symbols that let her shove him through to the Spirit World. Michael didn't know why, but it seemed a likely enough hypothesis. He was on the right track.

"Thanks. Did you happen to see where she went after that? If she turned left or right out of the alley?"

"Not sure." The homeless man chewed on his lower lip for a minute. "Right, maybe?"

"Thanks." Michael pulled the apple out of his pocket and tossed it to the man.

There was nothing else in the alley that caught his eye, so he exited, turned right, and resumed canvassing. When nothing came up, he retraced his steps and tried left. Also nothing.

Right. Back to doing things the hard way.

He worked his way in a widening spiral, following the grid of streets in a zig-zagging motion, until he'd completed two full rotations with nothing to show for it. If Hannah had been by any of these places, no one remembered—or admitted to—seeing her.

His search had gone bust. Again. Though it had led him to a familiar spot, so he decided to give in and cool his heels for a bit. His feet were killing him anyway.

Michael leaned back against the park bench. In front of him was the former church whose steeple had tried—and failed—to crush him and that boy. Christ, it seemed ages ago now. A different world.

The heat of the day was fading, but enough of it lingered oppressively in the air to make his shirt stick to his back. The scent of fresh-cut grass was sharp in his nostrils, overpowering the scent of garbage that might otherwise drift in from the closest streets.

That was New York.

Michael wasn't sure why he'd come back here. Maybe he was hoping for a clue of some kind. Why did the steeple fall? What about this place awakened a part of his supernatural nature?

Because he was certain now that he didn't save that boy with human levels of speed and resilience. Or was it just the fact that this was a church and he had wings like an angel? You'd think he'd feel some sort of peace or connection or *something* here.

But he didn't. He just had the questions running round and round in his head. Hannah. The Hidden World. Gabriel. A murdered billionaire. *Hannah* murdering a billionaire.

His sister.

What had happened in the handful of years that they'd been apart to take her down this road? She'd seemed scarred. She seemed hard. What had done that to her?

If it really was her and not just something wearing her face. Because that was something he had to worry about now as well. Shapeshifters. Spiritual possession. Magic warping the images that the cameras recorded.

Was any of that even possible? How was he supposed to know? Who was he going to ask?

Hannah? Gabriel? Certainly not Sara or Garibaldi.

Who could he even trust?

Michael had checked Hannah's old apartment. Someone else lived there now. Not surprising, and not surprising that they hadn't wanted to let him in to look for clues as to his sister's current whereabouts.

There was nothing in Tanner's files offering a lead as to where Hannah-the-terrorism-suspect might be holed up either. If there had been, the whole department would have been on it already. Michael had mixed feelings about that, but in the end, decided it was probably better that way.

Maybe there was some kind of magic that could find her, but again, if there was, he didn't know it.

Michael looked up at the church. Maybe he should pray for answers. Someone had to be listening, right? If there were angels and spirits and demons and all sorts else, someone had to be listening.

But did he want that someone to answer? There's the question. Because whoever or whatever there was that might be listening out there, Michael didn't think it was God. Not the one described in the bible, anyway. Not some all-knowing, all-powerful, kindly patriarch with the world's best interests, inexplicably, somehow, at heart.

As if in answer to his unspoken prayer, there was the sound of great wings beating. Where once there was empty air, a shadow, a flicker at the corner of the eye, was a winged figure. Though the wings vanished quickly after.

Gabriel.

"Hello, Michael."

"Gabriel." Michael eyed the man as he approached, then sat next to Michael on the bench.

"Looking for someone?" Gabriel's face remained enigmatic behind his ever-present sunglasses.

"Maybe. Why?"

How did this guy even know? Michael felt a growing unease with just how much he didn't know about this new world he was increasingly finding himself in. It was far too easy for someone to observe him with magic if indeed that was the case.

Not that he could talk, really, considering the surveillance he had access to with his agency.

"Your search is making ripples. It's not sending up flares—yet—but eventually I will not be the only one to take notice. Well, myself and your sister."

If that was true it meant Hannah was deliberately ignoring him for some reason. Did she know the agency was on to her?

Did she not trust him?

"What kind of flares?" Michael asked.

"Some mystical, more mundane." Gabriel adjusted his sunglasses. "You have to understand that there are... organizations here in the mortal realm that keep an eye on things. They have interests."

"Interests like my sister," Michael said. "Possibly interests like myself?"

"Possibly," Gabriel conceded with a small smile.

Michael rolled that over in his head a few times. What organizations were these? Terrorist ones? Secret societies? Cults? There was a lot of room for his imagination to run wild here, with what he'd seen already.

And all of that was assuming that he could trust Gabriel. When he didn't really know *what* the man was, let alone who he was or who he was working for.

All he really knew at this point was that the man had supernatural abilities and his sister didn't like him.

Michael studied the man's face. It was handsome, in a bland sort of way. Like someone had taken all the default parts of a man that made him good-looking and arranged them in a way that was aesthetically pleasing but called absolutely no attention to itself. There was an anonymity to Gabriel's good looks that made Michael suspicious. Possibly because he felt within himself that if Gabriel ever chose to take off those sunglasses and fully reveal himself the glory that would shine forth from him would be blinding.

It was a decidedly more-than-mortal feeling and Michael, so new to the hidden world, didn't know what to do with it. The painted wood beneath his hands suddenly felt just a bit less solid, a bit less real. What mortal material could support the weight of an actual angel?

So he chose to keep his distance.

"I'm not sure how I feel about drawing that much attention," Michael said, forcing a shade of easy banter into his tone. "I'm no one special."

"Everyone is special, in some way," Gabriel answered. "You, your sister, the people I work with, even the man that cares for this churchyard." Gabriel nodded to the groundskeeper trimming the verge off to their right.

"If you say so," Michael conceded. "Though I'm not sure that my sister and I are so special that we'd warrant this much attention." Never mind that Hannah may be a murderer and an assassin. "And speaking of my sister, I should get back to looking for her."

"I can take you to her," Gabriel said, extending a hand. "She won't be happy, but I can do that."

Michael stared at the offending limb. Did he trust Gabriel to do that, as a bare minimum? Should he even barge in on Hannah unannounced?

"No thanks," Michael said at last. "I think I need to find my sister on my own."

Even if that was easier said than done.

CHAPTER 15

Unexpected Help

"You look like hell," Tanner said, appearing out of nowhere to perch on the edge of Michael's desk. "I thought you took the day off yesterday to rest and recuperate. If this is what you look like rested, I'd hate to see you after an all-nighter."

"You've seen me after an all-nighter," Michael quipped back, "or at least you would have if you were able to stay awake."

"Ha! What can I say, I need my beauty sleep." Tanner grinned.

"You'd need to be in a coma for about forty years to put any shine on that mug of yours." Michael shoved him off the edge of his desk. "What have you got for me?"

Tanner tossed a manilla folder onto the desk. It landed with a heavy *thwack*.

"Speculation. We think our target is part of a larger organization. Priestly did some digging after Garibaldi rang 'round and shouted at a half-dozen different teams. This is what we have after collating all the information they sent us."

"All right." Michael flipped open the file. If Hannah really was working with an organization, it might be a new lead.

He only made it a few lines into the first page before he looked up at Tanner. His face betrayed none of the surprise he felt at seeing the organization's name that had been listed there.

"Are you having me on? "The Resistance?" What kind of terrorist group calls themselves that?"

"Check page seven. There's speculation that it's a simplification of their real organization name, employed for obfuscation." Tanner tapped the file. "In any case, there might be several new leads in here that might help us track down our suspect. Though if this is at all accurate, I think we'll just end up as part of a bigger task force trying to unravel the whole org. Not that we have enough information on it yet. Not sure why. You'd think something like this would be on our radar already."

"Yeah. That is odd." Michael flipped through several more pages. "And where did all this information come from, suddenly? It's all here, most of it looks legit, so why was it just all circulating with no one to put any heat on it?"

"Eh, maybe because they hadn't shot a billionaire before this?" Tanner shrugged. "That's a big hornet's nest to kick. None of the money people like having their comfortable lives disrupted. Especially with a sniper bullet."

"Would any of us?"

"They don't pay me for philosophy! I'll let you go through that. I need a coffee. Let me know if you have any questions." Tanner started to head off towards the office kitchenette.

"E-mail me any new docs that come up as you get them," Michael called after him.

Tanner just raised a hand in acknowledgment, not looking back.

Michael went back to leafing through the folder. The pages inside described a very large, very underground organization. There were hints that it might be global in nature, with key cells in Italy, the United States, Korea, South America…on pretty much every continent, actually, though there was nothing approaching even a sketchy organizational map.

Who were these people? Sure, there was evidence here, but it also seemed a bit too convenient. The picture of Hannah turning up, after they'd been chasing her for months with no slip-ups, just like that?

Michael felt unease in his gut. Something wasn't right here.

He needed to take this to Sara. Maybe she would have some insight on her end. Going off on his own, half-cocked, without sharing this information was a recipe for inter-departmental disaster.

Michael tapped his chin with the folder. And maybe he needed to take a risk, see just how much his new "partner" trusted him.

In any case, he was headed to the NYPD.

***

"Come on in," Sara said, closing the door to the small conference room behind him.

Michael glanced at the operations boards. Nothing much had changed, and they hadn't been updated to include the information on the wider criminal organization that Hannah may or may not be working with. Tanner had given him a bigger head start than he'd realized.

Overstreet, Sara's partner, glowered at him from behind a desk where the detective was going through a stack of reports.

"Brian," Michael greeted him with a short nod.

"Lieberman," came the response.

"Don't be so formal, Brian," Sara said, walking over to stare at the board, arms crossed in front of her. "Michael, what've you brought us?"

"A mess of trouble with hopefully some opportunity wrapped up somewhere in all the headache." Michael pulled out a copy of the information Tanner had given him and tossed it on a nearby desk. Hopefully it didn't get lost in the forest of other folders sprouting from the surface. "Looks like our suspect is a part of a larger organization, though which one and how large remains a mystery. Or at least a debate."

Brian had opened the folder and started leafing through it.

"This is a mess," the detective said.

"I know," Michael agreed, "but it's a new mess."

He gave both Sara and Brian a recap as they flicked through the new file. He'd wanted to take a different approach, ease Sara into the idea, sound her out on things before broaching the subject of Hannah with her, but with Brain in here, that would never work.

Michael would need to get Sara's strangely overprotective partner out of the way, first.

He squinted with his third eye, as he'd come to think of the process, just in case that prompted a clue. Overstreet was mostly free of strange spiritual parasites or haunting creatures from beyond the veil, though. The man was almost entirely mundane.

Almost.

When Overstreet looked at Michael his eyes flickered green. In that moment Michael saw tiny creatures that were mostly just grasping claws raking at the detective's eyeballs, but they didn't seem to have a solid grip on him.

Yet.

Michael really needed some kind of bestiary for these things. He could ask Gabriel...no. Not yet. He didn't know whether he could trust the angel. Not with Hannah's life and freedom on the line. He needed to sort that out, then he could go after answers to what Gabriel was. What he, Michael, was. And what that meant.

But first he needed a word with Sara, and that meant getting Overstreet out of the room.

He could ask the man to go for coffee, but that seemed obvious and rude. No, he needed something that would make Overstreet want to leave. Something like...ah!

"I don't suppose you've got anything on these guys in your systems, do you? The Resistance? I could go run a search if you'd like—" Michael offered.

"I'll do it!" Brian jumped in, spotting the chance at some easy glory. "We haven't gotten you a guest access yet anyway."

"You'd think law enforcement would be more efficient," Michael remarked as Overstreet rushed out of the office.

Sara snagged the folder out of her partner's hand before he could disappear with it. She crossed back to the board and uncapped a marker and started putting in some temporary lines of speculation, linking the picture of the subject to a new header, labeled "The Resistance."

Michael checked the door was closed and quietly locked it. He didn't want to be disturbed. He glanced back at Sara. She was still absorbed in sketching in the possible implications he'd brought in that folder.

"I've got one more piece of information," he said quietly, "but—let's call it a strict sort of need-to-know situation."

Sara turned to look at him. Michael still had his Sight active, and she had that same hyper-real focus she had before. There were no strange entities attached to her, and something about her just made Michael feel like he could trust her.

Even with this.

"Do I need to know?" She asked.

"I think," Michael paused, "I think I need you to know. I trust your judgment, and this—well, it's even messier than what I brought you in that." He jerked his head at the folder still in her hands.

Sara closed the folder and set it down on the desk.

"All right," she said. "Hit me with it."

Michael moved to take her place by the board. It was strangely hard to actually come out and say it. As soon as he did there would be no going back. Still, he forced himself. He reached out and tapped the photograph of Hannah.

"This woman?" He said. "I know her."

Sara just waited for him to go on. There was clearly more to it than that, if he'd waited this long to say anything. She quirked an eyebrow at him.

"It's my sister," he said, shooting a glance out the door to make sure no one was listening.

No one was.

"I haven't heard from her in years," he said quickly, and then the story began to pour out of him—the stake out, the near-miss, Hannah reappearing in his life recently but before the image of her proved her involvement with the case, the sense he had that someone at his agency was up to something, the inconsistencies in the research he'd brought with him. Everything.

Everything except the supernatural aspects of it all. That seemed a bridge too far, a weight too heavy on the fresh and fragile trust he was already testing to its limits. And, he found, he didn't want to tell Sara because he knew from experience it would make her a target.

The room was silent for a long moment after Michael finished talking. Thankfully, Overstreet still hadn't returned from searching the database for connections, and no one else had tried the door to the conference room. Michael waited for Sara to respond, knowing that there was a very real possibility that she might just take what he'd revealed to her, turn him in, and go after Hannah on her own.

Finally, however, she spoke.

"If she killed him, she'll have to take full responsibility for Hugs' murder," Sara said slowly. "I'm not going to circumvent justice for you."

"I'm not—"

"Let me finish." Sara tapped the folder. "I agree. Something here isn't adding up and I want to get to the bottom of it. There's too many weird things going on, and too many obstructionists. Drummer effectively cut our investigation off at the knees and then this alternate avenue turns up, out of the blue? Nah. Seems too easy. I want to know what's going on, and your sister—" her eyes flicked to the picture on the board, "—is smack dab in the middle of it. So yes, I'll help you find her, and together we'll figure out what is actually going on here. But I won't break the law for you. Bend, sure. We do that all the time. But not break."

"That's fair, and that's all I ask," Michael said quickly.

His back was sweaty. There were a lot of things that could still go very wrong. There was a whole supernatural element that Sara didn't know about and Michael had no idea just how much that might complicate things.

"You got any leads on where she might be?"

"Phone number, but I didn't dare run it on my end."

"Right. Makes sense." Sara chewed her lip. "I can do it here. I've got enough authority to log in and run it as a one-off. There are some other numbers on Hugs' phone I can run as well, to screen what I'm doing."

"Thanks," Michael said. "I really appreciate this. I know it's a lot—"

"Save it until after we figure out what's going on here. After all, we might still be hauling your sister's ass in for questioning."

Michael was saved from responding by a rattle at the locked conference room door. Overstreet had returned and was glaring in at Michael.

Sara laughed and waved for Brian to be patient. She drummed her fingers on the desk and then pushed off to walk over toward the door. As she passed, she looked up at Michael and murmured out of the corner of her mouth, "let me find Brain some work to do, and then I'll go run those numbers."

Michael nodded once, just a slight inclination of the head, so Overstreet wouldn't think anything was going on.

More than the detective clearly already did. Though likely not in the sense that he was thinking.

He should be tense, with Sara heading to the door to let her partner in, but he wasn't. Somehow, Michael felt in his bones that he could trust Sara, that she'd work with him on this.

She'd help him find his sister.

CHAPTER 16

The Winged Woman at The Pawn Shop

Michael looked out over the city. It was a breathtaking view from this height, here at the top of Hugs' building. He could easily see a small patch of green below, the park where the billionaire met his end. Sara had gotten the approval from the building management to investigate the roof and in light of Michael's reveal about the shooter, they decided it was worthwhile revisiting the scene, this time from a different angle.

The window washer's rig was still in place, though building management said it had been used at least once since the murder. Michael looked at it now with two sets of eyes, his mortal vision and the spirit sight that had shown him the small trail of metaphysical parasites that drew his attention to the rig in the first place the other day.

There was nothing left, so far as he could see with either set of eyes. Sara was crouched down near it, examining the ground for anything Hannah might have left behind. There weren't any shell casings, nothing so obvious. There were a lot of cigarette butts, but to the best of Michael's knowledge, his sister didn't smoke.

And even if she did, he doubted she'd be so stupid as to leave potential DNA evidence lying about a crime scene.

He'd held out higher hopes that his spirit sight might reveal a clue, but so far nothing had come up. Still, he kept at it. It was getting easy to turn it on and off, to glimpse through the veil. Though it was still unnerving. No matter where he was there were spirits of some kind, somewhere. Maybe it'd be different in the country, but here in the city? Absolute madness.

And they could see that he could see them. Often strange beings caught his gaze and held it. One or two even started towards him, but they always veered off before they got too close. As if they had seen something horrible looming just behind him, but whenever Michael turned to look there was nothing there.

Even now a pale woman was flying above him, with vast black and leather wings. Her hair was a spill of night and even from this distance, Michael could see the green-gold glint of her eyes.

Come to think of it, she had been circling ever since he and Sara arrived at the rooftop. A trickle of unease ran down his spine. Was that usual, or was something more going on? He was still too new to this to know.

"Find anything?" He called to Sara, making sure to track the woman's passage out of the corner of his eye.

"No," came the disgusted answer. "A lot of cigarette butts, some old rags, a half-empty bottle of cleaning solvent, but nothing that looks promising. Nothing to confirm your theory."

"I suppose we'll have to ask Hannah when we find her," Michael replied.

The woman was still circling them. Michael didn't look directly at her though. If she was spying it was best she didn't think him suspicious.

"If we find her," Sara said sourly. "Your sister is goddamn elusive. And I've tracked down a lot of murderers." Sara grimaced. "Sorry."

"It's all right." For all he knew it was a perfectly accurate moniker. "Any other leads?"

"A few. I went through that stupid folder of yours and cross-referenced some of the criminal activity mentioned in relation to this Resistance. They seem to work really hard to keep their noses clean, but they stock up regularly on weapons and they do a brisk trade in stolen artifacts, mainly from the Middle East. So I checked with some of the department C.I.s and gathered a couple leads from them. Markets, fences, flophouses, places we can check out."

"You made a list?" Michael thought that seemed like something Sara would do.

"I made a list," Sara held up her hands in surrender. "What can I say, I like to be organized."

"You'd never know it to look at your suspect boards."

"Do not mess with my suspect boards! Those things are perfect just the way they are. Do you know how many cases my suspect boards have closed?"

"How many?" Michael couldn't help grinning a bit.

"Don't go counting my victories," Sara quipped, switching gears. "We're not making nearly enough progress on the next one. Come on. We need to head across town and down. At least we don't have to go up." Sara kicked the ground. "There's nothing here, so we might as well move on. Come on." She headed toward the roof access door.

"Right behind you," Michael said, pausing to take one last look around the rooftop as he did so.

The winged woman was still circling in the sky above.

***

The pawnshop was one of those dusty storefronts endemic to the fringes of the island. Piles of pieces of lives, all stacked up in the windows to lure in bargain hunters and broke students, vintage aficionados and those needing to sell just a little bit of themselves to make it to next payday. An electronic bell buzz-rang as Sara pushed her way inside, Michael following close behind.

Inside the pawnshop was a veritable forest of shelves, all overcrowded with merchandise. Racks of clothing snaked around the perimeter while the back of the store held several plexiglass display cases with all manner of jewelry and other higher-tier items. A small flock of guitars was mounted on the back wall behind the counter. New York was a city of dreams, but most of them broke before they came true.

Michael reached out and sorted through a tray of odds and ends on the closest shelf. There were several belt buckles, a handful of polished stones, a pocket knife—even a slingshot, of all things. It was like a boy from the 1950s had come through and emptied his pockets. The knife looked to be Swiss army. Michael picked it up and began prying open the various attachments as he and Sara moved to the back of the store.

A bored-looking white man with a scruffy excuse for a beard lounged behind the counter, idly flipping through one of the

Metro area's many free papers. He didn't bother to look up at the sound of the bell and didn't bother to shift himself until Sara and Michael were nearly on top of him.

"Looking for something in particular? Or do you got something to se—" he trailed off as he caught sight of Sara's face. His eyes flicked her up and down then scanned Michael's bulk behind her. "What can I do for you, officers?"

"You know, actually, we are looking for something in particular," Sara said. "Isn't that right?"

She didn't have to look at Michael to know he'd pick up the cue.

"We are. Fancied a bit of antiquing." Michael froze his lips into a frosty smile.

"Maybe something from Jerusalem, or the Dead Sea area. You got anything like that?"

Michael could see the man had started to sweat. To be safe, he flexed his mind and looked at the man on more than the mortal level.

And had to bite his tongue to keep from reacting. The man was a literal pulsing mass of crawling, parasitic spirits. If spirit sight didn't overlap in a surreal way with his actual sight, he wouldn't be able to see the man at all for the chitinous, slimy buggers that had their mandibles sank deeply into this poor idiot.

"No-nothing like that. I swear!" The man stammered.

He was a terrible liar. Michael didn't even need an edge like spirit sight to see that. How the hell did this guy get a frontman job like this?

"Maybe you should check in the back," he suggested, letting the frost of his smile ice over his eyes.

The clerk's eyes nearly bulged out of his head.

Mentally, Michael frowned. There was no reason the guy should be having this severe a reaction. Was something going on with Michael's "secret" nature? One more question to add to his growing hoard.

"Oh, now, let's not be unreasonable," Sara cut in, smoothly picking up the "good cop" half of the routine without so much as batting an eyelid. If the guy was that afraid of Michael, she might as well work with it. "I'm sure the man knows *exactly* what stock he has in the back. Probably could tell you precisely how much it was worth, too."

There was a flicker of movement in the reflection on the polished counter. Something he saw with his spirit sight. Michael kept his eyes locked on the clerk, however. Now wasn't the time to get distracted.

"There's no need to have him check his inventory," Sara was saying.

"Re-really? I appreciate that." The man didn't relax, however. Michael was glad he wasn't *that* stupid.

"We can always take our business elsewhere. I'm sure someone else has a really nice stock of antiquities we could peruse." Sara pulled out a small photo of Hannah and slid it across the counter in front of the man, finger tapping. "You could probably even recommend a few. Point us in the right direction?" she paused and caught the man's eye with a bright smile. "Since you don't have anything like what we're looking for in the back room. Do you."

The man looked from Sara to Michael, uncertainly in his eyes. When Michael caught his gaze, however, the man quickly blanched and looked back at Sara.

"I—I suppose so, yeah. Give me a minute to think."

"Take your time." Sara drummed her fingers across the countertop. "We're not in a hurry."

"Got nowhere else to be except here. For now." Michael added, showing his teeth.

There was movement again in the reflections in the store. Michael still didn't move his head, but this time it flashed through the reflections gleaming on the black body of a Fender-Strat on the wall.

It was the image of feathered wings.

Familiar, feathered wings.

Michael didn't have time to dwell on what that might mean as the clerk had pulled out a pad of paper and was busily scribbling on it. Sara watched him closely, but her body language was relaxed. He suspected she was getting what she wanted.

"You should be able to find what you want here," the clerk said, tearing off the sheet of paper and folding it in half before passing it to Sara. "It's best if you get there early, though. They tend to sell out."

"Thanks for the tip." Sara retrieved the picture of Hannah and made it, and the slip of paper with the address on it, disappear.

Michael, never one to let the opportunity for positive reinforcement pass by, set the pocketknife on the counter and paid for it. Sara looked on, amusement plain on her face. The clerk looked at him like he'd sprouted another head.

Hell, that alone was worth what Michael paid for the knife.

Because he was standing directly in front of the cash register, Michael was in a prime position to see his reflection on the polished countertop change from his face to that of someone else.

Gabriel, sunglasses and wings fully evident, though the clerk at the counter gave no sign of seeing anything at all amiss on the counter in front of him.

The apparition of Gabriel raised a finger to its lips and pointed behind Michael just as the buzz-ring of the door blared out again. He glanced over his shoulder but turned back just as quickly. It was the demonic woman that had been circling them on the rooftop!

And the door made a sound. Which meant she was here, physically. Michael didn't know what that implied but he suspected that it couldn't be anything good.

"We got what we need?" He asked Sara in a low voice.

"Yeah, why?" She glanced up at him.

"Someone just walked in and she looks a little too interested in what we're doing. Dunno if it's anything, but it feels like something. Something to skip out on." Michael resolutely did not look at the winged woman as she prowled the aisles.

"Mmm. Well, I don't feel like being entertained. Let's head out. See if we can't lose our audience."

— CHAPTER 17 —

The Sword of Flame

The inside of the Crown Vic positively reeked of beef lo mein, chicken chow fun, and egg fried rice and Michael loved it. He wasn't usually one for stakeouts, but usually he was stuck in a sur-veillance van with three or four other people. It was hot, cramped, and Priestly always ordered the food and it was never this good.

"This is so good," Michael groaned between mouthfuls.

"Never let it be said I don't show my partners a good time," Sara said with a smile. Then she flushed, realizing what she'd said. "Stakeout partners, that is—stakeout partners!"

Michael laughed into his takeout container. It was a nice break from the tedium of the last several hours.

They had followed the lead Sara had browbeaten out of the clerk at the pawnshop and now were waiting in the car, in an alleyway, behind an innocuous-looking warehouse on the lower east side. Nominally it was held by an import/export firm dealing mainly in foodstuffs. In fact, it was entirely possible that some of the ingredients in the take-out Michael was eating right now went through that exact warehouse.

The irony was not lost on either of the detectives.

However, it seemed that concealed amongst the bags of imported noodles or boxes of sweet and sticky dates certain antiquities also made their way into the country. Michael and Sara speculated that Hannah, on the run from multiple local and federal agencies, would be running low on funds and would need a fresh injection. This was on Sara's list of likely options, the clerk at the pawnshop had confirmed her hunch, and for some reason, the name flashed briefly to Michael's spirit sight when Sara showed him the address the clerk had given them.

He had a good feeling about this.

Of course that was before the hours began to creep oh so slowly past, tedium piling upon tedium, its petty pace creeping from afternoon into night.

"I love this part of the job," Sara said, stowing her chopsticks in the takeaway container and shoving the whole thing into the plastic delivery bag. "The only time I can actually breathe. Otherwise there's just too much paperwork, leg work, office politics—it never ends."

"I hear that." Michael cracked a fortune cookie, eating the shell and ignoring the message inside. Normally he loved reading them, but right now? With all the supernatural shit going on? Seemed like tempting fate. "You get into—well, *I* got into this gig because I wanted to make a difference. To do something that actually helped serve some justice in an unjust world, but all you end up doing most of the time is paperwork."

Michael paused, thinking back over the past several days, thinking back to his childhood with Hannah and how fucked that seemed now that she was running around murdering people, possibly working with a terrorist organization or hell, who knows, maybe even a cult. That folder on The Resistance had all kinds of shit in it. This was not the Hannah he knew. He saw Sara looking at him out of the corner of his eye, face open, listening. She went hyper-sharp to his spirit sight again for a moment and suddenly he found himself saying more. Saying things that went a lot deeper than he thought he'd ever share with anyone.

"I grew up in a religiously-run orphanage. It was…a less-than-just place, though religion covered it up with a nice mask. It did teach me though that if you want justice, you have to find it yourself. There isn't anyone out there, up there, whatever, who is going to dispense it after the fact. And honestly, growing in there made me very certain that there wasn't anything more around, above, or below us than what we could see or sense or find. No deities, benevolent or otherwise. No guardian angels—" Michael paused. Man, were the past few days a head fuck. "—but now, with what's been happening—"

"Like the churchyard," Sara said quietly.

"Like the churchyard," Michael agreed. It was true enough and easier than saying he'd met a literal angel who may or may not be in service to some higher power. He hadn't actually asked.

He hadn't wanted to know, he supposed.

"It's making me wonder if there is something else out there," he continued. "Something, I dunno, bigger or more powerful."

"There's always someone bigger and more powerful," Sara said wearily. "You don't need a god to make that true. Just look at Hugs. He was big, powerful. One of the wealthiest and most influential men on the planet. Someone still took him out. And even if it was your sister, that doesn't mean she wasn't part of a larger organization. Hell, we're on a planet that we can only stand on because of forces all but incomprehensible to most of mankind, and that's just fucking gravity."

"True." Michael thought about that for a bit. "That's really fucking true."

"I didn't grow up in an orphanage, but my dad was killed—murdered—in our home. I was there when it happened, actually. Saw the guy—not the act, but the guy. That's where it started for me, all of this." Sara gestured at the car and the badge and gun at her hip. "So I get it. I get why someone might feel like they had to make justice happen on their own. Some of the systems we work with? They don't work. Some don't even exist. So yeah, I understand. I don't really agree, but I understand. It's the sort of thing that can really piss you off. Make you feel helpless or hopeless. And I get it. If I ever got my hands on Max Ashton," her voice trailed off.

"The guy that killed your dad?' Michael asked.

Sara just nodded. Michael remembered that first day at the precinct. The guy had said the name Max Ashton when Sara was interrogating him. Was she still looking for her father's killer?

"It's hard," he said, instead. "Just when you think you've got it figured out something jumps up to make you question everything. And even if you're a big fish in a small pond, there's always a fisherman waiting to hook you in the jaw. We're all always at the mercy of something bigger."

"Like Brian's ego," Sara said, unexpectedly puncturing the too-serious mood that had developed.

Sara grinned and Michael found himself smiling in return. Something about her—she just seemed to get him, even when she didn't know everything. Michael found he liked that. It was unexpected, to say the least, but it wasn't bad.

"Sorry to spill my crises of faith all over your leather seats," he joked.

"It's fine," Sara quipped back. "You can reimburse me for the steam clean."

They shared a laugh.

The conversation lightened a bit, after that, though it was no less "deep" for all of that. Michael shared a bit more about the orphanage, and Sara told him some stories about growing up with her aunt, after her father's death. It was a darker, more real version of the sort of first date conversation you'd get out in the "real" world, not that either of them thought of it that way, but that's what it was.

And it was nice.

"We've got movement," Sara said, cutting off the conversation and sitting up straighter in her seat. "Could be Hannah."

"We've got company," Michael said at the same time, catching a glimpse of leathery wings in the rear-view mirror. Then he saw the face attached to the wings. It was the woman that had been tailing them all day. "Shit," he muttered. "I think we were followed from the pawnshop."

"Are they after us or her, though?" Sara asked. "Shit!" She hauled open the car door as fast as she could, drawing her weapon. "They're headed for your sister."

If it was his sister. Michael hauled open his door. Didn't matter. It could be, and his spirit sight was telling him these people were dangerous.

There were four of them—no, six. Michael spotted another two landing on the rooftops to either side of the building they had been staking out. The woman that had been following them was moving in on Hannah—the suspect that *might* be Hannah. She had a huge bruiser of a man next to her with skin that looked like granite to Michael's spirit sight. Two others, both with the same leathery wings as the woman, were flanking to the other side.

"Freeze!" Sara shouted, clearly seeing something, though likely not the same thing Michael saw. "NYPD!"

The suspect started, but the—fuck it, Michael decided to just call them demons in his head—demons heading toward Hannah didn't halt. They didn't even bother to react. They just kept going.

Sara swore and moved in, Michael next to her. He thumbed the safety off his weapon.

Hannah—and it was Hannah, Michael could see now, her hood sliding off her head as she reacted to the approaching demons—swore and tried to make a break for it, running for the corner of the building. One of the demons lurking on the roof cut her off, however, jumping down to land right in front of her.

"What the fuck?" Sara said, before yelling again, "Freeze! NYPD! Down on the ground! Now! Final warning!"

The demons ignored her again.

A chill worked its way down Michael's spine. They seemed awfully casual about ignoring an officer of the NYPD with a loaded weapon. Too casual.

Sara raised her weapon and fired a warning shot. Michael didn't bother. He took aim at the woman with the wings, sighted down the barrel of the gun, and squeezed the trigger.

Nothing. He was close enough to know that should have hit. The bullet either bounced off, burned away, or was magicked out of existence. In any case, the demon tossed him a contemptuous glare and continued stalking toward Hannah.

They were careful in approaching Hannah. She had some kind of knife in her hand and to Michael's spirit sight it glowed white and gold. There was some kind of script on the blade but he couldn't read it from this distance.

Sara fired her gun as well, emptying her clip with a look of growing incredulity on her face when none of her shots managed to do a damn thing. Well, not quite nothing. It did prompt a response from the winged woman, who seemed to be in charge.

"Dullas," she said to the walking mountain next to her, "dispose of the rubbish. We can handle this one." She looked at Hannah.

Dullas turned and headed towards Michael and Sara. There was no way physics had any right to allow someone that big to move that fast. Sara stood her ground, changing out her clip expertly and taking aim.

Again, she emptied the whole clip into the guy and nothing worked. Michael charged the guy. If guns wouldn't work, maybe he could overpower him.

A fist the size of a dinner plate disabused him of the notion, fast. Michael's face hit the pavement and the taste of copper and salt filled his mouth. He managed to hold on to consciousness, however, and looked up just in time to see Sara's shin collide bodily with the region right between Dullas's legs.

The mountain of a man didn't even react.

"What the hell—" Sara managed before Dullas slapped her to the ground as well.

She didn't get up.

"Sara!" The name was a battle cry on Michael's lips as some long-buried instinct sparked to life. Flames of white and gold flickered across his fingertips as he pushed himself to his feet. As he stood, Michael clenched his fist around that spark of righteous fury and a long sword of pure alabaster flame erupted into being, hilt in his hand.

His shoulders erupted in a conflagration of pain as well and suddenly Michael could feel the air currents moving all around him, his balance first thrown off, then steadied as his body adjusted.

Dullas, his foot raised to bring down on Sara's unconscious body, paused, then turned to face Michael.

"Dullas, no!"

Michael barely registered the sound of the winged woman's voice, shrill with alarm. His vision had zeroed in on his foe—no, his senses had locked on the motionless form of Sara, the person he was defending from his foe.

He raised the flaming sword in his hand, leveling it at the mountainous man in front of him.

The big guy hesitated.

"Dullas! Retreat!"

The order snapped something in Dullas and he fell back, giving ground before Michael who advanced to stand protectively over Sara. The demons fled, each of them taking to the air one by one, save Dullas, who sank into the asphalt like ice cream melting on a hot day.

Michael wondered what the security camera footage would show, if there was any. There had to be one covering this angle. The criminals running the operation out of the warehouse wouldn't allow anything else, even if the city didn't have anything operating around here.

"Michael?"

He turned to face his sister, the sword in his hand flickering and vanishing. He had no idea why it did, or how to get it back. His shoulders suddenly felt lighter as well.

"Hannah," he said. "I think we need to talk."

"Fine." She looked from him to the unconscious detective at his feet. "Pick up your friend. I've got a place we should be safe."

CHAPTER 18

Hannah And The Resistance

Hannah led Michael around the corner to a stinking alley. There was more chalk on the brickwork. He paused; Sara still unconscious over his shoulder in a fireman's carry.

"You're not serious."

"It's just a shortcut," Hannah said impatiently. "A few steps in the spirit world can cover a lot of distance in the real one, if you know what you're doing."

"And you do?" Michael looked at his sister, the stranger.

"I've been doing this a long time. Come on!" Hannah walked through the portal, forcing Michael to follow.

Which he did. There were not a lot of options, and if Hannah got out of his sight, who knew when he'd manage to track her down again? If she could skip across dimensions, what hope did mundane law enforcement really have of nabbing her?

He expected Sara to wake up as they crossed the spirit realm. It would have been the least opportune time, but thankfully she stayed quiescent and missed the brief jaunt. It was only across an alleyway, through another chalk ring, and out on the inside of a warehouse.

As soon as he was through Hannah picked up a bucket of water nearby and threw it over the chalk circle, destroying it as the lines blurred and ran. There was enough there to see what it was, but the imprecision seemed to negate the magic, as the view of the spirit realm within the circle vanished.

"Here. Put your friend on the couch." Hannah led him over to a loft space that overlooked the rest of the crumbling warehouse. It was full of shipping containers but most were rusting away where they sat.

Michael spotted a line of glyphs chalked along the edge of the loft. Protection? Obfuscation? Whatever they were, they were clearly keeping Hannah safe, so he and Sara should be good here as well. For a while at least.

He settled Sara on the couch, then turned to Hannah.

"What?" She asked.

"What? *What?*" Michael stared at his sister. "You vanish for years—years!—I don't even know if you're alive or dead most of the time, then you show up out of the blue, shove me into an alternate fucking *dimension*, after—by the way—after you apparently murder a man in cold blood, and you have the absolute gall to stand there and as *me* 'what?'"

"You don't need to be involved," Hannah said.

The icy distance in her voice cut sharper than any knife could. Even one made of alabaster flame. Michael's eyes sparked annoyance.

"I'm doing this to protect you," she said when the silence got too heavy. "There's too many things you don't know about—"

"Also your fault," Michael snapped. "Gabriel—"

"Don't bring that asshole into this!" Hannah snapped back. "I expressly forbade him from involving you, but he still went and did it anyway, despite the fact that he was instructed not to—"

"Instructed? Instructed by whom?" Michael seized on the odd phrasing. It wasn't something Hannah would say about herself. "The Resistance? Is he a part of it as well? That would make sense. There's no way it's actually a mundane organization with the mess they put in our files."

"Your agency has a file on The Resistance?"

That, more than anything else in this fucked up day, seemed to shake Hannah.

"Should we not keep files on terrorist organizations that murder American citizens?" Michael stared flatly at his sister.

"Are you talking about Hugs? That bastard got what he deserved—" She cut it short and turned away to shield the welling up in her eyes. Whatever happened to his sister, whatever drove her to cold-blooded murder, was personal. But he had to know more.

"Yeah, I get it. There's more to the story. Things I don't know." Michael sighed. "Just fucking explain it to me then, please? I don't want to keep chasing my sister around the city, trying to arrest her." He paused. "Though I'm pretty sure I would have had you in the market the other day if Gabriel hadn't intervened."

"Probably," Hannah admitted, looking like she'd swallowed a lemon. "You're pretty good. Faster than I thought you'd be."

"Well, apparently I'm a lot more than I realized." Michael reached across his chest and massaged his shoulder with one arm.

"Don't ask," Hannah warned. "I'll—I'll tell you a bit more about The Resistance, about what we're doing, but only so you know to back off. Find a new case. Transfer to a different department. But you need to let this go, Michael. I'm serious. More than just your life depends on it."

"All right. I'll bite. Tell me about The Resistance. Tell me about what you've been doing." Michael leaned against an iron girder. "And tell me about Hugs. What did he have to do with whoever it was you lost?"

Hannah started.

"How do you know about Grace?" she stared at him like he'd sprouted a second head.

Why did that name sound familiar?

"I didn't—I don't, but I knew something was up." Michael tapped the girder. "But there's clearly something, so tell me."

"It's all the same story, really." Hannah fidgeted. "Some of it will sound vague at first. I'm not trying to be difficult, but there are things I can't say, not and keep the people I need to keep safe, safe." She smiled bitterly. "Not that I've always succeeded at that."

Michael grunted noncommittally. As one of those people, who'd been being "kept safe" by Hannah's silence, he wasn't sure how effective a tactic it was, but he'd let it go for now.

His sister was quiet for a moment. Michael let her gather her thoughts. Eventually, she started painting a broken picture.

"You've seen some of what's out there, just beyond the Veil," she began.

He'd seen a bit more than "some" to be honest, but Michael didn't interrupt. It'd only send his sister off on a tangent as she tried to "protect" him.

"There are all manner of creatures that share the world with us," Hannah continued. "Some we'd think of as good—scratch that—some we'd think of as benign. Some—some are outright evil. And a few of them are capable of crossing over to our world. Fairies are incredibly good at it, for example. Some just live here or are even partially human, like the vampires and the werewolves—"

Michael had to bite his tongue to keep from interrupting. Werewolves? Though why he should be surprised at this point…

"—and some spirit entities—demonic and angelic—understand the world well enough or have enough of a hold on it to form organizations to do their bidding. Go where they can't, for whatever reason. There are agreements older than most countries holding some things in place. I can't say I understand all of it myself, nor that you should be thinking about it anyway. You need to leave this life behind, Michael. Leave it—"

"No lecture on what I should do," he interrupted her. "You were telling me about you. What you're doing. And why you're a murder suspect."

"Right." Hannah looked off into the middle distance. "There's a powerful entity—whose name I won't use, just in case it draws his attention." She shot Michael a warning look. "And he has deep, deep influence in this world. You could probably call him an archdemon if you wanted. A Duke of Hell if not a King. And he has a group of servants who enact his will upon this plane—the mortal world, whatever you want to call it. They call themselves The Ten."

"And you're about to tell me that The Resistance opposes them?"

"They do, though that's not the name they always go by. There have been different ones down throughout the ages. The Resistance opposes any malignant supernatural forces that would prey on mankind, though recently we've had to focus more and more on The Ten and their puppet master."

Michael didn't miss the slip. Hannah definitely referred to herself as a part of The Resistance. He had the sinking feeling that this "Resistance" was going to turn out to be some kind of holy warrior cult or something. He'd worked around enough fanatics in taking down terrorist rings. He knew the signs.

"And how does Hugs fit into all of this? No, wait—" suddenly it clicked in Michael's head. "He's one of The Ten, isn't he? Who had more power and influence right now than the billionaire class?"

He thought back to Sara's list of Hugs' contacts, and the interview with Drummer—something about the whole thing never had set right with him. The Ten were all billionaires? He tried to grill Hannah for more details, but she insisted that he didn't need to know. That the less he knew, the better, actually.

"You need to back away, Michael." Hannah's voice was firm. "No good comes of you going down this path. Any more answers and you might not be able to turn back. I don't want to lose you too."

"Is that what happened to Grace?" Michael guessed. "Who was she?"

"She was…she was important to me. Leave it at that. She was important to me, she stumbled across something she shouldn't have, and then she vanished. All I know is that she died and that The Ten had a hand in it. All I see when I look for her magically are these eerie, golden fireflies. Ma—someone bad, something bad got to her." Hannah looked at him. "I couldn't take it if something like that happened to you, too."

"I've sprouted wings and I can conjure a flaming fucking sword," Michael all but shouted at her. "Seems a bit fucking late."

"Not yet. He hasn't seen you. He hasn't found you! You can still—" Hannah paused, realizing she was spilling more than she wanted. "You need to forget about all of this. Get a transfer. Move to another country. Take up fishing. I can get you enough money that you'll be safe—"

"I'm not safe if my own sister keeps hiding from me! Keeps lying to me!" Michael wasn't having any of it.

"It's for your own good! Look, I'll be fine if—"

"The hell you will! You have multiple agencies both federal and local on your tail! There are too many cameras to fool. We've got your photo from one, and the entire agency and the NYPD are after you because not only are you a suspected terrorist, you murdered a billionaire—cultists or not, those types of people have a lot of power and you're in their sights!"

"They're in mine, too," Hannah said darkly. "You have no idea what they're planning, Michael, and if I don't stop them—"

"What? What is going to happen if you don't stop them? They'll gut a few more industries? Sacrifice some dividends to their demonic master?"

"I can't tell you," Hannah clammed up. "I've probably said too much already. I need to get back to headquarters, figure out what to do if I've been compromised beyond use." She gnawed on her bottom lip, clearly worried about something.

"What? Can't you just whip up a magic portal like you did to get us back here?" Michael wasn't feeling very charitable. His sister had all but admitted to murder, being part of a crazy cult, and to hiding from him "for his own good."

"It's not that easy. Getting back magically would leave them open to attack—"

"From demonic forces, yeah. Which you won't tell me any more about." Michael shook his head. "Look, I assume you have some kind of proof that Hugs was up to no good. Even if it's not admissible in court, maybe there's something that would point us in the right direction so we could look into this conspiracy you're talking about?"

His sister had murdered a man. He didn't know what he was going to do with that. By all rights, he should be hauling her in right now, but with the demonic forces clearly after her—ugh. Something about it didn't sit right.

Maybe he could work out some kind of plea bargain. If she did have evidence of a conspiracy, and it was as bad as she implied it was, there might be some wiggle room. Maybe he was just kidding himself.

Michael didn't know how he felt or what he was thinking. But if he helped Hannah, he might get to the bottom of whatever is happening, and he might get a lead on this Resistance. He still wasn't convinced they were as benign as Hannah seemed to think they were.

"I'll help you get back. I can get transport, make sure we avoid cameras, that sort of thing. You don't even have to let me take you to this headquarters if you don't want me to. Just figure out a place that's close enough that you can get the rest of the way." Michael went over to see how close Sara was to recovering. "Just answer your goddamned phone when your brother calls. I fucking worry, and you being silent really isn't helping. If you can tell me this much you can fucking well stay in contact because I've fucking missed you, you fucking idiot."

"I missed you too," Hannah admitted softly.

"Too right you fucking did." He snorted. "Now here, help me carry her down and out of here. Where the hell is this place anyway?"

CHAPTER 19

Lower East Side of Nowhere

Hannah's hideout was somewhere on the Lower East Side. Michael propped a woozy Sara up and helped the recovering detective walk slowly along the sidewalk. Of course there were no cabs nearby, and the Crown Vic was several blocks away, which was no mean walk in a city the size of New York.

Michael glanced up at the street sign. They were on Delancey, not far from Essex street.

"Not far now," he said.

"Tell me again what she said about The Resistance," Sara demanded, blinking.

Her eyes were still a bit unfocused from the blow she took to the head. Michael went over what Hannah had told him again, leaving out the more supernatural elements. It had the unfortunate effect of making it all seem a bit more like a cult, and Hannah less sympathetic, but Sara was at least on board with the idea of following Hannah back to The Resistance leaders, maybe working out a plea deal.

"It leaves a lot of questions," Sara complained.

"You have no idea," Michael muttered.

"What?"

"Nothing."

Questions. All he had were questions! Two worlds' worth of questions. He'd give just about anything for some answers.

Sara stumbled against him, diverting his train of thought. Michael easily held her up, but then nearly tripped himself, the footing beneath his shoes suddenly uneven. He glanced down. The sidewalk had turned to uneven brickwork and the street next to them to cobblestone.

"I hate Lower Manhattan," Sara complained. "None of the streets run straight and there's always stuff like this. Who can walk on these things? Thank fuck I'm not in heels."

Michael hid a smile. Sara was clearly still suffering the effects of that blow to the head. She was much less guarded than he was used to. Not that he'd known her all that long, all things considered.

"Getting foggy too," Michael squinted around them. "That doesn't happen very often."

Above them, the streetlights began to come on, though in the thickening fog all they could really see were floating balls of light. The cobblestones beneath their feet grew slick with moisture, making their footing even less sure.

"It had better not rain," Sara said. "I've had enough of a day as it is."

Michael agreed.

"Is that moss?" Sara was looking down at her feet.

It was. Michael felt his heart begin to sink in his chest. Something was off. Cobblestones and mist, sure, but moss? New York was not a mossy place. It sprouted garbage bags, rats, and cockroaches, not verdant tufts of green.

"Come on," he said, spotting a bodega on the corner. That, at least, looked like something proper New York. "Let's get you something cold for your head."

"Sounds good to me." Sara winced.

Still supporting Sara, though the detective was needing it less and less as she recovered, Michael pushed his way through the door. The bell above rang out, once, twice, thrice, and Michael blinked in confusion.

This was not like any bodega he had ever seen. There were rows, yes, but it was more like rows and rows and rows, all piled high with produce, in shapes and colors that were, quite frankly, improbable at best. And the noise! It was a roaring cacophony all around him, much more akin to a crowded open-air market, or an incredibly cut-throat farmers' market.

He turned around to take them back out the door but it was gone! Behind him was nothing more but rows and rows of merchandise, though in that direction things looked more like vegetables than fruits.

Sara was looking around, confusion on her face.

"I must have hit my head harder than I thought," she muttered.

"Let's see if we can find something cold," Michael said, opting to act as if nothing was out of the ordinary.

He didn't know what else to do. They couldn't go back, so he led them forward. There had to be an exit somewhere.

Right?

"This looks delicious," Sara said, reaching out to pick up a luscious-looking fruit that had the shape of a plum but that rippled with the changing colors of a sunset.

"Don't eat that!" Michael said quickly, plucking it from her hand and returning it to the pile. He had a sneaking suspicion where they were and if he was right, it was probably best not to eat or drink anything.

Hannah had mentioned a goblin market, and this was looking to fit the bill. He'd been focused on Sara and their surroundings and was lost in the confusing welter of sound around them, but now that he was no longer looking panicked for an exit, other details were filtering into his consciousness.

Like the merchant behind that stall of fruits having six fingers on each hand and pupils that were slit like those of a cat. Sure, the guy was wearing a tracksuit, gold chains, and a New York 'Bills cap, but that didn't hide the slight points of his ears or the faint greenish cast to his skin.

"You want to buy a nice fruit for the lady? Sweet and juicy!" The merchant smiled at Michael and the man had enough teeth in his mouth—pointed and sharp—to outfit about three sharks.

Michael jetted away, Sara in tow. The aisles of strange fruits gave way to plants, and then wood, with all manner of strange wares crafted from the stuff. There were brooms and mops, both old-fashioned and the newest cheap plastic kinds mixed in all together. Old-fashioned rocking horses and wooden cars and cheap plastic toys, cracked and dirty, all mixed together from the last four decades, at least.

The proprietors of the stalls didn't get any less strange, either. If anything, they grew stranger. Men with rat's teeth and tails, women with cat's ears and long painted nails in all colors and shapes. All of them calling out and laughing and hawking their wares to the customers.

And there were a lot of customers. Michael recognized some demons and spirits and what he suspected might be a werewolf, but there were a lot of normal people here as well. Men and women that the strangest thing about them was that they were clearly New Yorkers. There were tall skinny kids in basketball jerseys and shorts. Old women with scarves over their hair carrying shopping bags full of groceries for dinner. A host of humanity surging around him, mixing with the strange fey beings and demons and other denizens of the spirit world as if it were the most ordinary thing imaginable.

In fact, Sara, too, seemed to be taking it all in surprisingly well. He would have thought the detective would be freaking out at some of the people—were they people? Yeah, people— here, especially after the confrontation with the demons outside that dodgy warehouse. But she was acting as if everything were completely normal!

"Excuse me," Michael asked the closest merchant, a woman with the grace of a spider's web and an ethereal beauty like mist, "how do I find the exit?"

"That depends," she answered in a voice like the hiss of rain across a pond, "what you are willing to pay. Or perhaps what you have bought. Or sold. Do you have pestilential persistent little memories that need trimming like gall from an oak?" She snipped a pair of silver shears right in front of his nose. "I can remove them for you, for a price." Her smile was impossibly large for so fine and delicate a face. "I will even include safe passage from the Market with any purchase. Imagine such a deal!"

"I, uh, just browsing, actually. Never mind." Michael moved along, pulling Sara with him before she could reach out and pick up any other merchandise.

He had the distinct impression that shoplifting—even accidentally—would not be a wise thing in this place.

The stalls—and the merchants—just got increasingly strange as he struggled to find his way back out, however. Memories and dreams, foretellings and curses—not exactly the kind of thing you'd pick up at your local farmers' market or flea. It got harder and harder to keep Sara from engaging with the merchants as well. She seemed determined to make a purchase.

"How did we even get here?" He muttered to himself.

"You both have a burning desire, a need, even," a wizened old gnome of a man said to them. He looked almost like a wombat in medieval clothing, his little body so round and his face so furred over with stubble. "That I'll answer for free, like. Call it a sample of my wares."

"Wares?" Michael just stared at the creature—the man—dumbly.

"Aye. Answers is what I stock. No matter the question or questions, I have a range of answers that will serve." The little man took a draw on a long clay pipe. "Quite the art, really, taking answers and mixing and straining and purifying the stuff until you have the essence of a pure answer, applicable to any question. Though that's the nice thing about the big city being so close. There are so many answers, and people always think they have all of them. They're willing to part with a good many for a reasonable price. Means I'm able to get my hands on the raw materials very cheaply, very cheaply indeed. That's why I can offer such good value to individuals such as your good selves."

"Us?"

"Yes. Both of ye were wantin' answers unless I miss my guess. I can smell it on ye. That's what brought ye to the market." He took another toke on his pipe.

True enough. Michael's world was a morass of questions in need of answers, these days. And if the merchant really could do what he promised, answer any question Michael might have, well, that might be worth the cost.

He grabbed Sara's hand as she reached for one of the bottles of clear and glittering sand upon the table.

"And these are the answers. The bigger the bottle the bigger the answer? Or the harder the question?"

"Something like that." The man puffed.

He didn't seem concerned that Michael and Sara might wander off, or fall prey to one of his competitors. They were shouting loudly enough. It would be easy to go to one of them, but Michael's gut told him that wouldn't help. This was what he wanted. Right here on the stall in front of him.

"You owe me some answers too," Sara said, poking Michael in the stomach. "You're not telling me everything."

Michael's shoulders twinged sharply, but he saw the little gnome of a man watching them through half-lidded eyes as he puffed away at his pipe and he didn't say anything.

"Yes, good lady, answers you may have, if you're willing to pay." The little man transferred his pipe from one hand to the other then moved it around to the side of his head. What Michael had taken for ears was actually a pair of lips, artfully twisted in a bit of a grin. The lips parted and began sucking on the pipe as the little man continued to speak from the mouth on his face, rather than the one on the side of his head. "You're even in luck. I can tell from here that the price you would pay for having the answers you seek will mostly be covered by the weight of the answers themselves." He smiled with his lips, all three sets that Michael could now see, but not his eyes.

The sight should have been terrifying. It should have been so completely outside of Michael's experience that it should have left him gibbering in either terror or amazement. Fey merchants. An alien market. The thing he wanted—needed—most, right in front of him.

It should have been all too much.

But Michael's horizons had broadened considerably in the past several days, and this gnome of a man was neither the strangest nor the most horrifying thing he had seen.

"If it's questions you have, it's answers I can promise," the merchant smiled from either side of his head, his twin mouths moving in unison. "And the price will be very reasonable indeed…"

CHAPTER 20

The Goblin Market

"How much is it going to cost?" That was the real question, though Michael wasn't quite sure he wanted to know the answer.

For all he knew the merchant would charge him for it as well!

What did he want to know? The truth about his powers? How to use them? Where he got them? There were all sorts of questions he could ask there, but not all of them gave him an immediate, practical benefit. Some would only make him feel a bit better or scratch the itch of needing to know. Hell, in the worst-case scenario getting an answer could lead to who knows how many more questions!

That was the real danger here, Michael realized.

But it was too good an opportunity to let it pass him by! There were a lot of places to get knowledge, and all of them had prices. Here, though, there wouldn't be anyone trying to keep him *away* from the answers, or lying to him.

"What are the best three questions I could ask?" Sara asked, eyes gleaming, before Michael could interrupt her.

That—that was a smart question.

"The answer to the questions will cost you," the merchant looked Sara up and down, "two truths and a lie. Within the next month, you will be forced to tell the truth twice when it is inconvenient, and lie once when you should most tell the truth. Is it a deal?"

Sara blinked. Whatever she had been expecting, that was clearly not it. Michael could see in her eyes that some of the reality of what she was seeing was starting to sink in. Tension wound its way up her spine like a string and he saw her reflexively twitch her hand toward her gun.

Thankfully she didn't draw it. There was no way that wouldn't end in disaster.

"Deal," she said instead.

The merchant's eyes glittered as he plucked several small bottles filled with glittering grains of sand—or rather, something that looked like sand—and began to mix them. His manner was careless but there was such a precision to his motions and movements that Michael was certain he was cutting the amounts to the precise grain. When the mixture was complete it was the same shade as Sara's eyes.

With a quick huff and puff of his cheeks, the merchant blew the powder into the detective's face. She blinked and Michael saw stars flash wildly across her eyes for a moment. Then she cocked her head to one side.

"Huh." She said. "I should have thought of that."

"Thought of what?" Michael asked before thinking better of it.

Fortunately, Sara was one step ahead of the merchant.

"I'll answer that," she said, holding one finger up in front of the gnomish man's face. "You're not adding anything more to his tab."

His tab? Michael bit the inside of his cheek. Of course! The little man had only said the first question was free! Nothing about any of the others. What all had Michael asked him? He tried to remember but couldn't.

Fuck. This was not going well.

"I should have thought to include affordability in the framing of my question," Sara said. "The best questions are often the most expensive ones. My number one? There's no way I'm willing to pay what it would cost for that answer. Though it was still a good deal." She looked sharply at the merchant, who sulked. "Judging by my other answers, I should be able to help you frame yours better. Then decide if I want to pay more for more answers."

"Like what?"

"I asked which questions were the best for me to ask. One of the questions best for me to ask was 'How can I get the greatest value from you for the least cost *that I am willing to spend*?', implying that there are questions that are of great value but whose cost is higher than I would want to spend to get the answer."

Michael's head hurt. No wonder Hannah had warned him off this place! A man would be lucky to get away with his skin!

"You didn't even get the answer to that question," the merchant complained. "How are you getting so much use out of just knowing what to ask? Most mortals can't wrap their head around this sort of thing."

"I—" Sara paused, then smiled. "I read a lot. I like stories with wishes in them. The skills transfer. And since I've now provided you an answer, you can take it off of Michael's tab."

"Oh, you're going to be a fun one, I can see that." The gnome grinned at her. "Smoothly and smartly done! Agreed."

"Think about what you need to know, Michael. Remember, the bigger the question, the bigger the cost." Sara glanced between him and the merchant. "And different questions are different sizes for different people." Then, after a moment's thought. "And don't worry about the case. I already know which question I'm going to ask about that. We'll get to the bottom of this! And I have a couple questions of my own to work on in the process."

Except there was no way that would work out exactly as Sara intended, Michael knew. She didn't have all the information. She didn't know everything Michael knew.

Not that that would stop her.

"Oh, that's a big question," the gnome said, looking at Sara. Then he looked at Michael. "Oh yes, this is going to be fun."

Michael's mind kicked into overdrive. What could he ask that would give him the answers they needed for the case, so Sara didn't have to ask her question? They'd run into dead ends chasing this thing from the mundane side, and he needed to know more about the supernatural side of everything, so maybe there was an angle he could work that hit both of those problems?

His wings. His powers. Hannah. The Resistance. The Ten. The archdemon threatening the world.

"Oh my," the gnome said softly, eyes glimmering as he looked at something only he could see. "So many questions whirring whirring whirring in that head of yours! What might they be, I wonder? No no! Don't answer that!" The gnome chucked. "You shan't catch me out twice so easily!"

Michael ignored him. Engaging with the merchant was a distraction. He needed to make sure he didn't ask more than he absolutely had to.

"Right. I'll list the questions and you list the prices," he said, after thinking for a bit. "Considering what I am willing to pay for this answer, who is the person I am most likely to catch that can tell me—no, that can get me closest to what I need to know to solve the problems I want to solve right now? Next, where am I most likely to find this individual in the next forty-eight hours? Who are The Ten? What are the aims of The Resistance? How do I utilize my—" he shot a glance at Sara out of the corner of his eye, "—innate abilities to their fullest capacity?"

"And I want to know—under the caveat that the price is something I'm willing to pay and will not do me undue harm—who is the one individual that can give me everything I need to settle this case and achieve the most just outcome possible?" Sara added. "Since we're getting quotes, I might as well ask now."

"I'll quote you your answer first, my dear, as the price will be bound up in his," the gnome looked at Sara and gestured to Michael. "All you need to do to have your answer is to accept what this one tells you, when he asks earnestly that you believe his words to be truth, no matter how outrageous they might seem."

Michael's stomach began to sink. The gnome turned to him as Sara was still blinking, trying to unravel what the merchant had actually said.

"For you,' the gnome said, "the price of this answer is bound up in itself, for you will pursue it, though it places you and those you love in grave danger." He snatched up a bottle, emptied it into his palm, and blew.

The dust caught Michael by surprise. Stars burst across his eyes and his brain swelled with a strange weight, but it almost immediately burst, flooding his mind with images that felt like memories of a life that hadn't happened yet.

He saw a church—no a former church. It had been converted to office space. There was a logo he didn't recognize but one that was easy to remember—and track down. It was on the front of the desk behind which was a secretary, a woman he knew. The demoness that had been tailing them! As he watched she looked up and smiled at a man whose face he couldn't see from this angle.

"Good morning Mister Kerbs," she said. "Praise Mammon."

If the man replied, it was lost in the swirl of reaction that surrounded that name. That name!

Mammon. Archdemon of greed. He was mentioned in *The Faerie Queene*. And the book had been in Drummer's study. Greed. Billionaires. The Ten? Something big enough to convince Hannah to scare him off?

Michael forced himself back to the present, to the grinning gnome in front of him and Sara standing next to him.

"And the price of the other questions?" He asked.

"Oh, it's quite simple, my friend." The gnome grinned at Michael, his teeth glinting whitely. "Answers of that nature are life-changing, and so the price is similarly life-changing. If you want those answers, the cost will be you answering *her* questions. Fully, truthfully, and without reservation. I expect you'll need to reveal yourself to her—your whole self, with nothing held back—" the gnome shot him a meaningful glance, spreading his arms wide, "in order to get the answer you truly need in exchange."

The words in Michael's throat died. How could he agree to that? He'd shatter Sara's world and for what? Extra danger in her life? The loss of her job? Because there was no way Sara'd let the demons and monsters get away from her when she could see them, and without a way to effectively combat them—Michael didn't like to think about what might happen.

There was no way he could pay that price. Maybe if it only affected him, but it didn't. This was Sara's life.

Was this what it had been like for Hannah? Judging by the gnome's cackle as soon as the question crossed his mind Michael wasn't far off in thinking it had been. Great. More complications to his feelings about his sister.

But even as he thought that he felt something that had been frozen in him crack and thaw, just a bit. He could see why Hannah was trying so hard to keep him at arm's length. He still didn't like it, but he could understand it.

A bit.

"Tell you what," the gnome said, "because you and your friend have provided me with such amusement, why don't I make you a special deal? You already have the easy answers, but I'll gift you the harder ones as well. You don't need to decide right now. The knowledge will be with you, and unlock when—sorry, if—you decide to pay the price." The merchant's eyes were mocking. "For both of you."

He didn't even wait for Michael's answer. He just plucked a large bottle from the stall in front of him and blew the contents across Michael's face. Before he could react, the merchant repeated the action with a smaller bottle, the contents of this one aimed at Sara.

The same starburst exploded across his vision, and his brain suddenly felt weighty, but there was no release. The pressure simply remained, though it faded into a background pulse, barely noticeable unless he prodded it with a mental finger.

"And I'll include the answer to your questions bout how to exit the market without being caught up in any more purchasing activity as well," the gnome said. "My gift to you. Use it well!"

Michael knew better than to say anything else. He caught Sara's hand in his own and pulled her toward the exit, the oath to which was burning a hole in his mind's eye.

Laughter followed them out.

CHAPTER 21

The Church of Greed

Mammon.

The name crouched in the back of Michael's mind like a serpent in a den.

It was also plastered all over the contents of the file in front of him. He'd had to promise Tanner a favor, a big one, to get him to run a search and analysis on the figure from folklore, mythology, and literature, but it was worth it. Tanner was a damned good analyst.

Mammon. It was the Hebrew word for wealth. Unlike Baal he didn't appear to be a pagan figure that had later become demonized by a major religion. Since the Middle Ages Mammon has been known as a demonic personification of greed. It was rumored that an offshoot of the Knights Templar became so consumed with lust for the wealth they looted in the Crusades that they secretly converted to the worship of the demon and founded a cult that persisted to this day. Sometimes it was conflated with the origins of the Illuminati.

Michael thought of The Ten. Of Hugs and Drummer. Of the faint pressure still in his mind that promised answers, if he just told Sara who and what he really was. What this case was really about, beyond the surface.

He was sitting in a dark sedan. Not Sara's Crown Vic, he'd left her at the precinct doing paperwork. The encounter at the goblin market has unsettled her to the extreme. He could see her grappling with what she could remember. And she remembered a large chunk of it, he could tell by the way she looked at him. By the way she kept almost asking him a question, then hesitating.

It was unnerving to see the usually unshakable Sara so off balance.

Across the street from him was the façade of a church, though it had recently been converted entirely to office space. It was the headquarters of a shell corporation owned by a conglomeration of other corporations, but having had the name Kerbs included in his vision, Tanner had managed to run down the connection.

Michael had known the name sounded familiar for some reason. Kerbs was a billionaire, even higher on the list than Drummer and Hugs, and the bulk of his fortune came from owning or controlling a share of most of the major payment processing platforms. Kerbs got a tiny sliver of 87% of the transactions concluded in a given day in at least the Western Hemisphere. He hadn't created the software, of course. He'd seen the potential in the industry's early days, joined a startup as a financial advisor, muscled out the creators, assumed full control, and now pretty much everyone thought he'd invented electronic payment processing.

His file was sitting under the one on Mammon that Michael was looking through.

Michael looked up at the church once more. Well, he'd gone through all the research in the folders, he was as armed as he was likely to be. Might as well head in and poke the hornet's nest.

He hesitated before making sure he had his badge on him. He'd want it if things went south, but flashing it would unleash seven kinds of holy hell on him from Garibaldi. In the end, he put it in an inner pocket, checked his concealed carry holster, and adjusted his tie.

His agency suit wasn't that far off from middle-management businessman. The plans for the place didn't have it crawling with security or checkpoints. Let's see how far he can bluff his way in before having to pull out any of his trump cards.

Michael cut across the street, stepped onto the sidewalk on the other side, and pulled out his phone as he pushed his way inside the church-cum-office. The entryway had been turned into a small foyer with a listing of the three businesses that now occupied the converted space and how to get to each. The floor plan was a mess. The architect had done their best to keep the stained glass windows whole and intact, but that meant some crazy shenanigans with floors and mezzanines.

Someone had found an antique lift and installed it, cage and all, but Michael opted to take the stairs to level 2. The building wasn't busy, and everyone he passed seemed to be consumed with whatever it was they were working on. He passed by without comment. If he wasn't their problem, he was someone else's.

Michael turned a corner, walking along a floor painted a garish panoply of colors from the sun slanting in through the stained glass window. Jesus wept on the cross to his left as he found the receptionist he was looking for.

It was the woman that had led the attack on Hannah. She sat behind the desk, talking on the phone and writing something on the ledger in front of her, not yet seeing him. To ordinary eyes, she was a pretty, late-20s woman in expensive heels and a smart, business couture dress.

To Michael's spirit sight she was a full-on demoness whose eyes were two pits of crimson flame and whose nails were glittering golden claws.

There was no sign of Kerbs. Not that Michael had expected to see the billionaire here, but there had been that chance. He didn't keep an office here, and it was a shell of a shell, the corporation that held this place in ownership.

What he could get here was answers, from the woman at the desk. He ran a few scenarios through his head, then walked forward.

"Excuse me," he said, "I was hoping you could help me."

"Hold please," the demoness said into her earpiece before looking up at him. "I'm sorry, we don't—" Her voice trailed off as she looked at him. Her eyes narrowed. "You. Why do you look familiar?"

"Perhaps because I'm a witness to your assault on a civilian at—" Michael rattled off the intersection nearest to the warehouse. "I've got a few questions for you. Now, we can do it here, the easy way, or—"

"I'm sorry sir, are you attempting to arrest me?" The demoness interrupted. "I'll need to call the company attorneys if that is the case."

"I could try," Michael said. "And you'd clam up, call the attorneys, and we'd duke it out in the interrogation room at the precinct, which we both know wouldn't do either of us any favors. I wouldn't get any of the information I'm after, and you'd likely get in trouble with your boss for causing a scene and potentially tanking the profitability of this nice establishment with an arrest scandal." Michael smiled blandly. "Or you could play nice."

"Or I could break your face," the demoness offered.

A fight. It seemed inevitable. Though Michael didn't really like his chances against someone in full command of their supernatural powers. His were still fairly untested, for all that the flaming sword he'd conjured had driven them off before.

Maybe he could use that. Michael tried to recapture the feeling of that moment. Maybe he could call forth the sword again.

But the feeling eluded him.

Fuck! He could feel it, just out of reach. The pressure in his head said the knowledge of how to use it was just a few words away too. If he dragged Sara into this. If he answered all her questions.

If he ruined her life.

"You don't want to mess with me," he said, trying to bluff his way through the blockage. "You and your little friends ran away quick enough the other night."

"What's your evidence?"

"How about my being an eyewitness and an officer of the law?"

"Then why aren't you arresting me?"

"You have information I want, and I'd rather have it than have your ass in jail."

"That's not a bad opener if you want to make a deal, but you'll need to sweeten the pot. How about you owe me a favor as well?"

Okay. She was a bit too cocky. Michael pulled out his badge to underline the seriousness of the situation.

"Look—" he began.

"You?" The demoness said after reading his badge. "You're the one he wants. Why are you—" she snapped her mouth closed, her eyes flaring.

"Am I interrupting something?" A new voice drifted over Michael's shoulder.

Sara's voice.

"I knew you had something," she complained coming up next to Michael. Her gun was out and pointed at the demoness. "Didn't know it was a lead on this one."

"Didn't know it would pan out like this," Michael temporized.

Fuck! With Sara here, his options just got a lot more limited.

The demoness looked from one to the other, her eyes narrowing. Then, without warning, she sprang toward Sara, golden claws aimed at the detective's throat.

Sara emptied her clip into the woman, but just as last time the bullets did nothing.

Michael's head throbbed. There had to be a way to fix that. Had Hannah said something about enchanted bullets? Or was it just the image of the one from Hugs's crime scene that was making his head hurt?

Gun not working, Sara instead hauled back and punched the woman in the face, diverting the claws that would have torn out her throat by a hair's breadth.

The demoness smiled at her, a small trickle of blood at the corner of her lip.

"Feisty," she said. Then her eyes widened.

Michael was standing next to Sara, a flaming sword in his hand. It had manifested with a thought, and if he hadn't seen Sara's weight shift in preparation to counter her assailant, he might have tried to intervene. But his gut told him to hold, that Sara had it handled.

The demoness made a break for the door.

"Don't let her escape," Michael called.

Sara was already ahead of him. She thrust out her foot and sent the demoness sprawling.

Or she would have, had the woman's wings not manifested and caught her. She still stumbled, but she was far from down and out.

Sara followed up with a spinning kick that arced up and came down on the demoness' low back, driving her to her hands and knees. Then she was forced to dance back as the secretary lashed out at her.

Michael had no idea if Sara could see those claws or not, but he was glad his partner had avoided them.

He stepped over to the door and closed it, turning the deadbolt afterward. They would have company soon. Shot fired. Someone had to have heard that and phoned it in, even if no one had come running to see what was going on.

Not surprising considering the kind of people that worked here.

The demoness was glancing wildly around the room, looking for another exit. She could probably crash through the window easily enough. Michael saw her weight begin to shift.

He stepped up to her, flaming sword in hand.

"Make one move and I'll cut your wings off."

The threat froze his enemy where she was. Michael slowly brought the point of the flaming sword to just beneath the demoness's chin.

"We could have done this the easy way, you know," he said with a sigh. "All I wanted was some information. Well, I suppose you gave me a bit, but you're going to give me a lot more before we're done. You're going to give me everything."

"Michael," Sara asked, "what the hell is going on?"

Michael flicked his eyes over to Sara for a split second, keeping most of his attention on the prone demoness frozen beneath the point of his flaming sword.

He had to tell her. He needed the answers. And the cat was kind of out of the bag already.

He couldn't tell her. It would destroy her life. There had to be a way to explain this and make her forget about it all.

But she'd asked. She wanted to know. She knew what she was capable of and, if she didn't know exactly what she was doing, she was no stranger to living under threat of violence.

And if he didn't tell her, she was going to get killed chasing this thing to the bitter end anyway. At least if he told her she'd know what she was up against, know what to look for.

Right.

"So, this is going to sound unbelievable, but bear with me…"

CHAPTER 22

Something's coming

"I'm half human and half…something else. You can call it an angel if you want." Michael talked fast. He knew they were going to have company very soon. "I only found out about this recently myself, and I know it's mad, but you've seen some of the things I've seen, so maybe you can imagine…"

And just like that, he knew what he could do. He'd answered part of Sara's question and part of the knowledge he'd bartered for at the goblin market came free in his mind. And without further debate, Michael put it to good use. He'd already started the reveal, he might as well go all the way.

"Lux et veritas," he whispered, and motes of white and gold light sparked to life in Sara's eyes.

"Jesus, Mary, and Joseph!" Sara suddenly stumbled back from the prone form of the demoness. "What in the hell—"

"She's either something from the Spirit World or she's like me, half and half," Michael stated. He remembered the inescapable feeling of truth that came with that spell. Hopefully it would help him convince Sara, help smooth her transition. "Sara. Sara, look at me. I'm still the same person I was before. The wings, the sword, it doesn't change the core of anything."

His partner looked at him, and Michael was relieved when she nodded. Sara was a bit wild about the eyes but she was trusting him. She was a pro. She'd hold it together.

Through this encounter, at least. Michael didn't want to take bets on how she might react when the pressure all around them stopped forcing her to hold everything in.

But he'd been honest. He'd revealed himself and answered Sara's questions. That was the start of something.

It was like a key turned into his mind and knowledge flooded the conduits of his brain. He knew enough to ask the right questions to pull the answers he needed from the demoness. Or to try and trick the information out of her.

"I'm nothing like you, *deschpach*," the demoness spat at him. "My blood is untainted by humanity! I serve the Lord Mammon willingly. Praise be to Mammon! Praise be to his golden eyes! Praise to the unblemished might of the diamond unyielding! Let his power fill me like wealth lurking in the depths of a mine, welling up from the deep." She began chanting.

Michael pressed the tip of the flaming sword to her flesh. It began to hiss and smoke and the demoness let out a blood-curdling scream.

The chanting ceased.

"We didn't come here for religious devotions," he said, "we came here for answers."

"Fuck you," the demoness spat at him.

"I command you in the name of The Resistance!" Michael followed a hunch.

"The Resistance?" the demoness laughed. "You're in service to that pathetic bunch of ragtag virgins?"

"You think The Ten is any match for them?" Michael sneered.

"The Ten has the backing of Mammon! They serve his greatness and are upraised in return! And soon, soon my Lord will have the power to enter this world directly. All will belong to him! All will fall before his might and their souls shall fill his coffers and none shall be able to gainsay him!"

Nice to have that confirmation.

"The Resistance will stop him. They've already begun to move."

"You mean the bitch that killed Hugs? Ha! His successor had already taken his place. Even if you manage to kill every single one of The Ten there are enough family members in reserve that Mammon's will be done. He shall—what are you doing?" The demoness looked at Sara, who was rifling through the contents of her desk.

"Well, if you're so important, there's got to be plenty of details here as to what your master's plan is." Sara started clicking at the terminal, pulling open folders and files. "Looks like it has something to do with PitCoin speculation, if this is anything to go by."

"I will kill you!" The demoness tried to lunge forward, only to be brought up short by the flaming sword at her neck. "Mammon! Lord Mammon! I call to thee for aid! Help thy servant do thy will upon this mortal plane!" She started to chant but cut herself off sharply at Michael's next words.

"You chant one more word and I will burn the tongue right out of your mouth." The sword in his hand flared.

The demoness just smirked at him. Michael felt the feathers on his wings stiffen, When had they manifested? He knew how, now, instinctively, the knowledge seeping into his brain as he shared more and more of himself with Sara.

"I wouldn't be so smug, if I were you," Sara called from behind the desk. "You said there were ten people serving Mammon to execute his plan? Well, thanks to Hugs we know who each of them are."

Michael shot Sara a glance. She shrugged.

"There were nine other numbers at the top of his most frequent calls list on his phone. All nine were registered to other billionaires, including Drummer."

"And Kerbs," Michael guessed.

"Yeah, how did you—" Sara looked at something on the screen. "Ah. That's how."

"I will skin you alive and turn you into a pair of pumps!" The demoness hissed at Sara.

"Lady, I doubt your master will allow you to live after what you've done here." Sara looked entirely unimpressed, though Michael was familiar enough with her to see that a lot of it was a front. Sara was operating under a strain. How could she not be, with all this information flooding in, eroding the foundations of her worldview?

But Sara was a detective and a professional. She wasn't going to let this opportunity to gather intel slip past. Especially since it looked less and less like the regular police force would be able to bring much force to bear on this. How do you handcuff a demoness who could melt the things right off and rip your head from your shoulders anyway?

"Hannah killed Hugs with a spell-etched bullet," Michael said. "I can probably enchant you a few to use in cases like this. She knows magic, and if she won't teach me the spell I'm sure I can pick it up from Gabriel."

The demoness hissed at the names.

"Gabriel?" Sara paused. "Gabriel Gabriel?" The archangel?"

"I dunno. Maybe."

"You don't even know?" The demoness tensed her body. "How little do you—I've been a fool! You're not nearly the threat you pretend to be, in spite of this sword and those wings." She shifted.

"Don't get any ideas," Michael warned her.

"You're no more than a babe! So fresh and new to your power. It's untested, your blade unbloodied!" A coil of flame appeared in her hands, sooty and red.

Michael reacted on instinct, thrusting the blade home before the demoness could become too much of a threat. He was aiming for her throat but he missed, the blade driving deep into her shoulder. She screamed, a terrible, wailing sound, and the flames began to slowly eat her alive.

She began to curse at Michael.

"I will kill you when I return! You have not seen the last of me fool. Demons never die! Banish me a hundred thousand times, I will always return, and I will find your little girlfriend there and rip out her spine through her mouth."

Michael glanced up at Sara. The detective was frozen in place, her eyes locked on the slowly immolating demoness.

"Hey," he called to her. "Look at me. It'll be all right. We've got one another's backs." He wished he could say The Resistance would help as well, but there was no guarantee. For all that Hannah was involved with them, and Gabriel seemed to be as well, it was still a foreign organization he knew relatively little about.

Though after today he knew a lot more than before.

"If there's anything left of you at all," the demoness suddenly went from frothing at the mouth to smooth and taunting. "When my Master is done with you. Praise Mammon! Hail and Welcome almighty King of Wealth! Hail to the Golden Throne! Hail!"

"Michael," Sara said, her voice rising, "what is going on? Something doesn't feel right."

"Something's coming," Michael whispered. He didn't know how he knew but he could feel it. Like seeing ripples on the water or sensing the pull of a tidal flow when wading into the sea, something was moving on the other side of the veil.

Something *massive.*

"He's watching you right now." The demoness laughed, a cracked and burbling thing. "He can see you—both of you—from the other side. Do you dare pierce the veil, Michael? Do you dare see who is looking back at you from the other side?"

There was a sound like the rushing of dark wings, like the explosion of a thousand crows suddenly taking to flight. Michael dared not look across the veil. He didn't know what was watching but he was certain he didn't want to lock eyes with it. Not now. Not in this state.

Sara was glancing over her shoulder, terror in her eyes. She couldn't see anything, but she, like Michael, could *feel* it.

And it broke her already weakened grasp on her composure. Between the attack, the goblin market, and the revelation that the world was so much bigger than she had imagined—to say nothing of the sight of a literal demoness flaming at her feet—Sara backed away.

"I don't know if I can handle this," she said. "This is too much. I—I need to go!" She turned to dash out the door, away from the feeling of those terrible eyes, away from the strange pangs of hunger she seems to feel under their weight. "Just leave me alone!"

And then she was gone.

CHAPTER 23

Max Ashton

Michael decided to give Sara some distance. He doubled down on investigating the leads turned up at the agency and let her and Overstreet run at things from their end without him for a while.

When she still hadn't contacted him after two days he took a detour after work to pass by the precinct. He was about to head in when he noticed that the building was being watched.

The watchers had horns and wings.

Michael veered over to the coffee truck, taking his time standing in line to carefully observe everyone in the vicinity. The supernatural suspects were easy enough to spot. They weren't trying very hard to hide themselves. They probably didn't need to, being invisible to most mortals.

The mundane operative watching the place, though; he was a surprise. Even more surprising was that Michael recognized him. It was the guy that had fled the murder scene—Michael had chased him out of Hugs' assistant's house!

Michael bought a paper to go with his coffee and found an out-of-the-way spot to pretend to read while he scoped out the surveillance on the precinct. There were at least four demons, two spirits, and the seemingly mundane man watching the place from the angles he could see.

When he was reasonably certain the man wasn't going to vanish, Michael folded his paper and made his way into the precinct, checking Sara's desk first and, when he didn't find her at it, the conference room where the case files were usually kept.

The place was in chaos. Three new boards had been crammed into the already tight space and pictures were stuck up all across each of them with notes in some kind of coded system. From the similarities and the presence of a snapshot of the mortal face of the demoness he'd killed two days ago, Michael guessed Sara had been trying to run down both sides of the case without tipping her hand to Overstreet.

Not that he knew what it felt like to try and keep a mortal friend in the dark at all, no.

Fortunately, Brian was out. If Michael was lucky he was on a doughnut run. The coffee had only made him hungry.

Sara stood with her back to him, muttering to herself as she glanced from a folder in her hands to the case board.

"Sara," Michael got her attention.

"Michael." Sara didn't jump. Didn't show any surprise or alarm at his presence. She simply turned to face him. "Good to see you."

"I hope that's true even after I tell you what I've just seen outside." Michael stepped fully inside the room and closed the door, locking it behind him. "You've got demons watching the place, and an old friend."

"Old friend?"

Michael could see the tension coil through Sara's frame.

"Well, not one you've met, so far as I know. I think you were a few steps too far behind me. But I saw him. The guy we scared off at Ms. DeSouzas's house? The murder suspect? He's outside staking out your precinct as we speak."

Michael crossed the room to look critically at the new suspect boards. Sara had her hand on the doorknob, eyes afire.

"There are about six demons watching the place as well, though, and of course a metric ton of civilians," Michael added. "We'll need a plan if we head out there."

Sara froze, clearly torn.

"If you've got a printer I snapped a pic of our murder suspect. It might be a bit grainy, but the zoom on these new smartphones is shockingly good." Michael pulled the slim rectangle out of his pocket and shook it enticingly, like candy before a kid. "We could even add it to your board. Draw some new lines. Because there is no way it's a coincidence that he was in the home of the assistant to a murdered, demon-worshipping billionaire and now—in the company of six honest-to-whatever demons—is watching this very precinct. Two days after we draw the attention of the Big M."

"Big M? You mean Ma—" Sara began.

"Let's not say the name," Michael cut her off. "Just in case. We've got enough trouble keeping unwanted eyes off our homework as it is."

"Fair enough." Sara pulled out her phone. "Send me the pic. I'll get a printout."

Michael did and then turned back to examine the boards as Sara slipped out of the conference room to make a physical copy of the photo and run it through the precinct databases. If this guy had a record they'd have a name in a matter of hours. Faster, if Sara had the clout to pull the right strings and didn't care who she might be pissing off by cutting in line.

He attempted to trace the connections on the new boards, but it was a struggle. He couldn't read Sara's notes, and while he recognized pieces, like the demonic secretary and the outside of the market building on Delancey, the interconnections eluded him. Even the lines connecting the pieces didn't help.

The door clicked behind him. Michael turned around, hoping it wasn't Overstreet. Lucky for him, it wasn't. It was Sara, and she had sparks flying from her eyes and a palpable aura of killing intent hanging around her like a funeral shroud.

"I don't need to run a search on our friend outside," she said. "I know who it is."

Michael blinked. Something had happened, clearly. Before he could ask, Sara answered his unspoken question.

"That's the bastard that killed my father. Max. Fucking. Ashton."

"I—huh." Michael looked at her. "If that's the case you're taking this surprisingly calmly."

"Like you said. We need a plan. If I go running out there right now, I'm liable to try shooting the bastard on sight and there are too many ways that could go south. I could hit a civilian." Sara paused. "And one of my answers from our market encounter might have given me reason to be a bit cautious here."

"Plus, demons." Michael chose not to comment on her reference to the Goblin Market. He was still grappling with the fallout from his own deal. No point getting mired in all that again now.

"Right." Sara took a deep breath. "You know, up until this moment I didn't know what to fucking think about all of that? That first day, I tried to forget it all. Push everything out of my brain except what I knew to be true and real and rational." She walked over to the new boards. "Then I realized I was never going to unravel this case looking at just one side of it. So I figured I'd try to make sense of it. There have to be laws binding these things—metaphysical ones, if not like, law laws." She sighed. "So I tried to make sense of it, logically. But I don't know the rules. The rules they use, they're different. Even if there are parallel dimensions or whatever in the science we understand today, I don't think they work by chalk circles and magic words. Let alone whatever you did to me to make me see all of that." She punched him in the arm. "Thanks for that, by the way. I'll have to think of a way to pay you back, properly."

Michael shuddered at the gleeful malice in her tone.

"But now? Seeing that asshole's face again? Knowing that he's somehow connected to all of this?" Sara shook her head. "I find that it doesn't matter. I don't care. I'm in. All in. And I think I was in even before you brought that picture in here. I just needed a little push."

"In that case, I've got something for you." Michael pulled two standard ammo clips out of his pocket. "I've done my best at enchanting these—etched the same sigils that Hannah used on her ammunition onto them. I'm not sure if it worked, but they're slightly more likely to be effective than your regular round when it comes to our new friends out there."

"God, how did you stand it, when you first saw through the Veil or whatever?" Sara shook her head. "All of those parasite things attached to just about damn near everybody?"

"It didn't last very long, the first time," Michael lied. "So I didn't have to deal with it all that much. Until I started seeing the things without the spell."

"How the hell do people deal with fighting these supernatural things without it catching the attention of anyone? That's what I don't understand." Sara shook her head.

"I'm not sure. I don't think the cameras we have are equipped to capture images of spirits. Look." Michael flipped through a few snaps he'd taken of the demons lurking outside. Nothing demonic showed up on the film. "It's like they don't exist to technology."

"Why can we see them, then? Even if it does take a spell? Just magic?"

"I dunno. They say eyes are windows to the soul, maybe it had something to do with spirit?" Michael shrugged. "But if we go out there and just open fire, we'll look like we're shooting at random, regular people. Or possibly thin air, depending."

"That's a bad plan," Sara said. "Let's come up with a better one."

"I say we forget about the demons. Focus on Max. We know he's a real person. I saw him. You know him. The camera shows that he's there. He might have some advantages, the guy was almost impossibly fast and disappeared without a trace in the blink of an eye, but I don't think he's a demon. Or a fairy."

"Right. Because demons aren't enough to deal with."

"I'm just glad we haven't had to deal with werewolves or vampires yet, honestly." Michael sighed. "I don't think I'm up to that yet."

"Well, you're not a teenage girl or a terminally angry man-child, so that makes sense." Sara grabbed paper and a pen and started sketching out a rough map of the outside of the precinct. "Show me where everyone is. Maybe you can draw off the demons and I can sneak up behind Max and nail him."

"Not a bad start." Michael took the pen and marked roughly where each individual was lurking. "Demons on the roof and here and here. Max is sitting on the steps of the plaza across the street. Good spot. Plenty of activity to cover his presence, no reason to be chased off."

Michael and Sara went back and forth for several minutes until they had a workable plan.

"Right," Michael said, "Let's see if we can nab this asshole."

***

But Ashton was gone by the time they made their way out of the precinct. Sara's reckoning would have to wait.

"We'll find him again," Michael said. "He's mixed up in all of this, somehow. One of our suspects will know something."

"Let's get back to the list then," Sara said. "There are some more billionaires we can shake down."

CHAPTER 24

The Ten

"Damn," Sara said, slamming her fist on the ornate railing. "Blocked again."

With the added context that there were ten billionaires—nine of which were all in the tenth's—Hugs's—phone—who seemed to also have a connection to Mammon and the supernatural forces messing with their lives, Michael and Sara had decided to investigate as many of the names on that list as possible.

It wasn't going well. After putting through a request to contact a large sample of the numbers on Hugs' phone—to cover their tracks and not make it obvious they were just interested in the billionaires—the duo had run into wall after wall. The billionaires had all lawyered up.

Michael and Sara were currently standing outside the building that housed the penthouse for the only other billionaire on the list that was currently in the city: Alloria Sadim. An heiress and serial divorcee, Alloria made the bulk of her fortune up in investments and shares of hyper-successful companies. Somehow, she always seemed able to get in on the ground floor. Nothing suspect about that ever turned up, for some reason, even though Michael had checked with the SEC.

Regardless, she wasn't talking.

The doorman was staring at them pointedly

"Thank you for your time," Michael said, taking Sara by the elbow and steering her outside.

Sara was rigid beneath his grasp.

"Just a minute," he said quietly. "I've got an idea." Michael led them outside and steered them around the block. Around the corner and halfway along to the next corner was a thin gap between the buildings. Michael stepped quickly into the small alleyway, Sara following.

"What are you doing?" she asked.

"I've been in buildings like this before," Michael said. "My ex's cousin and her husband lived in a place like this. You know there's an elevator that goes up and opens *into* each of the apartments? It's behind a locked door, but that's how all these rich people get rid of their garbage. They can't be hauling it themselves, and most of the residents in the building aren't so rich they have servants to do it, so the building staff carts it all away. Then it gets dropped somewhere...aha!"

There were a pair of large dumpsters, wheeled, blocking most of the small space in the alleyway. The cover on each was propped open and several large bags of rubbish were visible. He shot a glance at Sara.

"You can't be serious," the detective said. "There's no way we're this desperate yet. Finding anything useful in there would be like finding a rusty needle in a rotting haystack."

She wasn't wrong.

"There's also a back door which they almost always leave propped open." Michael pointed beyond the dumpster. "Not saying that we should break the law and bypass the front desk like this, but it's always possible a suspicious character happens past and some upstanding officer of the law needs to follow them into a building to make sure nothing nefarious is going on."

"A bit shaky and it's been done—"

"It's a classic for a reason!" Michael held up his hands. "Hypothetically."

"I don't—"

"Get down!' Michael grabbed Sara's arm and pulled her between the dumpsters, forcing her to crouch. The door he had been looking at was opening. Sara glared at him but stayed silent and watched.

A demon stepped out. Tall, reddish skin, massive flaring leathery wings. And a charcoal suit. He looked like security or a bodyguard. The demon flicked his eyes up and down the alleyway, turned, called the door, and drew a quick shape over it. To Michael's sight, a sigil of light briefly flared before vanishing again.

Then the demon turned and walked away, heading towards the other end of the alleyway.

"What did you see?' Michael asked when the coast was clear.

"Standard security looking dude. He locked the door and left. Why?"

"Demon," Michael said shortly.

"How do you keep seeing them?" Sara complained.

"Magic," Michael said with an eloquent shrug. "When I find someone to explain it to me, I'll explain it to you."

"You'd better damn well do more than explain. I need to see what I should and should not shoot."

Sara stood and headed towards the door.

"Better not," Michael said reluctantly. "I think he placed some kind of enchantment on it. If we touch it—I dunno. I don't think we should touch it.'

Sara went up to the door and squinted at it. Michael saw her fingers twitch but she didn't touch anything.

Michael followed, squinting to try and pick out the sigil again, that flicker of red light. All he managed to do was to give himself a bit of a headache. There was something there, he'd seen it, but calling that image back was beyond him.

More things he needed to learn. What else was he missing? Was there something he could do that would help crack this case wide open?

If there was, he wasn't going to find it here and now.

"We should go," Sara said as if reading his mind. "We're not going to get anything here, and I'm not going to go dumpster diving on the off chance there's something useful in there. And that security guard—demon or not—will be back soon enough."

The man *had* had the look of someone out for a quick stroll around the perimeter. Possibly he was looking for Michael and Sara even. The doorman had called up to check if Ms. Sadim was willing to see them.

"Come on," Sara said, disgust apparent on her face. "We're not getting anything else out of here today. Let's go grab some food and see if we can find a new angle from what we've already got."

There wasn't, so Sara instead drove them to pick up dinner and then to her apartment. It was on the extreme edges of the Upper West Side, just a scant few blocks from where the city turned into Harlem proper. She was on the fifth floor of a six-floor walk-up. The place was bigger than he expected, though, like most apartments in the city, it was in need of a good renovation.

The walls were a faded yellow, though they were hung with all sorts of brightly colored pictures. Butterflies and small birds seemed to figure prominently. There were some ancient specimens of furniture in the living room, and a small window that opened between it and the kitchen. A small dining table was placed beneath the window.

"I took over the place from my grandmother when she passed," Sara said as she tossed her keys into a bowl by the door.

"Rent controlled?"

"Don't I wish." Sara snorted and shook her head. "No. They drove out anyone that wouldn't agree to a rent increase. My grandmother got a good deal, though. I had a lawyer friend make sure of it. And when I took over the lease I kept it. Got some restrictions on how much rent can rise, and when, much lower than the average."

Sounded more to Michael like Sara was looking for an excuse to stay in the home her grandmother had lived in, but he was no real estate attorney. Not that he could blame her. There was a nice, homey feel to the place. It wasn't at all what he'd expected.

There was one thing, though, that was utterly Sara, and that was the massive cork board mounted on the wall by the window. On it was a replica of the suspect board from the precinct, but this one had yarn in multiple colors. Studying it, Michael guessed the red was for supernatural links and the green was mapping the mundane leads they'd had in the case. And no surprise where Sara's found the yarn, either. A knitting basket was sat next to the large armchair not far away.

"Do you want a fork?'" Sara called from the kitchen as she plated up the food.

"I'm fine with the chopsticks," Michael called back, most of his attention still on the board. "This is good work. Thorough."

He picked up a length of yarn and pinned it between a picture of a woodcut demon and the picture of the number 10 with a big circle around it and a piece of paper with the initials A.S. on it. Michael was glad to see that even in her home Sara was being careful.

When you mess with someone who has that much money it pays to be very, very careful.

"Food's up." Sara pulled out her chair and dug into her chow fun.

"Thanks." Michael joined her, starting with a spring roll.

There was silence for a few minutes as both dug into the food while it was still hot, broken only occasionally by requests for soy sauce or sriracha. It wasn't until they got to the fortune cookies that Michael and Sara returned their attention to the many problems at hand.

"We can't get anywhere near any of the suspected members of The Ten," Sara said, tossing her fork onto her plate with a vicious clatter. "They've got lawyers, security, even the department won't risk approving much in the way of surveillance."

"So we have to get creative," Michael said slowly. "We both know now that there are more ways than we're used to, to find information, or to conduct surveillance." There was more knowledge purchased from the goblin market tickling in the back of his mind, but Michael knew he needed someone to teach him properly. He knew more of what was possible, and even the basics of how, but part of that knowledge was knowing that if he screwed things up too badly, the magic could go very, very wrong.

That was one reason he hadn't tried repeatedly casting the spell that temporarily bestowed the sight on Sara. If he made a mistake he could easily burn her eyes out of their sockets.

Not a chance he wanted to take.

So he'd need Hannah—or maybe Gabriel—to teach him the finer points of spellcasting.

He shook his head. What a fucking trip. The world was so much stranger than he ever imagined.

"What're you thinking?" Sara asked.

"That I need someone to teach me more of what's possible." Michael drummed his fingers on the table in front of him, fortune cookie still untouched. He didn't quite want to tempt fate by opening it.

Sara must have agreed, as hers was likewise still intact.

"It'd be nice if the department—or your agency—would cough up a bit of support too," Sara said cynically. "Not sure that's going to happen though. Money talks, and that much money fucking screams."

"Especially with someone like Garibaldi," Michael said with a wry chuckle, shaking his head. "I've not met your captain, but I'm getting the impression that he's not much different."

"Money makes the world go around," Sara agreed. "Most of the department focus is on drug busts, gang violence, that sort of thing."

"Stuff that brings down property values when it crops up in a neighborhood." Michael reached out to toy with his fortune cookie.

"Exactly." Sara sighed and reached out for her own cookie, breaking it open with a sharp snap and crunching on the crisp exterior. She looked at her fortune cookie and barked out a laugh.

"You will have wealth beyond your wildest dreams." Sara shook her head. "Not likely, unless one of these billionaires takes a liking to me and puts me in the will. What do you think the odds of that are, after I've been running around trying to find out more about the murder of one of their fellow cultists?"

"I can't say I think the odds are very high." Michael grinned.

"What does yours say?"

"Change is on the horizon." Michael glanced at the back of it. "And my lucky numbers are 3, 17, and 24."

CHAPTER 25

Garibaldi's Plan

"Lieberman, my office!" Garibaldi barked across the office.

Michael saved the file he was working on and flipped the folders on his desk closed. He made his way to his boss's office, noticing as he did so that the rest of his team was filing through the cubicles towards the same destination. They arrived at roughly the same time and filed in.

It was a tight squeeze, and Garibaldi lounging behind that massive desk of his didn't help matters. Michael, front and center, cleared his throat.

"Sir?"

"We've had a break in your case. I'm deploying you as soon as possible to resolve the matter, with authorization of full force. We want this sorted, yesterday." Garibaldi passed him a folder and nodded.

Full force. Michael hadn't heard those words since…he shook off the memory and returned his attention to the folder. Michael felt the man's greasy eyes on him as he opened it, a sense of dread coiling in the pit of his stomach. And he was right to be wary. At the top of the folder was a picture of Hannah—grainy, security camera footage, but it definitely was Hannah.

He glanced up, keeping his face passive. Garibaldi was chewing on a cigar, a relaxed set to his shoulders and a disinterested look on his face, but Michael could see suspicion glinting in the man's eyes.

The asshole had been testing him! Trying to trick Michael into reacting!

Adrenaline pricked at the back of his neck. Something was very wrong here.

"Problem?" Garibaldi asked mildly.

"No, sir," Michael said immediately. "I presume all the details are in here?"

"They are. Go get prepped. You have to deploy tomorrow. Our lead says there will be a limited window of opportunity to nail that bitch." Garibaldi shook his head. "Can't believe *that's* the sniper that offed Hugs and got away from you lot." He glared at them. "Don't screw it up again, or I'll bust all of you so far down the ranks that you'll be digging paperwork out of your collective ass until you retire. Clear?"

"Yes, sir," they chorused.

"Dismissed." Garibaldi flicked a hand at them. "Except you, Lieberman. You stay."

Michael waited until his team filed out, keeping his eyes fixed on his boss and the folder firmly in hand.

"Sir?" He asked when everyone else had left and the door to the office had clicked shut.

"You're not going to have a problem offing the target just because she's a woman, are you Lieberman?" Garibaldi looked at him intently. "Because you let her get away once before."

"I had no idea the target was a woman at that time, sir, and I certainly would never purposefully allow a suspect to escape." Michael maintained his resolute posture.

"Well, I know at least one other occasion where you had no problem handling a female suspect." Garibaldi grinned lewdly. "And that turned out all right for both of us. Let's make sure this one turns out equally well, shall we?"

The man was totally fucking with him! Garibaldi didn't trust him for some reason. Well, there was a good reason not to, if he knew Hannah was Michael's sister, but how could the man know? Michael didn't even know, and there was no way they had her name and identity and weren't confronting him with it.

Unless it was a test. Or a trap. Though there was no real reason for either unless someone was pulling some very dark strings at the agency. Regulations would just have him pulled from the case and interrogated. What Garibaldi was doing either meant that they didn't know his connection to Hannah…

…or that they did, and they were trying to catch him in some kind of wrongdoing as well.

Michael blinked and shifted to looking at the scene before him with his Sight. He bit his cheek to keep from flinching. The last time he'd seen Garibaldi, the man had hungry things lurking between his teeth, and knotted strings around his blackened and rotting fingers. Now, it was even worse. Cords of sinew rose from every limb, glinting golden with fat, and the man's entire lower jaw was missing, displaced by a sucking, pulsating lamprey-like mouth, the pointed fangs glinting golden in the afternoon light through the window.

The eyes were the eyes of a predator, hungry and cold and calculating, and Michael could see his own face reflected in their obsidian depths. No. This was definitely a trap of some kind, and Garibaldi was in on it. There's no way this corruption could mean anything else.

"I asked if you were certain that there would be no problems this time," Garibaldi snapped, the sucking maw of his mouth all but slobbering over the words.

"I'm sure everything will go according to plan," Michael said, "sir."

Whose plan, well that was a different story. There was no way he was going through with whatever this asshole intended. There was no way that turned out well, for himself or for Hannah. Something in this office stank to high heaven and Michael was going to do something about it.

"Then I suggest you review the material, rein in your team, come up with a plan, and get ready for tomorrow. Dismissed."

Michael turned, narrowly avoiding a small gobbet of fat as it flew from Garibaldi's fingers and towards his face. He turned off his spirit sight as he left the office. He had no desire to see any more of his coworkers even a tiny bit like that, though he knew he'd have to have a careful look at everyone and soon.

Were there demons as well? No. He would have noticed, and if they knew he could see them they wouldn't risk sending anyone. They'd rely on mortals whose strings they could pull. Like Garibaldi.

Michael took refuge at his desk and carefully went through the file. The details on Hannah herself were sketchy, no last name, no known aliases, a few known criminal contacts—but nothing in here on her connection to Michael.

He shook his head. They really were testing him, trying to trick him into murdering his own sister. Though she was hardly an innocent. She'd killed one billionaire already and if this intelligence was correct, she'd be going after another one tomorrow. Funnily enough, the list of potential targets included all three members of The Ten currently in the city.

Or known to be in the city.

Michael made some notes. Looked out at the office around him, weighing his coworkers with a measuring glance and a bit of his Sight. Then went through his options. No matter how he looked at it, things were not looking good.

Fine. Decision time. Michael sat up and plucked the inter-office phone from its cradle. "Tanner? Meet me at my desk. We need to go over a few things for tomorrow." Then he pulled a sheet of paper free from its pad and began writing out a series of instructions, pausing every so often to tap the end of the pen against his chin in thought.

When Tanner arrived, Michael had nearly folded over the slip of paper and was looking through the file Garibaldi had given him. It still felt greasy under his fingers. He closed it and glanced up at Tanner.

"What's up, bossman?" Tanner's cheeky smile was bright as ever.

Michael looked the younger man over with his Sight. No obvious signs of corruption presented themselves. Not that he knew if that meant anything. Nor did it matter if what he was asking Tanner to do was questionable at best.

Best leave him with plausible deniability.

"I need these files pulled and brought to me. Use this ID number." Michael slid the slip of paper over to Tanner. "I need them immediately; every single one you can get your hands on. There isn't a lot of time left."

Tanner opened the paper and scanned it.

"Sure thing, boss. I can get these for you in an hour or so. Is this for tomorrow?"

"I'm looking a bit more broadly. I'm not sure about some of the details in this file. There are too many ways this could break." All of them bad. Michael tapped a finger significantly on the folder and shot Tanner a meaningful glance. "Jobs and lives are on the line. I want to make sure I can protect as many people as possible."

Including Tanner, hopefully. Michael felt bad about using the kid this way, but he needed those files and he had too many other things to do before the end of the day.

"Send me Priestly on your way," he said as Tanner got up to leave.

Michael pulled out his bag and carefully went through his desk as he waited. When he walked out of this office there wasn't going to be any coming back, so anything he wanted or anything he could use he needed to take with him now.

Priestly showed up before he finished. He shoved the bag under the desk and listed off several things he needed her to get for him, including a list of the journalists that regularly harassed the agency about human rights violations and corruption and their contact information.

"You think there's a sympathizer feeding the target information?" Priestly frowned.

"I'm almost certain there will be," Michael said. "I want to check, just in case."

What he actually intended to do was blow the lid off of whatever was happening here at the agency. He had enough evidence to give any half-decent journo a leg-up on unraveling whatever mess was festering at the center of things. Garibaldi was almost certainly on the take. Someone was pulling those strings Michael saw, and that kind of thing always left traces. Financial ones as well as supernatural.

"I'll also need a set of untraceable fund cards." Michael tapped the file Garibaldi had given him. "Put it under Garibaldi's authorization code."

"You think we'll need it?"

"Better safe than sorry, and if this folder means what I think it does…" Michael let the sentence trail off. Priestly would come to her own conclusions, and they'd likely fit his purpose better than any lie he could actually concoct.

"On it."

"Send me the others when you see them. Except Tanner. He's already got his assignment. Oh, and have someone send me up several thumb drives, big ones. I might need to prep overnight files for everyone."

Michael went back to his preparations, copying several files off of the agency servers and onto the drives that Priestly sent him. While they transferred he continued rifling through his desk, stowing nearly a hundred thousand dollars in untraceable operations funding in his bag, and generally raiding the office for anything useful that wasn't nailed down and he could get his hands on without drawing too much attention.

Fortunately, that list was a long one. Michael had seniority, a sparkling record, and was good enough at his job that he knew enough about how everyone else worked to nudge the system the way he wanted it to go.

If he was going to burn all his bridges here to get to the bottom of whatever was going down, he wasn't going to hold back. Unfortunately, he lacked the technical know-how to delete all the information they had on Hannah from off the servers, but he could at least mess the files up a bit, changing details on the source file. There would be hard copy backups, but everything would have to be double-checked and that would slow everyone and everything down.

And then he was ready. He was ready and he sat there at his desk, slowly sipping a cup of terrible coffee. It was insane, it should be insane. He was throwing everything away, and for what? A hunch?

But Michael's world had changed in the past couple of weeks. Everything was different now. He wasn't even the same person he was a month ago. Wasn't even the same human—if he was even technically human at all, really!

It made it really, really easy to let go.

What was he holding on for? His boss was a monster—possibly quite literally. The agency was being pointed at the enemies of rich and influential men, rather than at actual terrorists, because

Michael was less and less certain that Hannah and The Resistance were at all what he was being told they were.

It made him question all of his previous missions as well, and he fucking hated that. How many were actual targets that put the life and well-being of innocent civilians in danger and how many were someone using the agency to settle a score or remove some competition?

Michael glanced at the clock. He'd need to make a move soon. Too much longer and his team would expect a meeting to be called about the mission tomorrow. He reviewed his route. Which car he'd take, how he'd distract the attendant and switch the entry on the car so if anyone followed him they'd be tracking a different car, where he'd lose the chain of surveillance cameras around the agency, where he'd ditch the car, how he'd get to a place to lay low and stay safe, and how he'd make sure several journalists got the information he'd lifted off the servers. And on and on, spinning plans and likely scenarios in his head.

And to top it all off, he had magic he could use as well.

"Do you need anything else, boss?" Tanner asked as he walked past.

Michael shook his head.

"Thanks. I think I've got everything I need for now."

CHAPTER 26

The Path to The Resistance

Michael looked at the burner phone for the third time in as many minutes. It had been two days since he'd walked out of the agency, burning all his bridges behind him. What he needed was news. He was safe enough in the abandoned water tower he'd holed up in. New York City had tons of the things left over from earlier eras. Some still functioned, some just stood empty and decayed, waiting for the building's owners to tear them down or remove them as part of a renovation.

Not many did. It was cheaper to let them fall apart and then haul off the wood. And they made a great hiding place because most of them were accessible via the ubiquitous fire escapes clamped onto the outside of most of New York's larger buildings.

Plus he could fly, so he didn't even feel too worried about being cornered. No, what he needed was news. And the only place he was likely to be able to get it from was Sara. He'd have to break his silence and call or text her phone to get it, and that might put her in danger. Well, more danger.

He'd tried Hannah. No response. He had no idea if his team had gone through with the mission without him or not. No idea if Hannah had been confronted or not.

There also hadn't been any response from any of the journalists. He'd included a separate burner number and set up a remote access line to get messages from that phone, but nothing. Not even a nibble.

Fuck it. He'd scouted out a few other places to hide out. He could afford to possibly burn this one. There was a cheap hotel in the building below him. They'd assume he was hiding there if they bothered to track him this far.

Michael made sure all of his stuff was ready, then picked up the phone and dialed. It rang twice before Sara answered.

"Hello, hang on one minute." Sara's voice said. "I'll call you right back, hang on. I'm at work."

Then the line went dead.

Michael waited.

A few minutes later his burner phone rang. It was not Sara's number, but Michael knew it would be her.

"Hello," he answered.

"What the fuck were you thinking? Are you out of your god-damned mind?" Sara wasted no time and minced no words.

"They were setting me up. They were either going to trick me into murdering my own sister, or make me the fall guy for a whole mess of corruption at the agency when I intervened to save her. I chose option three: soaking them for six figures, grabbing evidence of the mess that place is in, and cashing out before they could screw me over."

Michael *should* have been keeping an ear out for the tell-tale clicks of a tap on the line, but he didn't. He trusted Sara and that was good enough.

Plus he had his escape route and new hideaway all set, so he was covered either way.

Sara swore on the other end of the line.

"I'm flying blind here, without you, you know,' she said. "I can't see all the shit you can, and your sister murdered another one of The Ten—"

"She did? Why isn't it in the papers? Which one?"

"They're keeping it quiet for now. But it was Sadim. The woman we attempted to interview just the other day. Hannah took her out just like she did Hugs, long-range bullet through the eye. She escaped again too. I don't think anyone thought she'd go for Sadim. If I was her, I'd certainly have wanted Drummer or Kerbs first."

"That's probably why she went for Sadim. If she didn't have someone whispering advice into her ear from the other side."

"There were some chalk markings at the site. Well, traces. I only knew what to look for because, well, you know. Almost everything was wiped away by some kind of water bomb she left behind." The sound of Sara's wry laughter came over the phone. "That one really confused the bomb squad I hear."

"After we helped her get back to The Resistance she goes out again and pulls this? What was she thinking?" Michael shook his head, though there was no one there to see it.

"You said there was something big going on. Maybe she feels this is the only way to stop it."

"Maybe." Michael set his jaw. "Right. Catch me up on everything else. I know you won't have much on the agency, but what do things look like in your precinct? Are you under any heat for my disappearance?"

It wasn't an unreasonable thought. They had been working closely right before he robbed his employer and vanished.

"A bit," Sara said evasively. "They don't have much to hang on me though. We weren't working together that long, all things considered. Brian's badmouthing you to the whole precinct though. Says he knew all along there was something off about you."

"Typical Brian." Michael might have been more generous if he weren't currently camped out in a rotting water tower on top of a charge-by-the-hour hotel.

Michael then went through his suspicions, how he thought Garibaldi was setting him up, what measures he'd taken to get incriminating information to several journalists that were usually champing at the bit to criticize the agency, and then listened as Sara caught him up on everything happening on her end.

"The chief is definitely unhappy," Sara said. "I'm under all kinds of pressure to wrap this up fast. He hasn't taken it out of my hands yet, but I think it's only a matter of time. I saw Kerbs's lawyer at the precinct today. I think there is a lot of pressure coming down from on high."

"They're afraid."

"And pissed. People like that aren't used to feeling like that. Someone is going to be catching it in the neck regularly until your sister is stopped. One way or another."

"You think the demons are still hunting her?" Michael sighed. "Yeah, I do too. And she'll have left some kind of trail they can follow. I was able to see the bullet path of her last shot, I bet they can do something similar."

"Where do you think she went, after?"

"Back to her base," he answered immediately. "I think things are going to be too dangerous for her to be running this on her own."

"It doesn't seem like she really has their support, the way she's been handling things."

"No, it doesn't. I wonder if they have some other plan." Michael thought of his sister's ulterior motive and scratched his chin. "Though they don't seem to be trying too hard to stop her. Maybe it's a lot of eggs in a lot of baskets situation. It can't be easy going up against demon-backed billionaires."

"That is a disgusting array of resources," Sara agreed. "So what's the next move?"

"I think I need to go talk to The Resistance."

***

Michael watched the old church from a coffee shop across the street. Even here, north of Harlem, the places were ubiquitous. You needed to get further out into the outer boroughs before the damn things lost their dominance.

At least it was convenient.

The church he was watching was smack dab in the middle of what used to be an Irish neighborhood. Some of the pubs still stood in the area, in fact. It had all the hallmarks of an old Catholic Church, though the sign outside was aggressively nondenominational.

It said a lot about The Resistance that their local headquarters was in a church.

It was a good cover. Plenty of reason for people to come and go at odd hours, no nearby neighbors to hear things as the closest residential buildings were all held at bay by the small but tidy church grounds, and this was New York where most people tended to ignore religion. They either worshipped the Almighty Dollar, Broadway, fashion, the arts, or any number of other small gods, but aside from the major tourist attraction style churches like St. Paul's, no one paid much attention at all to religion.

Michael had already seen several people entering and leaving that he'd mentally marked out as looking like more than the regular parishioner. No demons or angels, but the whole building practically glowed before his Sight, so there was clearly something going on there. Wards, probably.

He hadn't seen any demons lurking about, either, which was another point in the wards column. Though to be fair he hadn't seen anyone with feathered wings like himself or Gabriel either.

How uncommon were—his mind shielded away from the world angel—his kind? Or was it some kind of expression of nature sort of thing, and what looked like an angel and what looked like a demon was the same kind of spirit and the way they appeared had to do with the things they believed or the actions they took or the food they ate.

Do spirits eat? They certainly seemed to consume *something* from the mortals they attached themselves to. Was that what made the difference?

It was too bad that he hadn't had a chance to figure out how to pull an intelligence briefing on this place out of Tanner without raising any suspicions. He could really use some insight into potential entrances and exits right about now.

"Mind if I join you?"

Michael looked up. Gabriel smiled down at him and adjusted his ever-present sunglasses. Michael pushed the chair opposite him out from the table with his foot.

"Be my guest," he said.

Gabriel seated himself in one smooth motion.

"I see you've finally decided to come and ask me—us—for help."

"Who says that's why I'm here?" Michael said with a shrug. "Maybe I'm just trying to get my sister to answer her damn phone."

Gabriel laughed.

"Perhaps," the other man said, "or perhaps it is as I surmised. Or another reason that neither of us quite dare speak. I expect in any case, whatever the reason why, you still intend to ask for an audience with someone in that building. Is that correct at least?"

"More or less," Michael acknowledged.

Did he trust Gabriel? His instincts told him to, but these were new instincts, not the ones he was used to feeling in his gut. These instincts twinged across his shoulders and down to his back where his wings sprouted when they manifested. It was like calling to like, and that wasn't always something to trust.

After all, what human would blindly trust another human, knowing the world they all lived in?

But then, the world Michael thought he lived in wasn't the world as it really was. No, the real world was much stranger and more magical than he'd ever dreamed. So maybe trusting the new instinct wasn't all bad.

"I need to know more," he said after a moment. "And you said you were willing to teach me. And I need to know what's going on with Hannah. You're involved with that, too, based on the interactions the two of you have had. So, yes, I suppose I came here to see you."

"Then come on in, Michael," Gabriel said, rising from his seat. "I think we need to talk."

CHAPTER 27

The Art of No-Sword

Gabriel led Michael into the church, up the aisle and left before reaching the altar. There was an old wooden door there, which, when opened, revealed a disused vestry. Gabriel motioned for Michael to follow him in and then closed the door. When he did, there was a *click* from the wall and Gabriel pressed his hand against it, swinging open a secret passageway.

Michael sensed rather than saw the sigils at work which barred the secret entrance from any but the right individuals passing through. If you had access to magic, why not use it as security? Though there had to be a way to bypass that, at need. Hannah had figured out how to enchant bullets to pierce Hugs' magical protections, and Sadim's, after all.

"Through here." Gabriel pulled open the cage door of a vintage elevator and stepped inside.

Michael followed. The elevator dipped into movement as soon as Gabriel closed the cage. They descended at what felt like a slow pace and then came to rest with a soft bump. Gabriel hauled open the cage door and Michael stepped out into something that could be out of a war movie.

The place looked like an old-fashioned brickwork bunker, the kind used in period films. Bright white light spilled from the bulbs overhead, illuminating a moderate side room with corridors branching off in three directions.

How did something this size fit beneath that tiny church? How far beneath the city were they? Michael stowed the questions for later as Gabriel was already striding off down the right-hand corridor.

The corridors were populated, if sparsely, with people moving along them. Each one nodded at Gabriel. A few looked at Michael with varying degrees of curiosity.

Doors appeared at regular intervals, most of them ordinary looking, but a few that looked out of place, or that were ringed with sigils done in chalk, iron, or what looked like dried blood. Michael wasn't sure he wanted to know where those last ones led.

"Where are we headed?" he asked.

"First to meet Jesse, then to one of the athletics facilities to train," came the answer. "Through here." Gabriel held open a door and motioned Michael through.

Michael stepped through into an office that wouldn't have looked out of place at an Ivy League university. Mahogany bookshelves groaned beneath the weight of the tomes stacked within them, a massive desk with a blotter and several stacks of papers dominated the center of the room, and an aging man in a priest's collar sat with a quill—an actual quill—scratching across a piece of paper.

"Gabriel," the man said without looking up, "and Michael. What a pleasure." He carefully finished his line and then blew gently across the page. "So nice to finally have you both here."

Michael looked at the man with his Sight, just in case. And the man was clean. At least nothing attached to him was rotting or slimy or disgusting. There was a strange solidity to him before Michael's Sight, and when Jesse met Michael's eyes, Michael flinched away. There was a razor-edged purpose in that gaze.

"I'm not here to join you!" Michael just blurted that out. There was a fervor in those eyes that he had only seen before in religious zealots. That wasn't quite what he saw here, but it was close enough that it unnerved him.

"That's quite alright," Jesse said calmly. "I understand your connections here, do not fear. And I'm quite certain of your intentions, so fear nothing on that account." He smiled slightly. "After all, if you carried ill-intent with you over our threshold you would have burned to ash immediately. I set the wards myself, and I'm something of an expert."

"Ah," Michael wasn't quite sure what to do with that. "You must have taught Hannah, then."

"I can see why you went into law enforcement." Jesse's eyes were kind. "Hannah was an excellent student, even more so before she lost Grace. That was such a tragedy." He shook his head.

"But we're not here to speak of your sister. If you have questions, however, about our origins, what we do, about the evil that even now stalks you, Hannah, and your friends, I am here to provide them."

"Mammon?" Michael blinked.

"Indeed," Jesse confirmed. "But it would perhaps be wise for you to pursue your studies with Gabriel before we have an in-depth conversation on that subject. It's a complicated one, and some fortification of your mind and body would not go amiss before then. But you are welcome to Sanctuary here. You would not be the first to find solace within these halls."

Gabriel shifted and Michael suddenly got the impression that there was something more to Jesse's words.

"I shan't keep you boys, however." Jesse smiled and waved them away with his quill. "It was good to meet you, Michael. Do enjoy your time here."

Michael knew a dismissal when he heard one, so he followed Gabriel out of the small study. The door closed itself behind them and the lock turned of its own accord.

More magic.

"This way," Gabriel said, already striding down the hallway. "I'll give you the tour."

He took Michael through the facilities beneath the church. They were extensive, with storage for food, many bunks for sleeping resistance members, and various useful rooms. Michael was sure there was even more he was not allowed to see, and would not be allowed to see until he agreed to a more permanent position with The Resistance.

If he did.

"One last stop," Gabriel said eventually. "Then we can really get started on what you came here to learn. Right through here."

"Looking forward to it," Michael said, though not without a pulse of apprehension.

"Here we are." Gabriel flicked on the lights. They flicker and hum to life.

The room in front of them was some kind of training hall. The floor was firm but with a bit of yield, and there were all manner of swords hung on the walls. Michael spotted several kendo swords, a couple of katanas, and a selection of European-style long swords amongst the ones he could easily identify from a glance.

Gabriel stepped into the center of the room, removing his trench coat and tossing it over a coat rack. Michael followed his lead, not quite certain where this was leading. But hey, if it taught him something about his powers, he would be willing to give it a try, whatever it was.

"Pick a sword," Gabriel said. "Let's see what you've got."

He gestured at the walls, and, smiling, conjured a smooth blade of edgeless, white light. It was about the size of a long sword and had both hilt and pommel. In fact, looking at it, Michael could see decorative scrollwork of different colored light as well.

Michael flexed his fingers. Gabriel wanted to play it that way, did he? Fine. He could do that.

A sword of white flame appeared in Michael's hand.

"Good," Gabriel said. "I won't have to beat that manifestation out of you. But how long can you maintain it?"

The man immediately launched into an attack. Michael found himself driven back by a flurry of relentless blows. He managed to block each one, just barely, but he was quickly sweating and after the sixth or seventh attack the sword in his grip sputtered and flicked out of existence.

Michael found himself with the point of Gabriel's sword of light resting at the hollow of his throat.

"It's a start." Gabriel banished his sword with a flick of his fingers. "The first thing you must learn is that your sword is an extension of your will and your will alone. It's no magic trick, no confluence of energies or strange spell. It is pure, solidified will. The longer your will can hold, the longer your sword will remain unbroken. Once you've mastered it, you can fight without end, no matter the conditions or the number of enemies arrayed against you."

"How does that work? I'm still only one person." Michael flexed his fingers. Were they hot? His hand felt hot.

"You've clearly trained with a sword. You have technique and understanding. What you need now is to understand the art of no-sword." Gabriel smiled over that cryptic pronouncement like a cat over a saucer of cream.

Michael refrained from asking the obvious question. There was no way he'd give Gabriel that satisfaction. There had to be a riddle or a trick to it. That's how this kind of thing worked in the movies, right?

"You said it was the will, not the sword, so…" Michael flexed his hand and willed the sword back into existence.

Gabriel's sword flashed into being and blocked the blow that Michael had aimed at the other man. The angel tsked, and Michael could somehow tell there was amusement dancing in the eyes behind those sunglasses.

"Will, yes, but that is not all. You must also have purpose and know yourself, the true core of your being. Alloyed together they will show you the path to no-sword. There is a place, right on the edge of your mind, where consciousness ends and the unconscious mind begins. Your instinct."

"I don't understand."

"Attack me again," Gabriel said.

Michael did. Again he was effortlessly blocked.

"How did I block you so easily?" Gabriel asked.

"You're faster—no, well, you are, but you knew where I was going to hit before I did. Was it my eyes? Did I telegraph my intentions?" Michael attempted to puzzle it out.

"No, your eyes did not betray you, but you are getting close." Gabriel turned his back to Michael. "Again."

Michael immediately launched an attack. Gabriel wouldn't test him like this unless—Michael's sword was blocked again by Gabriel's.

"Find the edge of your mind. Your instinct will react faster than your conscious mind can. This is the art of no-sword. When you notice the sword that is moving to strike you, if you think about meeting the sword, your own movement will be undone and you will be cut by your opponent. Again!"

Michael attacked and this time Gabriel met his attack face to face and they sparred back and forth. Gabriel wasn't even breaking a sweat, and he took the opportunity to continue lecturing Michael as the two swords of light and flame flashed around them in their combat.

"If your mind is not stopped by the sword that moves to strike you, you can meet its rhythm, without thought or judgment. Again!"

Sparks flew. Michael lunged for Gabriel, but he easily slid out of the way of Michael's blade, plucked it from his hand, and swatted him on the backside with it.

"See? If you followed your instincts, you would have dissipated the sword of your will before it could ever touch you, rather than allowing your power to be turned against you." Gabriel lightly shook his fingers.

At least the flames had hurt him a bit. Michael took a small bit of satisfaction in that before conjuring his flaming blade anew.

"If you can master no-sword, you'll have no trouble easily mastering the rest of your powers. I will show you how. But first, you have to show me that you can grasp what I'm teaching you here." Gabriel leveled his sword at Michael. "Again."

Michael attacked, putting more force behind the blow than he intended. His frustration was bleeding out into his swordplay. A dangerous mistake.

Gabriel dealt with it easily, knocking his sword aside and slapping him lightly on the face in the process.

"Temper, temper," he chided Michael. "You cannot allow your conscious mind to take over. If you do, you will slip from the razor's edge between consciousness and instinct. You will be limited. If you put your mind on your opponent's sword then your mind will be taken by the sword." Gabriel gestured for Michael to attack again. "But if your mind is not the least bit detained and you move straight in and wrench your opponent's sword from him, then the sword that was going to cut you down will be the sword that cuts down your opponent. This is what is called No-Sword."

Michael slipped. He could feel the edge, but riding it was proving impossible. His mind kept slipping back, latching onto all manner of sensory input.

"You're trying too hard," Gabriel said. "Do not seek to put your mind anywhere, because as soon as you do it is bounded, limited. Find the edge and then release your mind and will into the universe all around you from that point. If your mind is everywhere, you will be everywhere, and there will be no sword that can hit you."

"That doesn't make any sense!"

"It makes precisely no sense until it does. That is no-sword." Gabriel twitched the point of his sword at Michael. "Right. Again!"

CHAPTER 28

The End of the Tunnel

Michael sipped his coffee, wincing both from the sunlight that lanced through his dark glasses and from the muscle aches. Training with Gabriel was not easy on the body. He was sitting on a bench near the church where he had saved the boy from the falling spire, waiting for Sara to meet him.

He hadn't wanted to, but she'd insisted. Michael thought it was too dangerous. She was sure to be being watched, but the detective had assured him she could slip any tail they placed on her, and that it was too risky to try passing files back and forth, even over anonymized phone connections.

She wasn't late. Michael was early. It still felt like she was late and Michael felt an itching between his shoulder blades. But he forced himself to calm down and sip his coffee. Nothing had gone wrong. Nothing would go wrong. He was just edgy being outside after so many days of safety beneath the church that hid the headquarters of The Resistance.

"Don't look so shifty," a voice said behind him. "You might as well hang a sign around your neck saying fugitive."

Sara, likewise in dark glasses with a hat pulled low over her forehead, sat down next to him, dropping a newspaper on the bench between them. Michael picked it up and slipped the thumb drive hidden within the pages into his pocket.

"Like you can talk," he said. "You look like a spy film stereotype."

"I wish. I'd make better money." Sara snorted.

"What've you got that couldn't wait?"

"Right, so part of the problem was tracking The Ten, right? But then I realized that one thing that all rich people jump to whenever something goes wrong…"

"They always blame the help," Michael said, immediately seeing where Sara was going with this.

"Right. So I pulled all of the information on their employees and ran that through the department resources, and used that information to put together a more detailed picture of The Ten." Sara shook her head. "These guys are rank. Investigations like this only turn up a fraction of the real dirt, and what I've seen—racketeering, bribery, insider trading—well, the details are on that drive. Not that any of it would stand up in court, but that's not the picture we're after right now."

"Any interference from anyone you can link to The Ten?"

"Not as such," Sara shook her head. "The link, that is. There's definitely interference. A lot of it. I've been gently tugging some threads there, too, and…" Sara trailed off, a troubled look crossing her face. "I hadn't realized just how compromised the department is. It's…extreme. Money talks, but in this precinct it's practically screaming its head off."

"Mmm," Michael said. There was a flicker of movement at the corner of his eye.

Spirits. They were moving around. It was distracting, but Michael wanted at least a chance of spotting any demons early on if they showed up.

"And it's not just the precinct that The Ten have bought up most of. They're spending a *lot* on political donations, too," Sara added. "Something smells funky there. Everyone at a certain level of wealth plays politics. Money buys power and power reaps more money. I get it. But The Ten have been hosting a lot of receptions and dinners and fundraisers, far more than makes any sense. They're pouring millions of their own money into these events. You don't do that if you don't expect a seriously big return."

"So Mam—the enemy is trying to do something with the government? Well, it's a center of power. Makes sense. But what is the real goal?"

"Something to do with PitCoin, I think. All of our billionaires are leveraged heavily in it. I checked though, and I don't see any bills on the docket that might impact cryptocurrency in any way."

"Keep looking? I'll check with my contacts in The Resistance. Maybe one of them will have some extra insight."

"What's that like?" Sara shot him a glance.

"It's strange. Not all of them seem to, ah, see things the same way I do, but all of them have stories about how their lives were ruined by 'agents of the enemy'. So, yeah, it's strange. Gabriel's been so busy teaching me that I haven't had time to pick his brain about what he thinks of all this."

"And Hannah?"

"Avoiding me." Michael sighed. "I think she's pissed that I'm not doing what she wants and forgetting about all of this."

"As if you could!" Sara shook her head.

It was nice that she, at least, completely understood where he was coming from.

Sara turned the conversation back to what she'd discovered and the theories she was forming. Michael took mental notes and resolved to dip into the money he'd stolen from the agency to get a cheap laptop to access the files Sara had brought him. He was about to ask Sara what she'd found about the link between her father's murderer and The Ten when a flash of light drew his attention to a gathering of the same spirits he saw hovering about the violent murder scene of Robert Hugs.

Something was going to happen, and soon.

Michael scanned the perimeter. A patch of pale metal half-glimpsed through the trees caused his stomach to sink. He recognized that van.

"Shit!" Michael said. "We've got company."

"Who?" Sara asked, immediately tensing for action but disciplined enough not to look around for what Michael saw.

"That's an agency van. Four o'clock. And with my luck, it's going to be my former team. It would be just like Garibaldi to send them out and bring me in."

"Shit. Sorry. They must have followed me."

"Or they've been running facial recognition and caught a decent angle on me. It doesn't matter how they found me, we need to get out of here, and you need to get back clean. They have to be after me. I'll draw them off. You slip off when I distract them."

"Like hell I'm doing that," Sara said hotly. "We both get away or neither of us gets out. I'm not going to leave you hanging. Besides, I need you. You've got the magic I need to fight these demons and cultists and what the fuck. I sound insane." Sara sighed. "Where's our exit."

She assumed he had one, and she assumed right. Michael had three exit routes planned. Though the third option, growing wings and taking flight, might not work with Sara along. He wasn't sure how well she'd take to being carried off in his arms.

He didn't even know if he could carry that much weight and fly. Though Gabriel had been teaching him that as well, he was still new to the whole winged thing.

Best not to risk it unless they had to.

Option one, through the church's side entrance and out the vestry window, was out. Michael knew the agency playbook and they'd have the place surrounded. Option three, flying, was a last resort. So that only left option two.

There was a large grate just on the other side of the small wall that bordered the churchyard-turned-park. The wall itself was only a couple of feet high, more a border than a deterrent to movement. The grate led to the tunnels networked beneath the NYC streets, the ones that vomited hot air up from the subway all summer and winter long. Usually they were secured, but Michael had made sure this one was loose in case he needed a quick escape.

And it turned out he did.

"We're going underground, literally," he said. "Follow my lead."

If the agency was listening with any of their tech, he'd just given them a big clue, but he was counting on the move being unexpected enough—and that they didn't have Tanner there to pull up schematics quickly enough—that it would give him and Sara enough of a lead to make their escape.

The flock of spirits swirling over the van shifted. Michael swore. They were moving!

"We need to move now. They're coming." Michael rose and vaulted over the bench, running away from the church toward the wall.

Sara followed, right behind. She wasn't quite as fast as Michael, but she was in excellent shape. The NYPD was supposed to maintain standards, but it rarely worked out that way. It was to Sara's credit that she maintained her fitness.

Michael hurdled the wall and while Sara caught up, he yanked up the grate. Sara didn't hesitate, she slipped down through the opening and used the pipes and handholds to quickly clamber down. Michael followed, yanking the grate closed behind him.

With any luck, they'd be out of sight by the time any of the pursuing agents came close enough, and they'd waste time trying to find which grate the two had used to make their escape.

The pipes carried wastewater and steam. Michael hissed as he burned his hands on one, using it to swing down to the cramped maintenance tunnel running beneath the street.

"Left or right?" Sara called quietly.

"Left," Michael said. "It runs that way a few hundred meters before linking up to the maintenance tunnels for the subway. We can make out way there, head down, and lose them in the maze that is the subway. Eventually we'll find our way to a platform we can hop up on and push out through the barrier. I've got a spare card if you need one."

"Let's get away from your friends first," Sara said. "They're still too close for comfort."

Michael nodded and followed as Sara led the way down the tunnel in the direction he indicated. It was too narrow to slip past her. Progress was going to be slow. Michael kept one ear tuned for sounds of pursuit. So far there hadn't been any sign.

He should have been listening in the other direction.

Sara came to an abrupt halt. Michael managed not to slam into her, just barely, and before he could ask her why she had stopped he saw past her shoulder and beheld the reason.

It was his team after them. Because of course it was. Who else but Tanner could have pulled up the city schematics fast enough? And who else but Stowe would be standing there, tall and broad and bulky enough to take Michael down?

And there was no way Garibaldi would let them off the hook after the stunt Michael pulled. Michael had hoped, but it was clear now that that hope had been false at best.

"It's over, Lieberman," Stowe called, gun leveled at the two of them. "You might as well surrender. You're not getting out of this."

CHAPTER 29

Someplace Safe

Michael stared at Stowe, at the gun pointing at him and Sara. He could feel her, just behind him and to the right. So far as he could see, with either version of his sight, there was no one else here in the tunnel.

So long as you discounted the engorged black slug-leech-thing that was attached to Stowe's back.

"Don't even think about it," Stowe said, his aim never wavering. "I'm fast enough to cap you both, even if you're quick on the draw. Michael knows how good I am."

He did. And Stowe was. There was a reason he had been Michael's first choice for boots-on-the-ground assignments. The man was fast. He wasn't smart enough to make a good leader, but he excelled at what he did.

And right now that excellence was standing between Michael and Sara and their escape.

"Who's down the tunnel in the other direction," he asked, stalling for time to think. "No one from the squad, I'm guessing, unless—"

"No one believed us when we said we should watch *all* the potential exits. So yeah, it's me and Priestly. Maybe you should have gone the other way. Then you'd have stood a chance."

"Didn't think Tanner would be able to grab the schematics that fast." Michael shook his head. "I should have known better."

"You *should* have known better than to go rogue! What the hell, man?" Stowe's hand tightened on his gun as his shoulders tensed. "What happened?"

"I saw what was really going on at the agency, at the station," Michael said. "Someone was trying to set me up—"

"Don't try that spy-fi movie bullshit on me," Stowe barged into Michael's explanation like a bull into a china shop. "You know the world we live in! You know what we do! People are going to die because of your bullshit!"

"People die every day regardless," Sara snapped at him. "And I hate to break it to you, but what's going on—"

"Nobody asked you!" Stowe shifted his aim to Sara. "Shut it or I'll do it for you."

Michael felt cold fire kindle in his gut and he knew that with just a simple flex of his will he could have a flaming sword in his hand in moments. Stowe would never expect it. He could kill the man before he got a shot off, maybe. Stowe had always been faster before, but Michael hadn't known just what he was capable of before, either.

But it was a risk. If Michael was wrong, Sara would die. And he found that he didn't want to risk that.

He didn't really want to kill Stowe either. He'd worked with the man for years now. He wasn't a bad guy. Had a nice wife. Bit of rough luck with her health though.

Michael's eyes flicked to the thing attached to Stowe. Grief, anger, despair—a lot of these spirits fed on those emotions. Gabriel hadn't been able to instruct him on a complete bestiary, but the angel had covered the basics, and the more Michael shared with Sara the more necessary knowledge he found himself mysteriously already in possession of.

"How's Elaine?" Michael asked suddenly.

Stowe's gun was immediately pointed back at him.

"Leave Elaine out of this," the man said dangerously. "You don't get to do that. You don't get to say her name."

Stowe's eyelid twitched. It was a crack in his cool façade. Somehow, Michael knew that there was more to it than the man's feelings for Michael or what Michael may or may not have done when he made his exit from the agency.

"She's worse, isn't she."

"I said *shut up!*" Stowe's grip on his weapon, normally perfect, poised, and smooth, shook for a moment.

"She's worse and—" Michael couldn't help but see the spirit gorging itself on his former friend. No, still his friend. Well, maybe still his friend. "—and you're taking money from someone to pay for treatment, aren't you? Is that why you're down here alone? No backup? No surveillance cam or drones?"

The thing on Stowe's back pulsed and writhed in dark delight. Whatever emotions were pumping through the man they were clearly intense and intensely negative.

"I said," Stowe's breathing became staccato, "don't. Talk. About it."

Fuck that.

"How much are they paying you, Stowe? Hmm? How much to betray your friend?"

"You left us!" Stowe shouted. "What the fuck kind of friend does that? What the fuck did you do at the agency? Garibaldi wants your head. Off the books. Big reward. But bigger for me, if I do it. Prove my loyalty. The team's loyalty."

"And who do you think is paying for that loyalty?" Michael shot back. "It sure as shit isn't Garibaldi. And it sure as shit isn't coming out of the agency budget. So someone else is offering that prized money up. Do you even know what strings are attached to it?"

"Shut the fuck up!" Stowe shouted, his voice echoing off the pipes and the cramped cement all around.

Michael flinched back. What if one of his other teammates heard? Priestly could catch wind of the situation and come running. And that he'd have to deal with both of them.

That was not something he wanted to do.

He didn't know if it was something he could do.

He had to calm Stowe down. He needed to talk his way past. If he couldn't…Michael crushed the thought.

"You know I'm right," Michael said, all of his attention focused on Stowe, ready to react if it looked like his words pushed the man in the wrong direction. "How many times did I have your back? How many times did I make the right call on a mission? How many times was it Garibaldi that got us into a mess with crappy orders, or asking for 'just one little thing that upstairs wants?'"

Stowe didn't answer. Michael could see the man wavering. He saw it both in his eyes and in the disgusting ripple of color that went through the thing attached to his back.

Then a pulsating wave went through the thing, like it was vomiting back into Stowe through the place where it has clamped on to the man, and the wavering stopped. Hate sparked in his eyes and his gun locked on Michael again, sure and smooth.

"It doesn't matter. You think you got it all figured out? Well, you don't. You have no idea what I'm going through, or what I'm willing to do about it."

Michael only listened with half an ear. Blood was roaring in his ears and his Sight was narrowing in on that *thing* on Stowe's back. It was doing more than just passively feeding. It was *influencing* Stowe. Cultivating his moods to produce more food, like a farmer enriching his fields with shit.

It was disgusting. And it was going to die.

Michael had no idea what cutting it off of Stowe would do. His instinct was that it was the right move, but it was just that—an instinct.

"I don't know, no," Michael said, voice soothing as he shifted his stance slightly. "You're right."

The problem was that the thing's head was attached to the back of Stowe's, at the base of his neck. Michael wasn't sure if spirit physiology worked like real life, but just stabbing the thing seemed like a bad idea. Who knows what poison it might pump into Stowe in its death throes? Or if it wouldn't burrow in like a tick. He needed to get it to detach, somehow, then kill it.

It hadn't liked it when Stowe wavered earlier. It was the positive emotions, he realized suddenly, with the clarity of knowledge bought at the goblin market. Stowe had remembered their past, their friendship, the good they had done for no other reason than it was the right thing to do.

The right thing.

"You're right, Stowe," Michael said. "Just like you were right in Milford when you saved that little girl. Like you were right in basic when you said it was all or none. Like you were right in Minneapolis when you said we had to get back to the van. You saved Tanner with that one."

It was working. Stowe's hand was quivering, just a bit, and Michael could see the pulses of brighter color rippling through the spirit's form. His fingers tensed.

Come on!

The thing still wasn't detaching. It was writhing in discontent, however. Michael needed to dose it with another rush of positive emotions from Stowe before the thing pulled its vomiting trick again.

Shit! Was it going to kill Stowe? Would it sacrifice its host like that? Michael scrambled for something else, another dose of positive emotions to flood the fucking thing with.

"Like you were absolutely right that Elaine was the one, and you were right to propose—what was it?—a month after you met? Best idea of your life, man."

That did it. The spirit leech on Stowe's back went positive rose with disgust and reared back its head, revealing a ring of bone-white teeth dripping with black gore.

Michael went for the head, conjuring a sword of flame and sidestepping Stowe's panicked reaction. The man pulled the trigger—he was a professional—but there's no agency training for responding to a flaming sword appearing out of nowhere.

The sword pierced the head of the thing and it fell away, writhing and burning away until there was nothing left but a smear of greasy ash in Michael's spirit sight. He immediately banished the sword. Stowe was staring at him, shaking.

Shock. It looked like it, anyway.

"Michael, what—"

"It's been a long day," Michael said. "For both of us. Lucky that you didn't see us while you were standing here, wasn't it? Too bad that Tanner's schematics must have missed a route that I managed to find in my earlier recon. Right, Stowe?"

"R-right." Stowe looked at him and blinked.

The man was pale, but he seemed lighter on his feet, somehow. Michael hoped that with the thing dead the man's life was a bit easier. Not that it would cure his wife, or get him out of that corrupt agency, but it had to be easier to deal with all that when there wasn't some brain-sucking Thing From Beyond pumping you full of who knows what psychic shit.

"Take care Stowe," Michael said, slowly edging past the man, motioning with one hand for Sara to follow. "Hopefully the next time we see each other all this has been straightened out and we can be friends again properly. Maybe I'll buy you a beer."

"I'd like that," Stowe said, clearly still dazed.

Yeah, there was definitely some kind of effect being freed from whatever that was. Stowe was usually far more guarded emotionally.

Though maybe that was the spirit's influence too. It can't be healthy, bottling everything up. Not when repressed emotions are like fine brandy—fermented and distilled in potency—to the worst beasts of the spirit world.

Michael kept an eye on Stowe as they backed their way down the tunnel until it forked. Then he took the lead again, ferreting them deeper and deeper into the tunnels, taking switchbacks and turnings in case Stowe came to and changed his mind.

"You going to tell me exactly what happened back there?" Sara asked when it was clear they weren't being followed.

"There was something stuck to him, feeding on him. I cut it away." Michael wasn't paying full attention, one eye always on the tunnels and most of his attention on the maps he had memorized earlier.

"Seems like there was a bit more to it than that. He was a member of your team, right?"

"He is," Michael said firmly.

Stowe, Tanner, and the rest weren't his enemies. Not yet. In spite of whoever was pulling the strings at the agency.

And if Michael had his way, his team would stay that way.

But that wasn't going to happen—he wasn't going to protect them, or Sara, or himself, if he kept reacting. He needed to act. Something was happening and they had pieces, hints, maybe even omens or portents, but what they really needed was some good old-fashioned actionable intelligence.

He said as much to Sara.

"Sure, but where are we going to get it? I have some leads, but a lot of what I have is back at the precinct, and after what just happened I don't think I can go back there."

Michael stopped. She was right. Damnit! He'd gotten her all messed up in this, even though he didn't want to.

The price he paid.

"So we go someplace safe. Plan our next move from there."

"And where is that?" Sara asked, clearly not liking where Michael was going with this.

"We need to get to The Resistance."

CHAPTER 30

Capturing a Demon

Walking into the church was easy. Moving through the pews and finding the small vestry door Gabriel had taken him through, that was easy as well. Closing that door with himself and Sara inside, that, that was more difficult.

Michael's hand hovered over the door handle, his mind flickering over the wards he had briefly seen, the words of warning so kindly and lethally delivered by the priest who had met him that day. What if those wards were not so friendly to Sara as they were to him?

"Well? What are we waiting for?"

"A leap of faith, I guess," Michael said, closing the door.

It wasn't like they had anywhere else to go. Especially with the power arrayed against them. The door closed with a click.

On the wall behind them, the wards blazed to life. Michael tensed, but then relaxed. The light from the sigils matched the sharpness around Sara to his Sight, somehow, and he knew she would pass muster.

And she did. They stepped through the wall with little to no fanfare.

Well, except Gabriel, who was waiting on the other side.

Sara got the tour. She took it better than Michael had, though she was wrestling with a bit less than he was. Plus, she didn't have to go through the gauntlet of introductions Michael did for some reason.

They could erase her memories. The thought came to him unbidden, a slice of bittersweet fruit from his bargain at the goblin market. Sara was fully mortal. She was more vulnerable to that thing called magic than Michael was, or ever would be.

The air suddenly seemed several degrees cooler.

"Problem, Michael?" Gabriel glanced back over his shoulder.

"No," Michael lied, forcing himself to relax, banishing the sparks dancing at his fingertips.

Then they were in a small lounge. Gabriel banished the other resistance members who were using it, closed the door, and sketched a quick silence ward so they would not be overheard.

"I take it things have taken a turn." The angel said.

"They have. I don't suppose Hannah is around?" Michael glanced across the room, though he knew she wasn't standing in it.

"She can be." Gabriel inclined his head and his eyes went distant for a moment. "She should be with us shortly."

They made small talk until Michael's sister arrived.

Hannah swept in the door like a thunderstorm across the square states. Her eyes snapped with anger and she pointed a finger directly at Michael.

"I *told* you—" she began.

"You were completely right," Michael interrupted. "I'm sorry I didn't listen more carefully to you. I'm not sorry I got involved, I wouldn't have wanted not to, but you were looking out for me, not trying to manipulate me, and—" he shot a sideways glance at Sara, "—I can understand why you felt you had to do what you did."

Hannah blinked, the wind completely taken out of her sails.

"Now, we need your help," Michael said. "Mam—a certain someone is up to something. Strings are being pulled at the agency. They were trying to get me to kill you, Han, and I may have overreacted in my departure. Still, what's done is done and I'm not going to cry about it. What I am going to do is find what, precisely, the other party is up to and bring all hold heaven down on whatever his plans might be."

Michael stood and began to pace.

"So we need names. Agents. Accomplices. Whatever. Sara has some, possibly more back at the precinct, if we could get anyone to slip in and retrieve her files. Gabriel, you and The Resistance have to have eyes on some likely targets."

"We do. I have, in fact, already got a list for you." The angel looked slightly unnerved for some reason. "We've had it for quite some time, but didn't realize precisely what it was intended for."

Michael let *that* slide for now. He didn't want to get pulled into a tangent.

"Hannah? I know you've been working on killing as many of The Ten as you can. You have to have a lot of recon, stuff you haven't even told The Resistance. Since it's clear you're intent on playing Lone Wolf." Michael crossed his arms and looked at his sister.

"I might," she conceded, though she acted as if the words were being forcibly dragged out of her by a team of wild horses.

"Then let's have them. Come on. I want a list to work from. Sara and I will go out, shake the tree, and find some nice juicy demon to squeeze for some actionable intel. Then we set to dismantling whatever this master plan is right down to the ground."

"Michael," Sara said in a tight voice. "Did you realize your eyes are on fire?"

Michael pulled out his phone and used the glassy black surface as a mirror. His eyes had completely been replaced by two pipes of white-gold fire.

He blinked.

They returned to their normal state.

"Perhaps reserve such moments of passion for times they are more easily channeled to your purpose," Gabriel suggested, a smile ghosting across his lips. "And for now, refresh yourself while Hannah and I collaborate to produce the list you require."

"Thank you," Michael said, sitting back down.

"Oh, it is our pleasure. If you can find us this information, we'll both be in your debt."

"Speak for yourself, feathers," Hannah snarked, arms folded defiantly across her chest. "My plan was working just fine."

"Hannah," Michael said. "Please?"

"Fine." She threw up her hands. "I clearly fucked up keeping you out of this, so I suppose I might as well help. At least you left that cesspool of a job."

Michael bit back the urge to defend his job, to say that they did good work, put bad people away. Then he remembered Garibaldi. The job that had got him his promotion. All the things he'd seen recently.

Was holding on to the belief that they did good work just another illusion?

Instead, he put on a casual face and kept the conversation light.

"Awww, there's the big sister I know and love," Michael said, the teasing tone of his voice at odds with the roil of emotions inside.

"Watch it, or I'll shove the damned list so far up your ass you'll have to go to the dentist to have it picked out of your tonsils."

Sara laughed uproariously.

"I like your family," she said.

Michael sighed.

***

Getting the list from Hannah without violence turned out to be the easy part. Capturing and subduing a demon, on the other hand, was turning out to be much more difficult.

There were mortal targets on the list as well, but Michael and Sara quickly discounted them as likely to lack key pieces of information. Even if they were in on the existence of the Spirit World, would they really know Mammon's true goals?

If Michael was a demon prince and the embodiment of greed who came to plague the Earth full-on Apocalypse style, he wouldn't share the full details with many mortals. Hell, he'd only trust his closest lieutenants with that information. Which meant The Ten, if they were willing to consider going after mortals, and some of the strongest demons Michael had yet to face, otherwise.

Not that he'd done too badly so far, all things considered.

He still had his head.

A whip of flame cracked next to his ear, driving that very point home. Michael fell back for cover behind a nearby car. He and Sara had tracked the current name they were investigating to a small chop shop on the lower East side. The owner had a diamond stud in his right ear, more gold chains than good taste would ever allow, and full possession of a suite of demonic powers that was giving Michael and his partner a run for their money.

Sara leaned out from behind cover and fired off two rounds—enchanted by Michael, so any demons they came across wouldn't be able to just shrug them off. One winged the target in the shoulder. The other missed, fortunately.

"We need him alive, remember?" Michael called to her.

"Then *you* go tackle him! He's out of my weight class," Sara hollered back.

"I will strip your bones from your flesh and feast upon your livers!" The demon roared at them.

The guy had a literal goatee and massive red-leather wings. He was a walking stereotype on both planes, mundane and spiritual.

At least the whip was unusual. Better than a pitchfork for that, at least.

Michael winced at the thing cracked near his head again. Worse in a lot of other ways though. His sword was—he thought—a superior weapon, but it did lack reach.

At least until he mastered the art of no-sword.

He hadn't done badly so far, this battle. He had managed to fend off the whip, keep it from cutting him too deeply, though he was sporting a small number of cuts that felt like cauterised razor slices.

He'd managed to block all the ones aimed at Sara. She was tough, but a whip made of hellfire was something else. Even if Hannah had loaded her up with a few defensive wards and spells.

The whip cracked at Michael's face again, and this time he managed to maintain the state of mind required by no-sword for long enough to slash through the whip, severing over half of its length.

He knew from experience that damage to a weapon of will was temporary, but exacted a toll in psychic pain on its wielder. The demon across from him was no exception. The man screamed at him in agony and rage, blood-red flames trailing from his eyes like tears.

The demon gathered them up and began to conjure a new whip of flame.

Michael didn't let his advantage go to waste, however. He pressed forward, Sara providing covering fire. With the whip slowly reforming he could afford to close easily.

Disabling his opponent with a sword made of fire would be more difficult, though at least his foe had the resilience of a supernatural creature.

Mixed blessing there.

Michael swung, a sharp overhanded blow designed to disable, aiming the flat of his blade for the demon's temple.

The demon dodged and lashed out with his claws. Back and forth they danced, Michael's attacks enough to keep the demon from refocusing his whip, but hampered as he was by his need to capture the thing alive, he was unable to swiftly end the combat.

Sara took shots where she was able, but chances were few and far between. Michael was too close to his opponent. When she did finally get a shot, it winged their target but locked the demon's attention on her.

He ripped the door off a nearby car and hauled it back to throw it at Sara.

If that thing hit her, she'd die instantly!

Michael felt a surge of energy flow through his limbs. A battle cry in an ancient language he had no idea how to speak leapt from his lips and pure instinct drove the sword of will home, plunging it through his foe's abdomen and out the other side, flames cauterizing as it went.

The demon screamed in agony, reaching out and digging his fingers into the metal frame of a nearby taxi being stripped for parts. He hauled it up by main strength and slammed it down on top of Michael.

Michael, eyes once more two pits of white-gold flame, slammed to the ground, his wings bursting into existence and wrapping around him like a cocoon. He felt the impact, there was no doubt about that. Probably even cracked a few ribs, but getting hit with a car hurt a lot less than he thought it should.

It certainly hurt a lot less than getting skewered through the spleen with a flaming sword. Michael looked over to where his opponent should be standing, should have fallen. That blow was a solid one; Michael had felt it.

Too solid, it seemed. The target had vanished, eaten away to nothing by the flames of Michael's sword. A smoking outline of cinders was all that remained.

"Well, that went well." Michael winced and shoved the remains of the car off of him. "Who's next on the list, I guess."

"I think we should try one of the ones Gabriel suggested," Sara said, leaning against a battered taxi. "Mine all seem to put up too much of a fight, and Hannah's are, well, they look like a bit much right now. Maybe if we had full tactical backup."

"What are the next three names?"

"Marie Kowall, a banker; Justina Faraldo, an entrepreneur and a start-up queen, whatever that means; and Richard Aurek, some kind of gold-digger social media influencer or something."

"The last one," Michael said. "He sounds easy enough to handle. I could use a cool down after this."

"Makes sense to me." Sara tried to haul herself up and groaned.

"Maybe we stop and get something to eat first."

CHAPTER 31

The Golden Boy

Michael and Sara sat in one of the ubiquitous coffee shops on the Lower East Side. It was close enough to Midtown to get tourist spillover, but far enough from the major hotspots that influencers and posers could feel like they were getting "real New York" to share with their "fans."

One influencer—their target—was in the middle of taking selfies of himself while a pair of fawning groupies were holding lighting equipment and adjusting the positioning of the tiniest cup of espresso that Michael had ever seen in the background.

"God I hate social media,' Sara muttered. "I completely believe this asshole is a demon of some kind."

"He's not the only one," Michael murmured. "At least one of his associates is as well. The one adjusting the cup. The other one might just be a flunky, or she might also be a demon, but with better skills at hiding than most."

The Sight was useful, but it was far from infallible. There were plenty of enchantments that could counter its effects.

Their target— Richard Aurek—had married into a cadet branch of one of the billionaire families that made of The Ten. He was a long way from the corridors of power, but Michael had to wonder just what Mammon had sent him to keep an eye on as part of all this. In addition, his social media accounts were all sponsored by PitCoin and he pushed the cryptocurrency hard in several of his posts.

He was probably captioning this one with something saying how he paid for this "exquisite experience" with PitCoin. So easy! So much value! All the hottest people are doing it these days!

"Can we get him away from his fan club?" Sara was slowly shredding the napkin in front of her into a small bird's nest of a pile on the table.

"I could follow him into the bathroom. There's no way even a demon is not going to need it after as much coffee as we've seen him slam back in the past hour." Michael rolled his eyes.

The getaway was set. They had a car and a plan, and each of them had a set of enchanted manacles. If they could subdue Richard, the manacles would keep him in line. If Michael could overpower his will, they'd keep him asleep as well. Long enough to get to a more secure location, anyway.

The problem was he wasn't alone, and they had to attempt to capture him while he wasn't at any of the homes he maintained around the city. Each of those places was a fortress with full security staff. Though this came with its own problems in the form of innocent bystanders.

Which is why Michael was sitting here contemplating following the guy into the bathroom.

Though it looked like he didn't have much more time to debate. Richard threw down his napkin, evidently *finally* satisfied with one of the photos they had taken. Michael tensed as the demon-in-influencer's-clothing stood up.

Be ready…

Gabriel? Michael glanced around but could not see any sign of the angel. Why was he contacting him now, of all times?

This one is more dangerous than you know.

Then why the hell not say something when giving Michael and Sara his name? What the fuck! Did everyone have to have a goddamned agenda? Was there some kind of rule about keeping secrets just to piss Michael off?

"Watch my back and be ready with the manacles," Michael said. "This could get complicated."

He didn't bother mentioning Gabriel's voice. It would just throw Sara off.

The coffee shop didn't have its own facilities. There were a set of shared ones that all the small little shops in the area used. Michael followed Richard as the man blazed forward, eyes on his phone, fingers flicking across the screen.

The men's bathroom wasn't large—three stalls on one side and two urinals and the mirror and sinks on the other. It was painted in a heavy-handed style that screamed "hip" while also being cheap.

Fortunately, it was also unoccupied.

Sparks danced across Michael's fingers, but just before he could summon his sword and attack, Richard spoke.

"Bold of you to come after me like this." The man turned to face Michael.

Richard's eyes had turned to two pits of molten gold and the metal dripped liquid off his fingers. His wings manifested as vast, black appendages with gold veins running through them, though his face remained the same, unlike many others.

"You like my look? It's because I'm half-mortal, like you. See?" He held up one hand and traced his jawline. "There's always something that gives it away. Like my skin. Or your great, clumsy movements."

Michael manifested his sword.

Richard laughed.

"Oh come on Michael! There's no need for that! Why, with my father's help, you can have anything you want. Why not simply ask? It's not like we can't meet your price."

Richard reached out with his fingers and the gold dripping form then touched the nearest bathroom stall door. The gold began to eat into it and slowly crept across it, transforming it as it went.

"There," Richard said. "That's more gold than you'll find anywhere in this city outside of the largest three banks. It won't last, of course, but we could make a deal and ensure this transformation is permanent."

Father? Richard was Mammon's *son*? No wonder Gabriel had warned him.

Michael shook his head to clear it. But this was also a prime opportunity. If anyone would know Mammon's actual plans, it was this guy.

"What would it take for you to come quietly with me and answer a few questions?" Michael asked. "What's your price?"

"Oh, you can't afford me! Only Father has the power to give me what I truly want." Richard began advancing slowly on Michael. Drops of gold spilled from his fingers as he went, slowly changing the tiles beneath him.

It was probably a good idea not to let too much of that get on him.

"And what's that?" Michael asked, bringing his sword between the two of them, mind racing as he took in the contents of the bathroom. What did he have to work with here?

"I'll show you mine if you show me yours!" Richard laughed. "Come on Michael! Help a guy out. What do you want?"

"Come with me and find out!" Michael lashed out with his flaming sword.

Richard laughed and smacked the sword away with his open palm. Droplets of molten gold splashed and sizzled across the tiles, spotting them with bright yellow glints.

"You'll have to do better than that, Michael! I think perhaps you should come with me. Father would like to have words with you, I know."

"Why?"

There was the slightest of beats before Richard answered.

"Another thing you cannot afford," the demon responded.

"Ha!" Michael sneered. "You don't know, do you? Does daddy not trust you as much as you'd like?"

"Shut up!" Richard's eyes flared.

The demon conjured chains from the molten gold dripping from his fingers and began to spin them about, fouling the strikes of Michael's flaming sword. Once, twice, thrice Michael attacked and every one was turned away, molten gold splashing across the walls and floor.

A drop landed against his skin, sizzling away and leaving a small spot of metal flecked against his flesh.

Michael desperately tried to fall into the mindset of no-sword, using it to block entangling attack after entangling attack, but they were coming hard and fast and Richard showed no signs of slowing down, his reservoir of will clearly at least as well developed as Michael's, if not deeper.

He was going to lose. Richard would turn him to gold and haul him off to wherever Mammon's agents were waiting, and then, once Michael returned to himself, he'd be at the archdemon's mercy.

A quality that was not known to be in ample supply in demons, and less in an archdemon.

Then the mirror rippled, cracks feathering across it, before the glass exploded into the bathroom, heralding the arrival of Gabriel.

"You!" Richard's face screwed up into a mask of hate and the demon began lashing at the newcomer with his chains of molten gold.

Together Gabriel and Michael pressed the demon, with a sword of light and a sword of flame. It was easier, but Richard still managed to keep them at bay, the chains he wielded moving almost with a mind of their own, independent of their conjurer.

How was the demon this good? Michael would have thought Gabriel would have been able to best him easily. He redoubled his efforts. They couldn't let this chance escape!

"You're too much spirit and not enough flesh, old man," the demon taunted Gabriel. "Your hold on this world is weak and growing weaker by the day! When my father's plan is in place——"

Richard's words cut off as Gabriel lunged for his throat, the blade of light narrowly missing the chance to carve the golden demon a second, crimson smile.

The demon hissed and lashed out with his chains, the wild and coruscating metal driving Michael and Gabriel both further back.

"I'm going to kill your protector, then haul you before Father for your punishment," Richard howled. "You will not stop his inheritance—or mine! The world will be ours and all shall worship at the golden altar of Mammon!"

"I'll make you worship at the porcelain throne, first." Michael feinted with his sword, allowing it to vanish a split second before the chains wrapped around it, then drove his fist into Richard's solar plexus as hard as he could.

The demon coughed in agony and a small bubble of golden blood burst from his lips.

"Oh, you'll pay for that," he said, glaring at Michael, the chains reorienting on him and lashing forward.

Michael was forced to fall back as the chains of gold lashed out at him, driving him back and seeking to coil around his wrists and ankles. His flaming sword countered each of these attacks until the environment betrayed him.

His foot slipped in a small puddle of water and Michael's balance wavered. In that split second both chains lashed out, one for Michael's waist and the other for his throat. If they had touched him, it would have been game over, his airways turned to gold in a matter of moments.

"Michael!" Gabriel lunged, shoving him out of the way.

The chains, not to be denied, chose to ensnare Gabriel in place of Michael, wrapping firmly around the angel and quickly staining his flesh gold.

"Quickly! The manacles!"

Gabriel held a hand out to Michael. Michael immediately understood, tossing the enchanted manacles to him. Gabriel caught them and with superhuman strength hauled Richard to him.

Chains bound the demon to the angel as much as the reverse.

Richard struggled but could not escape without freeing Gabriel or banishing the chains and leaving himself vulnerable. Instead, he tried to pour more and more gold over the angel he had in thrall, hoping he could turn him fully to gold before it was too late.

The demon didn't succeed. Gabriel's hands flashed out, moving with surety and skill, securing the manacles around Richard's wrists.

They flared with white-gold light and the demon screamed. Michael's attention was all on his friend, however. The angel was still wrapped in chains that were turning him to gold, faster and faster now, in spite of Richard being bound by the manacles.

"Gabriel!"

"Focus, Michael!" The angel said, visibly straining against the encroaching gold that was stiffening his body. "You need to get him and get out of here. Don't worry about me.

Eyes flaming, weeping tears of fire, Michael reached out and grabbed the manacles, sending his will through them like an inferno.

Richard's eyes went blank and his body went slack. Michael grabbed the insensate demon and slung him over his shoulder in a fireman's carry. The demon was heavier than he looked. Nothing Michael couldn't carry, though.

He slipped out the door and made his way quickly down the hall, projecting an air of authority ahead of him to clear the way. Something he developed during his time in law enforcement. Most people saw someone that looked like they were on a mission of mercy and got out of the way.

Mercy. That was not something Richard would have much of in his future. Not after what he'd done to Gabriel. Not with what he knew of Mammon's plan. No.

Michael was going to enjoy dragging the truth out of him.

— CHAPTER 32 —

The Price of Assistance

"Fuck!" Michael slammed his fist into the wall. A small spiderweb of cracks spiraled out from the point of impact.

He and Sara were in a secure room provided by The Resistance. Their captive was bound with blessed chains of lead and iron to a chair in the center of the room, blindfolded, gagged, and with a bag over his head. The demon sat motionless, though Michael could swear the asshole was fucking smirking at them from beneath that hood.

"It's not your fault," Sara said quietly, not for the first time. "Gabriel knew what he was doing. He saved your life and he helped secure the prisoner."

"Yes, but—"

"No." Sara cut him off. "You couldn't have done more than you did. You've got the skills you have, at the level you have them. Want to do better? You have to get there."

"I failed him! If I was better, faster—if I'd mastered no-sword—" Michael felt his gut twist.

He'd lost people under his command before, lost good people he'd worked with, before that. He'd even experienced a field promotion when his own commanding officer hit a spot of bad luck and ended up eating the business end of a bullet on a covert mission.

This was different, somehow. There was a link between himself and Gabriel he couldn't explain. He hadn't even really noticed it until Gabriel was turning to gold and fading before his eyes. Maybe it was their shared heritage. Maybe it was part of the way he had learned the art of no-sword. Whatever it was, this hit different.

"There's no point in crying about it right now," Sara said reasonably, disturbing his drowning thoughts like a stone cast into a still pool disturbs the water with its ripples. "Come on. Focus. We've got work to do. Gabriel wouldn't want this chance to go to waste, would he?"

Michael sucked in a deep breath.

"That's dirty pool," he said, shaking his head, "but you're right. I'm not helping anyone like this."

He turned to the prisoner but paused when Sara reached out and grabbed his arm.

"Take a minute," she said. "Get some water. Get your head on right. *Then* we do this. We can't afford any mistakes here, and this guy—" she shook her head "—he's gonna be tricky, I can tell. The ones with rich daddies always are. And this guy's daddy is one serious motherfucker."

She wasn't wrong. Michael nodded, reached out to squeeze her fingers back. Sara released him and crossed over to the other corner of the room and began talking to mid-air as if she were reporting to an unseen figure.

It was unnerving. Michael could completely believe she was talking to someone through a two-way interrogation mirror or hardline link. And he wasn't the only one. He noticed Richard twisting in his bonds, trying to catch what Sara was saying—or who she was talking to.

Let the demon squirm. It would do him—and their coming interrogation—good. Michael went to his bag in the corner opposite Sara and rummaged through it until he found his water bottle, taking it out and taking a big gulp of the tepid water.

It wasn't pleasant, but it did help center him. He studied their prisoner as he sipped. Sara was right. This was going to be one tough nut to crack.

Not that he didn't have a few ideas on how to go about that.

When he felt ready, Michael stowed the water bottle and signaled to Sara. The detective nodded and moved quickly and quietly behind their prisoner. At Michael's nod, she reached out and whipped the hood and blindfold off the demon.

Richard blinked in the sudden light, glancing around at his surroundings. His muscles bulged and he strained against the manacle and chains. Not that it did him any good. Not only had those bindings been provided by The Resistance, but Michael had also had Hannah inscribe protective circles around both the chair and the chamber.

It would take a miracle to free the demon, and demons didn't really get to benefit from those, did they?

"Hello, *Dick*," Michael said, his tone light and mocking.

He was banking on irritating the fuck out of his prisoner. And what do you know, his instincts were right. Richard's lips split in a hideous snarl and the demon's forked tongue lashed out, snapping to the left and the right in hatred.

He couldn't speak through the gag, though. Michael stepped forward. Richard lunged at him, jaw working against the gag. Michael pulled out a laugh, hoping it didn't sound forced, and casually slapped the demon across the face with his full strength behind it.

Richard's head jerked to the left and a small trickle of gold began to leak from his mouth. Michael tsked and blotted at the area with a cloth he'd dipped in sacramental wine.

Freshly blessed.

The gag was all that kept Richard's scream from deafening both himself and Sara.

"That's hardly gracious," Michael said, chiding. "Can't have you bleeding all over the place, now can we?"

Sara released the gag while Richard was glaring daggers at Michael.

"Now, that's better, right? Let's have a nice chat." Michael smiled at their captive.

Richard spat. Fortunately it was more saliva than blood. The Resistance wouldn't be scrubbing gold out of their concrete and rebar aesthetic tonight.

"I have nothing to say to you that I haven't said already." Richard worked his tongue against his teeth. "I'm going to get out of here, and then the two of you are going to learn the true meaning of pain."

"Is it scrolling your feed?" Sara asked. "Because I've already tried that and boy, when you're right, you're right. Your content's for shit, man."

"I will gut you like a fish and eat your liver like sashimi," Richard said in a poisonously sweet voice.

Michael slapped him again. Hard. The demon's head rocked back.

"Manners," Michael said mildly. "Now, you are going to tell us everything we want to know, and you're going to do so while keeping a civil tongue in your head. Or I'm sure Sara will be happy to rip it out for you."

Richard laughed, a scornful sound, ringing with disdain. He didn't seem to be respecting either Michael or Sara as a threat.

That was all right. That would change. For now, Michael let the demon talk. They'd get down to business soon enough.

"You're not going to break me with force. What? Beat it out of me? As if." Richard sneered at them. "And you're not going to kill me. Not only are you both—inexplicably—bound by, what, morals? Who has those these days? You both have another little problem. I've got something that you want. Kill me and you get nothing."

"You're half right," Michael said, letting silence fall after his words and forcing Richard to squirm.

Eventually, the demon couldn't take it anymore and asked the obvious question.

"What do you mean?"

"We're not going to beat it out of you. We don't have to." Michael smiled, a chilling expression as distant as the stars. "Why use actual force when you can just use the threat of it? It's worked for countries the world over and throughout history."

"Of course to do that we'd need something absolutely horrible to threaten him with," Sara chimed in, right on cue. "Do we have something like that?"

Michael made a show of pondering, tapping a finger against his chin before snapping his fingers in a *eureka!* moment.

"Do you know, I think we just might. Remember our trip to the goblin market?"

"How could I forget?" Sara smiled, though her smile was far nastier than Michael's. "So many strange and powerful things. So long as you are willing to pay the price."

Richard flinched at that. Michael quashed a flare of hope. The demon was nervous! His plan just might work.

"What was it we picked up there, again?" Sara wasn't quite so good at acting clueless as Michael, but it didn't seem to matter.

Richard was staring at the both of them, a look of trepidation on his smugly handsome face.

"This little trinket." Michael pulled out a rough fragment of stone.

He'd picked it up from the parking lot outside of the church. It looked absolutely mundane. Which it was.

But Richard didn't know that.

"The fuck is that?" The demon stared at it in horrified fascination.

His imagination must be working overtime. Michael hadn't even done anything yet. Though that was about to change.

"You've heard of the Philosopher's Stone, right?" Michael began tossing the rock from hand to hand.

"Of course I have," Richard sneered. "What am I? Headless? You know who my father is."

"Then you'll know that it's an incredibly difficult bit of alchemy to pull off," Michael said. "Mishaps happen a lot. In fact, what is it they say? The philosopher who seeks to turn lead into gold is more likely to accomplish the reverse?"

"That—that's not possible." Richard went three shades of white gold.

"Is it not? A lot of people would say demons don't exist. That magic is a fiction. That you can't get money from nothing." Michael leaned in. "Are those people right?"

"He doesn't believe us,' Sara said. She shook her head. "Maybe we need a little demonstration?"

"That seems like a good idea. You got any gold on you?" Michael glanced at Sara.

She nodded and pulled a plain band off her hand, setting the ring on her palm. Michael plucked it out of her hand, making a show of keeping it far from the stone in his other hand. He twisted it back and forth in front of Richard.

"It's gold, right? You can smell it or something?"

The demon's tongue flicked out. Richard stared at the ring and then, as if against his will, he nodded slowly.

"Good. It'll do for our little test, then."

Michael handed the ring back to Sara. With a flourish, then, he flashed the bit of rock in his hand—his False Philosopher's

Stone. Carefully he pressed it closer and closer to the ring, until it touched the metal.

He quickly released a small shower of white-gold sparks, glittering motes of will designed to distract Richard. The demon hissed and Sara palmed the gold ring and replaced it with an ideal one they'd had quickly cast of some lead from the hardware store.

"Huh. Look at that!" Michael exclaimed. "It's not shiny anymore. What do you think, Sara?"

"Looks like lead to me," she said. "Feels like lead. Grey, soft—" her eyes skewered Richard where he sat, staring in horror, "almost worthless. Here. Have a sniff."

She held the ring of lead out to Richard. The demon grimaced and shook his head. His tongue flicked in distaste.

Good. Michael had gambled that one of Mammon's broods, so obsessed with wealth and with gold flowing in his veins instead of blood, would have that kind of reaction.

"I wonder what something like this False Philosopher's Stone would do to a being with molten gold in his veins?" Michael asked the room, turning in a circle, arms wide. Then he zeroed back in on Richard and pulled out a switchblade, flicking it open to punctuate his next sentence.

"Let's find out, shall we?"

"Fuck!" Richard screamed, struggling so hard to escape that if his chair had not been bolted to the floor he would have toppled over backward. "You win! You fucking win, all right? Get that fucking thing away from me! I'll tell you whatever you want!"

"So glad we could finally establish the price of your assistance," Michael said with a feral grin.

He pulled up a chair, spun it around, and sat down in it, reverse-style with his arms folded over the back.

"Let's talk about your daddy…"

CHAPTER 33

The PitCoin

Hannah joined them once Michael was sure the faucet of information they'd tapped out of Richard wasn't going to run dry any time soon. She stood back and let them work, only offering the occasional comment to help direct the interrogation with a bit of intelligence that she or The Resistance had collected.

Michael had collected pieces: the existence of Mammon and the Spirit World, PitCoin, The Ten, key political figures being targeted. Hannah added more context: a conspiracy to somehow deliver ultimate power into Mammon's hands, allowing the archdemon to fully manifest in the mortal world and rule for the rest of eternity as its god-king. Sara chimed in occasionally with connections she noticed from her own investigations, particularly when Richard started talking about The Ten buying up politicians like it was a hellfire sale.

"Here, give me that." Sara grabbed a piece of chalk from Michael.

Someone in The Resistance had gone and fetched down a chalkboard from the church rec room above and several bits of chalk. The green expanse was crossed and cross-crossed with notes, connecting lines, and question marks as the three tried to piece together the shape of Mammon's plan.

Every so often Richard would snicker at their efforts, but Michael waving the piece of harmless stone in his direction—the False Philosopher's Stone—was always enough to shut the demon up, son of Mammon or not.

"So what have we got?" Michael looked up at the board. "PitCoin is cryptocurrency developed by The Ten on behalf of Big M to do…what?"

Richard rolled his eyes at the nickname the three had come up with for his father.

"No, it's easier to start with Big M himself," Hannah said. "Look. All power comes from somewhere. There's inherent power, like you have, Michael, when you draw upon your wings or summon your sword of flame—"

"Totally overcompensating, by the way," Richard interjected.

Michael menaced him with the bit of rock and Richard clamped his jaws shut.

"—or there is power that is drawn *from* some where or some thing." Hannah continued. "A lot of humans draw power from various beings we think of as gods, or demons, but a lot also draw power from ideas or concepts."

"The warlocks you mentioned," Sara said.

"Right. Spirits can draw power as well, either from human hosts who feed them their life or emotional energy—"

Michael had a sudden flashback to the horrible thing he had cut from Stowe's back.

"—or from a particular concept or law of existence that they have tied themselves to. Or were created with a tie to. I don't really know for sure. No one does." Hannah grimaced.

"I do," Richard taunted.

This time he shut up before Michael's hand could even twitch.

"The point is, Big M draws his power from wealth. The idea of wealth. The desire for wealth. How much wealth his followers control—"

"The Ten. Billionaires. That's a pretty big metaphysical punch." Michael tapped the False Philosopher's Stone against his chin.

"A lot. Plus Big M grants them wealth to use which they invest in various crimes, cons, and thefts—"

"Legitimate businesses!" Richard said.

This time all three of them glared at him and Sara went so far as to grab the stone from Michael's hand and take a menacing step towards the demon.

Richard shut up again.

"So PitCoin is what? Another way to generate wealth?" Michael glanced at Richard, expecting another outburst, but the demon was just sitting there, looking at them smugly.

"That, and more." Hannah tapped her piece of chalk on the political side of the board. "How much do you know about the national debt and the dollar as international refuge currency? Bear with me, I swear this is relevant."

Hannah knew her brother. His eye had started to glaze over already.

"Not much," he said. "The national debt is how much we owe—"

"A lot of it to nations overseas," Sara interjected. Then, when the other two looked at her, "what? I listen to the news."

"Right. Nations overseas buy dollars because it's seen as more stable than their own—or other countries'—currency. It's a safe investment." Hannah looked grim. "For now. Most of that safety is an illusion. An act of faith. When something shakes that faith, like a war or a debt crisis—"

"Which we seem to have every six months now," Sara muttered.

"—then the value of the dollar goes down as countries, individuals, and international corporations try to shift to a more stable currency." Hannah tapped the board. "Any guesses what the current leader in 'safe' currency is?"

"It can't be PitCoin?" Michael looked at the board. "It's not even real!"

Richard cackled.

"No money is real anymore,' Sara said. "It's kind of a pain for the forensic accountants at the precinct."

"Yeah, the gold standard was done away with ages ago." Hannah tapped the board with her chalk again. "Money is just faith given form. It's worth what it's worth because enough people believe it. If something shakes that faith, boom." Hannah dropped the chalk. "The dollar plummets, and everyone rushes to buy up what they think is the safest alternative. Control the safest alternative and you can control the world."

"Which is why Big M has people like this asshole pushing it," Michael said, jerking his chin at Richard.

"Hey!"

Everyone ignored the demon.

"And they've bought up plenty of news time and reporters, they've made tactical purchases from shell accounts, all pushing up the value and making PitCoin appear to be stable, on the rise, and the currency of the future. If the dollar fails, The Ten—and Big M—stand to win the greatest financial windfall in recorded history." Sara glanced at Richard and frowned. "Though judging by the look on his face, that's only part of the story."

The demon suddenly shifted his face to neutral.

"There's more to it than that?" Michael looked disbelieving. "What else? How is Big M gaining enough power to manifest in the real world from all that wealth suddenly dedicated to his worship not enough?"

"Because wealth is always about more than money. It's about power. Control," Hannah said bluntly, tapping a finger to her lips. "PitCoin uses unique coding and technology to track how much of it there is and how it moves through the monetary system. If most systems use it in the wake of the new dollar, and Big M has his minions push the agenda, it could replace a massive percentage of transactions. Big M would know who was buying what, from whom, and when. Think about what you could do with that much detailed information on people. The blackmail potential alone is worth billions."

"And not just that," Sara added. "If you control the main currency, it means everybody in the world works for you because you create and control what they want and need. Dependency breeds obedience, compliance. You create the millionaires and the billionaires and own them simply by giving or withholding. Control the creation and flow of money, which is the main expression of value, and you control the world. It's quite simple actually."

"Fucking hell." Michael looked over the board again. "And if that's what Big M is trying to do, then how does he do it? He's been buying up politicians, but even with ten billionaires backing him, there's no way he could get a total lock on all of the legislature in order to—"

"He doesn't need all of them," Sara said suddenly. "He doesn't even need a majority. He just needs enough of the key players—say the Speaker of the House, some members of financial committee boards, and a few others in key swing states, for example—to bring things to a standstill. He doesn't have to do anything other than tank the next vote to raise the debt ceiling. If that vote fails, with the world watching—and trust me, we've had enough of these recently that I *know* the world is always watching—that could be all the shock the system needs to tank the dollar and jumpstart PitCoin."

"Delivering Mammon himself unto the world," Hannah said solemnly.

A sudden chill swept over the room and Michael had the sudden sense that malevolent eyes were seeking him, as through a thick fog. He shot a glare at Hannah, who raised her hands in apology.

"Sorry. I should know by now to watch the names I conjure with."

"How about no conjuring while there's a demon present?" Sara glanced over at Richard, who had gone suspiciously quiet.

"Tell me, Richard," Michael said suddenly, "how close is your father to controlling the next vote? Must be damned close. Hannah clearly set the plan back by killing Hugs. I'm sure whichever senators and congressmen he bought up either upped their prices or got snatched up by the competition. I'm feeling this is what, kind of a razor's edge situation? You seem pretty sweaty for someone whose daddy is sitting firmly in the control seat."

"I will make you—" Richard started to rant but bit that forked tongue of his as soon as Michael brought the stone near to him.

"The only thing you're going to make is a smear of flaking lead on the ground if you don't start talking." Michael's eyes lit into twin pits of white-gold fire.

"He's got all the politicians he needs! I swear! So long as he—" Richard bit his tongue.

"Aw, come on now. You can't stop there! You're just getting to the good part." Sara stepped up and moved Michael's hand incrementally closer to the demon, inching the stone nearer as she did so.

Richard leaned back, desperately thrashing against his bonds.

"No! I can't! He'll do worse than kill me!"

"What?" Hannah drawled. "Will daddy cut off your allowance?"

"Is that really worse than all the blood in your veins slowly turning to lead?" Michael asked, pushing the stone a little closer.

It seemed that plot was about to run out its usefulness, however. They'd hit upon something that scared Richard more. The demon began ranting incoherently, forcing Michael to back off, lest the bluff be called accidentally by the demon's wildly contorting body.

"We don't need him," Sara said, tapping her phone screen. "Political junkies are just as good. I've got a breakdown here of everyone who might be a swing, what their voting history is, biggest donors, the works. It's even searchable. I can put together a list of the most likely—oh!" Sara's eyes widened dramatically. "Yeah. It's right here! Look at this—"

She tilted her phone, angling it so only Michael and Hannah could see.

"Oh, that's gotta be him," Michael said, watching Richard out of the corner of his eye.

The demon looked tense.

Good.

There was nothing of note on Sara's screen. Michael knew it was another bluff, but so far, so good.

"Are you sure it's not Senator Wasserstein?" Hannah said, playing along. "I always thought he seemed dirty."

Richard relaxed slightly. Michael's gut tugged at him.

"It's not someone who could be dirty," Michael said. "Anyone dirty can be bought, and they aren't going to all this trouble just to buy up some extra politicians."

Richard froze. Michael knew he was on the right track.

"No. They're going to do something else." Michael tapped the phone. "Who is the politician least likely to have anything to do with wealth, corruption, crypto—none of that stuff."

"Senator Smith," Sara answered. "I don't even have to look that one up."

That did it. Richard went, if possible, even paler. They were doing something to target Senator Smith.

"What happens if Senator Smith doesn't show up to the vote?" Michael asked.

"Automatic abstention, which means, if they've gotten one or two members of Smith's party to cross the aisle and vote with them or abstain, they could sink the vote!"

"And the dollar goes with it, PitCoin surges, and Big M ascends," Michael concluded darkly.

"What do we think?" Hannah asked. "Delay? Kidnapping?"

"Murder," Michael said with some finality, watching Richard out of the corner of his eye and shaking his head when the demon's reaction confirmed it.

The man clearly spent too much time on social media. He couldn't not share his every thought and emotion, somehow.

"Thanks, Dick," Michael said brightly. "You've told us just about everything we wanted to know! Unless there's some extra surprise that you've got squirreled away somewhere and you feel like sharing? Maybe the access codes for The Ten's bank accounts?"

"What? Why would I have those? If I did do you honestly think I would have married that airhead Britney? She's not even in the direct line of succession! She just had the biggest trust fund—"

"I don't know whether to be glad or disgusted he said trust fund instead of something else that starts with the same letter," Sara said, rolling her eyes.

"Let's just make sure there aren't any backup plans," Hannah suggested. "At least ones that junior here knows about. Some of The Ten, at least, are pretty canny. They might have alternatives in the works."

She cracked her knuckles.

"I've got a new spell I'd like to try out anyway…"

CHAPTER 34

The Critical Vote

The trip to Washington from New York would have been faster if they could fly, but there was no way Sara or Michael could risk boarding a plane, not with all of the agency's eyes looking for them. Fortunately, they were no longer limited by mortal means of transportation. With some help from Hannah, Michael took them all through the Veil, traveled a short distance on the Other Side, then stepped back into Washington. A trip that should have taken two or three hours when you included flight time and getting through security was accomplished in less than half that.

And neither he, Hannah, nor Sara needed to expose themselves to the authorities to do it!

The amount of spirit-enabled smuggling that must go on did not bear thinking about. Unless the goblin market had some kind of control, that was just a whole other mess to worry about.

But that wasn't his job. It wasn't even the job he had before walking out. No, his current mission was altogether different. And, thankfully, Sara had all the credentials, experience, and necessary knowledge to get them in to see the Senator, even without an appointment.

No mean feat, in all honesty.

Right now they were in the antechamber of the senator's office suite. It was well-appointed and tastefully done in strong colors with simple details. The exact picture of a thrifty politician who serves the people.

There had to be something, though. No one was a saint. There would be some kind of hook. Maybe not one Mammon could exploit, but it would be there nonetheless.

Sara was arguing with the head of the senator's security detail, a tall, muscled man with dark skin and an air of consummate professionalism.

It was just his bad luck that Sara was more determined than he was professional.

"No, I will not go over the intel with you right here, right now," Sara was saying. "We don't have time! We need to get in there and assess potential threats now. My department picked up this tip at the last minute and we're talking life or death!"

Collins, the head of security, sighed and put a hand to his earpiece. He nodded to Sara.

"We've just been cleared to go in. Thank you for looking out for the senator's well-being ma'am. It's too big a job for anyone, even the team I have." His eyes took on a challenging note. "And my team is the best."

"I don't doubt it," Sara said. "But even the best team can be caught unawares. Let's go make sure that doesn't happen, shall we?"

Collins showed them into the senator's office. Smith himself was behind the desk, adding his signature to a seemingly never-ending parade of papers handed from one aide to another to the senator. A third collected the completed documents and organized them in a neat stack in her arms.

"This is the detective who wanted to see you, sir," Collin said. "Senator Smith," he indicated the man behind the desk, then went around introducing the rest of the people present, all senatorial aides of some kind or another. "The senator's senior aide, Lucille, junior aide, Justin, and personal assistant, DeAnne."

Sara and Michael nodded at each in turn. Hannah stayed behind them, keeping silent behind her dark glasses and generally providing an extra air of menace and competence.

"I'm afraid you'll need to be quite succinct, ma'am," the senator said to Sara. "As you can see I can't afford to pause the business of state at the moment. There are several things I need to get done before the debt ceiling vote later this evening."

"I understand, sir." Sara nodded. "Though it's the vote we're here about. We've come into possession of some information that suggests you will be targeted, today, precisely because of how you intend to vote on that bit of legislation."

"You must be joking." The senator's pen stopped its scratching and everyone in the office paused to look at Sara.

"I'm afraid not, sir. It seems—"

There was a high-pitched whine and then a crack and shards of glass exploded out of the window.

"Get down sir!" Collin threw himself across the window to defend the senator, who scrambled beneath his desk. The aides scattered towards the corners, moving so quickly and smoothly without colliding with anyone or anything that it was clear they'd drilled for a moment like this.

Collins was shouting orders over the wire to his team as more bullets punctured the window. Michael and Sara had taken refuge behind the chairs. Hannah, further to the side, had pressed herself to the wall by the windows, gun in hand, mirroring Collins's position. Analyzing the bullet patterns, Michael was sure there were multiple shooters, at least two, probably three, firing from two different angles.

Overkill. They really wanted this man dead.

"Sir!" Justin, the junior aide, was gesturing to the senator. "You need to get out of here! The west exit is clear."

The west exit was also across the room from where Sara and Michael were taking cover. If the senator left by that route, they might lose him, and there was no way there weren't more agents of Mammon waiting outside. If they could afford multiple snipers they would have covered all the exits.

This was a thorough job.

"Go, sir! I'll cover you!" Collins shouted, shooting back at the snipers in a classic fire and cover pattern.

Senator Smith nodded and began crawling across the floor toward the door Justin was holding half open as the young aide crouched near the bookcase. Sara and Michael exchanged a glance and then began to follow, Michael praying that they didn't catch a stray bullet.

The distance between the chairs and the west exit suddenly seemed a very long one.

The senator slipped out the door, followed by Justin. The other two aides elected to stay where they were, safely behind cover. Sara and Michael made a mad dash for the door and somehow escaped without incident.

Almost without incident. Sara was wincing and holding her arm.

"Winged," she said. "It's fine. We need to keep the senator covered."

They rushed down the hall, leaving the office and its hail of gunfire behind them, but the hall was even worse. It was a long corridor made up more of window than of wall, tall sheets of panel glass glittering in the afternoon sun. The senator was running along it, almost pulled along by his aide.

He didn't make the passage unnoticed.

Bullets fired. Glass exploded. The hallway became a meat grinder. Michael flared his power, wrapping himself and Sara in his wings, blocking the bullets and the glass like they were nothing, his wings propelling him forward to where he could shield the senator and his aide as well.

They made it to the end of the hallway before they came face to face with another problem. A man in black tactical gear blocked their path, gun raised, a series of incendiary devices strapped to his belt.

"Cover!" Michael shouted, surging out ahead of the others.

Sara dropped to one knee, steadying her aim, and began firing at the target. The senator and Justin followed to opposite sides of the hallway and hugged the wall, grabbing what scant cover they could.

At least it protected them from the bullets still flying through the corridor above them.

Sara's bullets slammed into the man's body armor and stuck there, useless. Michael took a more direct approach. He manifested the sword of his will, flaming gold in the slanting light, and surged forward driving it clean through the man, body armor and all.

Demon wings flared, briefly, and Michael's sword was quenched in an icy darkness. His opponent was definitely one of Mammon's elite. That blow would have killed and consumed a lesser being.

A sword of darkness, trailing an icy mist, materialized in his opponent's hand. Sword met sword, a dizzying dance of death, as the two warred back and forth in the doorway. They would have been evenly matched, but Michael's initial attack had severely wounded his counterpart, giving him the clear advantage.

The sword of flame struck, severing the sword arm of the masked demon. The appendage fell to the ground and the blade dissolved into shadows. Michael followed the strike with a clean blow, severing the demon's head and sending it tumbling across the ground to rest near where Sara was kneeling.

Sometime during the battle, the hail of gunfire had stopped. Michael still pulled the senator and his aide through to the next room. Collins and his men joined them mere moments later. Hannah was with them.

"Your office is clear, sir," Collins said, "but we need to get you to a more secure location—"

"As long as it's one near enough that I can still make the vote," Smith insisted. "It's too important—"

"You really should think of your life, sir," Justin said. "Your constituents won't be better served by you throwing your life away."

"He's not wrong," Michael said. "But we'll make sure you get to the vote, senator. That's why we came. Hopefully this little incident puts your mind at ease in regards to our information."

"To a degree," the senator said, maintaining a very high level of composure for someone who was just shot at.

Michael wondered if the man had a military background.

"I still struggle to believe that a billionaire of any stripe would be behind this," the senator continued. "It doesn't seem to have enough profit margin in it for them." He smiled wryly.

"Sir," Sara said, "I think I have some additional context that may prove the rest of our information."

Michael hadn't noticed that Sara had picked up the head, carrying it by the balaclava like some kind of gruesome handbag. She set it down and carefully peeled back the covering material. Michael blinked. He recognized that face! It was the man they'd pursued at Hugs's assistant's house!

"This man is Max Ashton," Sara said.

Michael was probably the only one who noticed how tight her voice was, how white her fingers had gone.

"He is a known criminal, a murder suspect in the case of one Ms. DeSantos, the personal assistant of billionaire Richard Hugs, and regular associate of—"

"I get the picture," Senator Smith said, looking slightly green around the gills. "Why do you have swords, anyway? Wait, where did your weapon go?" he looked at Michael in confusion.

"I'm afraid that's classified, sir," Michael covered with a deadpan expression.

Fortunately, he was saved from Smith demanding more of an explanation by Collins, who insisted that they move the senator to a more secure room, deeper in the complex. The place was beginning to positively swarm with security as teams fanned out to find the assailants and entrances and exits were secured.

Michael and Sara followed the senator. They'd foiled the first attempt but Michael had absolutely no doubts that there would be others.

But they just needed to keep him safe until the vote. If The Ten were not expecting Michael and Sara as wild cards, they might not have anything available to counter. Mammon was a more complicated issue, but hopefully the archdemon would be sufficiently bound by his inability to influence the mortal world directly.

Though he hadn't done too badly, considering. The reach of an archdemon is long indeed.

Neither Michael, Sara, or Hannah noticed Justin, the Senator's junior aide, making a discreet phone call.

"I think we have a problem..." Justin said when the call connected.

CHAPTER 35

Protecting the Senator

Something was wrong. Michael couldn't tell what it was but there was a tingling between his shoulder blades as he stood there, next to Sara and Hannah, in the designated safe room where the senator was insisting on carrying on with work while security teams swept and patrolled the building.

The room was ornate, a far cry from Senator Smith's office. It was some kind of generic receiving room, designed to impress donors and supplicants alike with the majesty and grandeur of the senatorial hand. Donors wanted to feel reassured that their money had been well spent, that this was a person who could get things done for them. Constituents had a similar desire, though their entitlement came from the knowledge that—on paper at least—politicians served those who had elected them.

Too bad money—not people— elected more politicians. No wonder Mammon had made this place his playground.

Michael's eyes began to burn. His Sight was trying to tell him something. He checked his surroundings carefully before glancing across the veil, wary of things being slightly different and throwing off his combat reflexes should he need them at a moment's notice.

At first, everything looked the same. The room was still showy and grandiose, though the light from the chandelier above cast far more and far thicker shadows. There were a few spirits about, drawn to the aura of bloodshed and fear, just as Michael had expected, but nothing seemed unduly out of place.

Until he saw one of the shadows move. It coiled across the ground like a serpent with eyes of sooty flame, wrapping itself up and around the body of one of the security guards in the room before slipping into his mouth with a small intake of breath. The form of the man shifted before Michael's sight, just a flicker, and then the man cast a winged shadow, and embers of hellfire shone through his aviators.

Possessed. The demons were possessing the security detail! If they couldn't take Smith out from the outside, they'd do it from within! Literally!

Himself, Sara, and Hannah. They were clean. He knew that. He didn't see a demon in Collins yet, nor the Senator or his aide. Not that he could definitively tell. Possession seemed a lot more subtle than other manifestations from the other side. Like the demons could use the people they were squatting in like cloaks or shields.

One officer he could see was definitely possessed. There were four others. Michael's eyes flicked over them. He caught at least two flares of hellfire embers and what he was certain was a flicker of wing settling into the shadow of another. He couldn't be sure about the last man.

Michael made a decision.

"It's a trap," he shouted. "Collins, watch out! Protect the senator!"

And he manifested his flaming sword and beheaded the security guard closest to him. Sara and Hannah grabbed Michael's cue and followed, pulling their guns and firing at the other security guards. Two fired back. A third took aim at the senator but was thrown off his by Collins barrelling into him. The man went down with a sickening crunch, all but snapped beneath Collin's weight.

Michael's sword slashed through the shadow that issued out of the dying man's mouth and nostrils, cutting it in two and killing the demon before it could jump into Collins. The thing screamed as it died, an agonizing sound that made Michael's teeth itch and sent Collins's eyes rolling up into the back of his head as the man passed out from the sheer psychic chaos crashing across his brain.

Michael whirled. Sara and Hannah had dealt with the others. At least, they were all down. Michael couldn't tell if they were all dead or not. Had no idea if the one man he wasn't sure was possessed had been or not. If he'd been a casualty of friendly fire or not. Michael shoved the thought aside for later. For now, they had to protect the senator.

Senator Smith was standing, mouth agape, behind his desk, as Justin the aide crouched down next to it.

Apparently the young man's ambition didn't quite extend to throwing himself bodily in front of his employer.

"Are we good? Secure?" Sara had her pistol out and was wildly glancing around the room, trying to see the things she knew—or suspected—were there but could not see. Not without the Sight of her own.

Michael could have enchanted her. Given her the Sight temporarily, as Gabriel had done for him that first time, but Sara hadn't wanted to risk it interfering with her aim, trusting that Michael's innate abilities would serve them better. Keep them safe.

And it had. Just not quite so quickly as Michael would have liked.

"I don't know," Hannah said slowly, scanning the room while looking through the hole in a piece of smooth stone. "I can't see any others."

Michael felt that itching between his shoulder blades. No. That was not all of them. There was at least one more. And if it wasn't in Justin, who would have killed the senator already if he'd had a demon inside him, that only left...

"There's one inside the senator," Michael said with cold and creeping certainty.

"Very perceptive," the senator's voice answered him, shorn of its usual life and energy.

Michael turned to see the senator holding two guns, one each pointed at Hannah and Sara. He tensed, not sure if he could save both if the demon in the political meatsuit fired on them at the same time. The senator chuckled.

"You're fast, but you're not that fast. Not yet. I can tell." The demonic senator inhaled and flashed a forked tongue. "I can taste it in you."

Michael felt the sword of his will flare with anger.

"Oooh. You think a light show can stop what's going to happen? No. It can't. Just like none of you can stop the will of Lord Mammon. You've already lost. You just don't realize it yet. The accounting is not in your favor."

"It will be as soon as I cast you and the rest of your friends out from this place," Hannah snapped.

"You want to play exorcist? Fine by me. I like our odds." The demon in Senator Smith smiled with his borrowed teeth. "Can you clear the whole place? It doesn't taste to me like you have that much faith, that much magic. Or do you perhaps have a hidden patron we don't know about? Joan, perhaps? You seem the type that would appeal to that flaming virgin." He chuckled. "But then, if you did have that kind of backing, Lord Mammon would not have expended so much effort to secure victory here. He knows better than to throw good money after bad."

"If you've won, get to it then," Michael challenged. There had to be a reason the demon was playing for time. What was it? Why was he running out the clock?

Because he—or Mammon—was afraid that they could do something to tip the scales back against him if they had the time to think? The time to act? That had to be it.

"Oh, no. I think I'd like to play a while. It takes a lot of effort and a lot of sacrifice to possess a mortal. And they burn up so quickly once you do. No capacity, you know." That smile again. "So I'd like to enjoy it as long as I can."

Michael couldn't stop him. Not without being in at least two places at once, which was impossible.

Or was it?

With the art of no-sword, his will became the ultimate weapon. With the art of no-sword, he could effectively be in many places at once and strike from many directions.

Defend against any number of attacks from any number of sources.

Michael took a deep breath and sought the edge of his mind, the place Gabriel had taken him to, the place between everything and nothing, which could then be everywhere. It came to him, not easily, but Michael straddled the knife-edge of that existence and bent his whole being to mastering that verge.

Nowhere. Breath. Everywhere. Breathe. Two guns. Two targets. One instant hanging shining in time.

Michael could almost see it, from that place in his mind at the edge of everything and nothing. From there he felt that if he could just look in the right direction, in the correct way, he could see all of eternity, from the Beginning to the End.

Was that how it worked? From the edge of nothing that touches everything, you look through the infinite possibilities and find the one you seek, then bring yourself to and through it, manifesting your will wholly upon the Earth?

Was it just a more advanced version of what he did with his sword?

If so, it was easier said than done. But there was no time, on the edge between nothing and everything. There was time for Michael to think, suspended between ticks of the clock as he was.

Not that he could maintain this state indefinitely.

Nothing. Breath. Everything. Breath. Two guns. Two targets. One blade. One moment.

One will.

Michael's will.

The art of No-Sword.

There! For one shining moment, it crystallized in Michael's mind, and in that instant, he exploded into action. Twin swords of white-gold flame materialized in his hands.

The demon within Senator Smith fired instantly, but Michael, from the nothingness at the edge of everything, had already seen and begun to move. Two swords became four, and he sliced the bullets out of mid-air. Sliced right through the barrels of the pistols in Senator Smith's hands.

Almost.

Michael stopped the bullets. And he sliced through one of the pistols. He missed the other, his experience with this moment, this kind of combat, too new to control. He needed more time and more energy, and he ran out just before he accomplished his aim.

The twin swords of white-gold flame, so recently blazing as brightly as twin stars, suddenly flared to void-black darkness and sunk in on themselves, consumed by the nothingness of the edge that Michael rode.

An edge that cut deeper than any blade ever forged.

A scream burst from Michael's lips as the existential pain of absolute nothingness sliced into his palms, a line of nothingness finer than monofilament wire. He was lucky the swords consumed themselves quickly, without taking more of him with them. As it was twin lines of red crossed his palms where he had been cut, body and soul, by that edge of nothingness that he sought to ride.

"Well," the demon inside Senator Smith said, a look of stunned disbelief on his face, "aren't you a surprise. Fuck. And here I was looking forward to a fun fuckin' ride in this meatsuit. But you're good. Better than he said you'd be. I'm going to have to cut this short. Have fun, all, with the unholy hell about to rain down on you."

The demon smiled widely, swung the remaining pistol in his hand around, wrapped his lips around it, and blew the back of Senator Smith's head out all over the wall of his borrowed office.

Michael stared, stunned. Sara and Hannah stared, speechless.

Senator Smith was dead. The demon was gone. But the damage had more than been done.

"Fuck," Sara swore.

"We need to go," Hannah said. "Someone will have heard all of this and security is already swarming the place. They're going to think we were involved. And I'll bet most of them are going to be carrying a demon inside when they come for us."

"Fuck," Michael agreed with Sara.

Then they ran.

CHAPTER 36

Mammon in the Flesh

"We need to get out of here," Hannah said again, checking her gun and checking the exits.

Senator Smith's corpse was swiftly cooling, what was left of it splayed across the desk. Justin, the aide, was curled in the fetal position, rocking and keening in terror.

"Do we bring him with us?" Sara pointed to the aide.

Michael shook his head. The kid would be too much of a liability. Hannah agreed.

"We need to get to a secure location," Hannah said, checking her gun. "I had—" she glanced at Justin and thought better of what she was about to say. "I know a place. Come on."

Hannah took the lead. Sara followed with Michael bringing up the rear. He moved slowly. His mishap with the art of no-sword had taken a toll on his body beyond the cuts to his hands, which still bled profusely. He wrapped them in makeshift bandages torn from his shirt as they went, gliding from nook to cranny, moving behind cover and with the aid of the distraction of the security team still sweeping the grounds for assailants.

They were nearly out of the place when the alarm went off again.

"They've probably found Smith," Hannah said. "This way."

Michael let his sister and Sara lead the way, trusting them to lead through the mortal realm while he kept his Sight up and active, scanning the spirit world for any threats.

Spirits swarmed all around, and he could see the form of flitting demons in the sky above. Mammon's eyes. Mammon's agents. He passed the information along to Hannah, who nodded.

"I'll try to keep us out of sight until we can get to the car."

Hannah led them and Michael saw first-hand just why it had been so hard for his team to track her down. She seemed to have a sixth sense for cameras and timing—or maybe it was a spell. Whatever it was, she guided them quickly and easily through the crowd, across the lawn, and down to the parking structure.

Their car was unfortunately three levels down.

"This next bit is going to be tricky," Hannah said. "Follow me exactly. The blind spots down here are really slim. Too many concerns about bombs. Thank fuck it's still a government facility and the pressure to come in under budget outweighs the desire for perfect security coverage."

Money, again, determining the way the world went.

They were just a few yards from the car when the quality of the shadows changed. Michael called out, halting their progress. His Sight couldn't show him what was different, but he felt instinctively that it was.

His gut was vindicated moments later when six demons, beautiful and lethal with skin as dark as night and fingers ending in nails like gold razors, stepped from the shadows.

"Shit!" Hannah had her gun in her hand immediately.

Sara was even faster, drawing and firing in the time it took Hannah to brace herself. The bullet caught one of the demons right in the left eye, driving deep and killing him instantly.

The other five hissed and vanished back into the shadows. Michael summoned his sword, wincing at the pain that shot through his hand at its heat. It was like the wound on his hand allowed the fire to seep directly into his blood. He felt like he was burning from the inside every moment he kept that sword manifest.

"They weren't expecting that," Hannah said with grim satisfaction. "Though now they're ready. That'll make this harder."

"Can we make it to the car and leave them behind?" Sara asked.

There was the screeching sound of tearing metal and a pool of gas and oil began spreading out from beneath their car.

"I think that's a no," Michael said. "We need to—"

He turned and slashed with his blade, narrowly missing decapitating the demon that was lunging out of the shadows behind him. He was in no position to try the full no-sword technique, but that didn't mean his moment of success hadn't helped him grasp some of the lesser advantages.

Michael was going to be very hard to ambush from here on out.

The demons in the shadows darted out, harrying them around the edges. They were fast, too fast to land a blow on, but their need to avoid the weapons of Michael and his companions also made them less of a danger. They couldn't pause, dared not get too close to his flaming sword, and had to always watch their backs, in case Hannah or Sara buried an enchanted bullet in it.

Michael counted. He'd thought so! There were only four of the remaining five demons attempting to kill them. Where was the fifth? Michael didn't like it. The fucker could be up to anything.

Then something changed and proved he was very right to worry.

"Mi-ka-el," a new voice slid across the battlefield, freezing all the participants.

It was an old voice, heavy and stiff with disuse, or with an unfamiliarity for speaking in a world constrained by oxygen and physical laws. It was rich and shining, temptation and luxury, old mahogany and shiny new gold.

"Michael," the voice came again.

This time he managed to spot the speaker. It was one of the demons, the tallest, the one he had mentally labeled the leader as the battle progressed.

He was speaking with the voice of Mammon.

Can demons possess other demons? Maybe archdemons can. What a terrifying thought.

"Enough playing," Mammon snapped. "This ends now. You and your compatriots have interfered enough. I—"

A shot rang out. Sara had leveled her weapon at the demon playing host to Mammon and fired.

The bullet exploded into a splash of molten gold before coming within arm's length of Mammon.

"Now, now," he said. "It's not like you are immune to the comforts of wealth, are you Sara? I seem to recall that you like to splurge on fancy coffees. It's a justifiable luxury, yes? So you have enjoyed my favor. Now return it by standing there and being quiet."

Hannah began chanting.

"And you!" Mammon flicked a glance at Hannah. "You are certainly not opposed to paying far more than you need to for antique firearms. Imagine! What a thing to waste money on."

The archdemon's tone was mocking as he somehow froze Michael's sister in place as well.

A demon each moved behind Sara and Hannah and grabbed them tightly. Michael saw why as soon as Mammon returned his attention to Michael. The mesmerizing effect or whatever it was was temporary. Sara and Hannah began to struggle but to no avail. They were held tight.

"I have your companions, Michael," Mammon said, smooth as gold, "but if you agree to surrender yourself to me, then I will let them go. A simple transaction. You're not opposed to that, are you?"

"What? Why me?"

"You're the one who is in a position to stop me. Gabriel is gone, and The Resistance is a mere collection of mortals. Without your power, my plan will face no challenge it cannot overcome."

"No! Forget about us, Michael!" Sara shouted. "Priorities! He'll destroy the world!"

Michael froze. Because that was the question. What was most important to him? What did he truly value?

And was the world worth saving? It was so corrupted. He'd seen it even before his eyes had been opened to the other side, to how Garibaldi truly ran the agency.

But even if he wanted to save the world, could he? That was a big job for just one person. He could take this deal and save Hannah, his sister. Save Sara, the woman he—the woman he had somehow come to love, though it was only now he could admit it to himself.

Would he even want to live in a world that was saved, if the price was Sara's life?

Michael looked from Sara to Hannah and back again. They were struggling against the demons that held them, but neither could break free, nor gain enough leverage to bring their weapons to bear. He reached for the edge between nothing and everything and almost passed out as the pain washed through his soul.

He would need to heal before he tried to master no-sword once more.

Michael was out of cards to play. There was no option. He had to take the devil's deal.

But that didn't mean he couldn't try to better the terms. His trip to the goblin market had taught him that. Might as well make sure Mammon got the full payout on the dividends from that lesson. And maybe, just maybe, make it so Hannah and Sara could finish what they'd started. They were more than enough to save the world if he could tie Mammon's hands just a bit and give them an advantage.

"I'll surrender myself to you on one condition," Michael said. "If I agree to your deal, you have to swear that you will let Sara and Hannah go. You will not harm them, nor order or allow any of your minions to do them harm, now or at any time during the remainder of their lives. Sara and Hannah, my friend and my sister, they go free and you never act against them again, nor allow your agents to. If you swear upon the wealth that is your power, I'll surrender."

"Fine, but if I am to expend so much effort to gain one half-breed boy and ensure the safety of two paltry mortals, I'm going to need more from you than simply your surrender. I will require the gold of your fire. It shall serve me and increase my power!"

"Michael, no!" Hannah shouted. "You can't trust him!"

"Quiet you!" the demon holding his sister tightened its grip, cutting off her air. "You of all people should not care to lose your brother, for what he has cost you."

"Hannah!" Sara struggled, trying to reach her. "Let me go you asshole!"

"I am not a being given overmuch to patience, Michael," Mammon's voice said, heavy with warning. "I require an answer."

Michael winced. Not what he wanted, but he wasn't walking out of here with that anyway. At least this way Sara and Hannah would get out, and be safer, if not wholly safe.

Though what did Mammon mean, about the gold of Michael's fire?

"Do we have a deal?" The voice of Mammon, speaking through the lead demon, spoke again, impatience clear in his tone.

Looks like Michael would find out because there was only one way this was going to go.

"We do," Michael said, sure of his choice.

Chains of gold like adamant suddenly sizzled into being on his skin. A collar of black leather etched with runes of gold and sealed with a small padlock clenched sharply around his throat.

"Michael! No!" Sara screamed, the sound piercing and high even though Michael was finding it harder and harder to see or hear anything.

It was the last thing Michael heard as darkness rose all around him and swallowed down his senses completely.

CHAPTER 37

The Cave of Mammon

Sight and sound returned to Michael slowly, like he was bobbing in an ocean of darkness and only slowly being drawn to a shore of light by inexorable tides. His muscles ached and there was a burning pain in his forearms. That was what he felt first. This was followed by the dull throbbing of the wounds in his palms and the pounding headache sending spikes shooting through his eyes.

His eyelids fluttered, opening slowly. The world around him was light, painful light, and it took time to adjust. When they finally did, Michael had to blink several times, trying to dispel the obvious dream he was still trapped in.

He never did manage to wake up.

Around him was a cave of wonders, with the wealth of nations piled high in every corner. Priceless swords of art and artifacts of gold, money printed on every denomination and material, from ancient coins with square holes in the center to the very latest plasticine money from Canada. There were tapestries with real cloth of gold and pearls embroidered across their expanse, rolled up and stacked like so many corpses in a corner.

It was dazzling. It was disgusting. There was no way any one piece could stand out from the others, and the works of art all languished, held in bondage for their monetary value, their cultural relevance lost in a sea of currency signs.

The walls, the few scraps Michael could see through the towering hoard, were simple stone, uncorked by the hand of man. Stone, shaped only by primal forces and nothing else. A natural wonder eclipsed entirely by the unnatural accumulation of random elements given value only by common agreement. It was sublime. It was profane.

It was the Cave of Mammon.

Michael was held suspended above it, on some kind of platform he could not see for being upon it. The chains of gold, bound tightly to his wrists, held him semi-upright, resting on his knees. A penitent before the Throne of Mammon, which rose above the piles of treasure around it like an island from the sea.

Mammon himself sat upon his throne, a figure no bigger than any mortal man, yet somehow radiating a presence that clearly marked this as a being beyond mortal ken. As Michael watched, Mammon continually shifted through several different forms, though each had commonalities with every other. After a time, Michael was able to pick them out.

First, there were the eyes. The eyes always held a cold light to them, gold and glimmering. They were ruthless and cruel, but above all, they were *calculating*. These were the eyes of a being that weighed each and every thing around them, assessing the value and deciding in a split second what was or was not worth the price.

And every form was richly and wonderfully dressed. Made-to-measure suits, fine silken kimonos, designer watches, jewelry in all shapes and forms from throughout history—all of it costly and obviously expensive, verging on the garish in its display of wealth and power. This was not the place for subtle, or understated wealth and elegance. No. This was wealth as power, on display for all to see.

Every form, likewise, held a hint of the rot at the core of this obsession with wealth and power. The old white man whose yellowed teeth were stained with sin and too many imported cigars. The aging woman whose flesh was hollowing out from the chemicals in her cosmetics. On and on it went, the glimmering fruit with the hidden worm at the heart of it. Every form was different yet every form was the same.

"Ah. You're awake. Good." Mammon turned when he felt Michael's attention on him.

Michael tugged at his bands, testing their strength. The chains held firm, even against his supernaturally heightened strength. Though it was Mammon's world. Who even knew what rules held sway here?

"You will not break the chains that you yourself have forged," Mammon said with a small laugh.

"What? By agreeing to your deal? How do I even know you kept up your end?" Michael shot back, mustering enough defiance to lever himself to his feet.

Mammon gestured at the tapestry across from his throne. Michael had to twist in his chains to see it, and it yanked uncomfortably at his shoulders, but he could clearly see that it showed Sara and Hannah, in photo-realistic detail. They were in the parking structure, unharmed, arguing over the ruin of the car.

"You'll have to take my word that what you see is truth and not illusion," Mammon said, voice dripping with amusement, "but I assure you, my imagination could never be so pedestrian as to conjure such a mundane and seedy scene." The archdemon shuddered. "Not a single glint of jewelry on either of them! Barbaric. A few rings add so much, and they even act as brass knuckles in a pinch. I should think your sister, at least, would appreciate that." Mammon laughed again.

Michael tugged at the chains as if that would tell him whether or not the archdemon was lying. They remained strong as ever, though they looked deceptively delicate. Gold wasn't that strong a metal! How could it have this much power to hold him?

"I told you, you forged those chains yourself," Mammon shook his head. "We are all slaves to our desires, child, and you are no different. That link?" Mammon pointed and somehow Michael knew the demon meant the one three up from the surface of the skin on his left arm. "That one was forged the moment you opted to negotiate for a salary higher than you needed at your first posting. You're half human, Michael. You are far from immune to the entreaties of wealth—and all things have their price. You should know that as well as any. You've given up enough in your life to get what you wanted."

"What? No. That was just—I knew my worth!" Michael protested.

"The love of money is the root of all evil," Mammon quoted at him. "All these little mortals, swarming over the surface of the planet like ants, thinking that Lucifer—that hack!—is the most powerful and dangerous of us. As if! When they consume the environment around them like locusts, rip up whole mountain ranges and tear down forests that have been growing for thousands of years in their hunger to buy buy buy and lord their status over others of their kind. Destroying the planet entire because of their greed. Honestly! They think *pride* is the real sin here?" Mammon laughed scornfully. "No. My power is far greater, as you shall soon see, when my kingdom comes into its own upon that little plane you call the Earth."

"What does that have to do with—"

"Your love of fine steak," Mammon pointed to another link in the chain. "The time you opted to work overtime instead of meet your girlfriend. The flowers you bought for Sara? So recent, that one, you almost can't see it near the end of your chains. It might even be sunk halfway into the stone above your head." Mammon smiled, broad and yellow. "Need I go on? Time and again you chose wealth! These chains were forged by you and your hand alone. Therefore you cannot unforge them. And the manacles? Oh, the manacles!"

Mammon cackled.

Michael struggled. Was the demon right? Had he been so driven by greed?

"Which hand was it, Michael, that you used to strike down Grace?" Mammon's voice was suddenly very soft. "I think you'll find that the heaviest manacle resides upon it."

Grace? Why did he know that name? Why had it kept coming up?

Mammon must have seen the confusion on his face because a vicious grin split the archdemon's poisonously pretty face.

"Oh, you don't remember! That is too sweet, too delicious, really." Mammon all but cooed at him. "Little Grace. The mission that Garibaldi sent you on, solo, to take down a dangerous terrorist uploading spyware onto a key civilian corporate asset of the government? Surely you haven't forgotten the case that secured your promotion, have you?"

Michael froze. No. He hadn't forgotten. But the woman's name, Grace, that he had buried deep, along with the look on her face.

His blood went cold. She'd been raving about things only she could see! He hadn't believed her then, but now? With what he'd seen, with where he was?

"She really was innocent," he murmured.

"Oh yes," Mammon cackled, "but that's not even the best part! The best part is that Grace? Grace was your sister's partner. Her close confidant. Her lover. And you? You took all that away from her! You gave Grace away to a man who would see her to her death and that? That wounded your sister so deeply that she set out on a quest for vengeance. Of course it ended with dear Bobby getting a bullet to the head…" Mammon's voice suddenly soured.

No. Michael went white and his spirit flickered and faded. He'd been responsible for the death of Hannah's partner?

The cave faded away as a wave of nausea rose, threatening to overwhelm him. But Mammon was relentless. The archdemon just kept talking. Kept insinuating his words into Michael's ear, into Michael's mind.

"We are more alike than you think, Michael," Mammon said, his voice like golden honey. "Honestly, you should surrender to it, as you have surrendered to me to save your friends. It would do you a lot of good. The wonders I could show you! The wealth I could share with you, let you command in my name! Soon I will have control of the entire world. I'll need dukes and generals to serve under me, to keep order. Think on that."

The picture in the tapestry flickered then and Mammon frowned. The image changed from a parking lot to what looked like a congressional office. It was done in the same motifs as the floor of the House of Representatives. He wasn't a huge policy wonk, but Michael recognized it from the news.

Michael froze, a lifetime of needing to compartmentalize his emotions coming to his rescue. The pain and uncertainty were shoved into a tiny little box, though he knew he'd pay for it later, so he could focus on what was happening here, now. He hardly dared to breathe, not wanting to draw attention to the fact that he could still see what was displayed. He certainly recognized the wizened old man sporting large round spectacles that made him look like nothing so much as a constipated tortoise. He was known for his ability to command precise coalitions of votes to achieve the party's aims.

He did not look happy.

Not that he ever did, of course. Michael couldn't remember the last time he'd seen the man smile. He was issuing orders. Michael couldn't hear them, but he was tapping his finger against a tally chart, and Mammon was completely absorbed in events, so he could guess what was happening.

The vote wasn't quite so secure as Mammon had made Michael think.

"They need not win the vote," the archdemon murmured to himself, so quietly Michael almost missed it. "They need only stop the vote. If it fails, the dollar falls, and my kingdom on the Earth shall rise eternal. And still…"

Mammon shifted, uncomfortable on his throne. Then, coming to some kind of decision, the archdemon rose. With a thought, he was standing next to Michael. He placed one hand over Michael's heart and then reached through his chest and began to pull.

Michael screamed. The pain was incredible. The fear and uncertainty he had so recently sealed away so he could watch and think and plan his escape flew free from its box and began eating away at him once more. Michael thrashed, trying to get as far from the archdemon as he could, to free himself from that terrible grasp.

Mammon was relentless, however.

"Now, now," the demon chided, "it's not that bad. Besides, you agreed, and I think I want to have what I am owed now. In case I need it."

Streams of gold fire like tangles of thread coiled around Mammon's fingers as he drew the stuff out of what felt like Michael's soul.

"Beautiful," the demon murmured.

When Mammon was satisfied he had drawn all of it out, the demon unhinged his jaw and swallowed the unalloyed golden fire down in a single gulp. He licked his lips as his jaw snapped back into place.

"I have business to see to, but I shall return soon and we can resume our conversation. Be well, Michael."

Then Mammon vanished in a fall of golden coins.

Michael threw himself at his chains, thrashing and tearing at his flesh, not caring if he ripped off a hand so long as it would earn him his freedom. He raged and bled and raged and bled but the chains would not budge, would not even let him bleed out and die. That would not be in keeping with the will of Mammon, nor in keeping with the will of the one who forged them. Not truly.

Still, Michael kept trying until exhaustion and pain swelled like a black tide and he lost consciousness.

— CHAPTER 38 —

The Weak Link

Gold.

Gold was the first thing Michael saw when he managed to open his eyes again. Gold strewn all around, gold at his wrists holding him upright. Gold cutting into his flesh and drawing a trickle of blood from his flesh, red mixed with sparks of whirling white.

That was new.

What had happened? Michael blinked blearily and then it all came rushing back. Mammon. The Cave.

The chains that bound him.

He thrashed against them again, raging at his incarceration, embracing the pain, anything to take his mind away from the ugly truth that he had been the reason a girl had died, and not just any girl.

Hannah's partner.

Michael fell to his knees once more, the chains jerking him up abruptly before he could hit the ground. He blacked out again.

Twice more he came to and twice more he raged against his chains until he passed out. The next time he woke up, however, he'd exhausted himself to the point that he could no longer ignore his thoughts. They came boiling out of the darkness and began gnawing at him.

Michael hung from his chains, knees on the ground, gasping for air until he recovered somewhat. The gold beneath his fingertips as he clung to his chains for support was cooler now, outside of Mammon's presence.

He ran his fingers over each link, remembering Mammon's words. He had opted to work overtime, but only so he could afford to take Christine on a vacation she had wanted. Was that really greed?

Something pinched his fingers. Michael flinched back. What was that? He looked more closely. A tiny gap had appeared. The seam where the link had been forged! Michael tugged experimentally at it, but it didn't budge any further.

His mind raced.

Mammon hadn't lied, not entirely. Everyone was a mix of desires, but desire was not, in and of itself bad. Especially when one desired good things for other people, or for everyone. Maybe the problem was when the greed for wealth put the self above the rest of humanity.

Maybe that was the true nature of Mammon's power.

And if it was…Michael thought. What else had the archdemon said? Something about Sara and the flowers he had bought her. Yes! Mammon implied that Michael had done it because he wanted Sara for himself, but that wasn't possible. Michael didn't even realize the scope of his feelings for her until today. So he couldn't have been that calculating! That was an incredibly weak link in Mammon's chain.

Michael flexed again. This time he felt the chains respond, several links weakening and expanding. What else? Michael ran through his memories, plucking out every one where he had done something nice for someone else, every kind word, every selfless act. He was no saint, but there was no dearth of memories for him to draw upon, and each and every one made his skin tingle as the gold of his chains grew duller and duller, and became more and more brittle, until at last…

The chains snapped!

Michael roared in victory, a primal sound, and his wings answered, manifesting fully from his back for the first time since he'd awoken in the Cave of Mammon. His reflection was reflected in gold and glory and he could see that his eyes were two pits of pure white flame.

Pure white flame.

Michael conjured his sword. It, too, was of pure white, and, if anything, burned even hotter than before. The gold in it was gone, forfeit to Mammon by virtue of their deal. Michael smiled. The demon would regret this deal. Not only had it refined Michael's fire, the fact that the gold was gone meant the demon would be bound not to harm Sara or Hannah!

He flared his wings. Now all he needed to do was return to the mortal world and find his sister and Sara. Then they could see about stopping Mammon's plan, for once and for all!

Michael spread his wings and flew.

CHAPTER 39

The Tortoise

A ring of pure white flame suddenly opened in front of the stained and dirty brickwork that made up the back of the Golden Crescent restaurant in Washington DC. Ancient cooking oil, slopped over the ground by generations of overworked employees smoked but fortunately didn't catch fire from the supernatural flames that vanished as swiftly as they had appeared, leaving a tall figure standing unbent, unbowed, and unbroken behind.

Michael took in a deep breath of city air. Though it stank and was poisoned with petrochemicals, the scent of sewer gas, and too much afternoon heat, it was invigorating after the stultifying atmosphere of the Cave of Mammon.

He pulled out his phone and quickly dialed Sara. After a long conversation in which he answered increasingly obscure questions to convince her and Hannah that, yes, it really was him, he agreed to meet them at a nearby diner.

The night air was cool on his skin, especially his wrists where the golden chain had burned into his flesh. Michael actually enjoyed the walk. It gave him time to get used to his body. He felt lighter, somehow, but also denser. Not purified as such—could the touch of an archdemon ever be called purifying?—but annealed, maybe. Like a metal becoming stronger through the application of carbon grit and fire.

It was good to be alive! And free! Michael threw his head back and laughed.

Mammon had no idea what was coming for him!

There was a spring in his step as he pushed his way into the Comely Comet Diner. His eyes scanned the various seating options. Sara and Hannah should be here already. If they got a car somehow, anyway.

It wasn't a large place, but it was twisty with high-backed booths and tables jammed into all of the odd corners. There was that particular feel to the air, slightly greasy but vivacious, the mark of a good diner.

It was also surprisingly empty. Michael hoped that wasn't a bad sign. He wanted pancakes. Though fewer people made for fewer chances of calling attention to himself, it also made it easier to spot Hannah and Sara. They had claimed an isolated booth near the southwestern corner.

He paused, staring at his sister. She had no idea what he'd done, how he was involved in Grace's disappearance. How he was responsible for her life going off the rails.

And she wasn't going to know now. There was too much at stake. Aching, he pushed the truth back down into the dark and wrapped it in a box, locked it tight, and forced himself to forget about it. If he survived, then he could tell Hannah what had happened.

Now, there was a demon to deal with.

Michael passed the waitress, motioning that he was with them. The woman just stared at him with blank eyes. She didn't get paid enough to care, and diner tips, while regular, weren't usually that good, so why work at it?

He joined Sara and his sister, ordered coffee and pancakes when the waitress came by, and then settled in to explain what had happened. He told the story quickly, aware both that they had limited time, and that neither his sister nor Sara would be content until they understood what had happened to him. He skimped on the details, but gave them a summary, focusing mainly on what he had learned while he was in Mammon's inner sanctum.

Because that is what had given him hope, and the idea for a way to still save the world from Mammon's clutches.

"Right. I saw something when I was there, in the Cave," Michael said, refocusing the conversation. They were short on time if they were going to act. "We can still pull this off. It'll be highly illegal, morally questionable, and will have serious consequences, but it could work."

"I'm listening," Sara said cautiously.

"You had me at highly illegal." Hannah smiled wryly. "That's where I usually work anyway."

"Yeah, and it got you on several national terrorist watch lists," Michael reminded her. "Not really a sustainable modus operandi."

"No one has caught me yet!" Hannah crossed her arms and quirked an eyebrow in challenge.

"I would have if Gabriel—" Michael paused. It had been easier to say his name than he expected. "—hadn't intervened. I was this close." He held up a finger and thumb a tiny distance apart.

"Skip the sibling rivalry," Sara said, rolling her eyes. "Get to the crimes and misdemeanors."

"More like felonies with a potential side of high treason," Michael said. "Look. It's like this, right? The enemy's entire plan hinges on blocking the vote, right? Normally to pass legislation a bill would need a simple majority. 51 votes. But they've adjusted the rules. As long as there are more votes for than against, it will pass. Abstentions or absences won't count. The whole plan was to eliminate Smith in order to tip the scales one way, so…"

"…so we tip it back," Sara said slowly. "But not by killing anyone. That's a step too far."

"We don't have to," Hannah pointed out. "I can't believe I'm the one saying this, but all we need to do is kidnap a senator. One of the sure votes. Or one who was using their influence to make sure some of their fellow politicians would vote the way they wanted. If we choose the right target, we could shift things by several votes in our favor!"

"That." Michael pointed a finger at Hannah. "I guess it's at least a bit genetic."

"Say that I even consider this," Sara began slowly, running a glance over their surroundings to make sure no one and nothing could overhear them. "Who is the target? And what is the plan? Because this will not be easy to pull off. Especially with what happened to Smith. Every other politician in this city is going to be locked down. Like fucking Fort Knox."

"That just makes it fun," Hannah said.

"Behave," Michael admonished his sister. "We don't all get our thrills scaling buildings to escape justice."

"That just means you're boring."

"Can we focus please?" Sara tapped the table between them all, shaking the coffee.

Hannah and Michael both looked at her.

"What?" Sara glared at them. "You want *me*, the *cop*, to suggest the target?"

"You're the one with an interest in politics," Michael pointed out.

"Fine!" Sara huffed. "The best one would be—"

"The tortoise one, right?" Hannah volunteered. "He's in charge, right?"

"*Senator Mitchell* is, yes," Sara confirmed. "He'd be the most effective, but that could hurt us. Him disappearing might prompt them to reschedule the vote altogether and launch a full-scale manhunt. No. We want someone with influence, but not someone that big."

"So who would you pick?" Michael asked. "Hypothetically. If you wanted to disrupt the vote as much as possible."

Sara thought, idly stirring her half-cup of coffee. She added more sugar. Then more cream.

"It should be either Senator Cleeves or Senator Tyler-Price. Both of them have influence. There's no way they aren't strong-arming several junior senators to keep them in line, and they won't have the same security on them as other potential options."

"Is Tyler-Price the one that insists on carrying her gun with her in her purse? Even on the senator floor?" Hannah grinned. "I can almost respect that."

"We should go with Cleeves then," Michael said. "He's less likely to be armed, at least."

Cleeves was a young man, determined to rise in the party ranks. His influence in the chamber came mainly from his good looks and charismatic personality. As far as Michael knew, he had all the morals of a cat in heat, but that didn't really make him less effective as a politician.

"I agree," Sara said. "Tyler-Price is too unpredictable. People like that are the worst to try and handle. Cleeves is an asshole, but he's a pretty boy and not much else, from what I can tell. I don't see him putting up much of a fight."

"Too bad," Hannah said, running her finger around the rim of her cup. "I like a man to have a bit of fight in him."

"I did not need to hear that." Michael shook his head. "Right. Hypothetically—" He glanced around to make sure the waitress was still staring at her phone near the entryway. She was. "—how would we go about securing the target?"

They proceeded to outline and discard several plans. They were hampered by a lack of concrete knowledge, but between Sara's contacts in local law enforcement and knowledge of political procedure, Hannah's shady past and Resistance resources, and the insights Michael's time in the Cave of Mammon provided, they slowly sketched together the outlines of a workable plan.

And Michael tucked away two orders of pancakes over the duration of the discussion.

"There is something deeply wrong about all of this," Sara complained when they had finally settled on a plan. "I'm a cop, damnit. I'm supposed to uphold the law, not break it."

"Ends and means." Hannah shrugged. "Sometimes you have to do bad things to accomplish good ones."

"I'm not sure I should be taking career advice from the assassin and terrorist," Sara replied, though she quirked up one side of her mouth to take a bit of bite out of the words.

"*Suspected* terrorist," Hannah corrected.

"It has to feel good to be free of some of the restrictions at least," Michael said. "I know you have more of them to operate than we did at the agency, and even I've found it kind of refreshing to just…see something that needs to be fixed and go fix it."

"That's not usually why I break the law," Hannah said, "but I suppose I can see the appeal."

"That's exactly why you break the law," Michael said. "What are you talking about?"

"Well, yeah, but my way is less…" Hannah waved her hand at Michael and Sara, "coppy."

"Stop saying that like it's a bad thing!" Michael threatened his sister with his fork.

"Isn't it?" Hannah challenged. "How good was either of your workplaces, when you got right down to it? Hmm?"

"She has a point," Sara admitted. "Both the precinct and the agency are pretty full of corruption." She shook her head. "Not that that should be the way it works! And it's no justification for just striking out on your own like some kind of insane vigilante. You two are terrible influences!" Then she sighed. "But that's the only thing that seems to be effective in the face of insane supernatural entities and fucking archdemons, so, sure. Let's go do something wrong to make something right!"

CHAPTER 40

Ends and Means

The office of Senator Cleeves was garish and lavishly decorated, all red and gold, with period furniture for both the waiting room chairs and the receptionist's desk. Michael had seen pictures of the inside of the senator's chambers as well, and they were equally ornate. It had been a minor scandal a few years ago, in fact, considering that the taxpayer had to foot the redecoration bill.

Little surprise then, that Cleeves was bought and paid for by Mammon himself.

Michael wore the mind-mannered brown of a courier. It was a solid disguise. It gave him a reason to be in the office without an appointment. It got him easily past security. No one gave him a second look. There were always couriers running to and from the offices. The business of government and all that.

Sara and Hannah had gone to a bit more trouble with their disguises. Hannah was in a wheelchair, a knitted lace shawl around her shoulders that was enchanted to make her look like an old woman. A very rich old woman. Sara was dressed simply but professionally as her private, for-hire nurse.

The two had almost come to blows, fighting over who would have to sit in the wheelchair and play the old woman. Neither Sara nor Hannah liked the idea of pretending to be frail and weak. And to be fair, neither had the temperament to be really convincing at it. That illusion of Hannah's was doing a lot of heavy lifting.

"Priority item for the senator," Michael said, stepping up to the receptionist. "Is he available at the moment?"

The receptionist, a good-looking young woman with an earpiece held up one finger for him to wait as she finished the call she was on. Michael took the opportunity to glance over her form with his Sight.

Not a demon. Michael felt himself relax slightly. There were a few spirits around here, and gaping maws where her eyeballs should be, but she was mortal. Apparently, Cleeves didn't rate a supernatural bodyguard. Good. That would make this easier.

The woman finished her call.

"I'll accept the delivery," she said in a bored monotone. "The senator is preparing for an important vote and—"

"I know," Michael interrupted. "This is top priority related to that issue. I was told—"

"Excuse me, young lady," Hannah broke in, the illusion morphing her voice to a controlled contralto, something smoothed with decades of use into a tool to command the lower classes, "but I have been waiting here for far too long. Do you have any idea who I am?"

Michael stepped back as Hannah kicked off, providing him with a welcome distraction. The receptionist was trying to get the old woman in front of her to hush. Hannah was having far too much fun playing the role of entitled old biddy to the hilt, shouting about how the senator was in the service to his donors.

Because she was clearly rich and clearly entitled, the secretary was trying her best to placate the old woman without causing too much of a fuss. Politicians ran on donations and no one who worked for one wanted to ever, *ever* be the reason that a source for campaign funding dried up.

It was like using Mammon's own power against him, in a way. Michael smiled and slipped through the door into the senator's office unobserved.

Senator Cleeves was lounging behind his offensively oversized desk. He was staring at his phone, eyes glassy, headphones in, as his hands moved beneath the immaculate surface stacked with neat piles of files and folders, all untouched.

Unlike the senator.

Cleeves gave a start as Michael entered. His face went red, but before he could begin to bluster Michael walked forward, head slightly down as if he'd been looking at the parcel in his hands all along.

It was a relief as much as anything else. While the senator was fully human, his body was positively swarming with parasitic spirits. There were green lamprey-like things sucking at his eyeballs and chitinous things like bone spiders scurrying across his hands leaving trails of blood. Worst of all, the man was practically surrounded by a cloud of golden leeches with leathery wings, each of which repeatedly nipped down to have a little nibble at the man.

Michael had to turn off his sight just to get a clear view of Cleeves himself.

"Priority courier item, sir," he said respectfully as if nothing were happening. "I'm told to tell you it is in regards to the vote."

"The vote?' Cleeves asked, quickly struggling to return himself to presentability. "Let me have it." He held out a hand imperiously.

There certainly wasn't anything wrong with his poise, Michael reflected.

"Sure," Michael said. "Here it is."

He passed over the parcel. Cleeves accepted it and went to tear it open, but before he got that far his eyes rolled up in the back of his head and he passed out.

Whatever Hannah had dosed that package with it was strong stuff. Michael was careful not to brush up against it as he carefully wheeled the senator and his chair back and out of the way so he could access the man's computer. If he had any luck…yes!

It was unsecured. No password needed. Michael quickly brought up the man's emails and scanned through them, then did the same with his contacts folder, copying over several key names and numbers.

Cleeves was the head of a small knot of senators he was whipping on behalf of Senator Mitchell and Mammon. With Cleeves out of the way, Michael could send off a few discreet messages, letting those senators know ahead of time that Cleeves had no intention of showing up for the vote and would, in fact, be de facto abstaining from the issue.

Without Cleeves breathing down their necks, most of the other senators were likely to break away as well. Most politicians realized the problems that would arise if they failed to raise the debt ceiling, including a potential run on the dollar. Mammon might greatly desire such a thing but most of the senators? The people who had huge sums invested in their careers and in fortunes tied to the prosperity of this country, they wanted nothing to do with that.

It was only the mega-rich, Mammon's select faithful, that were positioned to take advantage of the utter chaos that would result from a broken debt ceiling and a default on the dollar.

Michael finished sending off the messages and cocked an ear. Hannah was still complaining, but the volume of her voice had reduced. She'd likely had to tone it down in order to let the confrontation play out longer, buying Michael the time he needed.

He turned back to the senator. The man was still unconscious. Michael went to heft him up by the shoulder and start to carry him out of the office when his gut twisted.

Something was wrong.

Michael immediately looked through the room with his Sight. The small horde of winged leeches was swirling agitatedly above the senator's unconscious form like a cloud of demonic starlings, shifting and changing, holding almost one shape, then almost another, until something in the arrangement *clicked* and Michael suddenly felt a familiar presence.

Michael? What are you doing back here, Michael?

It was Mammon. The sense of his presence was undeniable, but Michael had the feeling the archdemon couldn't quite focus on him. Maybe the leeches were too weak to bear the greater spirit's full power. Whatever the case, Michael knew what he was doing.

He smiled, raised both hands, and flipped the fucker off.

Then his sword of pure white flame was in his hands and he began raking it ruthlessly through the cloud of leeches, turning them into small, crispy curls of sizzling flesh that quickly burned away to floating grey ask.

They smelled absolutely disgusting.

Michael? Michael! Stop! I—

But too many of the lesser spirits had perished. They could no longer support the weight of Mammon's regard. The little things burst away and fled, leaving the one who had fed them so well for so long alone in the care of the terrible being with the sword of alabaster flame.

The bone spiders and eyeball lampreys stayed where they were, but neither seemed to have any particular connection to Mammon, so Michael left them. He didn't want to risk putting out the senator's eyes or lopping off his hands.

Yet.

Michael thought quickly. He moved the senator back into place behind his desk and propped him up in a casual pose, carefully closing the man's rolled-back eyes. Then he picked up the phone, hit the receptionist button, and issued a gruff command.

"Just send her in. I can spare a minute."

Michael then crossed the room, grabbed control of the door, and pulled it open just wide enough to allow Sara and Hannah inside. The receptionist said something, but Michael didn't hear it, closing the door firmly and locking it for good measure.

"Quickly," he said. "We need to get the senator out of here. Mammon noticed something is going on. Not sure how much."

Hannah sprang out of the wheelchair and transferred the senator into her place. She draped the shawl around his shoulder and suddenly the old woman was once again occupying her mobile throne.

Though now she looked like she was asleep.

Sara would be able to wheel the senator right out the way she came in. Hannah would take Michael's place as the courier, so all the logs would line up and the security camera footage wouldn't do jack to help anyone trying to track them.

"Spirits?" Hannah asked, looking around the office.

"Several. I took care of most of the problematic ones." Michael also scanned their surroundings. "If you spot any that look like little gold flying leeches, deal with them. Mammon seems to have some kind of connection to them. No telling how much they could be telling him."

Michael spotted one hovering near the bookcase and skewered it. There were probably more hiding just outside the windows, but so long as none were close enough to overhear them or track their progress, good enough.

As they talked, Hannah donned a charm and stole Michael's courier hat. Her form shifted into one that mirrored his and she grinned.

It was strange seeing her smile on his face.

"You're having too much fun with this," he accused.

"No reason not to." She shrugged. "If you don't love your work, it's a pretty miserable life."

"Yeah, well, you don't have to love it quite *so* much," Michael said.

"I'm ready here," Sara said, giving the senator in his wheelchair an experimental push. "Not that much heavier than you, Han. Go figure."

"Maybe you need to diet," Michael quipped.

"Maybe Cleeves needs to hit the gym," Hannah retorted. "The citizens of this country certainly pay enough for him to have access to that ridiculous one they all use."

"You've been?" Sara glanced over.

"I didn't kill anyone."

"Obviously not. That would have made the news." Sara shook her head.

"Missed opportunity then," Hannah tugged her hat down. "Ready? No point in standing around waiting for someone to catch us. And that secretary looked *pissed* to be locked out of the room. We'll need to keep an eye on her."

"You two head out. I'll play decoy, let them all come after me." Michael looked out the window, eyes scanning for enemies.

There were sure to be several out there, close by.

Sara left first, with Hannah playing the part of the gallant courier, holding the door for her and the "old woman."

"No more visitors," Michael called, approximating Cleeves's voice as best he could before closing the door firmly once more with a *click*.

Michael glanced out the window. Yeah. He was going to have company soon.

Spirits had begun to swarm like locusts before his Sight. He'd managed to get someone's or something's attention! Probably Mammon, but possibly one of The Ten or Mammon's pet demons. Now to make good use of it while he could.

Sara and Hannah had made their respective exits. Michael waited for them to be well and truly on their way, checked to be sure the door was locked, and rolled his shoulders. Then he threw open the windows, summoned his wings, and leapt into the sky.

Let them try to catch him!

CHAPTER 41

Deadly Mind Games

Michael landed atop a residential building, one of the smaller ones. It was only six or seven stories high. His shoulders burned with the effort of flying. It felt amazing, even when dodging demons and attacking spirits, but he was not yet used to it. Something to work on, if he survived this.

He took a deep breath and massaged his left shoulder. The tips of his fingers tingled with the pure-white sparks that danced across them. The sword of flame felt even more like an extension of himself now, an extension of his own will. The place in his mind from which he accessed the art of no-sword was easier and easier to find. It still slipped; he still struggled to stay in that place, but it was easier to get there.

Michael was certainly getting a lot of practice, and it seemed like he was about to get some more. Two demons landed on the rooftop to either side of him. One was a lithe man, slim and oily looking, while the other was a woman that wouldn't have been out of place on the Olympic hammer-throwing team. Both had eyes like molten gold.

That put Michael immediately on the edge. Gold said Mammon. Between the leeches in Senator Cleeves's office and the other spirits and demons he'd dealt with between there and here, gold meant danger. Gold meant Mammon might take a hand at any moment.

"Where's the senator, half-breed?" The woman all but growled at him.

"Senator? I'm confused." Michael pretended confusion, hoping it would irritate the woman into making a stupid move.

It did. She loosed a scream and lunged at him. Michael easily dodged, his wings carrying him to the side, but his instincts flared and he reached for the edge of infinite possibility that was the art of no-sword.

He grasped it just in time, seeing that the other demon, the skinny one, had slipped into the shadows and was going to rise out of Michael's own shadow to try and stab him—a disabling strike.

Interesting. They really did need him, presumably to tell them where the senator was.

Alabaster fire flared in Michael's hands and he easily countered the demon's blade of shadow, though he frowned when the contact struck golden sparks rather than dissolved the darkness entirely. Something about that particular hue...

"Lord Mammon has gifted us with a measure of your own power, half-breed," the skinny demon gloated. "Your weapon is useless."

"Not entirely," Michael said, blocking a strike from the woman. "And I suspect that even if Lord Mammon gave you some of my power and some of his own, you'll struggle to use either without a head."

The demon hissed at his bravado.

Michael lunged, driving his sword forward in a series of quick, furious attacks. The demon fell back, scrambling for the nearest shadow and disappearing into it.

Yeah. They may have a bit of extra power, but there was no way they had anything like invulnerability. And if Michael could cut them, he could kill them.

Especially if they were trying to take him alive for information. Michael had no such compunctions, no such restrictions. Though there was an opportunity here if he could manage it. A bit of information—

Michael's train of thought was derailed by the pile driver the woman drove at him, the full force of her considerable strength behind it. He dodged again, slipping beneath her grasp and flicking his sword toward her exposed midriff.

He scored a thin line of blood, but she was fast, for all she was the size of a mountain and moved like a steam train. She managed to twist just enough to minimize the wound. She hissed in pain.

"You'll pay for that, little man," she promised him.

"I thought you needed me to answer your questions," Michael taunted. "Can't do that if you knock all my teeth out."

"Drilgir can pull it out of your mind if he has to," she said, cracking her knuckles. "Lord Mammon needs the information. He doesn't need you. Not anymore." Her eyes glimmered with a familiar shade of gold—Michael's shade. "He has the most useful part of you already."

"He'll have trouble doing that without a head," Michael repeated his earlier threat even as he slashed his sword of flame toward a nearby shadow. No-sword had shown him Drilgir emerging from it a split second later.

With Michael's sword in the way, the demon opted not to.

Michael leaped backward, angling himself upward, to catch the edge of the nearby water tower perched on the rooftop. He hauled himself up on the ledge and secured his footing. Fewer shadows, and the high ground if he had to hold off the female demon.

"Sulara," Drilgir snapped, "pull your weight!"

"I am! You're the one who hasn't even come close to landing a blow yet!" Sulara launched herself into the air.

Michael swore. He could see that she was better at flying than he was. Mid-air combat would put him at a disadvantage here. Though his skill could level that playing field to a degree. Enough to handle them both, though?

There was no sense of Mammon's presence, yet. The archdemon's attention must be elsewhere. On the vote? What time was it? Michael glanced at his watch. He needed Mammon to focus on him, not on repairing the damage he and his friends had done to the archdemon's plans.

"It'll take more than fancy flying to get anything out of me," Michael called. "And you can see Cleeves isn't with me, so you'll get nothing there either."

"You know where he's stashed, though," Drilgir said, lunging out of the nest of shadows tangled between the legs of the water tower. "And I'll pry it from your screaming mind as you howl your way to madness."

Michael slashed with his sword, once again drawing sparks as their blades met. He pulled through the motion, graceful as a dancer, and pirouetted into that space at the edge of everything and grabbed for the mindset of no-sword.

He managed just in time, and Drilgir had not let up his attack, this time, attempting to keep him pinned as Sulara swept in from the side.

Michael's wings flared, steadying his balance as another sword appeared in his off hand. Twin swords of snow-white flame burned through the afternoon air, drawing golden ichor from each of the demons.

Then he stumbled. The weight of Mammon's regard suddenly slammed into his consciousness. The archdemon was looking at him now!

Michael let himself drop, falling to the rooftop once again, letting Drilgir and Sulara swerve awkwardly to keep from hitting one another.

He schooled his mind. There were secrets within that he couldn't allow Drilgir to catch sight of. How the fuck was that fair, anyway? Mindreading? Michael was still too new to this world, there were too many things he didn't know.

Michael poked at the part of his brain that once held the knot of information he'd purchased at the goblin market. There were faint ideas there, small residues of memory. Nothing explicit, but maybe something he could work with.

There were layers to it. There were layers to the mind as well. Even if Drilgir could eventually drill down deep to Michael's most tightly held secrets, to do so he would first have to pass through the upper levels of Michael's thoughts.

So he'd make sure there was an attractive answer right there for Drilgir to see, if the demon did get lucky. He wouldn't be able to access the art of no-sword, this would be too distracting, so it was a gamble, but better that than betraying—Michael quashed the thought and put his decoy firmly in place.

No risks.

Michael slashed wildly above his head, predicting that Sulara would dive down right after him. He was right and the demoness was forced to pull up. Then he angled himself to a section of the roof free of shadows other than his own and turned so the sun was at his back.

His shadow stretched out in front of him. Sulara was off to his left. If she moved behind him, he'd have a problem, but for now he had a line on each of his enemies.

"Stop running!" The demoness bellowed and charged at him again, summoning twin axes of sooty red flame.

Sulara flung each at him, one after another, and they turned into spinning disks of red death. Michael parried one, then the other, only to narrowly manage to deflect the unexpected third. A fourth and fifth came whizzing toward him as well.

How deep was this woman's will? Or was she just channeling pure rage in its place? Those fires burned erratically and hotter than expected.

Shadow! Movement at the corner of his vision triggered a reflex in Michael and his sword of flame slashed downward. There was a screech of agony and Drilgir's hand went sailing across the rooftop to land in a small puddle of gold ichor. The blade of shadow grasped in its fingers began to slowly dissolve as the hand, separated from its owner, finally began to spark and catch fire.

It burned whitely.

"You'll pay for that!" Sulara cried, launching herself bodily at Michael.

Fuck. Michael dropped the mantra running through his head for an instant, long enough to reach for the edge of everything and nothing and the art of no-sword. Sulara moved toward him, time began to flow like honey, and Michael's will erupted into twin swords of blazing white fire.

The first, Sulara parried easily with her axes, but the second caught her by surprise, blooming from Michael's off hand and rooting itself in her neck. Michael twisted his wrist and Sulara's head went flying through the air.

Then he began frantically chanting his mantra again, because in that split-second he had dropped his defenses to reach for no-sword, he had seen Drilgir moving in the shadows.

Pain like a viper's bite struck him through the ankle. Drilgir's nails had pierced his skin, drawing blood—and perhaps a bit more—from Michael.

Michael answered the indignity by bringing both of his swords down toward the demon. What had the demon seen? The thought screamed through his mind, sending his heart hammering almost through his rib cage.

"Ha!" Drilgir leapt backward, evading the blow Michael had aimed for his head. "Not much in there. Easy to see what you were hiding!"

Michael's heart froze in his chest. If the demon had seen the true outline of his plan...

"See you in church, half-breed," the demon mocked before slipping into the shadows, one hand still clamped about the stump at the end of his right arm.

All that was left behind were a few drops of golden ichor.

Church. Resistance Headquarters. That had been the mantra running through Michael's mind. "Don't let them find Resistance Headquarters." The sense of the place was threaded through it, inevitably, and the demon might have found some of the defenses in Michael's mind as well. It was impossible to separate everything out.

But still. There had been no mention of Cleeves. No mention of Hannah.

Or Sara.

Michael wanted to breathe a sigh of relief because it sounded like his plan was still safe, but he couldn't afford to. Mammon might still be watching through other agents. There were plenty of spirits all around, always.

So Michael ran to the edge of the roof and leapt off, his wings carrying him up and on, as he made a beeline for Resistance Headquarters.

He had a feeling they'd welcome his presence soon enough.

CHAPTER 42

The Resistance Under Siege

The church that housed The Resistance headquarters was surrounded in two worlds.

It was a subtle thing in the real world. Michael could see a couple of vans parked strategically nearby, a few people whose body language said subtly to him that they were undercover officers of some kind, things like that. What kind of action might be planned Michael couldn't say for certain, but something was up. There were too many resources deployed here for it to be any other way.

The Spirit World was much more obvious when he turned his eyes to look beyond the veil. Flocks of spirits swirled above the church, though something—probably the wards—kept them from getting too close. Flickers of gold could be seen here and there in the moving masses, likely agents of Mammon. There were demons present as well, some in locations that even looked familiar to Michael.

He paused to confirm. Yes. Some of the people he suspected of being plainclothes agents were also demons. Mammon was definitely investing some serious resources here,

Good. Let the archdemon waste them. Though if he also wanted to deal a serious blow to The Resistance, this might be it.

Michael gnawed on his lower lip. This was actually a lot larger a response than he expected.

Help them, Michael.

"Gabriel?" Michael's head whipped around, but there was no sign of the angel, in either the real world or the spirit world.

He strained his senses. The voice had only been a whisper but he had been so sure it was Gabriel. Was he alive, somehow? Or speaking to him from, what, Heaven?

Michael still couldn't quite bring himself to countenance the idea. Even having seen the Cave of Mammon—or perhaps because he had experienced it directly—Michael didn't have the sense that Heaven, at least as the church preached about it, was a real place.

But what did he know? These were uncharted frontiers he'd only discovered recently. But with Gabriel gone, there was no one left to explain these things to him.

Not unless he was willing to return to the goblin market and barter away who-knows-what for more knowledge. Michael shivered. No. That was not a cost he was ready to pay.

Michael stepped through the Veil to the Spirit World. Reaching so frequently for the edge of nothing and everything had somehow made this easy as well. Where before he'd need an elaborate working of runes and spells like Hannah, now he moved between worlds with just a flick of his wings.

He summoned his sword with a thought and launched himself into the air. Mammon had invested a noticeable amount of power here. Michael was going to make sure that that investment went bust. It wouldn't bankrupt the archdemon, but hopefully it would bloody his nose a bit.

Michael winged his way to a small swarm of spirits circling on the outside of the mass coiling around the church, held at bay by the wards. Drawing closer, he could see they were similar to the winged leeches that had swarmed around Senator Cleeves. These were larger, however, and most lacked the gold coloring he expected. A few flashes of gilding deeper within the mass, however, convinced him Mammon was still pulling the strings here, somehow.

This close to the church Michael could see larger spirits driving swarms of smaller ones against the wards of the church. Spirits flared and sizzled, and the wards flickered in and out of visibility, faster than his eyes could track the shapes that made up the magical protections.

Some kind of attack designed to break them, eventually.

Well, Michael could make that tactic a lot more difficult. He just needed to burn through a chunk of the assembled spirits here. So, sword flaming in his hand, Michael began to swoop through the spirits, grasping the edge of no-sword as frequently as he could to rain down absolute carnage around him. Soon ash and ichor rained down around the perimeter of the wards and Michael swooped and dived through the spirits like a hunting hawk through a flock of starlings.

His predations did not go unnoticed, however. How could they? Spirits were burning, flaming out of existence across the sky above the church, and several demons were surrounding the place besides. Soon, Michael spotted three winging their way towards him, each with glimmering golden eyes, though the feeling of Mammon's presence remained absent.

Michael was ready. The art of no-sword burned at his fingertips along with the flame of his weapon, and these demons were not so skilled as the two that had so recently cornered him on the rooftop.

Once he had dealt with them, Michael glanced to the church. The wards glowed without interruption now, and the crowds of spirits had thinned greatly. A few glimmering flickers of gold told him Mammon was still at work, but he had bought the wards time.

Now to see what he could do in the real world as well.

Michael landed and stepped back into the real world through the veil. It felt right to do it that way, for some reason.

The first thing he noticed was that there was increased activity from the plainclothes agents he had noticed before, and several more unremarkable vans were pulling up into positions around the church.

Something was about to happen.

But the feeling of Mammon's attention was still absent. That bothered Michael. He needed the archdemon looking at him. He'd need to do something dramatic to get that attention.

After he figured out what was going on here in the real world.

Invisibility would have been nice, but that wasn't a trick Michael had learned yet. But he knew how these sorts of operations worked. He knew what communications gear would be employed, and had a very good idea of how to go about tapping into that network.

Michael studied the massing agents, walking quickly around the perimeter of the church until he found a likely target. A man was standing on his own, out of easy sight of either of the two unmarked vans nearby that contained waiting tactical teams, or possibly a command nexus.

That would do.

Michael moved along the sidewalk, angling himself so that his target never got a good look at his face, in case the agents had been briefed about Michael's dramatic exit from his previous employment situation. He almost needn't have bothered. Most of the man's attention was on the church, his eyes locking on everyone going in or coming out. Those were his suspects, his targets. Michael was just another guy on the street.

He should have paid more attention to his surroundings.

Michael slid in behind the man right after walking past, locking his arm around the agent's throat and quickly cutting off any hope the man had of making a sound or drawing a breath. There was a bit of a struggle, but Michael now had more than mortal strength in his arms and the man went limp and unconscious quickly.

Lowering the man to the ground, Michael made sure he was safely bundled out of sight beneath some nearby greenery, and then plucked the earpiece from the unconscious man and affixed it to his own ear. The radio he clipped to the back of his belt and covered with his jacked.

"—teams 5 and 6 are in place. Confirmed. Teams 5 and 6 are good to go. Waiting on confirmation from local law enforcement about deployment of their forces."

Things were about to kick off, but he still had some time. He was about to click through the other frequencies when a familiar voice answered the woman who had just been talking in Michael's ear.

It was Tanner!

For a moment Michael just reveled in hearing the familiar voice in his ear, as he had before on so many missions. Then his mind caught up with not only what Tanner was saying but how he was saying it.

His old team was in charge of this operation?

"—tell them to get the lead out!" Tanner snapped, more irritated than Michael had ever heard him. "We don't know exactly what this terror cell is planning but all indications are it's a major action and it's happening imminently. Make sure everyone has an image of Senator Cleeves on hand. I don't want any mistakes! There's no room to fuck up on this one—"

So Mammon had fallen for Michael's trick. Good. He felt a smile split his face like a razor.

It didn't last long. The archdemon had also pulled in Michael's old team. That they were still here—or that Tanner was, at least—meant that Garibaldi hadn't buried them all for Michael's desertion, which was good.

That Tanner was clearly in charge was even better. There's no way Garibaldi would risk a mission like this being led by a potential traitor, not with the higher-ups breathing down his neck as much as they had to be right now. No, Tanner and the rest of the team had to be safe, had to have passed whatever tests Garibaldi had put them through, after.

And if Tanner was here…Michael resumed his pacing around the perimeter of the church, keeping out of sight as he did. Was Garibaldi stupid enough to send his team out in his old van? The man was lazy and never changed anything if he could help it. He called it protecting taxpayer dollars, but it was just as much about his own sloth as anything else.

Not that one. Nor that. Michael glanced from license plate to license plate. He'd been in the damned van often enough that he should recognize…there!

Michael turned on his heel and went into a nearby bodega, watching the van through the window as he quickly browsed along the few aisles. His mind gnawed at the trap Mammon had set for him. He had friends on both sides of this conflict, and Tanner and Priestly and the others being here meant that Mammon had to have a hand around their hearts.

If he were the archdemon, how would he—?

There had to be someone new in that van. A demon at Mammon's command. It couldn't be hard. A few donations, advancing the career of the right person, and Michael himself had left a hole in the team that demanded to be filled.

It would be too easy.

And it made Michael's work here exponentially harder. Because his team were good people, and there was no way Michael could bring himself to sacrifice them, even for the greater good. He just couldn't do that.

Fucking demons. Michael resisted the urge to spit. No. He needed to deal with this. And quickly.

His eyes scanned the shelves, a crazy idea coming to him all at once, fully formed in his mind, like something out of the dreams of a deranged frat boy.

Michael grinned. He could get his old team out of harm's way, take what was likely one of Mammon's strongest pieces off of the board, and send the attack on The Resistance into disarray all in one move, if he did this just right.

He started grabbing items. He'd need to move incredibly fast to pull this off, but fortunately he was faster than any man alive, right now, so that shouldn't be too much of a problem.

He'd need an accomplice, but that should be easy enough in a city like New York as well. Michael grinned and struck up a quick conversation with the man behind the bodega counter. People always knew people who were looking for a quick bit of work. And if it was easy, too? Why not?

In very short order Michael was equipped with everything he needed and had a young man following him, eager to earn a few more hundred-dollar bills like the one Michael had already slipped into his hand.

Something about that felt right to Michael, using money to hurt Mammon, even if it was indirect.

Michael's lips tightened. The archdemon wanted to use his old team against him? Fuck that. Michael would figure out a way to save his friends, save Resistance headquarters, yank Mammon's attention back here, where he wanted it to be, then give the gilded old goat the ass-kicking of the millennium.

CHAPTER 43

Unholy Shit!

"We're going to prank my friends," Michael explained to his hired minion as they walked. "They're hanging out in the back of their van over there." He pointed to the surveillance van he was sure Tanner and the rest of the command team were sitting in. "Keys are tucked up underneath the seat, there's a little box velcroed there. Take 6th, turn right, and drive us to the parking garage—" Michael rattled off instructions, including giving the guy a quick exit plan, so he didn't risk any confrontation if Michael's "friends" didn't "take it well."

"I got you." The young man smiled. "I know what to do. You can count on me."

Michael peeled off several more bills and passed them to the guy with a smile and a laugh. He barely even had to force it. Part of him was looking forward to this.

For more than one reason.

There was no one sitting in the front of the van. Standard procedure. Someone lounging in a van attracted attention. A nondescript parked van drew less.

His minion signaled that he was ready. Well, no time like the present. Michael held up a finger, counted to three, then nodded for him to go.

Michael took a deep breath and reached for the edge of nothing and everything. This was going to strain his budding mastery of the art of no-sword to the utmost, but he couldn't afford to have this turn into an extended car chase. Possibilities flickered before his eyes, branching fractals of the movements his sword *could* make. Michael pressed past them all. None were enough. A bead of sweat broke out on his forehead.

There!

His sword of alabaster flame flared to life for just a second in his hand. Michael thrust it forward, twisting himself through dozens of possibilities simultaneously to strike them all with a single blow of his sword. One sword, one moment, a multitude of targets.

There was a scattering of retorts from all directions as dozens of tires popped and hissed into uselessness on each of the security vans surrounding the church. Michael let the sword vanish. No one would be following them now.

Michael took a deep breath, and brought himself to the edge again, in case the first thing they did when he stepped in was fire at him, then hauled the door open and stepped in, slamming it behind him and thumping the ceiling twice to signal his driver.

The engine roared to life. Good. They hadn't changed where they kept the keys. Garibaldi had chosen laziness over security.

Not that there were that many options for storing keys in the cab of a van.

"Michael?" Tanner was staring at him. "What—"

The sentence cut off as the van made a sharp turn.

Michael's eyes flashed over the scene in the interior of the van. Tanner and Priestly were here, yes, but the rest of his team was not. Made sense. The rest of the team was generally more mobile anyway. There was a third person in the command chair, however. Michael presumed it was his replacement.

She was tall and lithe and her eyes glimmered a malicious gold as Michael looked at her. Yeah. She definitely was one of Mammon's get.

"Attention," she snapped, smiling wickedly at Michael, "this is—"

His sword flashed, searing through the cable that connected the microphone to the transmitter. If she'd had an earpiece like Tanner preferred, he might have had trouble, as it was, he cut her off from her radio communications easily.

"I don't think you two are hanging out with the right crowd, these days," Michael said easily.

The van jostled as his driver took another turn too sharply. Michael reached out and easily braced himself with a hand. Tanner and Priestly were hanging on for dear life and his replacement was glaring daggers at him, though she was similarly unbothered by the rollicking motion of the moving vehicle beneath them.

She was a demon after all. Michael kept a close watch on her.

"Tanner," the demoness said calmly, "radio our situation to—"

"Won't work," Michael cut in. "No one is coming after us. And that signal no longer has an antenna to boost it." He flicked a significant glance up at the ceiling of the van.

It was more bluff than anything else, but if it worked, it worked.

The demoness narrowed her eyes at Michael, then, in a flash, she moved, knocking Priestly aside and pulling Tanner between herself and Michael—a human shield. A dagger of sooty red flame, flickering gold at its core, appeared in her hands, pressed against Tanner's throat.

"Where is the Senator?" She demanded. "Tell me now or your friend gets a new smile."

"Safe," Michael replied, his sword springing into existence. "If you'd like to make sure he—and you—stay that way, I suggest you let my friend go."

The van lurched again and the edge of the demoness's blade sizzled against Tanner's throat. The young man screamed and jerked backward, throwing himself into the demoness. It wasn't enough to unbalance her though.

Michael took a deep breath and reached for the art of no-sword. His concentration shattered, however, when the golden eyes staring at him suddenly took on an ancient and malevolent dimensionality.

Mammon stared out at him from the demoness's eyes.

"Michael," The demoness spoke with Mammon's voice, "return the Senator to me, now, or your friends here will die. You have grown remarkably in skill, that is true. You even managed to escape my domain, no mean feat. Congratulations. But you cannot hope to face me."

"You're not here," Michael said. "You're a long-distance phone call with a bad attitude."

"That doesn't mean I'm not more than capable of ending this mortal's life as easily as you might snuff a candle," Mammon replied.

Michael shot a glance to Tanner, meeting his glance and trying to communicate to the young man that everything was going to be all right. Priestly was lying motionless on the floor. She was breathing, but Michael couldn't see anything more than that. She was unconscious, in shock, or faking it until the chance to act presented itself.

She was also the safest person in the van right now. He needed to get Tanner away from the possessed demoness. There was a spark from that part of his brain that had held the packet of knowledge from the goblin market and the beginnings of a plan took shape in his mind.

"Fine," he barked, causing Mammon to raise one elegantly shaped eyebrow and move the sizzling knife further away from Tanner's throat.

It was still more than close enough to end his life, however. Michael wasn't confident his art of no-sword was a match for Mammon, yet. Not sure enough that he was willing to gamble with Tanner's life.

"I'll make another deal with you," Michael said. "A binding one. You release Tanner, now, and I promise to tell you everything I know about Senator Cleeves's current location and the evidence going out to a select few journalists I think I can trust that will tank PitCoin's market share and value."

"What?" Mammon stared at him.

"What? You didn't think we'd figure out your plan?" Michael shook his head. "You're getting old. Must be slipping. Maybe world domination isn't really for you. Think about taking early retirement. Retire someplace nice and warm."

"Tell me now!" Mammon snapped, eyes suddenly turning into pools of liquid gold. "Tell me now or I will end his life!"

The demoness's face was a contorted mask of pain and fury, the two expressions warring across her visage as tears of molten gold welled up in her eyes and left scorch marks as they trailed down her face.

"That's not the deal on offer, Lord Mammon," Michael emphasized the title. If he was going to make a deal, best make it right. Demons were tricky.

Not as tricky as goblins, but not bad.

But Michael always was a fast learner, and he'd gotten some particularly useful lessons since his eyes had been opened. He knew how to make a deal. He knew what Mammon wanted, and he had a pretty good idea of a few personality flaws he could play on to manipulate the archdemon.

All the power in the world didn't make a blind spot go away.

"Let the man go. Promise he will come to no harm at your hand, directly or indirectly, or by the hand of any of your minions, and I will tell you what I know of Senator Cleeves's location and what I've done to tarnish your precious PitCoin."

"There's nothing you can do," Mammon said, a drop of molten gold running from the demoness's eyes and falling to sizzle on the floor of the van. It would eat through and then fall to the concrete of the parking structure beneath them. They weren't moving any longer. This was as safe as Michael was going to get in terms of fallout and being out of view of the local security cameras.

"If there was nothing I could do, Senator Cleeves would be sitting in session with the rest of the Senate right now, getting ready to vote on the debt ceiling, but he's not, is he?" Michael pressed. "I escaped the Cave of Mammon. I shattered those pathetic chains you attempted to bind me with. I think you need to revise your estimate of just how dangerous I can be."

Michael willed his sword to flare more brightly.

"Besides," he added, "you're not even here. You're puppet master inside a swiftly dissolving shell. Your demoness doesn't look like she'll last much longer at this rate. I reckon I can take you, as it stands."

Tanner was staring at him, eyes wide with hope and fear. Michael had no idea what the young man was seeing, without the Sight proper, but between the flaming sword in Michael's hand and the sheer sense of Mammon's presence, it was kind of a miracle Tanner was still conscious.

"Very well," Mammon hissed. "You have a point. This vessel is flawed. You have a deal."

"And I swear upon my sword I will keep it," Michael said, keeping to the niceties. "Let Tanner take Priestly and leave, and then I will tell you what I know."

Mammon withdrew the dagger, now completely a thing of golden flame, and allowed Tanner to scramble over to Priestly. He gathered her up in a fireman's carry and staggered out of the back door of the van.

"Michael," he said as he passed, "is that—"

"Go," Michael said quietly. "We'll get a beer later and I'll explain."

As much as he thought he could, anyway.

"Where is Cleeves?" Mammon's voice was growing hoarse. "Tell me now! I abjure ye by the accord between us! Tell me now and tell me true!"

"I don't know where Cleeves is," Michael said, a vulpine grin spreading across his face. "Last I saw him he was in the care of an officer of the law and an assassin, though. They were headed West; the Senator was hidden by the illusion of a wealthy female donor and was being pushed around in a wheelchair."

Mammon stared at him. Two more drops of molten gold rolled from the demoness's face to sizzle on the floor of the van.

"You dare," Mammon breathed. "You dare cheat—"

"I didn't cheat," Michael snapped, voice harsh. "I told the truth and I've kept my word to you. I cannot tell you where Cleeves is because we made sure I did not and would not know! He's beyond your reach, and there's no way you'll find him before the vote."

"I don't need Cleeves!" Mammon bellowed. "He is insurance, nothing more! An investment I wish to reap dividends from."

"Even so, your little crypto project won't survive the bombshell we've cooked up for it," Michael taunted the archdemon. "Your little puppets may have stopped my efforts to expose corruption at the agency, but all that did was show me who I couldn't trust. I know better now who will take action."

"You have stolen from me, Michael," Mammon hissed. "Stolen from me and I will have recompense. Even if I must throw good money after bad. I will rip the iron from your blood and forge coins of it, gilded with the gold of the power I have already taken from you."

The demoness's form began to bubble and hiss, burned away by the gold boiling within her veins. There was a series of sharp cracks as bones exploded from her flesh, mammoth and golden. Red-gold muscle wrapped itself around them, then skin as fine as parchment and supple wings as fluid and oily as black gold erupted from her back.

Michael blinked. Mammon himself was tearing free from the shell of the demoness he had possessed! He was manifesting on the mortal world directly!

Unholy shit!

CHAPTER 44

Unchecked Greed

The doors of the van blew outward as if a bomb had gone off. Michael followed shortly after them, propelled by a blow from the newly formed body of the archdemon.

Michael flared his wings and drove the flaming sword of his will deep into the concrete, arresting his movement and regaining control of his trajectory. He came to rest lightly on his feet, one hand out against a nearby sedan to steady himself.

Mammon shouldered his way out of the ruins of the van, the last vestiges of the demoness he had once possessed and then consumed falling away in wet gobbets of flesh. The archdemon flared his wings and a wave of power rolled out from him, setting off car alarms and causing radios to blare into life, as supernatural energy filled the circuits that normally would run high with electricity.

…we're getting early reports of market chaos as a run on stocks is beginning. We haven't seen a hunger for buy-ups on this level since…

…this breaking story, of a bank manager who suddenly grabbed a gun from his own security team and attempted to rob his own bank…

…hints of a bribery scandal…

Unchecked greed was loosed on the world. This was the brave new world Mammon would usher in and rule over. The archdemon's presence was amplifying humanity's baser instincts to unheard-of levels, and, Michael suddenly knew in a flash of knowledge as the last of his barter from the goblin market flared up and ripple through his mind, it was also the aftereffect of the truly massive amount of power Mammon must have had to expend to fully cross the veil and manifest in the real world.

Michael really had pissed him off!

He had no more time to think on the implications, however, as Mammon summoned chains of churning gold, one in each hand,

and lashed out with them like whips. Each of the links was barbed, and the speed with which Mammon lashed them about him made the thought of charging the archdemon not dissimilar from the idea of charging a sentient chainsaw.

Michael's jaw clenched. No choice. He'd wanted Mammon's attention and now he had it. His job here was to keep the asshole busy until the vote was over, and Sara and Hannah could take care of their half of the plan.

He took a deep breath. He reached for the edge of everything and nothing and summoned the art of no-sword to himself. No wavering. No hesitation. He had to find that place and hold there, or Mammon would tear him apart and feast on what was left.

Chains of flaming gold lashed out, testing his defenses, and Michael met each sally easily. White flame sheared through lengths of chain, and splatters of molten gold sprayed all around the two combatants. But there was always more chain, always more gold. Mammon's hoard was eons in the making, and The Ten alone supplied him with staggering reservoirs of wealth to burn for power.

This was just the beginning, however, Mammon flexing muscles long unused. Millennia existing only as a spirit meant it took time to acclimate to physical reality, to muscles and blood and bones, even if those were made of gold.

The chains began flying faster, moving of their own accord mid-lash like striking snakes. Michael danced on the head of a pin, wings flaring and moving him faster than any mere mortal could hope to, and drawing arcs and circles in the air as he flew and ran, braced his feet and parried the chains, thrusting toward Mammon whenever an opportunity presented itself.

They were few and far between.

What is the weakness of greed, Michael?

Gabriel? Michael didn't look. He couldn't look. Any deviation in his attention and the chains would penetrate his defense and wrap him in death dressed in golden flame.

But that didn't mean he couldn't heed the words offering him advice, Gabriel speaking to him from wherever angels go after death.

Greed could not resist going for the things it desired, if they were placed before it in a tempting manner. Mammon wanted the world and had a plan to take it, but Michael held some card that could ruin that. It wasn't quite the same but hopefully it was close enough that he could take advantage.

"Bit sluggish there, Mam," Michael called. "Not used to physical reality? Or did you just eat something that didn't agree with you?"

Mammon hissed in irritation and lashed out with his chains.

Michael danced out of the way, shearing through two more sections of golden links.

"At this rate, you must be consuming your net worth at a ferocious rate. Careful, if you're too spendthrift you might fall off the Top Ten Richest Assholes list!"

"You are becoming more trouble than you are worth, half-thing," Mammon growled. "I will—"

"You don't get to dictate my worth," Michael cut in. "I know it, and there is no coin on Earth or in Hell that you could use to purchase its equivalent." Michael panted through a cocky smile. "You can't afford me. You're not rich enough where it matters."

Mammon howled in fury, the flames of his weapon flaring a deep red-gold, and the archdemon redoubled his efforts.

Michael parried and dodged, surfing the edge of everything and nothing, looking forward and riding a wave of instinct. It was not perfect. He was not perfect. His eyebrows were singed by crimson flame, the barbs of gold drew blood once, then twice, then three and four times. An archdemon's fury was no laughing matter.

He dodged behind a car. A chain of gold blasted through the metal frame of it like it was tissue paper, shredding the metal and showering Michael with shrapnel, sharp and hot.

None of it pierced his skin, however, which was beginning to glow with a pure white light. He was half-spirit, and what was a spiritual existence if not an expression of will—or greed, or lust, or charity—more than anything else?

...a crime wave seems to be sweeping the streets, we have increased reports of armed robbery...

...a riot broke out earlier at the retailer when the manager suddenly and without notice tripled prices...

...stock market in chaos as there is a massive fluctuation in valuations across the board, driven primarily by erratic behavior from...

The radios around Michael continued to blare out examples of greed running wild throughout the city.

How long could Mammon sustain this? It had to be costing the archdemon something to materialize here, otherwise he would simply have done so earlier. Drawing this confrontation out might be another way to hurt him, Michael realized.

But he didn't want to just hurt the archdemon indirectly. This asshole had threatened him, ordered his servants and minions to attack him—to attack Sara! Michael's blood pulsed with the need to hurt Mammon. To draw some good old-fashion blood. To feel the archdemon writhing on the point of his sword.

And Gabriel had given him the tools. Given him the hints.

Michael reached for the art of no-sword, finding that edge of everything and nothing, and this time when he gained the place, he looked not only for physical attacks that were coming, for physical attacks he might be able to land, but at the words he could use, the insults, the taunts, the tantalizing hints that he could throw out to distract the archdemon, to find that gap in defenses that he could then exploit with the art of no-sword.

"I'd say that cheap tricks were beneath you, but I guess that's all you can afford," Michael called out, lashing out with his sword at the same time.

Mammon's fury met him and the two increased the pace of their confrontation, Michael dancing on the edge of everything and nothing, calling our insults and jibes, slashing links and lengths from Mammon's chains, molten gold flying.

It cost him. Small wounds accumulated. Burns. Lacerations. His will was strong but far from indomitable. Still, Michael persisted. He was close. He could feel it.

Then he saw it. A gap in the coiling chains. A hole he could exploit, if he was fast enough. Michael's wings flared and he launched himself into an attack, slipping through the defense and spiraling around Mammon, averting attacks with well-placed blows from his sword, staying in the eye of the hurricane of chains coiling around the archdemon until he was perfectly in place.

He was inside the reach of the chains, as they coiled around and past him. The sword of his will flashed, moving with the speed of thought, and drove itself into Mammon's chest—where it suddenly stuck, the flame held back by the strength of Mammon's golden skin. The flesh around the point of the sword bubbled and melted and ran, but it took time for the metal to melt, and while it did Michael's momentum was gone.

Mammon's eyes locked onto his. The chain in the archdemon's left hand vanished and he backhanded Michael, sending the half-angel flying across the parking garage. The intervening space flashed by, too fast to register in Michael's ringing mind, until he slammed bodily into a black van, the force of his flight crumpling the metal around him and driving the van bodily into a cement support pillar. The car alarm wailed and died in a quick gurgle.

It was like getting hit by a Mack truck. If Michael's flesh were not suffused with his will, it would have broken his jaw, possibly crushed his skull. As it was, every bit of him ached and there was the sharp, coppery taste of blood in his mouth.

He couldn't take too many more hits like that. The force of it had slapped him completely out of the right mindset for no-sword. He reached for it, but before he could get there, his ears pricked up. A bit of good news tugged a smile to his lips.

Michael raised a hand to his lips and wiped away a trail of blood that trickled from them and he pushed his way free from the wreckage of the van around him. Broken glass crunched beneath him, but so much power burned through him now it had no power to cut his flesh. He grinned at Mammon, the archdemon whirling his chains around him in the lead-up to another attack.

"You really should pay more attention," Michael said.

"What?" Mammon's eyes narrowed.

"Don't you listen to the news?" Michael threw an arm back, driving his fist through a nearby window and turning the volume up on the car radio.

…Senate has voted with Congress, ending the standoff and agreeing to raise the debt ceiling…

"Sounds to me like you spent too much time chasing after me and not enough attention on your little plan." Michael spat out some blood. "Your plan has failed. Sorry about that. Maybe you can write the loss off on your taxes."

Michael's smile fell away, however, as the archdemon locked eyes on him. Murderous intent, bloody and stifling, rose all around them, sending waves of primal terror pounding through the parking structure.

"I will end you for this, Michael, and your torment shall be a thing they sing hosannas of in Hell until the end of days," Mammon promised him, eyes bright and burning gold.

CHAPTER 45

The Edge of Everything

Mammon began to chant, words in a strange and burning language rolling off the archdemon's tongue. Pools of gold began to grow from the spatters of metal Michael's conflict with Mammon had splashed about the parking garage. When the pools grew large enough figures began to rise from each, demons and demonesses, spirits of all shapes and forms, though each of them had a glowing gold chain wrapped somewhere around them.

Michael gripped his sword tightly and reached for the edge of everything and nothing. Mammon was calling in backup and he had none. All he had was the memory of Gabriel and the art of no-sword.

A feral smile crept across Michael's face. He'd make sure it was more than a match for anything Mammon could muster. Numbers mattered nothing to the master—or even the journeyman—of the art of no-sword.

He didn't wait for them to finish appearing. It was clear what Mammon would order them to do. There weren't choices in the matter, and if they had not managed to shake off the golden chains that bound them, as Michael had, there wasn't much chance that they'd manage to do so now.

Mammon was concentrating on the words rolling off his tongue. The chains whirled around him, a deadly defense. He could try to take another shot at Mammon while the archdemon was distracted, trying to penetrate the chains, but the first ranks of those beings summoned by the Master of Greed were already moving into defensive positions. The hulking ones, at least. Those of a leaner, hungrier cast were eyeing Michael.

An attack would come soon. So he might as well begin things. Michael willed a second sword to flame into existence in his off hand. A true master wouldn't need it, but for now, he would take any help he could get.

Michael twisted his foot on the ground to brace himself, looked down the line dividing everything from nothing, picked his targets, and exploded into action.

The wind moved through his wings, and he read as much about his surroundings from the air currents as he did with his eyes. There were three dozen forms already present, a third of them hulking brutes taking up defensive positions around Mammon. The rest were a mixture of long and lean and short and fast.

All of them were deadly.

Numbers. Too many numbers. Michael needed to whittle them down first so he didn't get swarmed. He could only maintain his concentration for so long. His will was not inexhaustible.

He plucked three targets from amongst the ranging possibilities. There was a thin woman with golden coiled snakes for hair. She's had no eyes, fortunately, or Michael might have worries about being turned to stone. There was an amorphous cloud of leeches, similar to the ones he'd driven away from the church. And there was a pale and elegant man in a silk suit whose smile held elongated canines and teeth-stained ivory.

Michael surged forward. One sword struck. Three heads rolled. Three golden chains broke and scattered links across the garage floor.

Then things got dicey fast.

The other beings summoned by Mammon all exploded into action themselves, none wishing to be next on Michael's list of victims. Michael suddenly had to dodge and parry as well as thrust and cut. But through it all, he held to the art of no-sword.

Blood and limbs flew. When he could not easily kill, Michael tried to maim, to hamstring, or to blind. Anything to make it harder for Mammon's side to focus in on him.

Cut and slash. Parry and riposte. Breathe. Ride the edge of everything and nothing. Be the art of no-sword.

"Worthless!" Mammon raged at his summoned help. "Your debts to me will never be repaid until that angel is dead or before me in chains! You wish to be free? You wish for my patronage? The wealth I can offer? Then *deal with that angel!*"

"Maybe you should do your own dirty work," Michael shouted, dodging a blow from one of the massive thugs in tight formation around Mammon.

He breathed. No-Sword spoke. Michael adjusted his blow and another head flew free from its shoulders. A gap in Mammon's defensive wall opened.

"Is it worth it?" Michael spoke again, this time to the minions Mammon had called to serve him. "Looks to me like all you're getting for your service is pain, blood, and death."

His blade lashed out again, spearing a demoness through the eye, punctuating his point with her death-wail.

Mammon's chains lashed out, nearly decapitating him, but Michael deflected the blow. He was rushing along the edge of everything and nothing, his will propelling him forward, keeping the flames of his sword brightly burning, and his skin glowing with a protective light.

He was getting to some of them. There was obvious reluctance among at least half of the summoned spirits and demons. Michael needed to push harder. Force them to break and run.

His arms were getting tired. His eyes were beginning to burn from the strain of focusing on the line between everything and nothing.

"How much is your life worth?" He roared. "Did Mammon purchase your deaths? Did he buy your loyalty? What favor did he grant you that you're willing to grant him your lives and your freedom? Do you value yourselves so little?"

The glimmering gold of the chains binding the wrists of several of the summoned beings dimmed. One or two links even seemed to go grey.

Michael remembered how he had broken free of Mammon's chains. Perception mattered. Values mattered. Motivations mattered.

Desires mattered.

Michael's eyes glinted and he shouted once more.

"Are you really being paid enough for this?"

That rippled through the assembled demons and spirits. If they were in debt to Mammon it was because they were, at their core, greedy. And greedy beings of all kinds hated to give more value than they received in return.

"This task is more than I owe," one of the demons cried, clawing desperately at the chain on his wrist. "I will not fight without greater compensation!"

One chain broke. Then another. Spirits and demons fled back across the veil, reducing the number of remaining supporters around Mammon by two-thirds, at least.

Michael struck then, whittling the remainder down to a mere three. Two hulking brutes and one lean and hungry demon with eyes like iced emeralds.

The hulk to the left hefted a car and flung it at Michael.

The angel dodged, spinning out of the way. The art of no-sword whispered to him and he flung the sword in his right hand directly ahead of him and to the left. It buried itself in the throat of the other hulk.

"I'll double what Mammon is offering if you turn on him and help me take him out," Michael shouted, something in the emerald eyes of the lean and hungry demon prompting the idea.

The lean demon froze, only to be decapitated by Mammon's chains a split second later. The archdemon was taking no chances, and he clearly knew the kinds of beings he had called into his service.

Michael found himself, panting, facing off against Mammon and one monstrous pile of lava. The parking structure was littered with blood and ash, most of the body parts already having burned away in the white fire of Michael's sword.

"That must have cost a lot," Michael drawled. "Sorry about that. Well, not really, but it's polite to say so."

The lava monster launched itself at him. Michael stepped to the side and drove his sword deep into the central mass of molten rock. There was a *crack* and the heat suddenly dissipated, the magma beginning to cool.

Then, pain erupted down Michael's left shoulder as Mammon's chains of golden flame slashed at his wings. Michael tore himself free before they could coil about him and trap him in place, but only at the cost of several more lacerations.

So began a furious battle between Michael and Mammon. They were far better matched than he might have feared. Michael's familiarity with the world, his nature as half-mortal which grounded him in the physics of the place, and Mammon's relative inexperience on the physical plane all combined to level the playing field.

Cars exploded from the blows they exchanged but neither managed to do more than scratch the other. It was a matter of Michael's will versus Mammon's power, and the question was which would give out first. If either broke off combat, they might escape, but the ongoing conflict would remain, and neither was willing to surrender.

Not yet.

But it was clear that if something didn't change, the battle would just grind on. Not an attractive prospect to either combatant. There was no telling on whose side the backup would be. If The Resistance arrived first, it would go ill for Mammon. If the Ten managed to scramble their forces first, it would become more and more difficult for Michael. He had handled a few dozen extra foes, but no one's will was inexhaustible.

"Enough!" Mammon's roar shook the parking structure to its foundation. Window shields—the few that were still intact—shattered. Concrete cracked and crumbled. Car alarms flared to life and were quickly stifled by the fury radiating from those syllables.

"This game is proving nothing," Mammon said. "And I will not waste more time here. But you, Michael, my business with you is far from over. I challenge you, here and now, in accordance with the Old Laws. Face me! You have wronged me and I am allowed to claim justice. I shall have it in the form of satisfaction from you, or from one of the other two you conspired with to rob me of my rightful victory today."

He meant Sara or Hannah! Somehow Michael knew that the powers Mammon was invoking wouldn't be put off by a bit of running and hiding. If he, Michael, didn't step up to the challenge

Mammon would probably have little trouble chasing down his sister and Sara.

Michael's mind raced, combing through what he knew and guessed, what his hard-bought and hard-won knowledge told him. And he didn't like the answer. He was going to have to take up this challenge.

For Sara. For Hannah.

A spark of white-hot rage kindled in his heart.

For Gabriel.

For himself.

Mammon had, in his greed, taken so much from him. Michael was owed payback as much as Mammon was. That had to count for something.

"I accept," Michael said.

"Excellent. The choice of weapons falls to you, then," Mammon said, a vicious smile flashing across the archdemon's face. "What shall we use for our duel, then?"

"Our wills," Michael said, flaring the pair of flaming white swords in his hand. "What else?"

"Then the choice of battlefield falls to me," Mammon crowed. "And I choose to meet you beyond the veil. Follow, then, and meet your doom."

Mammon's form began to sizzle and dissolve into liquid gold. It poured off him in waves, peeling back, layer after layer, revealing muscle and then bone. In moments there was nothing left but a pool of swiftly cooling gold that began to dull even as Michael looked at it, until there was nothing left but an irregular splotch of dull grey metal that he suspected was lead.

The archdemon was gone, but Michael knew he waited just beyond the veil. He took a deep breath. Nothing for it.

Time to step forward into the final battle.

CHAPTER 46

Beyond the Veil

Michael's phone rang before he could do anything else. It was a burner, cheap, but apparently solid. It had survived the battle with nothing more than a cracked screen.

Good reason to go old school. No smartphone would have made it through that.

"Hello?"

"Michael! Are you all right?" Sara's voice echoed over the line.

"I'm fine," he said. "It was—it was a thing, but are you and Hannah safe?"

They were. Michael took a few more minutes establishing details and providing a quick summary of the battle with Mammon.

"So we won?" There was more than a little disbelief in Sara's voice.

"We ruined Mammon's plan, for now," Michael said, "but he's still a threat. A big one."

He didn't say that he had to step across the veil in a few moments to try and end that threat. He didn't know how to say it. He didn't want to say it.

Not to Sara.

Not when it meant he might not be coming back.

So he said what he could. Something he'd been thinking about for a bit, had probably known, deep down, for longer.

"I think we should celebrate," Michael said. "Whatever else this was, it was a victory. For us. For the country. For the whole world, really. Though I'm not really sure how to celebrate something like that, really. No one else really knows. Well, The Ten probably do, and The Resistance will understand. Not sure I want to party with any of them though, to be honest."

Michael let out a small laugh.

"We could celebrate," Sara said. "You and me. Hannah if you want."

Michael let the suggestion of a private celebration, just himself and Sara dance before his eyes for a long moment. That would be… that would be everything, really. After what they'd gone through.

If he made it back, after facing Mammon's challenge.

"I'd like that. Pizza and beer?" Michael had to push a bit to get the sound of a smile in his voice.

"Pizza and beer," Sara replied with a laugh. "Maybe a movie."

"What would you like to see?"

Michael drew out the conversation, talking options for their ideal celebratory date, because that was clearly what it was. He built up a picture of it in his mind, then wrapped it away in his heart, hoping it would bring him strength.

"You sure everything is all right?" Sara asked, not for the first time.

"Tired," Michael replied. "I took quite a beating, kicking Mammon's ass."

And he was about to take an even bigger one. He didn't know how long he could delay taking up Mammon's challenge, but his time was most certainly running out.

"Where should we meet you?" Sara asked.

"The place in Brooklyn," Michael said. "You know the one. Does pizza like both Italian style and Louisiana style. They've got great food."

"Not really known for their beer, though," Sara replied, teasing.

"Food is more important than beer. We can always go someplace else for a beer. Besides, there's a movie theater not too far away. We can see what's playing."

"All right. Hannah and I will get the senator back, then head to New York." Sara rattled off how long she thought it would take them to get back.

"Great," Michael said. "See you soon."

He paused, then, realising he might not make it back alive, said one thing more.

"I love you," he muttered softly.

Then Michael hung up the phone, not knowing if Sara had heard him or what her reply might have been. Well, time was up. The world across the veil called.

He took a deep breath, rolled his shoulders, and moved to step from this world into the next.

***

He failed.

Michael had tried to follow Mammon, stepping across the veil. And step across the veil he had but hadn't managed to follow the archdemon. There was no sign of him.

Not good enough, little angel. Come to me or forfeit!

Mammon's voice seemed to mock him, appearing from nowhere, ringing like gold in his mind.

Michael clenched his teeth and stepped back. And forth. And back and forth. Why wasn't it working?

Will. The art of no-sword. Could that carry him to where he needed to be?

Worth a shot.

Michael took a deep breath and centered himself. He reached for the edge of everything and nothing because somewhere along that line had to be the battlefield where Mammon waited.

It was different, this time. Harder. Michael tried to push through, stepping quickly as soon as he caught a glimpse of starry night sky and vast golden wings, but the universe spun beneath his feet and he felt a wrench in his core.

Michael collapsed to the cold concrete floor, blood painting the grey as he coughed. No. Right idea. Wrong execution.

Mammon's voice taunted him again. Michael ground his teeth and forced himself up with shaking arms. He could do this! He would do this.

It took him two more tries and a good pint of blood before he caught the trick of it and finally succeeded.

It was different, this time. Before when Michael had stepped beyond the veil and into the Spirit World it had been, more or less, a reflection of the world he had left behind. This time, however, when he stepped beyond the veil he stepped directly into a sea of stars.

Before he could wonder at the difference, Mammon's voice reverberated through the darkness.

"Welcome, Michael, to the arena that will see your death. Despair not, however. I shall place your burning bones in the sky as a constellation of stars, so everyone who looks up from that pathetic little rock will see it as a monument to your failure and a testament to the price of daring to cross me."

Mammon burned amongst the stars like molten gold. His wings stretched impossibly wide, blocking out whole galaxies. Around him were arrayed the full might of his assembled forces, mocking and jeering, horrible, twisted beings of the spirit world warped by unchecked greed and avarice. Green and gold and black they were, and the sight would have turned Michael's stomach if he were any more human than he was.

But Mammon had also mentioned Earth, and it, too, was present. It floated beneath Michael's feet, rocking slightly from his perspective as his wings churned the aether of the space around him and heat him aloft before and betwixt Mammon and the archdemon's forces.

It was a perfect blue-green marble, shot through with white from this perspective. So small. So strangely delicate looking. Michael stared. It did make countries and wars, squabbles and grubbing for money all seem so pointless and petty. Somewhere, down there, Sara and Hannah were returning the senator to his office. Somewhere, down there, was the pizza restaurant he'd agreed to meet Sara at. So small and yet so important.

How could Mammon bear to look at it?

Or was that the problem? That it was an affront to his demonic nature like this, and he felt the need to reach out and tarnish it because it glowed like a jewel in the darkness and tormented the darker denizens of the Spirit World with its beauty?

Michael ignited the sword of his will in his righteous right hand and looked across the gulf or space toward his foe.

"So is this the fair fight you challenged me to, or are you going to break your word and let your little minions play as well?"

Michael shrugged. "By all means, do. Be in violation of your oath. Either way, you lose."

Mammon bared his teeth and the assembled demonic figures around him danced and jeered.

Michael summoned the art of no-sword to him and looked for the realities in which he bested Mammon's army single-handedly. He caught a glimpse of a demon behind him lunging forward to claw him to ribbons with its bare hands.

His sword of alabaster flame slashed out and the demon wailed as it dissolved into nothingness there in the dark between the stars.

"No. Honor." Michael said, flicking his sword as if he were removing blood from it, though there was none to remove. The flames had seen to that.

"Merely a test," Mammon replied easily, green tongue flickering through his lips. "We have to make sure you are who you appear to be, after all."

"Always trying to get something for nothing, even if it's just the confirmation of something you already know." Michael shook his head. "No wonder you were so easily defeated. You can't make the small sacrifices—like trusting my appearance—in order to secure the big wins. That's why you failed."

"You are why I—why the plans of my Ten were foiled," Mammon ground out.

Michael rolled his eyes.

"Can't even take responsibility for your own actions? What kind of sorry excuse for a leader are you?"

"You will not sway my army with such words," Mammon snapped. "Not here. Not on this side of the veil. I *own* them, utterly."

"Then it was you who attempted to subvert the rules of the challenge, by attacking me from behind?" Michael's eyes shot sparks. "Which is it, demon? Either you are in control and are trying to weasel your way through a challenge you yourself offered because you are a crass and craven fool, or you are not nearly so powerful as you would have me, and your followers, believe."

A susurration went through the assembled army of avarice surrounding Mammon. The archdemon's face twisted into an even uglier visage, if such a thing was possible.

Michael smiled in the face of his enemy's fury.

"You will find I am fully in control, little halfling," Mammon said, his voice as cold as the void that surrounded them.

Michael let himself drift, the jewel of the world beneath his feet. The glow of it at the edges of his vision strengthened his resolve. He was fighting for something that mattered. All Mammon had was greed. The archdemon was clawing for something he wanted, did not deserve, and did not rightfully belong to him.

"I will defeat you here," Mammon said, voice like a gilded razor, "and then I will lead my army down to the world below, the world you so cherish, and I will take it by main force. Your blood will draw a gateway, half-thing, between the Spirit world and the world of flesh. As you are both, we shall pass through you and everything you love will be mine."

The thought drove an icy spike through Michael's spine. He shoved the thought aside, melting away his fear with the thought of Sara, and Hannah, and his team. He stood there, between Mammon and all the world, to make sure that humanity was able to determine its own destiny.

"You may try," Michael said lightly, "but you will fail. I beat you once, you son of a bitch, and I'll beat you again. All that's changed is the scenery." The sword in his hand flared like a star itself. "And once I've gutted you, I'll mow down your army like a farmer reaping wheat. You've seen that as well. And here I don't have to worry about property damage."

"Impudent whelp!" Mammon's hands clenched and chains of flaming gold manifested in them. "I am Mammon! I am greed and avarice and the burning desire to possess! Without me, all of human history would be nothing! Without the thirst for profit, without the comfort of gain, there would be no industry! No progress! No invention! I am the flywheel that drives humanity, they are my investment and it is time that I had my due. Neither you nor any other shall stop me from taking what is rightfully mine."

"Thing is, it's not yours," Michael called back, his voice echoing off the nearby stars. "Humanity has wonder and industry all its own. Greed doesn't drive shit for the many." Michael knew he was exaggerating but knew twisting the knife would serve him better here. "So much of science came about because of philanthropy, from people genuinely wishing to improve the world without personal gain. The man who invented synthetic insulin? He sold the patent for a single dollar just to be sure everyone would have access to life-saving medicine. Pasteurization, vaccination, these are all things which began out of the goodness of humanity, before greed attempted to steal them for itself, for personal gain." Michael spat. "You're a perversion. An aberration. You offer nothing to humanity, save degradation and ruin."

Come on you old fucker. Make the first move, and make it a mistake. Michael's eyes were locked onto the archdemon, waiting for any sign that he might break.

Pulses of fury rolled off of Mammon and the stars almost seemed to shudder in their orbits.

"You will lose and you will bow before me before I tear you asunder," Mammon howled. "I am all that beats in the dark heart of humanity! I am the drive to live, to feed, to grow great! I cannot be slaked and my might cannot be stopped! Even in your heart I dwell and you cannot defend against me. You may have slipped your chains once, but this time you will not. I will reach out my hand and tear my way into your soul from within your own heart. You will bow before me and all shall worship at my victory!"

"No," Michael said in a voice that carried to the cold and insensate stars, "I will win because I am willing to sacrifice myself to save what I love and you are not. Greed is incapable of self-sacrifice. You are incapable of giving anything your all. And so you will lose."

Mammon, his flesh of gold so suffused with fury it glowed roseate in the starlight, loosed a howl of fury that sent a nearby nebula into swirling disarray and launched himself at Michael!

CHAPTER 47

The Final Battle

Time slowed, there on the edge of everything and nothing, as Michael reached for the art of no-sword. Chains of gold, forged by greed and as sharp as hunger, slowly lanced toward him, propelled by Mammon's arm and Mammon's will. Everything moved as through black honey, slow and purposeful and as inevitable as an avalanche.

There, on the edge of everything and nothing, Michael was able to look around him, to see behind him even without eyes in the back of his head. He was surrounded. An army of demons and fallen angels hung there in space, not just a ring around him but a full sphere. There was no direction he could look and not catch a pair of malevolent eyes wishing, devoutly, for his end. Green and gold they glimmered, and they seemed as countless as the stars in the sky.

Before Michael was the titanic golden figure of Mammon, face twisted and frozen into a mask of fury by the slow nature of time as Michael was experiencing it. And even then, the archdemon was moving fast, far faster than any of the lesser demons surrounding them. Though time was dilated, Michael was still bound by it.

The chains flashed forward. Michael found the place from which he could parry and swung his sword. Flame clashed with flame and Michael found the sword torn from his grasp, the razor edges of Mammon's chain drawing lines of blood from his sword hand.

Instantly he summoned a replacement, even as his first sword faded to sparks, and sent a vicious riposte back at Mammon.

The chains met him, turning aside the blow. They moved more quickly here, unrestrained by petty things like physics and gravity. Here where the spirit was the greater part of the foundation of reality they snaked around, defending their master.

Michael summoned a second sword into his free hand and began circling Mammon, looking for a gap in the archdemon's defenses. Once, twice, three times he lashed out with his swords but every time he was caught and countered by the spinning chains of gold.

The archdemon laughed as a trickle of blood flowed down Michael's cheek.

"Weak, half-blood! You are weak! Even here, in the Spirit World, you bleed! Pathetic." Mammon followed up his words with a contemptuous backhand of an attack.

It didn't connect but it drove Michael back, almost to the sphere of jeering demons, as he dodged.

The places across his skin where Mammon's chains had bit stung, and cold fire slowly ate its way deeper and deeper into his flesh from every nick and cut. With them came whispers, crawling into his blood and flesh, clawing their way to shriek within the vaults of his mind, insidious accusations of pettiness and greed, of avarice and all the ways in which he had failed.

He saw Grace again, her eyes pleading with him, her voice screaming her innocence. He saw how he'd failed her, saw the wound he'd left with Hannah. It clawed at his gut and scratched at his focus.

Michael reached for the art of no-sword, but time and again he found himself using it to block the attacks from Mammon's lightning-fast chains. Whenever he did find a gap to attack in, the archdemon's speed and strength allowed him to shrug off the blow.

Nicks and cuts accumulated on every inch of Michael's exposed skin, and the unyielding white light of his will began to dim ever-so-slightly as the battle raged on. The demons laughed and jeered at the show, pressing closer and closer, shrinking the size of the arena within which Michael and Mammon did battle.

If it kept up he'd inevitably be driven within the archdemon's reach and those chains would slash and bind him.

Michael gritted his teeth and looked for something different as he practiced the art of no-sword. He could be in many places at once, hit in many places at once. And even if the next attack didn't hit Mammon, perhaps it could advance a larger goal.

The swords flickered in his hands and Michael stepped into and through the movements of the art of no-sword, dancing on the edge of everything and nothing. An inferno of alabaster flame erupted across the darkness between the stars where he did battle with Mammon, a hundred points of flame lancing out toward and around Mammon.

None landed when it came to the archdemon, but that would have only been a bonus. Michael was far more interested in the hundreds of demons that died or were maimed by the backlash of his attack. The infernal horde shrieked in rage and pain, but they all drew back, once more widening the arena within which Michael and Mammon strove against one another.

Mammon laughed darkly.

"Kill my entire army," he mocked. "It will do you little good. There are thousands of souls dying daily on that Little Rock beneath your feet that are eaten up and consumed by greed. Each of them will become a soldier in my army, a coin in my ever-growing hoard."

The burning chains of gold lashed out once more as Mammon continued to attack. Michael parried where he could, shouldered the pain and agony and the whispers of the blows that found their way through his defense.

He would not falter here! He could not. Too many people were depending on him.

But bit by bit creeping despair was eating away at his will. Each nick and cut delivered another voice to the chorus of hatred in his mind, whispering at him, calling out his failures and mistakes. Sure, he scored several hits on Mammon as well, but the archdemon was in his element here, even if this wasn't his prime place of power.

Michael felt his wings twinge, felt himself wobble for a fraction of a breath. A trickle of blood from a wound on his wrist crept across the back of his hand and sizzled in the snow-white fire of his sword.

Then the weapons of the archdemon bit once more.

It was like being in the Cave of Mammon once more. It was like being chained by those manacles of gold and—Michael stilled and the stars around him froze in their courses as a single thought seized hold of him and carried him inexorably to the edge of everything and nothing.

This was exactly like his fight to free himself in the Cave of Mammon. The powers were the same! The voices whispering in his ears and assaulting his soul were the same!

Mammon was the same.

And therefore the key to victory had to be the same.

"I am not what you say I am," Michael whispered first to the voices cawing in his mind. One by one he sent a bolt of alabaster flame through them, silencing them with memories of sacrifice and selflessness.

The swords in his hand flared brighter. His skin shone more fiercely. His will renewed itself.

The chains of Mammon struck once more and this time Michael parried them effortlessly, whispering remembrances of good deeds and virtues at them through his blade. Memory became will became flame and the chains that blazed so resolutely gold began to flicker, here and there, with snow-white sparks.

It was a curious reversal of what Mammon had done to him, in the Cave. There, the archdemon had ripped the gold from his aura and used it to enhance his own power. Here, the white of Michael's pure intentions began to eat away at the shining golden fire of Mammon's weapon, of Mammon's will to power.

Mammon didn't notice. Not yet.

The sword in Michael's left hand flicked out, shearing through a small length of chain.

"I am of the blood of angels," he said. "My virtue is counted not in gold."

The sword in Michael's right hand flashed out, burying itself in Mammon's shoulder as the chains writhed helplessly around the archdemon.

"I am of mortal blood, sorrow, and salt," he said. "My ancestors rose through selfless acts of community and communion, as did all of humanity."

The demonic horde around them fell silent, drifting in space like so much dust and gas, motionless and rapt before the glory of the lights before them. Mammon spat invective at Michael but the words of the archdemon held no sway over him. They passed over and around and through him and fell, unheard, into the darkness between the stars, never to be heard again.

Everything and nothing stretched out before Michael. He found himself moving faster and faster, surfing along the edge, riding the knife-edge of it all. Mammon slowed from impossibly fast, to simply superhuman, to merely mortal.

Or rather, Michael accelerated to meet him.

Mammon lashed out, his chains coiling and snapping like whips or like beaten dogs.

"I—" the archdemon began.

"You," Michael cut him off, "you are nothing. You create nothing. You add nothing to the sum total of creation. All you can do is subvert and subtract, and thus, you yourself are worth less than nothing."

The swords in his hands flashed out again, shearing through more lengths of chain, drawing yet more golden ichor from the archdemon's body.

And Mammon gave way. He fell back before the righteous might of Michael's sword. The entirety of the archdemon's weapon now danced with alabaster fire, the glimmering gold of Mammon's will eaten away and consumed by Michael's.

"You call me half-blood. You say it is my weakness, but it is my strength. I understand both sides of the coin. I am of both worlds. I have lost, and I have loved, and I am the stronger for it. Stronger than you can imagine." Michael advanced, moving faster and faster.

Mammon turned as if to flee, but Michael moved with a speed akin to that of light in the darkness, and the darkness in Mammon was no match for it.

The demons all around them were like flies in amber. The chains in Mammon's hands falling to fine, white ash as Michael's will burned them out of existence. There was nothing left between the archdemon and Michael.

Nothing to keep him from his doom.

Michael struck, the sword of his will burning with the heat of an exploding sun. White flame flared and the gold of Mammon's skin was no match for the heat of Michael's blade. The will of the half-angel prevailed over the might and malice of the archdemon, and Mammon's head went spiraling off into the darkness between the stars, an expression of shock locked on the swiftly-cooling flesh that turned, even as Michael watched, slowly from the bright glimmering yellow of gold to the dull grey of lead.

The army of demons surrounding them, those that survived, shrieked and fled, vanishing into the darkness, stepping back through the veil into the real world, or simply exploding in small bursts of emerald and golden flame. Michael watched them flee with a strange dispassion.

He didn't have the energy to feel anything. He was wrung out, every molecule of energy and willpower spent during the battle with Mammon.

His eyelids grew heavy and the mortal part of him screamed for breath, here in the vastness of space. He floated, turning softly, in the void, until Earth rotated into view in all its blue-green majesty.

Michael felt his lips twitch, attempting a smile, but he simply had no energy.

Were the stars going out? The pinpoints of light were being swallowed by the blackness. But the Earth still shone before him. Safe. The Earth was safe. Hannah was safe.

Sara was safe.

Michael lost his grip on consciousness then and fell utterly into the darkness.

CHAPTER 48

A Kind of Date

A crescent of light broke the darkness where Michael floated. The crescent widened and Michael began blinking furiously as the late afternoon sunlight seared his eyes. The stars were gone.

Where was he? He was surrounded by something soft and scratchy at the same time—cheap blankets. There was a regular beeping sound and a strange pressure on one of the fingertips of his right hand.

Michael blearily looked around. It took a while to fight through the bone-deep weariness that still pulsed through his form, but eventually he recognized where he was.

He was in a hospital.

There was a pale blue curtain pulled mostly around his bed, so he couldn't see who else may or may not be in his room. The bed was near to the window, though, and the cheap plastic blinds were partially open, allowing the sun in.

In the light of the day, the memories of fighting Mammon seemed like a surreal dream. Had that really happened? Michael would have spent more time questioning it if his hands and arms weren't all covered with small scars, souvenirs from Mammon's barbed chains of gold.

They even seemed to glimmer faintly in the light, as if some of the gold had been trapped therein. Michael flexed his will, slightly, causing his skin to glow. Alabaster light flickered, briefly, then went out.

Even that small effort exhausted him. But there had been no sparks or threads of gold in the aura of his will. Mammon hadn't infected him, though nor had he regained whatever it was that Mammon had taken. All there was, was pristine white light.

"Ah. You're awake. Good." A nurse appeared, raking the curtain away with a screech of the suspension track. "Let me just see here…"

She bustled over and checked the various machines attached to Michael, felt his wrist and his forehead, and made a couple of notes in the chart at the foot of his bed.

"How are you feeling?" She asked. "Last time we spoke you seemed very out of it."

Had he said anything? He didn't remember.

"A bit fuzzy," he said. "Still exhausted."

"Well, that's to be expected, after what you went through." The nurse moved along briskly. "Speaking of which, the officer that brought you in is here. She's gone to the cafeteria for a cup of coffee, but I'll let her know you're awake as soon as she's back."

Then the nurse bustled out.

Michael couldn't blame her. Hospitals never had enough staff, and with recent events, there had to be a slightly higher than usual admittance rate. His thoughts slowly spiraled down and out in that general direction. He didn't have the energy to stop the darkness from drawing him down.

"Hey."

That one word, in a familiar voice, roused him from his stupor. Michael looked up and smiled. It was Sara.

The detective was in plain clothes, though her badge was attached to her belt. She'd loosened her hair, Michael noticed. It wasn't in its customary ponytail and it fell around her face in light brown waves.

It looked nice.

"Hey," he managed to croak back. "Where am I?"

A look of panic flashed across Sara's face.

"I mean which hospital am I in," Michael clarified, falling into a coughing fit after rushing to speak. "I know where I am in general."

"St. Michael's, midtown," Sara answered, before smacking his foot lightly through the hospital blanket. "Don't scare me like that!"

"Sorry," Michael said. "How did I get here? The nurse said you checked me in?"

Sara glanced over her shoulder, then rose and moved out of sight for a moment. Michael heard a door close.

Must not be anyone else in this room, then, he noted absently.

"You just appeared, bleeding, on my apartment floor. I'd literally just walked in after leaving Hannah and there you were. You didn't wake up, so once your wounds stopped leaking fucking fire, I wrapped you up and brought you here. So really I should be asking you what the hell happened." Sara crossed her arms.

"Get me some water?" Michael reached up to massage his throat. "I'll tell you. I just—dry." He let his hand fall to the bed.

Sara brought him some water and, after a few sips, Michael went through the whole story, from his end of things, moving quickly past the phone call where he had declared his feelings for Sara then stepped into a whole separate world right after to face down an archdemon and the potential death of both his body and soul.

He wasn't going to get away with it, he knew, but he was so tired that all he cared about was putting off the reckoning for a while.

Sara let him tell the story, her face going tight, white, and pinched at several points. Once or twice it looked as if she might say something, but in the end, she always bit her lip and let Michael continue.

There was no way she wasn't compiling a list.

"And that's the last thing I remember," he concluded, finally, before reaching for another glass of water.

"So he's really gone?" Sara shook her head. "Seems impossible."

"I mean, he was defeated, beheaded, though what that means to something like that..." Michael managed a shrug. "We stopped his plan, though. And while I don't doubt some other petty demon will figure out how to tap into the power of greed to fuel their ascendancy, I don't think we need to worry about it any time soon. But yeah, Mammon's gone."

Something about those words sat uneasily in Michael's stomach, but that may have just been the medications he was on.

The plan had been stopped. Mammon was gone. He was alive and Sara and Hannah were safe. That was what mattered right now.

"What's happened here while I was out?" Michael asked, redirecting Sara's attention away from the "I said I love you" elephant in the hospital room.

"We returned the senator," Sara began, "after making sure Hannah had enchanted his memory to cover up any, ah, problems." She shook her head. "No wonder you had so much trouble trying to pin her down when you were chasing her. There's no way modern law enforcement has enough tricks to match what she's got spells for."

Michael chuckled weakly.

"That's my sister." He shook his head. "Not that I'm much better, these days."

"You might be better off than you think," Sara said. "I haven't gotten to what's been happening with The Ten and their influence. Or your boss, Garibaldi."

"Oh? Please tell me it's good."

"Could be better," Sara admitted, "but most of The Ten have strategically relocated out of the country and left their lawyers to deal with a sudden raft of investigations. Out of nowhere, it was like someone took the brakes off the SEC and IRS. Every member of The Ten that I was able to check on is in severe financial difficulty, and suddenly there is a lot of chaos at the precinct, and from what I hear, at your agency as well."

"Must be the lack of Mammon's power and influence," Michael said. "If you're used to having magic smooth the way, I imagine the sudden lack would be pretty rough to deal with." A shit-eating grin crept across Michael's face. "What a shame."

"Couldn't happen to a nicer bunch of assholes," Sara agreed. "And your boss, Garibaldi, he's caught up in the middle of it all. Holding the whole bag of corruption while the big bosses fuck off to try and avoid consequences. Sounds like Garibaldi is being raked across the coals while they write a new, bigger book to throw at him."

Sara launched into specifics while Michael listened with half an ear. It was stuff he should know, stuff he wanted to know, but he was still so bone-weary that it was a struggle to focus. He should care. Should wonder if there was any way to get his job back, in spite of the way he exited, but he just couldn't bring himself to care. Not only was it a lifetime ago, a calling he wasn't sure he even had anymore, but he was absolutely shattered.

It was a struggle just to keep his eyelids open and pay attention to the woman he loved.

Eventually Sara noticed and trailed off.

"I should let you rest," she said.

"No," Michael said, "not yet. I'm not—" He wasn't ready to be alone, to face what his dreams might bring when he finally fell asleep for real, not whatever senseless coma he'd been in since returning from the spirit world.

"Stay," he said at last, tentatively reaching out and grasping Sara's fingers in his hand. "I'd like you to stay."

Sara squeezed his fingers in return and shot him a look.

"So are we talking about it now, or after you get some of your energy back," she asked, a frank look in her eyes.

"Do we need to talk that much about it?" Michael hedged.

"Yes," Sara said firmly, but as she looked at Michael's face her own softened. "But we can talk about it later. And about your titanic lack of good sense, dropping a bomb like that then fucking off to another plane of existence."

Yup. Michael was in for quite the spirited "discussion" once he recovered.

He couldn't find it within himself to mind, though. In fact, he was looking forward to it. Or he would be if he weren't so exhausted.

"Fair enough," he said. "Something for later." He had a thought. "After pizza and beer."

"Fine," Sara said. "Makes sense. Might as well take the victory celebration full on, without anything else hanging over it. But after—" she squeezed his hand again.

Michael found he didn't want her to ever let go.

"So you don't hate me?" he fished. He really wanted to know what she might have said in response to the end of their last phone call, but again he couldn't quite bring himself to come right out and ask.

He's faced down an archdemon for the fate of the world, but this? This was roundly defeating him.

Though in his defense he *had* just faced an archdemon. Who could be expected to be suave and unflappable after something like that?

"No," Sara said softly. "I don't hate you. I don't think I ever could. It's…" she paused and colored slightly, "it's just the opposite, actually."

Michael smiled as tension he didn't even realize he was holding suddenly left him, a weight lifting and leaving him more energetic than he'd felt since waking.

"Is that so?" He smiled.

The conversation danced around the issue a bit more before they both decided to move it to lighter subjects. They talked about nothing of any importance, just filling the air with conversation and goodwill. They chatted about families and friends, swapped funny stories from their younger days, and did all the things that people normally do on a first or second date.

Then the nurse reappeared and put an end to the afternoon.

"I'm sorry," she said, "but visiting hours are over and I think our patient needs to get some serious rest."

Sara rose, not even trying to pull rank or throw the weight of her badge around. Michael thought about raising a protest, but his surge of energy had long since faded and he felt sleep calling to him.

"I'll be back tomorrow," Sara said. "I'll bring some of your clothes and anything else you'd like."

"Some decent snacks," Michael asked. Hospital food never quite cut it. Too healthy.

"I'll do that. But don't forget, you still owe me pizza and beer." Sara smiled wanly and left, the door closing softly behind her.

Michael smiled, feeling a warmth inside that had nothing to do with his wounds or the alabaster flame of his will.

He had something to look forward to, now.

CHAPTER 49

Fragile hope

Michael leaned back and closed his eyes. The sun was warm on his face and the wood of the bench he was sitting on dug into his back in a pleasant way. Ever since he'd taken to flying so much he kept getting knots back there. Sure, he'd probably get used to it in time, but for now the pressure on the tangle of muscle fibers was more than welcome.

He was sitting in the churchyard again, the same one where he'd saved the boy from the falling stones. Something about it drew him back, again and again.

Sara would meet him here after she finished work, but for now, Michael was just enjoying the sun and his slow recuperation.

His phone rang.

"Hello," Michael answered without checking the caller ID.

There were only a very few people who had this number, so he didn't really need to.

It was Hannah.

"Just letting you know that I'm headed to Europe for a few weeks," his sister said. "Maybe a couple months. I'll let you know when I get there."

"Thank you," Michael said, a smile tugging at the corners of his mouth.

There was silence on the other end of the line, but Michael could tell she was there. Hannah had surprised him, really, when he'd told her about Grace and his involvement in her death. She forgave him. Said it wasn't his fault and that he didn't know.

"You don't get mad at the knife," she'd said. "You find the hand that wielded it and cut it off, and we did that. I'm just glad to know Grace got some justice. Even if it was indirectly."

"I'll see you when you get back," Michael said in the here and now.

He knew better than to push. And he knew better than to take her at her word. Though he trusted she'd stay in contact. That was about all, though.

If Hannah was telling him over the phone that she was headed to Europe, you could bet she'd be somewhere in South America. Not that he could call her paranoid, exactly. He'd seen enough of the mortal side of things chasing her, and over the past few days he'd gained a lot more insight into the supernatural side of things—and the spirits and demons that were out for Hannah's blood in their own right.

His big sister pissed off a lot of people—entities?—on both sides of the veil.

He bantered back and forth with Hannah a bit. She kept trying to end the call and Michael took perverse pleasure in keeping her hooked, minute after minute.

She'd been absent from his life for too long and he knew that as soon as she hung up it was anyone's guess when he might hear from her again.

Michael eventually surrendered to inevitability and allowed Hannah to end the call, but not before extracting a promise from her to contact him more often. He even threatened to fly to her under his own power if she didn't.

"And don't forget," he said, "I'm never without a blood connection to you. I can and will scry you out."

"I should never have taught you that trick," Hannah complained.

Michael laughed.

"Love you, sis," he said.

"Love you too!"

Then Hannah was gone with the *snap* of an old-fashioned flip phone.

Michael returned to basking in the sunlight and using the bench to ineffectively massage the knot between his shoulder blades.

"Mind if I join you?"

That voice…Michael opened his eyes and squinted against the sun. A lackadaisical smile and a pair of dark glasses greeted him.

Then there was a sound like vast wings beating and someone was sitting next to him.

"Gabriel," Michael said. "Why am I not surprised?"

"Because it takes a very specific weapon or set of circumstances to ensure that a true angel or demon stays dead," Gabriel answered. "And you realized it, on some level."

"You could have told me," Michael rebuked him. "I thought you were well and truly dead and gone."

"I saw a bit of that," Gabriel said. "Sorry. I tried to offer a bit of help here and there, though it wasn't easy." The angel grimaced. "Picking your essence back up after something like that is…not fun."

Michael reached out and clasped Gabriel on the shoulder.

"Glad you're back."

"Good to be back." Gabriel pushed his glasses up his nose. "And congratulations. Seems you got along all right without me."

"Could have been better," Michael grimaced and rolled his shoulders. "Probably would have made it through with fewer scars if you were still knocking about."

Gabriel threw back his head and laughed.

"I think you did better than I could have done," the angel said. "After all, I've had centuries to fight old green eyes. You managed to shorten him by a head on your debut confrontation. Don't sell yourself short. You did amazing work."

"I had a good teacher," Michael smiled. "The art of no-sword. I might have gotten a bit of a handle on it, there by the end." Then, more seriously. "Thank you. Without what you taught me— well, I wouldn't be sitting here talking to you now."

"I try," Gabriel said with false modesty and a sly grin. "Or perhaps I only reminded you of that which you already knew but had forgotten. Do not sell yourself short!"

Michael laughed and squeezed Gabriel's shoulder. It was a good time to be alive, and a good place, too. Though there was a slight shadow sitting between him and Gabriel.

"Does this mean he's going to be back?" Michael didn't look at the angel, keeping his gaze studiously on the church.

"Probably," Gabriel answered. "Though whether or not he'll return quickly enough to reclaim the mantle of archdemon of avarice is an open question. There are a lot of ambitious spirits and demons out there and one of them might be able to claim that mantle for themselves. It's not like the darker parts of humanity are going anywhere anytime soon, and that is a lot of free power just begging to be claimed and used."

Michael let out his breath in a slow hiss. The thought that Mammon could return, even after all that was…heavy. The thought that he might have to face the archdemon again was…it was more than his still recovering mind wanted to handle.

Oh well. That was a problem for another day.

"I suppose I've beaten him once, so if I have to do it again, there's that," Michael forced a bit of levity into his tone. "And hopefully this time I'll have you standing next to me when I do it."

"I'll endeavor not to get myself beheaded next time," Gabriel said drily.

"How're things with The Resistance," Michael changed the subject. "What are they doing now, with Mammon out of the way?"

"You think Mammon is the only archdemon with designs on the world?" Gabriel's voice was amused. "That greed is humanity's only problem? No, there are plenty of other meddling demons and spirits to keep us occupied. That and keeping watch for the return of Mammon or his successor. There won't ever be a lack of work. Not unless humanity gets a whole lot better, on average, real fast."

"I wish I could say I thought that might happen," Michael said with a sigh. "But Mammon wasn't *making* people act out of greed, was he? He was just fanning the flames and taking power from those actions."

"True," Gabriel said, "but hope springs eternal."

"Is there an archangel of hope?" Michael asked. It stood to reason that if demons could draw power from humanity's baser emotions, angels might be able to do the same with the positive aspects of human nature.

"There has been, time and again," Gabriel said. "It's a fragile thing, hope. Not everyone can channel that power. It's effective when done well, though."

Before Michael could ask any more questions, Gabriel rose.

"We can talk more later. You know where and how to find me." Gabriel's wings flared into existence. "We should fly together sometime. But for now, well, I think you're expecting someone, aren't you? And I have more catching up to do." Gabriel smiled. "Coming back from the dead always has so much paperwork that comes with it."

There was a sound like vast wings and Gabriel was gone, leaving Michael blinking in the afternoon light once more.

"Michael?" Sara moved into view. "Been waiting long?"

"Not waiting," he replied with a smile. "Just enjoying the sun—and the time off."

"Your shoulders still tight?" Sara sat next to him and reached out to massage them for him.

"Yeah, thanks." Michael relaxed into her touch.

He could tell her about Mammon's possible return, later. That was a problem for tomorrow's Michael and Sara. Today, today he was just going to enjoy himself.

He'd more than earned it.

They sat in silence for a while, watching people walk around the small green space surrounding the church: businessmen and women, parents and children, teenagers sulking through on their way to someplace less lame.

"They don't have any idea," Sara murmured. "None of them know how close they came to living under a demon's boot. None of them know what is living all around them, just beyond the veil."

"They won't believe you, even if you do tell them," Michael said sadly. "Some can't. Some won't. You'd convince a few though. Not sure if those are the ones you want to convince, to be honest, but you could convince a few."

"Not my job," Sara said lightly. "Though I'm not sure how much longer I can be a detective, knowing what I know and not able to do much about it."

"You could bring a new perspective to your work," Michael offered. "Maybe solve some cases that otherwise wouldn't get resolved. Evidence might be dicey at times, but every little bit helps, right?"

"Maybe." Sara stopped massaging Michael's shoulders long enough to roll her own. "Maybe I'll retire and go private. Pretty sure I could make a mint as one of New York's premiere supernatural sleuths."

"It's a pretty rare skill set," Michael agreed. "Though where would we get startup funds?"

"We? Why's it we now?"

"Who else are you going to get to regularly enchant your sight?"

"Pretty sure you still have a nice chunk of change after walking out on your last job." Sara suddenly had a calculating look in her eyes. "Enough to get started. Wouldn't take much. A license. Some cheap premises. Might not even need that, nowadays. Who uses an office anymore? Everything's online."

"I mean, I'm game if you are." Michael turned to look at Sara, eyes sparkling. "Even if it means you clean out my savings."

Sara swatted him with a free hand.

"It won't take that much," she insisted again. "And it might be nice to be working in an environment that's free of bribery and corruption."

"Unless you count doughnuts," Michael said. "I imagine I'll have to bribe you with doughnuts to get any kind of receipts or bookwork out of you."

Sara growled and punched him in the shoulder.

"See? I'm right." Michael smiled. "If I weren't you'd have said something, not punched me."

"Fine. You're right. Even a broken clock," Sara said, before turning to ease herself into Michael's side, nestling comfortably next to him.

Michael reached out and put his arm around her.

"What do we do if we end up with a case where Hannah's the culprit, though, that's the real question," Sara said suddenly.

Michael groaned.

"That sounds like a problem for the Michael and Sara of the future," he said. "Though it is starting to sound like we're really going to do this."

"Yeah, we are." Sara sniffed. "But I knew that before we started talking. You're just a little slow."

"Very funny." Michael turned to look at her. "You know what? You talk too much."

"So do something about it," Sara challenged him.

"All right. I will."

Michael leaned in and kissed her. Both worlds fell away and it was like riding the edge of everything and nothing. If he had his way it would never end.

A perfect moment, suspended in time.

Thank you for choosing to buy this book; we appreciate it!

If you enjoyed it, then please consider leaving a review on Amazon.

Stay informed of new releases in the Archangel series and get all the latest Black Mike news and info sent to your inbox. Join Black Mike's newsletter at black-mike.com.

Many thanks!

AUDERE BOOKS

Made in the USA
Columbia, SC
27 January 2023

10713987R00205